MASTER OF DRAGONS

Dragon Core Chronicles Book Three

LARS MACHMÜLLER

MOUNTAINDALE
PRESS

ACKNOWLEDGMENTS

Wherever you live, certain life lessons will stick with you. For me, they are often quite simplistic in nature. Be a friend to your friends. Don't be a dick. Don't put that on fire.

"Pay it forward" was never one of those. Not until I met the LitRPG community. The number of people who have helped me along the way is staggering – people who, had I known who they were, I'd have been too timid to approach. But this genre embraces its own, and I love it.

Shemer Kuznits alpha read my very first book. Jeanette Strode helped me find my first editor. Taj El has beta read every single one. So many writers, narrators, editors or other full- or part-time professionals have given some of their time to prod me in the right direction.

I could have messed up royally tons of times. Still might. Heh. Still probably will, at some point. But knowing that I have these people at my side is heartening. And you can be damn sure, I'll have their backs too! LitRPG forever – pay it forward!

CHAPTER ONE

"The greatest gift of leadership is a boss who wants you to be successful" –
Jon Taffer

God, I'd missed sunlight. Reborn as a shadow dragon, I was supposed to be the embodiment of darkness, prince of shadow and all that–but this was the real deal. The stress practically oozed off of me. I'd come so very far in such a short while, and I'd finally made it. Top of the world, mom!

I glanced to the side, and my wings wavered briefly before I regained control. There's a trick to flying. Putting it to words isn't the easiest thing, since it's tough to define with human analogies, but if I were pressed hard, I'd boil it down to "think with your muscles." It's like learning how to ride a bike. You know how your body works, but you need to learn how to use it in a new, frightening manner.

I tried to relax into the sensation of keeping myself afloat and level without tipping to either side. This in itself wasn't tough. The winds were what made it difficult. At the moment, I was beating my wings, struggling against the erratic gusts of wind near the very top of the Scoured Mountain, enjoying the feeling of the sunlight shining down on me.

Heh. The flying by itself wasn't the only thing to make me nervous. I was improving. No, my company might have had something to do with my state of mind. With an effort, I ignored the looming presence at my side, leveled out against a particularly strong draft of wind.

Right next to me, buffeting me with heavy waves of air, flew Selys. Dragon of dragons, ruler of the mountain and, until mere hours ago, my enemy. In flight, she was even more impressive, handling her massive, red-scaled body with a grace that should be impossible with a frame that's longer than an eighteen-wheeler. On the earth, she made me think mostly of muscles, claws and teeth, but here, her easy movement turned her into winged destruction, an angel of fire.

"I was ready to destroy you. In fact, I very nearly did. To think how much you could have cost me."

Her voice penetrated my mind with a presence that almost hurt. I had yet to pin down how her attributes were divided, but her Mental Powers were impressive. At least, I didn't have to try to lie to her anymore. Those games were over. "I know, Selys. You are aware that I didn't mean for any of it to happen."

"Oh, I am aware. Had I sensed any real treachery from you, you would be dead now. I sense a lot of other things from you, but not treachery."

She was right. I wasn't considering betraying her. I was concentrating very hard not to focus on the *very realistic* risk that at some point, for the good of my people, the world, and humanity in general, I'd have to go against her. Face down the most powerful force in the damn mountain. Yeah, I was *not* considering treachery so hard I might sprain something. I was definitely aiming to find an alternative less likely to leave me as bloody paste.

She continued. "I can work with you. We will talk about the future soon. For now, however, look down."

I did as she said, taking in the sight of Fire Peak and the rest of the upper layer of the Scoured Mountain. It was an impressive sight. The area was maybe eight miles end to end, with Selys' ruling city placed dead center in the middle. The plateau surrounding the capital was leveled and flat, all other approaches smashed and ground to dust, holes in the earth filled in and growths removed, reducing any chance for enemies to approach the place in secret.

The capital itself took my breath away. The entirety of Fire Peak was hidden behind a rough wall, tall, wide and coarsely made. While the red-brown clay brick constructions of the houses inside were chaotic and haphazardly flung up, the avenues leading through the city as well as the towers spread throughout were an elaborate structure only visible from above, like a multi-layered wheel with all spokes pointing inward, equidistant and straight as a ruler.

As I'd walked along the busy streets earlier this day, I felt that the structures had been allowed to grow unplanned–but watching with a bird's-eye view, I could see how far from the truth that was. In the center of the approaching avenues, like a spider in the web, stood the fortress, dark, heavy, and colossal. It was strange to think that, just hours ago, I'd been fighting for my life inside that very fortress. Speaking as a shadow dragon, I didn't really love the layout. The streets were too wide, the approaches too open. Where were you supposed to ambush any attackers from?

Regardless of the tactical shortcomings of the city, the fires and smoke still rising from the battle that had ended earlier did nothing to diminish the impressiveness of the tableau. Right near the gates, a large pile of bloody corpses showed where Selys' defenders had managed to hold the undead abominations back, eventually being overcome, leaving the gates wrecked.

From there, the carnage inside the streets clearly showed the path the necromancer's monsters had taken, leaving a reddish-brown, corpse-strewn path directly toward the fortress. A few hundred feet in front of the towering palace, however, the ground was covered with bloated, blackened corpses–the remains of the unliving minions who had died along with their master.

Crazy. Hell, the entirety of my time in this life was lunacy. First, I'd been reborn into the body of a dragon, and had found unlikely allies, both among the lowest of the low and former defeated enemies. I had fought for survival repeatedly in an attempt to catch my bearings and survive in a dragon-eat-dragon world. Later, I'd been forced into servitude of the Soul Carver, a messed up shell of a former human, who decided that necromancy was the only way to take over the world, until Selys and I had finally managed to take down the twisted spell caster in a long, horrible fight. I could hardly believe that I had survived, let alone grown in power—enough that the powerhouse at my side seemed to actually accept me as her successor. And somewhere, my followers hid. My new family. Mixed races, old enemies, brought together for one purpose. Formerly weak and downtrodden, now… more.

My glance shot sideways. She caught my gaze, eyes boring into mine. Her mental voice demanded. "Tell me what you think of the sight."

I responded immediately. I still did not know what to think of her, but so far I had found that she valued honesty above diplomacy. "It's an impressive sight. I'd not expected this level of craftsmanship inside the mountain. Looks very defensible, too. On top of that, the planning it must have taken to ensure the streets and towers are spaced as evenly as they are… that hasn't been easy. A lot of the houses themselves are not that well-built, but the walls look extremely sturdy. You'd be hard to take down."

"Defensible. Yes. It is that. Powerful, too, as I will show you soon." A low rumble emerged from her – laughter. "Power. That is the very point of it. When you reside inside Fire Peak, people *know* that you are in charge. The very placement at the top of the mountain, in the center of everything—that show of power alone grants you legitimacy. Everything else I have done only adds to it, ensuring that everybody under my reign acts according to my will. *This* is why I have stayed here for so long. If you remain in control and maintain your position, you are granted power above and beyond the expectations of most creatures of Deyra."

I did a double take at that. I knew people were aware about Deyra, the goddess who supposedly granted every minion inside the mountain power, but still. Talking about a deity like a fact of life… it was the weirdest thing. Something to consider for later. For now, I sensed an opening. "Yet you are not satisfied, Selys."

Her lips pulled back, displaying a terrifying row of incisors in a horrible smile. "As I told you earlier, my little shadow son, no, I am not satisfied. While the power of this place is immense, it imposes limits on you. After all the years I have resided here, I yearn to throw off the chains and *grow*. Ultimately, while the mountain grants you all that it holds, it also acts as a prison, entrapping you, making you focus inward and center your vision on the mountain itself, when instead your ambition should be focused out *there*." She beat her wings and started to climb.

I followed her, climbing higher and higher toward the bright eye of the crater. I moved at a safe distance and focused on keeping my flight safe and steady, a task that became harder as we braved the peak where heavy gusts of wind pushed against us. I did not feel confident with my flying yet. In comparison, Selys moved like a natural predator, not struggling in the least, even as gale-force winds buffeted the both of us. To my relief, she alighted on the edge of the crater and looked up toward me. I impacted the ground with a running landing and almost tripped over a boulder. "Sorry. I haven't had many opportunities to spread my wings."

She shook her head, once. "Inconsequential, for now. You will need to practice. There is no excuse for a lack of aptitude. Inside this place, that equates to weakness–a weakness any enemies will abuse. And make no mistake–should you follow in my footsteps, the entire mountain will become your enemy. Enemies working under your rule, perhaps, but they will still be plotting your demise every step of the way. As it should be. Go. Fight. Thrive. And leave your enemies behind. Like Deyra demands."

I didn't point out that her interpretation was pretty different from that of the other species inside the mountain. My attention was blown away by the awe of the view of what surrounded us. On all sides surrounding the mountain, a harsh, imposing wilderness spread, showing nothing but forest and mountains as far as the eye could see. And the dimensions... clouds half-covered the horizon, mountainous forms, larger than skyscrapers.

Some of them were traveling across the barren edges of the climb below us. I had an idea of the size of the Scoured Mountain before, but watching it from the outside somehow made it *real*. The Scoured Mountain towered over all neighboring mountains, leaving them looking like small hillocks. It must be larger than that massive volcano on Mars.

Again, I marveled over my eyesight. I could see everything. Below me, a huge, hawk-like creature circled, focusing on a pond further below, where two heavy, horn-clad beasts smashed together in play or battle miles and miles away. At this distance, they must be the size of elephants. I gawked. What really blew me away was the lack of civilization. "There is nothing nearby? No buildings, no other sentient races?"

Selys sneered. "My saving grace. I did not grow up inside the mountain. It is... a different world. For all my minions within these confines of rock and soil, it is easy to forget that the outside exists and that our existence is but a tiny part of the realms. Out here, survival is harsh, nature less forgiving and growth is much harder to come by. It is still a necessity to move out here, unless you wish to remain confined down there forever."

She raised a claw, pointing in the direction of a series of shattered mountains. "There lies the Eastern Demise. That is what the humans have named the range. To my knowledge, no one in the Realms is aware that anything east of the range has any value, much less holds a Blessing of Deyra." A frightening grin spread on her face. "I have ensured that any who come to explore fail to return. Oh, but I will make sure to educate them, soon." She spread her wings, glaring into the distance and then subsided, looking back to me. "Not until you have earned your place, however. Come here."

Carefully, I walked over to where she stood. She was right next to the drop. Beyond her, the edge went straight down, far enough to make my head spin. I was sure dragons didn't experience vertigo, but it was hard for me to ignore the countless feet of empty air beyond. She waited impatiently. "I did not bring you up here merely to show you the world. There is something you need to understand in order to be capable of reigning over the mountain." She placed a clawed foot on the ground at the very edge and rocked it back and forth, dislodging a pile of dust and small rocks and pushing them off into the crater.

I frowned. What was she doing? Showing me that she didn't care who she hit? Wait. "Are those... bricks?"

She nodded. "Dragons were not the first to discover this place. Neither were the Dworgen or Urten or any of the lesser beasts who yet dwell here. No, this was the work of the Corren. Bless the tasteless creatures. Who do you think mined out the tunnels inside the mountain?"

My mind raced. "Oh. Wow. So, the extensive tunnel system that spread all over, and the old ruins that are still around. It's all theirs? Fire Peak, too?"

"Exactly. The tunnel systems do change constantly. Collapses, natural expansions, mindless animals tunneling through the dirt. This all alters the setup of the terrain, obscuring the remains of their works. But the majority of the constructions remaining inside still originate from the presence of the Corren. We can thank them for our present situation."

I considered it. Suddenly, some things stood out to me as obvious. Dirt passages that, out of the blue, were replaced by broken brick for several corridors. Those weird square rooms I wanted to explore on the second layer. Hell, maybe even something like Creive's domain. There were probably tons of other examples of their work spread out below me.

Selys continued unperturbed. "They are one of the few humanoid races that avoid all other sentients, and were it not for them keeping their distance from all civilizations, this place would have been discovered by others long ago. Now that they are gone, not many here remember their presence. Inside the mountain, the sight is rarely set on the past, but rather on the here and now. Regardless what you might think, the crowning achievement of the Corren is not Fire Peak. Rather, it dwells in the access to power they have left behind.

"Some of the power granted to you, should I allow you to take over, is quite literal. At the very center of the mountain emerges the Blessing of Deyra. The life-giving, boosting, heal-ing, *powerful* essence of our creator herself. Preserved inside the core, it travels upward through the earth, sealed, compressed and enhanced by a marvelous crystalline construction, ending up as the best-kept secret of Fire Peak. There, the mistress or master of the mountain connects directly to the Blessing, absorbing the power of Deyra."

I frowned. "But the Talpi informed me that anybody in the Scoured Mountain would be able to access Deyra's gifts. I have seen it for myself. The benefits that all races here gain, the boost when I built a hoard... what am I missing?"

She huffed. "The gifts are powerful enough in their own right. Still, in comparison, those are but remnants. Traces left over for the lesser races and aspirants to the throne to scrabble over, while the holder of the Blessing reaps the true rewards..."

I kinked my head to the side. "And you would leave all this behind? Give it to me?"

The carnivorous grin on her face left no clue as to whether this was benevolence. "Yes. If you earn it. I will not do it without safeguards, either."

I flinched at the sound of that. I recalled the Soul Carver becoming enraged at the prospect of the oath she wanted him to swear. Still, if it earned me and my minions a place of our own, I'd take it. "I will do what I need to do."

"Good. Because this ruin of a mountain pales when you compare it to one of the *real* Blessings out there. And with the power I have taken for myself, I mean to seize them all for my own. Come. Let me show you Fire Peak."

CHAPTER TWO

The sensation of throwing yourself into open air with miles of emptiness below you is beyond comparison. The initial raw fear combined with the following feeling of being able to control the descent and enjoy the ride… Yeah, chalk one bonus point to the natural awesomeness of being a dragon! Flying about inside the larger tunnels and caves was one thing, but this... I now knew why wing gliders, parachuters, or whatever the adrenaline freaks were called insisted on tossing themselves out the open door of airplanes. The rush was real.

We set down outside the city wall near the gate. This time, I aced the landing, taking a single additional step to gain my balance. Selys was already waiting for me next to the wall, and I hurried over, frowning at the rough workmanship. She indicated the structure. "Why do you think I had this erected?"

I frowned. Was that a trick question? "Erm. For protection? So any attackers would have to fight through the gate and give any of your defenders an advantage when they attack from above?"

"Yes. Also, to intimidate. Whenever anybody approaches for the first time, they see the wall towering above them and *know* that whoever is inside is better than them. It is the largest construction in the mountain outside my fortress, and it lets others realize how small they are."

I let a claw slide over the surface of the shoddy brickwork, nodding. Of course. The quality of the wall in itself was nothing to speak of. It was massive, sure, standing at least 60 feet in height and a third of that in width, and the fortifications above looked suitably intimidating, but I had no doubt my Talpi could make short work of it. Hell, we might not even need the shamans. "Have you considered enhancing the structure? Adding traps and so on? I believe my Talpi would be good at that."

She waved the thought away. "It would be a waste of time. This is a classic failing in shadow dragons. You feel the need to imbed every available square inch with traps and hiding places. You will need to be more pragmatic. The effort needed to strengthen every foot of the wall would be insane - especially when it is not the main defense of the city."

"It isn't?" I stared incredulously at her.

"Follow."

We entered through the front gate, guards shuffling to let us enter, bowing and kowtowing at our passing. Heh. At Selys' passing, at least. I was sure there were still some hard feelings that my presence had led to them outing themselves as inefficient protectors. Still, looking at the massive armored figures as we passed by, I wouldn't want to tangle with them by myself.

There were multiple races, but they were definitely chosen for size and strength. Even the smallest of them looked stronger than my largest Crawl. The ones who carried golden armor looked particularly fearsome—it was some kind of distinction, I guessed. Right inside the gates, we turned left, following the wall at a leisurely pace. Selys seemed to be enjoying herself. She sometimes nodded in satisfaction at the occasional golden-armored beast.

The difference between the outskirts and the remainder of Fire Peak was astounding. Where the center was erected more like a proper city, with the clay houses rising several stories with little space in between to make the most of the space, out here, single-story constructions battled for supremacy with large warehouse-like structures.

"Who do you allow to live here?" It had been on my mind since we started the tour, and I still couldn't quite figure it out. There seemed to be no system to it. Tiny creatures that would never be able to stand up against some of the ferocious guards scurried along the streets next to huge beasts with no rhyme or reason.

Selys smiled. "That is one of my greatest accomplishments. Right from the start, when I took over Fire Peak with an unimpressive surviving force and my pet in tow, I decided to not handle everything myself. Instead, I focused on telling my underlings what I wanted and let them sort it out. If they fail, they reap the consequences."

A pleased rumble emerged from her. "They rarely fail anymore." We walked for a minute in silence before she started talking again. "I have few rules. I want my city to be kept pristine. The Scurriers take care of that. I want my buildings to be sturdy. That is for my Earth Force to handle. And I want my Guard prepared, well-equipped and imposing. In short, I created the basis, now they oversee themselves."

Earth Force. That sounded like a science fiction crew of sorts, or maybe that horrible old cartoon where love was a super power. Around me, I noted a new sensation intruding on us. A scent of... blood. "What are we approaching now?"

"It does have a presence, does it not?" We stopped and she indicated a side street that led down to a huge open area, where the smell of blood and sounds of animals threatened to overwhelm the senses. "We will not be visiting. Those are the Stocks. My hunters and gatherers reside there. They raise most of the meat we need and capture what else I desire."

A couple of blocks further on, we turned right and moved further toward the center. Soon, Selys stopped next to one of the tall towers that dominated the city. "What can you tell me about these towers?"

A test? I backed up a bit, taking in the construction. The material of the slender, ten-foot-wide tower looked to be molten in some way to create a solid surface. I circled around, moving close enough to let a claw slide over the surface. I needed to apply pressure to mark the material. It must have been a full eighty feet tall, peeking over the city wall. I couldn't see the top from down here. I turned toward Selys and lifted my wings from their resting place on my back, asking, "Can I look?" She inclined her head, and I flew up to circle the upper part of the tower. Up above, a small, winged humanoid almost fell out of the tower as my head rose up next to him. The open platform gave a full 360-degree view of the surroundings. The only thing breaking up the open surface was a simple pedestal holding a bright, glowing piece of rock. I activated my Mana Manipulation, letting my translucent pseudopod range out to touch the pedestal. That was it. Both the piece of rock and the pedestal itself burned with magic. It smacked of... destruction. Fire.

I sank down slowly, mind deep in considering the possibilities. When I looked up at the towering form of Selys next to me, it was hard to miss the smug look on her face. She no doubt expected me to come up with a blank. "It's a defensive structure. Maybe an offensive one. No clue what it does, but the guy up top is probably the one to control it. At a guess, I'd say it's to attack any fliers. Oh, and I doubt that any of your builders made it."

The momentary look of surprise on her face confirmed my guesses. Her eyes narrowed. "The function of the Fire Web–you might be able to divine that by looks alone–but how can you tell that my builders have not constructed them?"

"Everything. Material, craftsmanship... heh, tools, even. You can tell at a glance that there are no tool marks in whatever they used to construct it. So, either they know more about construction than my minions, which I doubt, or somebody used magic to erect the towers. It looks like what my shamans can make when they really apply themselves. And since I haven't seen any of the buildings inside the city looking like this..." I let my voice trail off.

"I am glad to hear that your critters are more useful than their reputation says. You are mostly right. Yes, the Fire Web allows the keeper on top to use his mana to direct bolts of fire at any winged attacker. In addition, the towers can act in concert to torch the skies, erect a protective shield of flame that will keep any enemies from entering."

My eyes shot to the tower and onward to the next one. The towers ran along the wall, surrounding the entire city. "So, you mean..."

"Yes. Any attackers will be held back for almost a full day, allowing for time to arrange the defenses and prepare for anything. As for anybody caught in the web, they will be scoured from existence."

I thought back to the heaps of undead. They had almost made it all the way to the fortress. "That is absolutely amazing. I can't believe how much stronger than my current constructions that would be." Perhaps it was better not to pry... ah, fuck it. So far, she hadn't punished my curiosity. "Why didn't it activate when the Soul Carver's minions attacked, then?"

Selys' glare bore down on me. Okay, maybe all curiosity wasn't welcome. "While the keepers are allowed full control of the fire attacks, I am the only one who can activate the flame shield. As you might have noticed, I was otherwise occupied."

"Oh. My apologies. I didn't realize—"

"Forget it. You could not know. It is a limitation of the application. Strength-wise, however, you are correct. This is above and beyond what a regular hoard will grant you. This is but one of the special gifts the Blessing of Deyra grants."

Our walk resumed, and Selys showed me the intricacies of Fire Peak. I gave her my utmost attention, not only in order to understand how they worked, but also to see how I'd be able to change it to a society I could live with. There would be much to alter. For while the intimidating red dragon insisted that everything flowed without her interference, there were still a lot of moving parts that required prodding, intimidation, and nudging in order to work. And the current city was one based on and revolving around violence. But could I adapt that? Somehow use it against Selys? I tried not to let my thoughts revolve too much around the subject and let Selys catch a whiff of my ideas.

There is always a lot to learn about a superior when they show you the worksite you're going to spend the next long time getting accustomed to. Which details do they focus on? How do they present the challenges? The coworkers? The project? I gleaned a good deal from Selys' attitude.

Sure, *she* could move a claw, and even the smallest of her minions would spring to act on her smallest whim. But everybody below her were various degrees of slaves, influenced by the threat of violence from her or her minions. The output produced by the workers in the city was impressive, but the undercurrent of slaves scurrying along underfoot to handle the menial labor made no secret of the exploitation.

And it was everywhere.

The foundry? Buff, soot-covered workers were chained to the bellows, while empty-eyed creatures carried provisions to the smithies in a lean stream. The magic school? An apparently enlightened small group of magic users, led by a small, scale-covered humanoid with dragon-like features, insisted on using living targets as they showcased their aptitude. The leatherworks on the edge of the city were hard to look at, with the despondent workers carrying open, bleeding sores from handling the toxic materials. Hunters. Builders. Everywhere, the groupings were centered around pleasing Selys' tiniest whim and fixed in a constant competition to avoid becoming the next ones to be downtrodden or punished.

While she claimed indifference to the goings-on in the groupings below her, she was attentive and missed little. Simply by looking over a series of armors laid out, she discovered impurities in the ore and directed the smith to reforge them.

She singled out a group of hunters that had gained in levels too quickly and told their superior to punish them appropriately. Everywhere we went, she paid attention to her surroundings and impressed me with her quick thinking.

Also, while she might disparage the importance of the mountain in the grander place of things, she still wanted me to understand, in-depth, how the machinery worked. She didn't want a temporary replacement. She was genuinely invested in making sure the mountain would go on working without her, even if her intention was just to have a safe fall-back zone if her plans on the surface went south. This was good. From what she'd said earlier, she also wanted to go out into the world and put all humans and humanoid races under her yoke. That was... less good.

Hours later, we were circling back toward the entrance. The wounds that had been troubling me were slowly closing from my natural healing abilities. I was feeling better, if in massive need of rest. The days leading up to the battle had been demanding in themselves. I had spent a few hours after the battle, watched over by her jumpy guards, but it couldn't really be classified as "rest." Now, my head was filled to the brim with new information, my legs were dragging, and I had trouble keeping focus.

Selys turned toward me, growling. Apparently, I had missed something. "I was going to take you around to the masons, but we are cutting it short. You need to work on your endurance. You are showing weakness."

I bowed my head subserviently. "Apologies. It's been a long day—week, even."

"Excuses are worth nothing. Improve."

"I will. I work hard. I'm not a shirker."

She nailed me down with her gaze for several seconds before giving a single, grudging nod and moving on. We were in the eastern part of Fire Peak now, midway between the fortress and the walls. A duo of workers moved past us, carrying a dead guard between them, stripped of armor and weaponry. The blood on their clothes gave a hint to their destination – the guard would probably help fill the larders. No mercy in this place and no waste.

Selys slowed down. "I will ensure you hold to your promise. For now, see to your minions. Tell them that they are not in danger, for now. They acted well in ambushing the Soul Carver's horde." One outstretched claw indicated a portcullis ahead. Behind the portcullis lay a wide courtyard. Inside, a large group of heavily armed guards of all sizes and races were gathered, keeping their weapons and attention fixed... on my people.

CHAPTER THREE

"Home is people. Not a place. If you go back there after the people are gone, then all you can see is what is not there any more." – Robin Hobb

I never thought I'd see anybody act happy at the sight of a dragon, but as my people spotted me, they completely lost it. After a few seconds of prodding and shouting between themselves, their cheers rang out through the streets. The guards looked like they believed themselves to be under attack, until they saw Selys and me and relaxed ever so slightly, though they still kept their weapons trained on them. That didn't dampen their exuberance in the slightest, though. Whistles, growls, and cheers filled the streets and grew in intensity.

The same could be said for me. A huge wave of relief sent me leaping across the plaza to them, brilliant smile on my face.

Selys shook her head. "They will stay in the city, under guard, until our business is resolved. Come see me in the evening. Rest. You will need it. I will send food."

"Thank you, Selys and *thank* you." For not killing me. For helping me get rid of the Soul Carver. For giving me the chance of creating my own society. I didn't voice my thoughts, but it looked like she caught the intent.

"No need to thank me. I grant no rewards freely. What I give you is earned." The massive dragon turned her back on me, and I could only admire the sinuous grace in her movements as she stalked away. Her Agility score must be beyond comparison. And Strength. And… my mind was wandering.

Shaking my head, I turned back toward my people and approached them. As I walked closer, the smile on my lips slowly dimmed down, as my mushy brain caught up to the fact that they didn't know that Aelis had died. For an instant, I felt the need to… not approach. Just lie down, get some rest, and avoid the subject. But I growled deep in my throat and joined them nonetheless. I meant what I'd said to Selys. I was not one for shirking my duties, and I sure as hell wasn't going to start now.

As I got closer, the guards backed slightly away, leaving me an open path to join them, and a handful of minions parted ways from the large group to meet me. The first one there was Arthor. The Talpus shaman was tall for his kind, and his spotted brown and white fur was dirty and bedraggled. The rest looked bone-tired and a couple of them sported wounds attesting that their flight and subsequent battles had been hard-fought as well. Some were completely out of it with nearby Talpi attending to their wounds.

Arthor's demeanor ignored all that, however, giving him a stateliness and gravitas that belied his messy appearance. "Dragon. Did Aelis make it?"

I shook my head. "No."

At my words, a murmur rushed through the group, but Arthor simply massaged his brow. "We feared as much when she was caught. Are we in danger?"

"Not right now. Possibly not at all. I'm relieved to see that you are all looking well. Whatever you've done to get here, well done. For now, we should use the time to relax, heal, and sleep. I'm dead on my feet and summoned before Selys in the evening.

We should make the most of that time." I grimaced. "Talk. Remember Aelis."

Arthor looked behind him and said something softly to some of the other Talpi, before turning back to me. "We will. Aelis would want you to take care of yourself, too. Pfah. You can't very well look presentable if you're all covered in blood and... whatever that all is." He waved a paw at my body. "You sleep. We will wash your scales. Not me, though. You reek."

I didn't debate. I didn't even look. The events of the last few days finally crashed down on me, and I curled up in a ball, rested my head on my tail, and slept.

Hours later, I was awakened by a sharp tug on my head. I lifted my head, looking up to locate what was causing the pain and seeing nothing. Then, shaking away the bleary aftermath of sleep, I noticed other signs of movement, barely registering along my length. Glancing down, my mouth opened in an unwilling grin to see the perpetrators: a small group of Crawl and Talpi pups who had been using my sleeping, now relatively clean, body as a playground. I carefully lowered my head toward the ground, and the pull disappeared, along with the small, chubby Crawl, who let go of my horn and instantly sprinted up my tail to start climbing my body again.

For a brief moment, I ignored them and stayed unmoving as I watched my people from between lidded eyes. All told, they were looking better than I could have hoped. Some were wounded and most were both dirty and bedraggled. Something had changed, though. I saw a young Crawl sitting patiently next to a Talpus, repeating his movements, using some kind of wide grass stalks to weave a container of sorts.

A short series of growls had the offenders scamper away at a sprint to hide with their parents, and I saw Roth standing there. The thickset, muscled Talpus looked impressive with the two-handed sword slung on his shoulder and he looked me over, whistling slightly. "You look a mess, Onyx. Anything permanent?"

I let my gaze slide over the mass of impact wounds, scorch

marks, cuts, and stabs from the battle with the Soul Carver. "No. It looks worse than it is. I'll be healed in a handful of hours. How about you?" The thickset creature was liberally covered with cuts, and dark ichor spattered most of his legs. The sword was spotless, however.

The grin on his face betrayed it all. "Oh, I'm good. The Soul Carver's minions didn't do so hot, though." He inclined his head to the left. "Come on. The others are waiting."

The usual gang was there. Creziel, the smaller of the Talpus shamans, looked completely unhurt, drumming his paw on his leg while he avoided my eyes. Arthor was also ready, and I could sense the impatience oozing from him. It felt wrong, however. Two spots were unfilled. The unflinching, silent presence of Erk was gone, since he'd been killed in an ambush a few days earlier—and Aelis. The formal, caring backbone of our group, always serious and helpful. I missed the tiny scout already. I was only missing one more presence, right until the white-grey blob came floating in from behind, coming together in our midst to form a shining, androgynous haze. Timothy formed a translucent hand to wave at me. "Hey, old-timer. Glad you made it."

"Same to you, Tim." My gaze moved on to take in the other two.

Grex, the Imp leader, was easily recognizable. His dirt-colored skin had a triangle-shaped orange spot on the chest, making him stand out from his brethren as he bobbed about, tiny wings working overtime. As if that weren't enough, his constant mental chatter left no doubt as to when he was present or not. "I'm glad, too. Glad we're leaving. I've seen Imps in Fire Peak. They don't look happy. Oh no. This is a bad place to be small. Even though we were not small in the battle. We were giants. We're taking off, right?"

I smiled at him. "It's good to see you made it too, Grex. And you," I focused on the final participant. The Crawl was young, but didn't hold the clumsiness of early childhood as the Crawl pups. She hadn't started growing the hideous protective folds and rolls of hardened skin that characterized their race. She stood to the side of and behind Tim, as if she were hiding behind his presence. "You are Gert, right?"

She nodded. Timothy was the one to respond. "Yeah. After Erk passed, she volunteered to take over to talk on behalf of them all. I thought she should be part of the discussions. She has been learning fast."

"Good idea. So, let me start with my story, and then you tell me how the hell you managed to decide to attack the Soul Carver instead of fleeing like we'd agreed."

I didn't leave anything out. They took it in silently, even though I could sense their emotions as the story progressed. Their surprise as they learned that Aelis had actually been brought back alive. Their outrage, as the Soul Carver trapped her in invisible chains and used her life as a blackmail tool to coerce me into serving him. Finally, the mixture of sorrow and pride as she decided to take poison and end her own life rather than have the Soul Carver succeed in his plans to obtain the mastery of the mountain. I finished my story with a shrug.

"Selys, well, I might not exactly be adopted into the family. Still, she accepted the way we managed to kill or subdue all other dragons here. Now, she's spent some time introducing me to the intricacies of life in Fire Peak, and she's promised to give me the final details soon. It may sound like we've already made it, but she is holding something back. I doubt it's going to be a cake walk."

Timothy grinned, but quenched it quickly. "Easy. He doubts that it'll be easy. And I guess that's as good a time as any for me to take over the story-telling."

I blinked, looking at the see-through form of the human ghost, or ectoplasm, his new evolution. "Sure. Since when did you become the spokesman?"

His form blurred slightly, and his mental voice didn't sound as confident as he continued. "Since I was the one who talked them into attacking, I'd say."

I couldn't quite contain my shock. "You? *Et tu*, Timmy? Why would you do that? You had already gotten away."

I could feel the resolve building inside him as he faced me. "Well, we've had a few discussions on the subject, haven't we? You're pretty good at planning, but you rarely plan long-term."

"Get to the point, Tim. You know I like my talk as plain as that ugly, see-through mug of yours."

"Well, you were right. We had gotten away and were waiting for you. Or waiting to see what would happen, really. Soon, we realized that you hadn't made it, though, and we had to decide what to do. Your plans were decent–"

"Decent?" I fumed. "Rebuilding a society where these people can live together and gain strength? You call that *decent*?"

He nodded. "Yeah. Because it failed to take the aftermath into account. Think it through, man. So, we managed to get away without the soulstones. We were doing alright. Some were wounded when we fled, fighting to get away. Still, we made it. We'd be able to flee. That would save us from the Soul Carver being able to track us down, right? Yet he was still on the loose, though, batting for Selys' throne. If he managed to actually kill Selys and take her place, he'd be in a position to spread his influence over the entire mountain. In short, our long-term safety was severely questionable. So we decided to do what the Talpi do best."

"That was my decision, dragon." Arthor cut in. "We might not be the strongest, but we can hide and scout with the best of them–and we only needed to know one thing."

Roth grinned unabashedly. "Is the scary undead bastard crazy enough to attack Fire Peak, or would he stay in hiding near the entrance to the upper layer? Well, you know the answer to that." He made a punching motion. "Creziel and Arthor, along with the scouts, located a small opening into the upper layer, which we widened into a side tunnel. Not large, but enough to spy on Fire Peak without exposing ourselves. A while later, we spotted them marching on the city."

"The Soul Carver's minions." I shook my head in disbelief. "And somehow you thought that taking them on was a great idea. Fighting the forces of one of the worst powers in this damn place."

"Nonono. Fighting would be silly. But fun. We are small. They were huge. Does he not understand?" Grex bobbed about in the air, pure joy coming from him. "They were not fighters. They were... targets. Targets are more fun."

Arthor broke in. "What our excitable friend there is trying to say, lizard, is that the Imps finally proved their worth. Over longer distances, with a lot of air for maneuvering and with large targets, they are deadly. You may recall that the Soul Carver liked his minions huge. Well, at a distance, that just makes them better targets."

His dark grin emphasized the sense of satisfaction coming from him. "He did send a few fliers, too. Those cost us a few wounded. Still, once we had taken down the flying creatures, we pulled back and hid, let the Imps handle the rest." A rare smile bloomed on his face. "You saw the Soul Carver's minions. They were tough and took a lot of attacks to take down, but they couldn't get to the flying critters, and our own ranged attackers were too fast for them. We beat them. Even so, we were too late."

Grex flew higher to float above us all. "Too late! Yes! They ran from the Imps! We are too powerful."

Roth rolled his eyes. "Get down here, you jumpy insect, before the guards spit and roast you." He shrugged. "More like the Soul Carver or his minions decided going against us wasn't worth the price. He sent a handful of the ugly things out to distract us while the rest went for the fortress... and we weren't fast enough. At least with our attack, the defenders smelled their coming and managed to end some of them before they smashed the gate down. Well, once that was done, things got boring."

Creziel intervened. "Not boring. Tense. We had no clue what was going on, and we couldn't see what was happening inside the city. We rested as well as we could, kept an eye on the city, and waited. Well, and once Selys' guards ranged out along with that sorcerer of hers to find us, we decided we had better show ourselves."

Too much. "What? I mean, fighting from a distance–clever and all, even if it was a crazy risk, but why would you expose yourself?"

Timothy blurred apart, then came together, forming a timid smile. "That would be me again. I convinced them that it was the best idea, that if Selys had won, we needed to get out there, prove that your forces aren't a threat. It worked, too, right? So, go ahead and tell us we did good!"

I glared at him, then took in the rest of the group. They were all, including Arthor, waiting expectantly for my response. I let a low growl build in my throat and bared my teeth at them. "You were all reckless. Suicidal. Horribly stupid." Slowly, I formed my grimace into a grin. "I'm also goddamn proud of you. And thankful. If it weren't for you, the Soul Carver's minions might have made it to the fortress to help him fight Selys and me, and that would not have ended well. At the very least, you've done a lot to convince Selys that I'm on her side. So thank you. Sincerely. And don't *ever* fucking do it again!"

I continued, less abrasively. "I haven't talked about this much. I'm not really the type. Back on Earth… well, I had a family there. Wife and daughter. Heh. Boy, did I screw that up. I wasn't there, didn't pay attention, was always working." I cleared my throat with a noisy rumble. "I don't spend a lot of time thinking about what could've been. Don't really see the point. But if I were to point out a single regret, that'd be it. Not being there for my family."

This would be where one of the smartasses of the group, Timothy, maybe Grex, would jump in with a funny jab. Silence. They were listening, unguarded. I continued, facing them all. "Well, I'll just go ahead and say it. This time around, I'm not letting my family down."

For a moment, there was complete silence. Then, Roth huffed, got up. He walked over to me, looked me up and down. "So, scaly. Family, is it? I think I would've remembered if my dad had a set of teeth as ugly as yours." He grinned, then patted my front leg. "I'll take it, though. I've always wanted a crazy uncle who could beat up half the mountain."

I bared my teeth at him. "Crazy uncle, eh? I was going for for strict family father, but... you know, I'll take it."

The others laughed and the discussion moved elsewhere. The emotions stemming from them were something else. The warmth and acceptance flowing my way affirmed my decision in a manner simple speech couldn't. I was surrounded by family.

We took a while to chat about less important things. Who had gained in levels? Everybody—mostly the Imps, ranged attackers, and shamans though. Some of the others had been forced to fight, when they ran from the Soul Carver's minions, but the majority had been clever about it and ran away. Grex had reached level 10 and gained a feat that converted his fire-bolts into larger, more powerful versions. He was more than ready to show us, until we finally talked him out of it. Surprisingly, Laive also managed to hit level 10 and gain a new feat from a struggle with an undead wolf pack. The feat she'd chosen was a first for the tribe and excellent for our needs.

[Nature Sense
This feat grants you a sense of communion with plants. With practice, you can learn to feel plants, obtain easier access to their functions and secrets, and help them to better thrive.]

Creive, my blue dragon vassal who was near his own hoard at the other end of the mountain, must have gained in levels, too. Going through my notifications, I could see that he had not been resting on his laurels. The xp gains were numerous and... pretty damn impressive. A hundred here and there, but it added up to... 2,300 experience points total. That was almost 10% of a level for me. Not bad. Looked like he was ramping it up lately, too. When I checked in on his domain through the map, all I got was a skeleton crew, busy carving up a few large monster corpses.

Timothy, after a while, asked for help. "I have a choice here, old man. I actually hit Level 15."

"Oooh – new feats, then? Wait, I haven't even heard what you got at Level 10?"

He flexed his translucent arms, making the biceps grow to an implausible size. "Bragging time, then. Level 10 was a team player feat. I got [Improved boost] AND a new skill. [Improved boost] doubles the positive effect I inflict on anything I touch. That means right now, I can give a small group of Talpi the equivalent of a ten-level boost."

I gaped. "That's *huge*. If the boost is that good, the skill has to be underwhelming, right?"

Tim's grin grew and grew in size.

I huffed and stretched a wing, waving it through his form. "Alright, brag away."

"[Explosive Redistribution] It costs me 200 mana - that's almost half my mana. Totally worth it, though. It lets me manipulate my essence, turn it into a bomb, and I basically explode… and reappear somewhere else."

"No! Are you serious?"

"Yeah. It feels super weird, but you don't want to be on the receiving end. I used it against the Soul Carver's minions. It was super-effective."

I nodded, wide-eyed. "You'll want to use that only as a last resort, though, or you're leaving yourself ripe for the picking. Still, that's another killer. So… you decided the first one for yourself, but now you want my advice? How come?"

He shrugged, bobbing a bit in the air. "Well, the picks for level 10 were easy choices. But these… well, there are three feats, and they're all pretty amazing, if I should say so myself. I'm not quite sure which path to choose, though."

They were awesome, to be true, and I could see his dilemma.

[Defensive Pillar
Adds an additional 50% to your Mental Power and remaining mana whenever you stand still for more than 10 seconds.]

[Improved Essence Control
Your ability to stretch, focus, and concentrate your essence is improved. The precision and range at which your boosts and debuffs can affect others is improved by 100%.]

[Improved Speed.
Given that an Ectoplasm does not have an actual body, the speed of your movement is derived not from your Agility, but Mental Power. Your Mental Power is increased by an additional +50% for the purpose of determining your speed.]

"Wow. Those are impressive. I see your point, though. Pretty different routes to take. So, basically, do you aim to be the unmoving, but hard-hitting powerhouse, somebody who can buff or debuff entire companies, or are you looking to be fast?"

He grew an unsteady frown. "Yeah, that's the question now, isn't it? I'm not a fan of having to stand still too much if we're in combat – that's just asking to be struck down."

"That takes selection number one out of the equation. I mean, we could probably work up some routines between the two of us, but... no? Okay."

Timothy's features faded, leaving him blurred, like an old TV right on the edge of the signal reception. "The essence control one is damn tempting. I'm getting better at managing this sorry excuse for a body, but it's still *slow*. Being able to reach out quicker, affect people faster, affect *more* people, both when I'm in the middle of combat and buffing... yeah, that'd be a boon." He frowned.

I nodded. "Mmm-hm. Also, you'd finally be able to switch that cursed thing for a face that doesn't scare the cute Talpus pups."

"...You're such an ass."

I sketched a bow, spreading my wings wide. "Thank you. I do try."

He laughed, and his frown disappeared. He continued, pensive. "It's just… We're in this for the long haul, know what I mean? And I've found that increased Mental Control and simple repetition *both* help me improve at handling myself. So, in time, with enough practice, both my control and my speed will climb, regardless. I don't know if the range and control would be worth as much as the speed."

"Honestly? No sass this time. I don't think so. I mean, Improved Speed. It sounds a lot less flashy than the other choices, and it's harder to pin down, but it's solid. You'll be increasing your speed by an additional 50% *and* the increase grows along with your Mental Power, which, coincidentally is your main ability? Yeah. Screw buffs. You'll be able to dodge like nobody's business, outmaneuver anybody. That's not even the most important part. This will allow you to *run away*. You said it yourself; we're in for the long haul. Take the feat that lets you live another day."

Once Tim left, I finally took the time to look over my own status. The starting point wasn't half bad. The experience from the battle with the Soul Carver in itself was unmatched. Even when we defeated two dragons at once back in my lair, we hadn't come close to the wealth of experience I gained from the Soul Carver. 54,000 experience points took me all the way from level 23 to level 26.

I received my three automatic points to Agility and six to Mental Control, after which I quickly distributed my attribute points. Strength, I ignored, as per usual, leaving me with fifteen points to divide between Mental Power and Toughness. Frowning, I decided to go all-in on Mental Power. As long as I had my Mana Crystal necklace for healing myself, I could sacrifice some Toughness for additional power.

[Personal Info:
Name: Onyx

Race: Young Shadow Dragon. Level 26 – experience toward
next level: 8600/26000
Size: Very large

Stats and Attributes:
Health: 570/570
Mana: 860/860
Strength: 32
Toughness: 57
Agility: 79
Mental Power: 86
Mental Control: 120
Mana regeneration rate: 2040/day
Health regeneration rate: 57/hour]

The results were... definitely to my liking. My Mental
Control was through the roof, with Mental Power and Agility
not too far behind. Toughness was trailing, but my use of Mana
Crystals made up for this somewhat. My only really crappy
attribute was my Strength, by design. While others frowned at
the thought of a dragon with low Strength, I'd rather be able to
run away really fast and wear my enemies down at a distance.
Leave it for physically overpowered dragons to sparkle and burn
prettily while I ran circles around them and carved them down
to size.

There were different ways of approaching survival as a
shadow dragon. A classic, apparently, was creating an ambush
specialist–a hard-hitting close combat monster who excelled in
surprise attacks and could run circles around their enemies all
day long. Me, I preferred this version. Shadow Control, Shadow
Whorl, and Create Illusion–all focused on confusion, obfusca-
tion, while I used my breath weapon, Weakening Fog, to sap the
power of any attackers. Oh, and Bestow Camouflage to hide
my own minions. Mana Manipulation was... still a bit of an
enigma. That one might become more useful in time.

I'd chosen my feats to double down on the above, emphasize

my strengths and take the edge off my weaknesses. Hardened Scales and Improved Magic Resistance let me weather some additional beatdowns when the battles turned ugly. My new-ish feat, Shadow Meld, did the same too, weathering half of all physical damage when I was hidden in shadows. I hadn't had the chance to try it out in practice yet. Then, I had Improved Power and Improved Spell Control to make my skills hit harder, come faster. Finally, there was my very first choice, Path of the Wise, which increased my Mental Control as I leveled, increasing my control over skills and letting my mana regenerate faster.

If I were to find something I could really use to improve at this point, it was something with oomph, some nuclear ability I could use when the gloves were off. I could already handle lower-level enemies with ease and felt safe going up against most single beasts in the mountain one-on-one. The massively strong, resilient ones, though... I could do with additional firepower. I was hoping my new feat could provide that.

One notification made my future survival suddenly seem a lot more likely. A major flaw of mine had been that I could only manipulate shadows within my own domain. Now... things were looking up.

[Congratulations: You have improved a racial ability: Shadow Control becomes Improved Shadow Control.

Wherever there is light, shadows hide for you to manipulate. You are no longer restricted to being inside your domain for your Shadow Control to function.

Your ability to manipulate shadows has become second nature. You can remove them, deepen them, and have them move like living creatures with a single thought. The ability is limited by the size of your hoard and your Mental Power and Mental Control.]

I didn't get the choice of a regular feat, though. No, what I received was something bigger, more pervasive.

[Congratulations. By reaching level 25, you have unlocked access to your first Defining Feat. Choose one of the following:

[Codex of the Self. All strength comes from within. Your attributes gain a one-time increase of 50%.]

[Codex of the Trainer. All strength comes from those under your thrall. From now on, your minions gain 50% additional experience.]

[Codex of the Builder. All physical strength is as nothing, compared to the constructions you leave behind. Construction time and cost of all buildings is halved.]

This was the same thing as the first feat where I had to decide which attribute would grow automatically each level. Yet, this time, it was bigger than myself. Or at least, it could be. Codex of the Self was appealing. Still, it also felt somewhat shortsighted. Even with the massive boost I could get, I would likely not be able to measure up to something like Selys. Compared to the long-term boost Codex of the Trainer would give, which had no upper limit, it fell short. It was the last one that really tempted me. Codex of the Builder. With my mana regeneration, that would pretty much equate to being able to build anything I wanted at record speed, enabling me to put up a new domain in a couple of days? It was a siren call.

I selected [Codex of the Trainer] with a sigh and silent nod at myself. In the end, it wasn't about the buildings or the legacy you left, but the people you built it with. Heh. And now, those people would grow even more impressive.

Once I was done, I adopted a serious mien and cleared my throat. Then, I addressed them all. "Alright. We're not going to beat around the bush. Losing Aelis... hurts. Not only because of who she was, but also due to her knowledge and preparation. We need somebody to take responsibility over the scouts. I know who I'd recommend for the task – but it's for the Talpi to decide. Whoever it is has big shoes to fill."

Arthor huffed. "We do not use shoes, dragon. Regardless. No need to even debate this. Wreil. Come over here."

A slouched figure looked up from where he was resting, then moved closer. The dark-furred Talpus was tall, but his slouch had him appear lower. I hadn't talked much with him. From the wide smile on his face, he clearly didn't mind the attention. Everybody seemed to like him, too.

Arthor didn't wrap it up. "Wreil, you've heard about Aelis. You know what's going to happen. You're, what, two levels higher than the second best of the scouts?"

As he broke into our circle, he slouched even further, his paw grasping hard at his necklace. "No. Leith's same level as I am. We're both three levels higher than the next one."

Grex burst into laughter. "He is? Leith is good!"

The tall shaman waved off his concerns. "Pfah. I've met Leith. He's not a good choice."

Wreil bowed his head, earnesty and nerves battling for supremacy within him. "I can do the scouting. You know that. I... I can't be Aelis, though." I spotted glints of bone within his paw.

I smiled at him. "Nobody is asking you to. But we *do* need somebody to take responsibility for the scouts, and the task of choosing the right scouts for the job, making sure they're engaged correctly at all times, sent to the right places. Would you do it?"

He looked up at me. His paw clenched around the necklace, and I spotted the items that made the sounds. They were teeth, incisors of different kinds, painstakingly arranged on a leather strip. He held them hard. Reluctance oozed from him. "I guess. Besides, Leith would piss everybody off."

I nodded. "Thank you, Wreil. Now, we have other issues to

talk about. There are things I want us to handle better in the future."

Roth jumped up and pointed. "Looks like the future will have to wait for the future. Your escort is here, Onyx."

I looked up. Selys' pet was here, striding toward me with confident steps.

CHAPTER FOUR

We walked in silence back toward the fortress. I did not expect some sort of male bonding with the sorcerer after we had taken down the Soul Carver, but... a word of thanks would have been nice. I mean, I had saved his robed ass from being immolated. Nothing in his looks or movements displayed that he had any emotions. Hell, it looked like he had come straight from the cleaners, with his red robe completely smooth and clean and the golden mask polished to a reflective sheen.

When we arrived at the huge, gloomy, castle-like structure, it was like visiting it for the first time. On this occasion, my mind wasn't caught up in battle plans and self-recrimination, and I didn't have the Soul Carver to contend with. As a result, I could take the time to look at the place. It was actually quite bright on the inside and stylish, with the ever-present color scheme of red and gold. I couldn't help but smile a bit at the shinies. Lamps, vases, bright murals. It seemed like gaudy was the popular theme for red dragons.

Today, we took another route through the fortress. At first, I thought that it was a common misdirection to make sure that the visitor couldn't remember the path, but then I realized that, of all people, Selys would be aware that I could always follow the path in my mini-map. Looked like we were going somewhere else today. I didn't mind. I had no interest in reliving the experiences of the battle with the Soul Carver, especially with how close I'd come to dying.

Fifteen minutes of walking in silence through extravagant halls brought us to a set of nondescript large Stone Doors. The only special thing about the room was the placement. From the mini-map, I could tell that it was smack in the middle of the fortress, possibly of the mountain itself. We stood in absolute silence for a full minute in front of the door, and I was about to ask what was going on when I heard low noises like water rushing at the edge of my hearing. Then the sorcerer moved, flinging the doors open and standing to the side. "Enter the Blessing of Deyra."

Theatrical son of a bitch. I nodded and entered, bowing deep when I saw Selys inside. It was not a large room. In fact, with both Selys and myself in there, it felt slightly crowded. It was also completely unadorned, smooth walls and ceiling covering the nondescript, square room. Nondescript except for one thing. In the center of the room, a large bowl was carved into the floor. Something within the depression glowed, giving off a blue-red tinge that covered the walls and ceiling in undulating colors, not unlike a projector set to hippy-mode, painting the entire room with living, breathing waves of light.

Walking into the place was similar to settling into a very warm bath tub. A moment's sense of overwhelming heat followed by a deep, thorough feeling of relaxation. I let out an involuntary sigh.

A low rumble erupted from Selys. "The first time is an interesting experience, is it not?"

I nodded and moved slowly toward the bowl and sat down, looking closer. Inside, a liquid rested, unmoving but for the lights within that seemed to have its own life. "It really is. Is that what you were talking about? The Blessing of Deyra?"

She nodded. Her presence was less intimidating than it had

been earlier. Almost... reverent. "They say that once, long ago, Deyra walked among us and lived in all things. She was the living embodiment of every single drop of water and pile of dust. It was a time of kinship, equality, and love, where all manners of creatures lived together in harmony. With every breath of air and every mouthful of fruits and plants, you would take in a tiny bit of Her essence. Uncounted years of plenty and growth, of easy access for everybody to the most sacred of things. All beings were able to obtain almost unimaginable heights simply by living, breathing and eating."

She huffed. "Of course, this was not to be. I have heard many versions of the story, but the common denominator is this—dragons were said to be the first to understand the pathway to real power. Because, if you eat a piece of fruit holding a piece of Deyra, you gain merely the power inside that piece. But if you consume a creature that is already rife with Deyra's essence, the gains are much higher." She *hissed* with her eyes closed. "Those are rumored to have been the best ages for dragons, letting us rule over all lesser creatures with impunity, taking their essence and gifts as we saw fit. Some were quick to follow our example and gain power. Others scurried and hid underfoot. Ah, but I would have loved to be born back then. But of course, they were vain, believing that they could get away with their transgressions against her."

Selys' face carried a smug grin. "Deyra did not appreciate our quick thinking. Some species say that we were twisted into our current forms as a curse. The envy of lesser species. Others say that Deyra was shocked by our decisions and retreated from her watch. Whatever the reason, when she pulled away, she also took most of her blessing with her. Plants became less, simple nourishment, bereft of her energy. The days of plentitude ended, and we were left alone, rudderless and motherless, with only each other for company.

"We were not ones to mewl and cry in complaint, though. With Deyra gone, we were allowed free rein to do as we pleased. We thrived and grew. The other races fared worse. While new generations were still welcomed and introduced to the world by Deyra, they were left struggling, almost incapable of true growth without access to her essence. As the millennia passed, however, all races began to struggle."

"Dragons, too?" I asked quietly.

"Dragons, too. While we were the real powers of the world back then, we were also children of Deyra. We wanted to fight and grow. Once we had thinned the herd of the choicest meals, the only creatures with actual power that we could absorb were-"

"Other dragons." My mental voice was akin to a whisper as I tried to envision the idea of global dragon war.

"Exactly. And these dragons were not the paltry imitations of today. Even I am but a pale shadow of the monoliths of the past. Picture living, not for centuries, but for millenia, feasting on creatures rife with her essence." Selys shook her head, eyes aglow with an inner fire. "In their struggles, they tore the world apart. Swaths of land were laid barren, covered in ashes, layered in ice, or cloaked in permanent shadows. Even as some of us grew, many perished."

I had to ask. "Dragons, I mean we, do not live as long as back then?"

She expelled breath from her nostrils in a noisy huff. "Oh we do. If we survive." Selys settled her massive head near the glowing pool and lapped at the liquid within. A tiny shudder moved through her body. "You can imagine what happened next. We were far from alone in the world, and even at the top of our might, there were always challengers who wanted to fight us to take our power for themselves. At first, the challengers were mostly the larger species. Wyverns. Frostborn. Elementals. Any being who consumed enough of Deyra's essence to grow in strength and dared challenge us. We fended them off with little trouble, though, and ruled the lands with an iron fist, keeping the lesser races as thralls. Still, compared to the other creations of Deyra, we were dwindling, and our spawn were pale imitations of ourselves, bereft of the access to Deyra's gifts. Growth for newly fledged dragons had become much, much harder. Over the next centuries, our kind struggled to maintain our power as our thralls challenged our reign. I will spare you the details. Yet, with few exceptions, we were forced to move into the wilderness, fleeing from the trouble of having to constantly defend ourselves against all comers. Cowards. That was what led to our downfall. That, and the humans."

"The humans?" I sat up straighter. She had mentioned them earlier, but never went into any detail. Even though I wasn't technically a human, I still *craved* to hear more about my kind.

"Yes. Our thralls. It was all of the humanoids, really. We kept them to serve us, because they were weak and easily controlled. Or so we thought. The humans have always been the most prolific and the first ones to group together. Annoying critters. You will know by now that all creatures are born with a fixed scale of importance. If you are high in the hierarchy, you grow faster and earn better skills and feats than the lower, less important creatures.

"This is natural and it is *right*. Should a weaker creature have the same rights and possibilities as one of us? Of course not. They should serve us or serve as food, as our mood sees fit. The humans were the first to truly challenge that right. They are not strong and adequate at best in their gifts, but they are numerous, inventive, and so *horribly* adaptable. They fled the safety of our protection and started banding together, forming their own places.

"Of course, we burned them as they were built, but there were always *more!* What started out as outposts in far-away regions soon grew into actual kingdoms as they started challenging the powers throughout the realms. Emboldened by their audacity, other humanoids took lessons from them, casting off the rightful hierarchies and slinking away to form their own cultures."

Selys looked lost in thought for a while. Then she growled. "We were too slow and complacent. Ages of being on top let us doubt their power and the rate at which they spread. Once the dragon rulers left across the lands took heed of the spreading humanoid kingdoms and groupings, they were too late. While they were weak, they were many, and so inventive. With tools, magic, and tactics, the former invulnerable rulers were forced to flee or be outright killed.

Burkan of the Light was taken down by Dworgen, the group of dwarf-like deep dwellers that came to rule the north. Corisan the Venomous was outmaneuvered by the rune magic of a cult of humans. The Living Flame herself was forced into the frozen wastes by elves and never heard of again. With each of these defeats, our kind grew weaker and our descendants less able to take on the growing presence of the humanoids. The only thing that saved us from extinction was the fact that they war among themselves as often as with us."

"What about other strong creatures like ourselves?"

"What?" Selys looked confused for a bit. "Oh, they have probably had a bad time of it, too. There are settlements of them out there, here and there, like the Frostborn Maze of Tergal, but they are few and far between. That is beside the point, however."

I bowed my head. "Sorry. Please continue."

"What is important is that, a few centuries ago, the humanoids discovered that Deyra had not disappeared from us entirely as we thought. No, there were areas where her powers shone forth into the world."

"...like the Blessing of Deyra?"

"Just so. And for those who know how to access her gifts, the possibilities are endless."

I tried to picture it inside my mind as she explained. Like... lava creating volcanoes where the tectonic plates allowed for the superheated mass to break through, so did Deyra's Blessings spill out in certain places. With a world dominated by warring humanoids and riddled with monsters, they started learning about areas where the power gain was stronger than usual. What would happen? Some would learn of this and try to use it to their advantage. Then...

"The power balances are shifting?"

A low rumble of approval arose from Selys. "You have an interesting mind. Yes. Where the factions around the world wise up to the fact that there is power to be tapped, the world rearranges itself. Factions rise and fall in unforeseeable ways, depending on who gets access to the Blessings. But the important factor is this: Those who have learned of a Blessing use it for their own gains and keep it secret. The knowledge remains isolated, and nobody has yet made a serious move. Before I came to the mountain, I captured and interrogated many humanoids and they said the same - it has not devolved into open war." She huffed. "Yet. It has been a few decades since I came here, but I doubt the situation has changed much in that little time.

"You aim to be the first to command more than one Blessing?"

Selys' grin grew monstrous as she stretched her neck toward the ceiling. "I mean to win them all! I will locate the Blessings that are still hidden, like this one, and take the rest by force. I am going to reclaim the world for dragonkind. Controlling the Blessings, we will be able to regain the hold on lesser species, like we used to."

"We?"

She nodded, eyes looking down on mine. "Yes. We. I will leave the worthy among us in charge to rule while I take over the rest of the world. My offspring, such as you, if you prove capable, or some of the few remaining survivors. There are others I may reach out to. As for you, Onyx, you have outgrown the kin in your clutch and managed to impress me with the Soul Carver. Yet, that is for nothing if you are unable to keep control of those beneath you. This is why I brought you here today."

Suddenly, the blue-red colors of the walls were distorted as the room was filled with a huge map, showing the entirety of the upper layer of the Scoured Mountain. "The power inside the mountain is focused here, at Fire Peak. You will learn more about exactly what that means. However, you will also have to adjust to one simple fact. While the Blessing of Deyra grants the rightful owner the largest boon, it affects the remainder of the Scoured Mountain. Enough that, even at your strongest, you would not be able to contend against their collective might, nor keep up with their growth. This is why I maintain them in a stranglehold, make sure my minions are devoted to me and not their own tribes."

I nodded. That made sense. In the end, I was but one dragon, and the mountain was filled with creatures, growing faster than everywhere else not influenced by a Blessing. Even with the entirety of Fire Peak behind me, control would be difficult, especially when Selys left.

"This is why you need to maintain the hierarchies and keep your underlings in their place, as I have done." The map switched, expanding to show a much larger area, riddled with tunnels, caves, and natural phenomena. I wanted to stare at it forever. The detail was amazing, and the number of places it showed portrayed exactly how well Selys knew the mountain, compared to myself. The winding passages we were looking at didn't look too familiar.

"Where is this?"

"This is the layer right below ours. The opening that led you upward is here." She indicated a tiny, slanted tunnel on the map and I nodded thoughtfully. They looked recognizable, with what little I had explored down there. The rest of it, however. Heh. It'd probably be a day or more to travel across, even if it was near the top of the mountain. Of course, the tunnels were still covered in gray, given that she wasn't there in the flesh. But three large areas stood out, the living colors showing that she was able to explore them through the map right now, should she so choose.

I took a guess. "Those three bright spaces are where your vassals live?"

"Yes. The largest groups of non-dragons inside the mountain. Each of them is able to tap into the Blessing in their own limited way, like you did with your hoard. They may not be as powerful as your hoard, but the Blessing will still afford them limited advantages over weaker groupings that are unable to access Deyra's powers directly. None of my vassals alone would be able to challenge me for sheer power, especially taking the defenses in the city into consideration. Combined, their might overpower even that of Fire Peak... except, I have them well in claw. This is the issue. I *could* leave you in charge right now. But the moment I take my absence from the mountain, my control over my vassals will fade. Knowing them, you would be challenged as soon as they figured out that there is a new force in charge." Her aura was suddenly tangible, intimidation oozing from her.

"That would *not* do. I will not accept having my plans ruined by an incompetent who is unable to hold the lesser races of the mountain in place. While you have impressed me with your growth and capabilities, you also show weakness. You allow your underlings to act as if they were close to your equals. You do not punish those who speak up against you. You did not even secure access to the hoard of your blue sibling when you had him beat."

She sneered, disgust obvious in her. "In here, weakness will be taken advantage of swiftly. So, unless you convince me that you can be strong enough, I would rather hunt down my consort again, carry a second clutch, and search for a new successor. A few years may make a dent in my plans, but losing control of the Scoured Mountain would ruin them entirely.

"So, I charge you with this: You need to bring these three tribes under your control and have them accept your dominance. I grant you a month. You will do this without my assistance and interference. If you manage this, I will accept your vows and grant you dominance over the Blessing in my absence. If you fail, you were not worth my time to begin with." The map faded away, leaving only the weight of Selys' countenance as she glared down on me.

Wow. Okay. No pressure at all. Thanks, Selys. "I will do it." The words sprang from my mind, even as I reeled. Heh. It wasn't like she was giving me an option here anyways. "When do I leave?"

"In the morning. I will provide you with food for the journey." She stretched her neck and spread her wings wide. The huge wings reached the walls on either side, and the moving colors painted her with a demonic tone before she moved, and her looks softened. "Let it not be said that Selys is ungrateful. Before you leave, I will allow you to have a taste of what can become yours. Go on, my child. Drink from the Blessing."

With an additional glance at her towering presence, I carefully moved forward toward the bowl. Lowering my head, I looked down into the depression, filled with unmoving liquid. Inside the liquid, colors moved, as if of their own volition, and I almost believed that I saw shapes moving about below the surface. "Here goes nothing." I thought and let my tongue roll out of my mouth, lapping carefully at the liquid within.

The sensation was unfathomable, hard to describe. I could only compare it to... it was like... picture seeing a loved one after too much time apart. That pit in the stomach that leaves you almost short of breath, even if you know it's all in your head. Then imagine the sensation you get, when you partake in a spicy meal that is *just* strong enough to leave you gasping for breath, but it's still *so* good.

Then picture those sensations traveling over the entire body in waves. I had been mostly unaware of all the smaller hurts and agues from the battle the day before. Now, they came back to me, as the waves washed them away, leaving my body feeling both lighter and stronger. Cold, heat and pleasure rushed through me, leaving me momentarily unable to talk or even think. Before I knew it, I had drained the bowl and stumbled back, numb and overwhelmed.

Selys laughed. The coughing rumble of her belly laughter filled the chamber as she shook with glee. "I know what that is like. Now, leave me. I will see you off tomorrow."

I was barely able to gather my thoughts as I left the chamber, accompanied by the human pet who was waiting outside.

Like awakening from a heavy slumber, I slowly forced myself back from the overwhelming sensations, and I was left with an unusual clarity of mind, finally able to look at the list of notifications that popped up after drinking the liquid.

[You have partaken of the Blessing of Deyra
The Blessing expands your connection with Deyra, allowing you to approach the utilization of the maximal capabilities of your species for learning. Your body is similarly boosted, increasing your natural attributes, regeneration rates, and learning capabilities.
- Your attributes are boosted by +48%
- Mana regeneration rate doubled
- Health regeneration rate doubled
- Experience gain doubled
- Additional constructions available
Time remaining: 71 hours, 58 minutes]

Holy cheat skills, Batman! That was incredible. No wonder Selys was so goddamn dominating. If she had spent years upon years inside the mountain boosted like this *and* gaining twice the experience than she normally would? That fully explained why she was so much stronger than everything else. Huh. And those 48% were probably because she took a mouthful herself–might have been a full 50% otherwise. So, if I managed to become her successor, this would be mine? Pretty goddamn powerful incentive.

I was lost in my own thoughts while we navigated the walkways of the fortress, completely ignoring the splendor and decoration. When we stepped outside the building, the sun had traveled beyond the edges of the crater, leaving Fire Peak swathed in shadows. We started on the walk toward my minions, when my guide suddenly spoke up. "Why did you save me?"

Shaken out of deep thoughts, I didn't follow him right away. "Huh. What?"

In the fading light, the golden mask of the powerful human sorcerer hid his expression, but his eyes cut right into mine. "When the Soul Carver attacked. Why did you decide to save me?"

I gathered my thoughts. "Two reasons. First was that you seemed the strongest of Selys' guards."

"You could not know that." he challenged.

"I guess I couldn't. Still, the others succumbed fast, while you held on. It was a guess, and it paid off. My second reason..." I debated not saying it, but for some reason, it spilled from me. Perhaps it was the fact that this was the only human except the Soul Carver and Timothy I'd talked with in this world. Perhaps I was still shell-shocked from the near-religious experience of the Blessing. "It's that I used to be a human myself. I died in the world I came from and was reborn here. I guess I felt some sort of kinship with you—a need to protect you, like you were one of mine."

The tall human froze in place next to me and stared at me. The seconds passed until he finally shook his head in disbelief. "You are serious." Silence grew back, and I started to look around. We must have looked suspicious, stopped like that, right in front of the gates of the fortress. Finally, he began walking, looking down. "You will *not* tell Selys about this. I cannot imagine how she would act if she knew, but it may not be enjoyable for you. She holds no love for humans. Besides, you and I *do* have something in common. Because I'm not a Human anymore. That stopped when I swore an oath to Selys. Now I'm only her pet. A monster like you."

That put a dampener on the mood. We crossed the city in silence, finally arriving back near my people. "I was given orders to tell you the following. Pay attention or let it be on your own head. First off, the Soul Carver's minions carried his hoard when they entered the city. You have been allowed to keep it. She has only removed a few items she deemed dangerous."

Very fucking generous, since it was my hoard in the first

place. I inclined my head graciously, though, and didn't say anything.

"On top of this, in her generosity and in recognition that her plans might have been postponed, had she been forced to deal with the Soul Carver by herself, she will grant you a single boon. You are allowed to ask for an item or minion within reason."

I didn't breathe, didn't pause to think about it. "I need a healer. Somebody who can join my ranks and keep my wounded people healthy." Even if I didn't have the current load of wounded minions to take care of, it had been a serious lack ever since the early days.

The sorcerer waited to see if I added anything, but then inclined his head. "That should be within my capabilities to arrange. Selys said that you are to leave in the morning. Before that, you will have your healer." Then, without further words, he turned and walked away.

Behind the ring of nervous guards, Roth was training, throwing clawed punches at the air. Belying the flurry of blows and evasive maneuvers, his mental voice rang out toward me, cheery and loud. His fur was matted with sweat as he grinned at me. "Have fun?"

CHAPTER FIVE

"Our wounds are often the openings into the best and most beautiful part of us." – David Richo

The rest of the day flew by. The news that we would have a healer was welcomed with open arms. The scope of the mission we had before us? Not so welcome. My minions were still reeling from the uncertainty, stress, and shock of the time under the Soul Carver. I instructed them all to rest and recuperate as well as possible, and that the healer would take care of the remainder before we were to leave in the morning. I hoped that whoever he or she was would be able to deliver on it.

In the evening, I asked Arthor and Timothy to join me for a chat. Arthor looked much better already. Some rest had done him well. Timothy was silent, pensive.

We debated the details of the task we had before us, then I concluded. "We won't be going into battle, though. We're leaving for home."

Arthor sniffed at the air. "We're fleeing? Are things looking that bad?"

"No. We need to take the time to rest and think, however.

Our people have gone from one battle to the next. We need a break. If we move straight into battle right now, we *will* fail."

Timothy agreed right away. "Yes. It will allow us time to plan, both for the long and short term."

Arthor, on the other hand, was less certain. "Pfah. It sounds like a waste of time. We will lose at least a week like this, having to go back and then retrace our steps, plus however long we spend at home. We could use the time more efficiently here."

I nodded. "Yes. We could. But we need to be smart about this. And, let's face it, our people aren't doing too well right now. We need to rest, train, and build up our forces uninterrupted. We can't face three of the strongest forces of the mountain in battle as we are and hope to emerge victorious. If we spend two weeks resting up in preparation for that, I'll count it well-spent. Also, I want us to finally have a long discussion about the future. We need to act, not just react all the damn time." I had one more reason I wanted to go home, but I wouldn't say it. It was only a hunch. But if I was right, it could mean a world of difference.

The shaman looked behind him. A large part of our people were sleeping. Those who weren't were moving on with their day, keeping themselves busy or talking. Still, it was only too easy to find the wounded, or those who sat or lay, staring at nothing with shell-shocked impressions. Only the pups seemed to be entirely immune, and even they had sudden bursts of crying or whining.

He turned back with a grimace. "You are at least half right. We're used to running for our lives and living on the move. The mountain leaves no room for worrying about the future. I will grant you this: the past months *have* been especially hard on us."

I stared him straight in the eye. "So, let us go home. Let us heal." He took a deep breath, then nodded. His shoulders visibly relaxed as what must have been a huge burden on him finally released and I couldn't help but add, "God knows we've earned it."

The following day, Selys' pet was there to see us off. He kept his promise regarding the healer, too. To my surprise, the healer was neither a he or a she—but an it.

"What *is* that?" I glared down at the slowly moving pile of caustic-looking layered goop that rested on the floor. There were no body parts there, nor bones. It looked like somewhere between flowing lava and the nuclear waste they portray in comics, painted a dull brown and oozing along the cobblestones.

"An Ergul. I am the one holding its mental leash at this moment. You will need to keep it beside you until it becomes your minion. It only reacts to mental commands, and once it's bonded, only to yours. Right now, anybody with the necessary mental capacities can command it."

Anybody? I'd have to keep it close then, so nobody could just take it away. "Okay? Is it hostile? What can it do?"

"No. Its simple mind has been broken. It has no hostility. Should you die, it might become aggressive again, but then, that would not be a concern for you anymore. It is... I'm not sure how to explain it. It eats or dissolves meat and other materials and can reform that into what is needed."

I blinked. That sounded... really creepy. "How does it work?"

He shrugged. "I haven't seen the Ergul in action. Try it out."

I looked from the large pile of goop and back to my minions and sent my thoughts outward. "So, this creature is supposed to be able to heal us. Any volunteers?"

A bit of scrambling later, and they came to a compromise. We centered on a sleeping Crawl who was out cold with a nasty injury. His shoulder was a mess, hardened skin perforated and smashed in several places, sporting deep, reeking half-healed wounds. I recognized him as one of the Crawls who'd almost been slaughtered in the ambush from heavy-set, but agile, Ethium. Focusing on the creature, I sent a mental command to the Ergul. "Go ahead. Heal him."

With disturbing speed, the slime being bubbled toward the

Crawl. Starting from the feet, it oozed over his body, widening out to engulf the entire, ugly humanoid. I almost asked the sorcerer if it was likely to suffocate the Crawl, but relented. He said it was a healer. I would have to take his word for it. When the entirety of the squat Crawl's body had disappeared beneath the oozing form of the Ergul, a small tremble ran through its entire mass.

A few seconds later, the slime... concentrated, for lack of a better word, flowing together to settle in on top of the damaged shoulder. There, its ugly mass started shaking back and forth, wobbling with the violence of the movement, while a barely perceptible light gathered in the center of its mass. Then, as suddenly as the shaking had started, it stopped and the slime flowed off the Crawl.

As one, we moved closer to the downed Crawl, and a surprised rumble escaped me. I don't know what I expected, but this was not it. The wound was simply gone. Not only that, the surrounding flesh looked healthy, and the unhealthy stench coming from the Crawl's wound was slowly fading. Where the wounds had been, flesh had flowed in to fill the holes. It wasn't perfect. The Ergul could obviously not replicate the creation of the hardened layers of skin, and the Crawl would suffer from a lack of armor in the healed spots, unless his body would be able to recreate the armor eventually. Also, it looked like the process had devoured some of the muscle mass on the Crawl, leaving him slightly lopsided. Still... I shook my head in amazement. Where, a minute ago, his breathing had been labored and broken, now it was easy and relaxed. I had no doubt the Crawl would wake up healthy and hale.

There were no teary-eyed goodbyes here. I thanked the sorcerer for the healer and we loaded up the assembled hoard and took off, marching homeward. When I looked behind me, at the dark fortress overseeing Fire Peak, the overall sensation running through me was not one of fear or doubt. I would probably be wise to fear the coming challenge, but I didn't. I had my people at my side, and the future was looking up. And we were going home. That ,more than anything else, plastered a wide smile on my face.

CHAPTER SIX

The ensuing travel was, in many ways, the same as the trip out. We scouted ahead, were cautious and made haste as well as we could. Regardless, it felt like the two journeys couldn't be compared. The mood was great, for one. We had no over-hanging threats, and Selys' challenge lay far enough in the future that we were able to relax slightly. And that we did. While we made sure to remain focused on our safety, the mood slowly improved as we trudged down the mountain.

Before, the Imps' nature had been an annoyance, their constant chatter underlining how their carelessness set them apart from the rest of us. Now it felt different, even contagious, and they earned the occasional hard-won smile from us as they roamed the tunnels, playing among each other carelessly. Oh, and they kept up. That was another miracle. They might not be able to keep up at a forced march, but the tiny fliers had improved enough that they were actually capable of keeping up with the hardier of our minions, even at a decent pace.

We didn't scout out the vassals on the second floor. We had no desire to alert them to our presence yet–that would come in due time. The only person we sent elsewhere was Leith, a perpetually sour, dirty Talpus scout. He went to inform my blue dragon vassal, Creive, that I had indeed survived and might call upon him soon.

I did note an interesting change with our scouts. I didn't know who had instigated it, but they weren't Talpi scouts going out by themselves anymore. There were also at least two Crawls tagging along now, and often an Imp flying above them all. According to Wreil, they had learned that having them as a defensive measure if something went wrong wasn't a bad play, even at the cost of some of their regular stealth. Our dysfunctional family was, little by little, growing more like an actual family, albeit a strange one.

We even took breaks now and again, enjoying the lack of overwhelming threats or threatening slave drivers. For myself, I took the chance to practice my flying. Whenever the ceiling was high enough, I'd float, fly, dodge or maneuver, trying to get the hang of advanced flight. It wasn't ever going to be impressive until I managed to find a place under open skies or a huge cavern the size of Creive's, but every little bit helped.

During our first real break, I decided to follow the conventions of how a dragon ought to behave and spend the time to meticulously go through the hoard and see what Selys had stolen, with my minions lingering nearby to see the result. It was a positive surprise. No doubt, she had kept the best and most powerful items of the Soul Carver for herself. But it would seem that her idea of what comprised a good item differed from mine.

Grex's eyes boggled, and he laughed uproariously as he pointed at a short wand from the pile. "Mine! I need that. Onyx, can I?"

I carefully inspected the device. "Wand of Middling Winds. Really? Are you trying to become a mage? Or blow enemy fliers out of the air?"

"Nonono. Weak wand, you see. Many uses, but not much power. Use it on myself, blow away from attackers. Turn faster."

I tried to picture the energetic Imp if he had a way to move about in the air even faster and failed. This might end up causing his demise, but my curiosity demanded I let him try.

I nodded and looked at the piles before me. On one side lay the items from my old hoard. Nothing had gone missing that I could spot. There were more than thirty new items, of various shapes and powers. Most were simple, huge weapons. The Soul Carver had been pretty direct with regards to his undead. None of them were amazingly powerful, but a few of them...

I singled out a few to give to people who deserved it. One was a staff sling, with a +3 Agility modifier. Another, a magical throwing axe infused with the ability to return to the wielder at the cost of mana. Apparently, Leith, the cranky Talpus scout, had a throwing skill, so we set the throwing axe aside for him, while the staff sling went to one of the ranged fighters. The rest were simple items with +1 or +2 modifiers that I'd definitely dish out in the case of a battle, but for now, we'd stash them in the hoard.

We were having a break in an abandoned hallway, on an old, worn down brick road, when I decided to gather my companions and bring up a sore topic.

"When we talked about the reason for going home, I said it was because we needed the break, to recover. That was the truth, but only a half-truth." I took a deep breath, then continued. "Fire Peak was not the place for that discussion. However, we had to get out of there, because we are now set on a path that is likely to bring us into conflict with Selys."

The onslaught of exclamations and, in one case, descriptive cursing, was not unexpected. I craned my neck to look at the tall shaman who glared right back at me. "You can handle the truth, Arthor. It's one of the attributes I admire in you. You don't need coddling, but rather, you face the facts. Well, accepting Selys' task avoided a conflict with her. However, I believe that conflict *will* come sooner or later, regardless of what happens."

Arthor crossed his arms right away. "Explain yourself, dragon."

I looked at them all in turn. It was hard to imagine that, a few short months earlier, I would have seen all of them as monsters or some really interesting new kinds of pets. Now, however, they were as close as anybody I'd ever known, barring my ex-wife and daughter. I did not relish having to once again throw their future into uncertainty.

"It is true. Our situation is not looking too good. I believe that at some point, there will be blood between us, and I would rather that we face it well-prepared." I grimaced. "I do not like it any more than you do, but let's look at the facts. There is no certainty that we can handle the challenge that Selys has set before us.

"We might have to flee. Should we make it, however, I'll be facing the oath that the Soul Carver refused to swear. What do you believe will happen then? Do you believe that she will grant me free rein, let me loose to handle the mountain as I see fit. Or, will I be forced into servitude and compelled to follow the rules and systems that Selys has set in place?"

I did not need to sense their crestfallen emotions to know what the answer was. The silence and their averted gazes spoke volumes. I shook my head. "It's not a given. How does the oath work? Is it a formality, weak enough that I can swear it and still be able to work toward a good society for all of us? If that is the case, though, why would the Soul Carver refuse to swear? No, I believe that, at some point, we *will* be forced to make a decision: submit, flee, or fight. And if it comes down to a choice between submitting and fighting, I would rather fight for a free future for us than bow and accept slavery. One taste of that under the Soul Carver was enough for me."

The sensations coming from my people were mostly subdued and morose. After a moment of silence, Grex was the one to float toward the tall ceiling of the hallway and speak up. "This will be *fun!*" The tiny Imp whirled around us, cackling with glee. As he watched the others staring at him, he threw up his hands. "What? Don't tell me you don't want to do it. Throw off the chains. Bring 'em all crashing down. Fire 'em up! Fire 'em up!"

A moment's shocked silence ensued until Roth started chuckling, and suddenly his laughter rang out into the dark cavern. Shortly, the rest joined in until we were all cackling with the absurdity of the tiny creature throwing his challenge at the mightiest beast in the mountain.

Roth pointed at Grex, wiping tears from his eyes. "That settles it. I like you. You're going to get yourself killed, but I like you." He turned from the jittery Imp who was still grinning like a loon and faced the other Talpi. "While he and the other Imps are attacking, I'll be well over here, where we have a chance of survival. Who's with me?"

Creziel ignored Roth's antics, looking straight at me. "Onyx. Would you *prefer* to fight Selys over fleeing?"

I gave him a fond smile. He had come a long way, daring to ask something as direct as this. "Not at first, but yes." I held up a claw, forestalling any arguments. "I hope to see Selys off on her quest, while we use all the time we earn to prepare ourselves, grow, and reduce Selys' influence and power. I also plan to learn what exactly the oath covers, then use whatever loopholes I can find in it.

"At this point, we have nothing but speculation about the oath. Even so, if it kept the Soul Carver from taking up the place that he wanted, it must be magical in nature." I held up a claw. "Should we manage all of this, we might build a decent place to live for ourselves for some time. Yet, even if we do create our own society, Selys *will* destroy it at some point. If we back out and stay away from her, she will chase us and hunt us down. Why? Simply, because everything she plans goes against what we want.

"I have already told you what she is planning—to rule the world. Not just the mountain, the entire world. Enslave all humans and other humanoids, forcibly take over all Blessings of Deyra throughout the lands, and install her own offspring to handle them under her rule. The only other viable alternative would be to flee the Scoured Mountain entirely, and that would still leave Selys in charge of the Blessing here. And you know what? Any situation that leaves Selys in charge and us enslaved or running for our lives doesn't sound that excellent to me."

Arthor's eyes shot daggers at me, and the rocks floating around him looked like they were poised to fly my way. "You're saying this like we don't know how to hide. Dragon, even if Selys decides we're her mortal enemies, we can find a hole to escape her notice. You would drag us into this conflict?"

"With your eyes wide open? Yes. Not against your will, however."

They were silent for a while. Creziel was the first one to talk. "So let me get this straight. What you're saying is either we fight Selys for a better world, run away and hope we are not found, or bow our necks and forget all about it?"

I grimaced. "I'm not saying we need to face her down right *now*. Still, yeah. That's how I see things."

"Do we have a chance against her? I do not mean in subduing the ones on the second layer. I mean against Selys herself." I felt nothing but honesty coming from the tiny Shaman.

I gave him my most earnest smile. "If we get the time to grow? I believe we do. We have already earned enough levels and trained hard enough that we have moved past the limits anybody would usually attribute to our races. We can continue training, earning new powers and improving our equipment to the point where our combined might will be able to face any other race inside the mountain. In fact, I have just earned a new feat that pretty much ensures we should earn the strength to handle things in the long run."

Roth sneered. "That's not the point, though. If we fight Selys, we won't be facing off against one other group. We'll be dealing with *all* of them."

Arthor interrupted. "Pfah. Use your tiny head, Roth! That isn't likely. The lower layers aren't used to dealing with Selys, and they'll flee rather than face her. And the tribes on the upper layers who live accustomed to her rule... we're supposed to handle them ourselves first, aren't we?"

I nodded, happy that Arthor saw the point. "Exactly. Who knows what will happen in our conflicts with those groups? At worst, we will have the chance to fight them, weaken them. At best, we may gain new allies."

"That still leaves us with the entirety of Fire Peak pitted against us. And Selys."

"True. And that is not a happy prospect. Still, that is only if we have to fight Selys before we manage to even the odds. And even if it does happen, we would not face them head-on. We would fight them our way with traps, ambushes, and illusions. Make them suffer every step of the trip and shrink away before they could strike back at us."

Arthor insisted. "Do you think you could fight Selys and win, though?"

Annoying little critter. He had a way of being insightful and right. "No. I do not plan to, either. I wouldn't face her. I would bring the mountain down on her, harass her with spells from afar, attack through hidden openings and never ever allow myself to be trapped."

Arthor grunted. "At least you know your own strengths, and ours. Good. We will need time to discuss this. I do not know if we are ready to face the forces of Selys, but the vision of a future where we can be free—entirely free—is tempting. We will talk about it."

I bowed my head. "There is no need for a decision yet. We may soon reach a point where we need to decide, however. So talk and think. "

As Tim and I watched the others walk away, he asked. "Do you think they'll come around?"

"No clue. They've lived forever on the lower rungs of society. They might not be able to understand how much they've grown."

"Sure." Timothy was silent for a long while, until he

suddenly blurted out, "Seriously. Do we have a chance? I mean, really?"

"Honestly? Yes. Whatever else we've learned about the mountain, one thing is certain. Everybody we've met is crap at tactics. Most of the races, even the ones led by dragons, seem unable to come up with anything more convoluted than a sneaky ambush or a head-on attack. We can use that. Still..." I shuddered. "I hope I won't have to face Selys in battle... ever. She's scary."

"Yeah. Here's to hoping she leaves, and we get to convert all her allies to our side."

"Agreed. Heh. Or we'll wake up and this was all a dream."

He stared at me, blinking. "Wow. If that happened, I'd have to spank my subconscious."

CHAPTER SEVEN

"Sometimes I wonder whether the world is being run by smart people who are putting us on or by imbeciles who really mean it." - Laurence J. Peter

The answer to my question regarding what we were going to do with Selys came two days after our departure in the form of a cranky shaman. Our travels up to Fire Peak had been hard, stressed, and filled with caution, since we couldn't allow the Soul Carver's forces to be spotted. Moving down was different. *We* were different. Higher-leveled, tougher, and more aware of our strengths. Our travels had continued with few incidents, and we were almost at the lowest layer of the mountain. This far down, few monsters dared challenge us or even posed a threat, and the few groups of monsters that we encountered we handled with little delay.

I could tell straight away from Arthor's demeanor that this was not a courtesy call. Even if he hadn't radiated focus, the way he held himself was a dead giveaway. His usual sardonic grimace was absent. "Dragon," he halted and addressed me.

"Arthor." I lowered my head so he could look me in the eyes.

The Talpus didn't waste any time. "We have discussed your proposal." His face twisted. "Pfah. Fight or flight. This shouldn't even be a discussion for a Talpus."

"But?"

"But you have messed up all natural responses. I am not surprised that the Imps would join your stratagem; they have little self-preservation. As for the Crawls, I would not expect them to have the brains to know what is best for them. Roth is not a surprise, either. But he is not the only one. Even Creziel believes in your plan. Pfah. That new feat of yours, Codex of the Trainer, doesn't help. They are adjusting their sights, seeing new heights they can reach." He glared at me. "If we do join the struggle, what assurances do we have?"

My answer was instant. "You know I cannot promise anything. I will, however, give you my word that I'll give it my all to ensure that we make it. And, if things go bad, we *will* flee rather than face annihilation. We are going to do this our way. And if all goes well, it won't be an issue for years to come, while we grow and thrive."

He took a deep breath. "Alright. In that case, we will join you. But I will tell you this once and once only. Talpi know the value of flight. It has been the basis of our survival for our tribe for generations. Still, at your side, we are learning to appreciate other approaches. Working together. Aiming for greater things. Pfah. I am babbling like a pup eager to ambush his first Hermit Rat. What I mean to say is this: Your actions have earned our trust. Do not misuse it."

I didn't respond to that, meeting his gaze with my own, unwavering. After a brief pause, he nodded and our talk went on to more practical issues.

The rest of our return trip was uneventful. What few monsters we met were low-leveled and weak, with one exception, a single Orugal which we managed to hit with an ambush so devastating the powerful monster never even managed to pinpoint our presence. All told, where the last trip to Fire Peak took us almost five days, the return trip was less than three. The experience gains were quite decent, too, with the Orugal granting most of the 2300 experience I got and an additional 500 from Creive. He was on a *roll*.

CHAPTER EIGHT

The homecoming was sheer joy. Everybody spread out into our lair, finding their places with cries of satisfaction and thrilled sensations. At first, I withheld my pleasure, waiting to see what had happened in our absence. The moment I saw the Gallery of Illusions still active, however, I released a roar of triumph and joined the others as they charged toward our home. I wasted no time in re-establishing the hoard, then went straight on to investigate the damage.

The actual physical damage from when the green and blue dragons had attacked was still very much front and center, but it could have been a lot worse. There was little structural damage, and what was left was mostly clean-up and superficial burn marks, chipped tiles, scorched walls, and the like.

It was the first chance I had to see in practice what happened when you removed a hoard and let the place stand. I had feared it would be more profound. The worst parts were the farms. The Growth Boost had run out, and all this time without watering had taken its toll on the crops. They weren't all dead, but definitely flagging. Laive and the others had their work cut out for them.

Judging by what remained from the Soul Carver's lair when I had first entered the place, and what had happened with Timothy trapped inside the Soul Circle, I had an idea, but I finally got it verified. I was right. I loved being right! Since all constructions needed mana to exist, the moment you removed the hoard that formed the link between them and Deyra, they stopped receiving mana and started draining their reserves. Once they ran out of mana, they simply went poof, leaving no sign of their former presence.

Our timing... well, it wasn't bad. Not at all. Sure, all the Shadow Towers had evaporated, but over half of them had already been ruined in the fight with the two dragons. All Stone and Shadow Doors were gone too, as were the Growth Boosts and Habitats. Everything with a mana cost below 200, basically. The rest, however, remained. I was especially glad to see the Training Chambers and Sorcery Chamber still up. Our people would be able to go straight back to training right away, and with my insane mana regeneration, it would be a matter of a handful of days, at most, before we had the domain back to the conditions from before that crazy necromancer had gatecrashed our party.

As I supervised the Crawls unloading the, by now, pretty massive contents of the hoard from off the backs of my Clenchers, the sides of my mouth couldn't help climbing up. The very second that the first item hit the ground, I got the request to establish the hoard. I clicked yes, mentally preparing for the incoming deluge of notifications, as they kept unloading items and my hoard grew in size and efficiency, with the changes that entailed. The system didn't disappoint.

I breathed a silent sigh of relief. I knew in my mind that, since I'd already established one hoard here, doing it again shouldn't be an issue. But watching it spring into being and forming a connection with the constructions inside the throne room ensured that I wouldn't have to start from scratch. That was one giant pain in the neck averted.

I went through the details regarding the hoard one-by-one,

skimming to see if there was anything new. Habitat, Training Chamber, doors and towers - no, no, no, and no. It was all repetition of what I already knew. I mentally swiped the notifications away, faster and faster. Hoard Defense, Sorcery Chamber, Gallery of Illusions, The rooms and their upgrades were the exact same as when we dismantled the hoard.

I maintained one single, final notification.

[Criteria to upgrade hoard:
- Reach a minimum of level 25
- Improve contents of the hoard
- Own at least 30 Mana Crystals
- Create one of each constructions]

Huh. Nice. That had seemed a lot more unreachable the last time I looked. I needed to build one of each kind of available construction. That would mean... six, total. Then a handful of Mana Crystals - okay, eight - and improving the contents of my hoard on top of that. Yeah, I was getting that. Just needed to get the basics up and running first.

For a moment, I considered bringing in everybody to discuss how we were going to spend the time here, but then I reconsidered. I was going to allow people a chance to rest and recuperate, like we talked about, then tomorrow we could see about prepping to ensure that we'd be able to stand our own against whichever monsters we'd have to face.

As for me? I still had one issue. I glanced left at the one detail that was different from how I'd established the room. Right next to the throne, swirling lazily, remained the bright colors of the Essence Siphon the Soul Carver had constructed. Holding my breath, I selected Inspect on the Essence Siphon– and to my great relief, watched the details of the construction appear immediately.

[Essence Siphon
This Siphon works to transform the spilled lifeblood of any

being into temporary power for the creator. As the domain improves, so will the boons and duration of the increases.

- *Duration of temporary increase is doubled.*
- *On top of the increases, lifeblood will also replenish the life and mana of the creator. If he is already fully healed, the health and mana will be added as temporary points on top of his current points.*]

Amazing. I had feared that I'd be unable to use it due to some class restriction or because it belonged to the Soul Carver and not me, or that it wouldn't reconnect to my hoard properly or something. Now that I had it, I knew that people could actually combine constructions in the same hoard. I would, theoretically, be able to talk Creive into building amazing Lightning Towers and other blue dragon productions inside my hoard.

For now, however, that was beside the point. The Essence Siphon by itself was unlikely to be a game-changer. Sure, it could prove invaluable in a head-on fight, but I was trying to avoid those, if possible. However, with the Siphon still here and recharging mana, that had one very important implication. Because the Soul Carver had created exactly two constructions while he was here, and the second one could very well make a difference.

Time to tell if my hunch was correct.

With a spring in my step, I hurried toward my old room. With the Stone Door dissipated from lack of mana, I rushed through the opening, only to hit the brakes at the nauseating sight of the contents. When the Soul Carver was there, it had been a disturbing place to enter, since he used the room to repair and improve his undead creatures. Even when he wasn't inside, it looked like a deranged butcher's shop, with body parts arranged neatly on the stone tables.

Watching him take his minions apart and reassemble them was even worse. I hadn't thought to appreciate whatever magic he maintained that kept the body parts from spoiling. Now, I did. This very moment, the place looked like the birthplace of the Plague. Half of the room was alive, crawling with bugs and maggots, and the remnants he had left behind were more fluid than actual parts.

I sprayed the place with a Weakening Fog, moving my head from right to left to ensure that I caught everything, watching in grim satisfaction as the entire room stopped flying, slithering, and crawling. I then strode in, ignoring the crunching sounds from under my claws and Inspected the markings on the floor. This could be totally worthless or it could be -

[Mana Focus

This construction allows you to enter your mana and apply it, concentrated, in the forms of runes on the face of weapons or other appliances. The runes will allow you to add magical effects onto any inorganic material. As the domain improves, the mana costs will decrease and possibilities improve.

● *Using the Mana Focus will now be cheaper, draining less mana.*]

Yeah! Unless I was reading this wrong... it had to mean what I believed it did, right? I had no intentions of messing about with necromancy myself, but applying mana to weapons or other appliances—how could that be anything other than enchanting? I walked to the Training Chamber down the west corridor and plucked a clawful of the training spears from the stone container in the corner.

I asked two of the Crawls training inside to come with me and help clean the room. They showed no emotions at first, but when they saw the horror-movie worthy pile of insects and maggots sprawled on the floor, they went right to work. I tried to ignore the squelching chewing noises that accompanied their clean-up duty, focusing my attention on one of the weapons. It really was of crappy quality, not usable for anything besides training purposes. The piece of roughly carved bone was still clearly formed like the femur of a small bipedal creature, and a rough piece of leather held a dull stone spearhead in place. So, how to approach this?

So far, I'd found the menus that were available with some of the constructions to be less than helpful. A little explanation would be nice, but apparently we were playing on hard mode. The Mana Focus was no exception. [Select item for mana infusion] was the only explanation given. With a mental shrug, I placed the spear on the table before me and mentally focused on the [Select] button.

Right away, my mana started ticking down. At first, I couldn't see any change, though I could sense the mana being whisked away from me. Within seconds, I spotted a subtle glow forming around the simple weapon. Half a minute later, that glow covered the entire length of the bone. Slowly, ever so slowly, it seemed like the mana started to permeate the spear itself, imbuing the spear with an inner glow on top of the blue surrounding haze that had grown to envelop the entire shaft and spearhead.

Interesting. Since nothing else happened, I stayed still. By now, I'd lost the first 50 mana, and the flow gave no sign of diminishing or stopping. The glow from the weapon grew into an almost blinding sheen, and I soon had to squint my eyes to protect myself from the radiance of what I was creating. Then, while I was considering my next move, a splintering sounded from the haft.

"Oh crap!" was the only thing I had time to think, then the splintering noise erupted into a loud crack as the spear burst apart in a blue explosion. The pieces flew everywhere, and I was pelted by the remains, taking a strip of health damage in the process. Blinking, I just stood there for a full minute, while I assured myself that there was no permanent damage. Then, with a shudder, I grabbed the next spear. Okay, so that wasn't the way to do it. Time to experiment.

An hour later, the room had almost been cleared of insects, my mana was below two thirds, and I'd ruined another practice spear, fortunately when the Crawls weren't nearby. Still, I'd been enlightened with several useful tidbits of information. For one, there was a definite point of no return, where I couldn't load any more mana into an item. Second, finding the tipping point was a matter of experimentation.

Not only that, but, it worked. It bloody worked! The last time, I'd managed to break off the stream at the exact right time and was left holding an item that now harbored a slight inner glow and granted a +1 to Mental Control. I was practically salivating with this thought. That would mean that, with practice, I'd be able to imbue every single weapon we had with magical capabilities. I'd also be able to do it a hell of a lot faster than my hoard currently did. Hell, and given that the Soul Carver had used this room to fix his minions, there had to be even *more* possibilities hidden here. I had no intentions of mucking about with experiments on flesh–that was too disturbing. Unless, what happened if I poured mana into meat? Would that make something like Dragon Meat? Could I create my own way to cheat the system and gain attributes from eating imbued flesh?

Ten minutes later, I had to admit to myself that the last myth had been busted. I could not make my own mana-imbued meat. Horrible shame. I shook my head, dislodging the other ideas. Those were theories for tomorrow. I was definitely going to test them all, but I couldn't allow myself to be sidetracked by every random idea that popped into my mind. I looked at the remaining spears on the table ahead of me. There were still so many things I needed to learn, but I was having so much fun!

Back on Earth, I had loved the classic games where you were able to achieve random rewards through crafting. The only thing I needed to make this day perfect was the ability to quicksave and load, so I could make sure I got the stats I wanted, because here I didn't have unlimited resources. Lacking that... I needed vast quantities of items, instead. Grinning, I made my mental voice ring out into the lair. "I need everybody to bring items. Spare weapons, equipment, tools, and jewelry. Everything that we're not using that's not of top quality, bring them to me inside my room right now."

Within minutes, I was surrounded by a small pile of crap,

and when the rumor spread about exactly what I was working on, people practically sprinted off to fetch more items. Apparently, the chance of ending up decked out in a full magical setup outweighed the risks of having their weapons and armor ruined.

For the rest of the day, I lost myself in experimentation. I had already learned a handful of lessons from the way items improved inside the hoard, and I needed to extrapolate from that. First off was the fact that better-quality items were able to grant better bonuses. It took me little time to confirm that this amounted to the item being able to hold more mana. The cracked stone hammer in front of me reminded me that it would probably be a while before I had the ability to intuit 100% when I'd "filled" an item to the brim. Nevertheless, I had no doubt. A well-crafted spearhead was able to hold maybe twice as much mana as the practice spears, resulting in a +2 bonus, just like in my hoard.

Of course, figuring out some of the details brought nothing but more questions. And I leapt into it, working at a frenzied pace and jumping from theory to theory. It felt like this was going to be the cheat skill I needed; my access to first-class stone craftsmen combined with my insane mana regeneration would ensure that I would be able to churn out magic items at an incomparable pace. I struggled to keep my mind straight and focused on everything I needed to learn, even as I created item after item. Then, I realized I was being obtuse and fetched Timothy. Why try to handle the mental math myself when I had a friend who reveled in this sort of thing? A short introduction had him awed, and as I filled him in on what I'd learned so far, he started grinning like a loon and nodding along. Ten minutes later, he had a young Crawl placed next to him, learning how to create those Quipu strings in a manner to showcase the possibilities and limitations of the Mana focus.

We burned away all my mana along with the remaining hours of the day. I was soon relegated to focusing on the creation, while Tim took over the theorycrafting entirely. Soon, he had me pushing the limits of the system, while I focused on improving my capabilities at the manasculpting. Roth agreed to act as guinea pig for us when it came to testing out the items, and the results were beyond overwhelming.

We only had one *really* disheartening result. You couldn't stack several items that gave a bonus to the same attribute. There would be no bundling of Agility items to make our Scouts preternaturally fast and difficult to hit, no stacking Mental Power items on our Shamans to make them supernatural nukes. If you carried several items boosting the same attribute, only the strongest would take effect.

I'd been hoping that, since these runes granted bonuses in a different way from those in my hoard, we could have one of each boosting the same attribute. Sadly, no.

Apart from that, it was all a big discovery party. First off, there were no actual size limits. The factor that decided whether an item would be able to become enchanted and the possible strength of the enchantment was some combination of material and quality. In short, shoddy armor was as likely to break as a badly crafted necklace. As long as a ring was exquisitely crafted and made of good materials, it would be able to hold a surprisingly powerful boost. Even a decently crafted finger ring managed a simple +1 bonus.

We found two other smallish speed bumps. There were limits to how much you could equip. It would have been a completely unbalanced system otherwise, but I was still disappointed. Just a bit. Still, the limits were... generous. You were able to receive a bonus point per two levels. That meant that Roth, who was currently at level twenty-two, was able to gain a total bonus of eleven points to his attributes or damage.

Keeping in mind that the tiny Talpi only gained a single bloody attribute point per level, that would make a huge impact on their power. The most important thing? There would be no shortage of items. Most people already carried a few items that would be able to hold an enchantment. Creating the additional items needed in order to ensure that each of my minions would hold between five and ten magical items was doable. Even Arthor agreed that it would be worthwhile for me to focus on this over construction.

I was no closer to controlling the outcome of the enchantments. Whatever I created was a crapshoot and the chance of creating an almost useless (for now) +10 to damage healed was just as likely as a bonus to Strength. Still, I started wasting less mana as I learned how to focus properly on the process, allowing less of my energy to leak away into thin air. I learned that the combinations available were limited and, I was thrilled to discover, almost all of them were useful. The enchantments could affect the five different attributes, increase melee, ranged, or magical damage, add protection *from* those types of damage or buff the damage healed and healing received. Finally, they could also affect health or mana directly. All told, fifteen different possible outcomes, and with eighty-eight minions, with each their approach to... everything, there were scant few enchanted items that wouldn't be happily snatched up. The remainder went straight to boosting my hoard.

I felt the last bit of my mana drain out of me as I granted a +1 Toughness bonus to a heavy atlatl. Not the best attribute for a ranged spear thrower, but it could have been worse. I sank to the ground with a huff. "That's it. No more for today!"

"Awww. Is the widdle dwagon tired?"

I groaned as I looked at the annoying cloud who hovered over the shoulder of the Crawl. "If you ever start using your Mental Powers, you'll learn that it's actually hard work." Ignoring his sputtering protests, I continued. "How is the needlework progressing, love?"

Timothy's form solidified and a glare shot daggers at me. "You know, I have no trouble imagining why you're divorced, old-timer."

"Low blow, Timmy. Low blow. Heh. Not bad, though. How are we doing? I got kinda focused there with the final couple of items."

He waved at the small pile of items on the floor next to him.

"We are doing *great!* Arthor and Creziel will be able to create rings for everybody within the next handful of days. They will be simple, but well enough crafted to hold +1 enchantments. If you keep up the tempo and don't take too many breaks, I'd say you should be able to finish with all the items within time of us having to leave again and leave us with a wide enough assortment that everybody can choose only items that are at least vaguely useful to them. Arthor, Creziel, and I are going to help where we can, but… our mana regeneration is nothing compared to yours."

The excitement of my discovery was slowly fading as I realized the amount of work that lay ahead of me, but I nodded. This would be a serious step up for us and it needed to be done. "I'll take any help I can get. It's quite easy to tell that this is going to consume mana like a… a mana sponge. Yes, that was weak. Please ignore it. Thing is, Tim, these items are going to be crazy powerful, but we'll have to balance them with any constructions. So… any suggestions on what we should and shouldn't build?"

Timothy's form went indistinct as he thought. "We're staying for a week, right?"

"Yes. Ten days at most."

"In that case, I'd say ignore most of the constructions and focus on enchanting. We don't really need Habitats to heal up since we're not expecting to fight down here right now. Maybe create a single one for the pregnant females and to buff our builders. Same goes for Shadow Towers. We can do without. As for Growth Boosts, the crops aren't going to grow as fast as we're used to, but as long as we keep them watered manually, they'll probably make it. Besides, Selys gave up plenty of supplies."

I nodded slowly. "I tend to agree. Heh. When we leave, we might be gone for long enough that the low-mana constructions are going to disappear again, anyway. So, focus on the physical cleanup and save our mana for the items. I like it. Good thing the Training Chambers and Sorcery Chambers still stand. We can't afford to stop growing! Apologize for the detour. Anything else?"

"One single thing, but you'll love it." A pair of smirking, floating teeth solidified in the middle of his vague outline. "We tried adapting a piece of armor, and the items work on the Clenchers, too!"

"Oh. That *is* excellent.' I imagined a group of Clencher cavalry, Clenchers and riders fully kitted with magical items, bearing down on their enemies. "Well done, Tim."

"I know. Like I said, spreadsheets rule!"

CHAPTER NINE

"Go to the ant, O sluggard; consider her ways, and be wise." - Proverbs 6:6

I lost myself in the task of outfitting every single minion in the lair, spending my waking hours with the Mana Focus. This made the tiny, featureless room the unofficial center for all discussions and the replacement of the throne room for the time being. Soon, I had improved enough at imbuing items with mana that I was able to hold a conversation while I worked. An actual conversation, not one of those chats you have with the wife when you're busy, where you go "mm-hmm" and hope she doesn't say anything you were supposed to actually absorb.

Creziel asked me to join him in the Gallery of Illusions after some time. We looked over the detritus from the battle with the two dragons. God, it felt like it was ages ago already. I was thankful that my minions had gathered all the bodies for food long ago, or we'd be looking at a slaughterhouse. Even so, the remnants of the battle still lingered. Dark patches in the dirt showed where blood was spilled, rocks had cracked open where the attackers had shattered the openings in the walls to get at our Shadow Towers, and soot-colored impacts remained from where their electricity-wielding attackers had shot their lightning attacks indiscriminately.

Regardless, the tiny Talpus at my side beamed positivity. "This will be but a day or two of work, Onyx. If you re-establish the Shadow Towers, I can fix the openings with little issue, maybe add a few additional traps. I do believe that we could do with at least one extra pit trap near the entrance. Maybe we can widen some of the other tunnels, add-"

"Sorry, Creziel," I interrupted, "I'm afraid your work will be a bit more extensive than that."

"Some misleading... why?"

"You know what happened in the battle against the dragons. The Gallery did an amazing job at holding back their lower-leveled minions, but when they came in large numbers, we were forced back. Afterward, when the dragons showed up, the Gallery and our assembled defenses did absolutely nothing against them. And now that we might end up facing off against Selys or her minions..." I let my message trail off.

"Oh. I believed that we were not going to face her down, Onyx?"

"You are completely right. But I still want us to prepare for a worst-case scenario. And regardless of whether Selys herself shows up or not, she has her faithful sorcerers and more than enough numbers to overwhelm us, like the two dragons did. We need to expand. Think larger. Larger rooms. Larger traps."

Creziel's merry disposition faded and was soon replaced with a deep frown. He walked into the center of the Gallery, deep in thought, staring at the walls as if they had insulted him personally. "Yes. I see your point. We do have some issues. We cannot widen the walls too much toward the other tunnels that lead to the new Farm or the old passages to either side. If we do that, we will reach outside the effect of the Gallery itself, and enemies can bypass the entire thing."

I grit my teeth. "That *would* be a problem. We need the confusing effect to be able to defend ourselves effectively." The frown on Creziel's face grew deeper. "I wouldn't feel so down-trodden, though. While we may not be able to expand to the sides, we still have other directions. Heh." I stared pointedly at the dirt ceiling hanging maybe twenty feet above.

Creziel slapped the rock outcropping next to him. "Of course. I can't believe I didn't think of that. If we expand upward, any Shadow Towers you create will be out of reach of most close-combat fighters. We have enough soil and rock above us that we can expand at least twelve feet further up."

"Now you're thinking. We need to think larger still, though. We must have some traps that would work against dragons or other powerful monsters. And we need to enlarge the room enough that our Imps can help in a fight. They are at their best when they're not crammed into close confines."

The tiny Talpus paced, eyes gleaming. "Yes. Yes! If we open up the room entirely, they will be able to fly about and bombard any invaders from above. Then we could include escape tunnels, small enough that larger creatures would not be able to follow. Oh. And keep some walls and large pillars to hold up the ceiling and make it difficult for larger attackers to move about. Erect Shadow Towers up above, where they are even harder to spot. And we could…"

"Now you're thinking right, Creziel. We may need to expand the tunnel leading to the Throne Room, too. Having the Clenchers charge near the pit trap was efficient, but again, once the dragons arrived, it was pretty much free for them to waltz toward the throne room."

He nodded, deep in thought. I could practically *hear* the gears grinding inside his head. "I… will need to think. This is going to be hard work for Arthor and myself, however. And the builders. The volume of earth that we have to shift here is… significant."

"I understand. But I believe that a concentrated effort here could mean even more to our safety than a handful of additional hours of training. Now, I need to get back to my enchanting, but you just shout if you want my help or opinion on something. Also, check in with me before you come up with any final plans."

The coming days bled into each other as I lost myself to the rune crafting. Any item I was done with, we dumped inside the Hoard immediately in the hope that maybe they could get additional boosts there before we left. My work became constantly more and more natural to me, and after a few days, I could *feel* the innate limit of an item like pouring water into a cup blindfolded and sensing from the weight when it was full. Once I reached that level of ability, I was able to zone out and keep on working flawlessly, even as I spoke with people. This wasn't any special talent on my part; anybody who has worked with their hands is used to dealing with repetitive tasks.

Thankfully, I had the occasional interruption that kept the worst of the monotony at bay. Roth came to discuss aspects of training. Tim joined me to talk about leveling, feats, or simply to pass the time. Even Laive popped by from time to time to discuss farming. There was plenty of necessary work to restore the farm, continue on the second one, and improve the watering system so we would be able to leave it for a longer period of time and keep ourselves self-sufficient when it came to our plant-eaters.

Those discussions often left me feeling ambivalent about the whole thing. With the conflicts hovering ahead in our near future, I found it hard to focus on the details of growing mushrooms and the like. But even so, I did enjoy thinking about a possible, more peaceful, future, after all our struggles. Only once did Laive take me completely by surprise.

"You will need to do something about Povel."

"Povel?"

"What do you mean, Povel? I have agreed to his demands, even encouraged them. It's hard to argue with his results. Still, he keeps ramping up experimenting, and I have to spend more and more time and effort trying to grow what he needs."

I held up a claw. "I'll have to stop you right there, Laive. I really don't know what you're talking about. Povel is... a builder, right? Brown and grey pattern?"

"You... don't know? Truly? I was sure it was your doing. And what he said..." Her words trailed off, as the sensation from her turned into a blend of annoyance and consternation. "Povel, he... yes, he is one of my kind. A builder and a lazy one at that. Lately, he's taken to creating food for all of us. Comes around insisting that we need to create more herbs and plants all the time, asks for help *experimenting*. How was this not something you came up with?" She wrinkled her nose and huffed. "Him cooking means he works less, but we all let him. His food... Well, it's different from what we're used to. Better. He is so insistent, though. Annoying."

So *that* was where it had come from. A few times, I had been served the odd meal that was... different. Treated with herbs, cooked, fried... something different from the regular dried rations we tended to have for the carnivores, or fresh meat, whenever our hunters managed. I clicked a claw on the floor, thinking about it. I didn't have to think long. "You'll help him as much as possible."

"But the time-"

"No. This is worth a little time and sacrificing some space in the garden. If his demands are truly unfair, come to me. But improving our food isn't only good for our spirits, it also strengthens our bodies. In fact, have him talk to Timothy. That floating sack of knowledge is bound to know all sorts of things about nutrients and what have you." I looked her right in the eyes. "Besides, do you really mind having meals that taste better than Talon Rot?"

She relented quickly after that.

Most of my minions kept their distance. They knew what I was working on and what it could mean for our strength, and left me to it. I did experience one delay, but one I did not mind at all. It started out with noise. By now, I was well used to the types of sounds ranging through our domain. The usual everyday shrill cries of the Talpi. The guttural, harsh voices of the Crawls. The chittering and constant babbling of the Imps. The nuances and underlying emotions were also becoming easier to follow. In general, however, there would always be a certain level of noise ranging through the domain, testament to the high number of denizens in our domain.

What made me decide to leave my enchanting and check out what was going on was a buzz, an intensity and sudden increase to the everyday sounds that permeated our home. I didn't have to go far. By now, the Talpi had moved into the new Habitat I'd established inside the room where Tim's old magic circle used to be. The closer I came, the clearer the sounds became, and if the sheer number of Talpi present didn't have me intrigued, the sensations coming from them piqued my curiosity. Because they ran the gamut, from joy and elation over confusion to dislike and disgust.

Creziel stood outside the room, slightly apart from a group of Talpi who were chatting away in their high-pitched voices. He stared intently through the opening. From inside, I could sense the smell of blood, but it didn't appear like any danger was evident. "What's going on, Creziel?"

He jumped, turning and blinking at me a couple of times before gaining his senses. "Oh. Onyx. I... It's nothing, really. Just a birth. They are all healthy."

"*Just* a birth, is it?" Something was off here.

I could practically smell his nervousness as his gaze dodged between the door opening toward me and back again. He took a deep breath. "No. There is more. Perhaps you should see for yourself, but..." Creziel stared at the ground, uncertainty roiling from him. "Please let me go in first and explain. And please do not hurt her."

Hurt her? What the hell? I stared in bafflement at Creziel's back as he entered the room and entered into a hushed conversation with somebody inside. Moments later, he emerged again, looked at me and nodded, standing aside. I ducked my head to enter the opening. Heh. The last time I'd been here, the large doorway had been tall enough to fit me without issues. This might become a problem eventually. I ignored the voices from all around and the sudden increase in the intensity of their emotions and moved closer to the nest.

Talpi built nests for their pups. Perhaps it was the wrong word, but it looked like a nest. It was a circular dirt construct with raised edges, lined on all sides by dried moss and grasses, cloth and leather, a hodgepodge of all sorts of soft materials they had been able to scrounge up to create a comfortable resting place for the newborn and their mother. The smell of blood and other fluids burned in my nostrils as I raised my head to look into the nest to see... harmony.

It was a wonderful, life-affirming image. The Talpus mother, one of the builders, wide and strong, rested on her side with her eyes closed while the newborn pups, mewling and squirming, struggled for supremacy and a place at the mother's teats. It was one of those images that had an innate level of cuteness that, even if you didn't care about animals, you'd still have a hard time scrolling past it without a single "awww."

I failed to see the problem here, though. They looked like every other litter of pups I'd seen in the domain to date. Maybe... I took a closer look. No. All looked hale and healthy. As was usual with Talpi, the color schemes ranged all over the place from brown to black with a few lighter splotches here and there. Huh. One of them did look a bit bigger than the others. Maybe... I selected Inspect and chose the larger pup... and froze.

Personal Info:
Name: ...
Race: Evolved Talpus Pup. Level 1 – experience toward next level: 0/1000
Size: Very small

Holy crap. This *was* something new. And unexpected. The pup hadn't received his attributes on display yet. That didn't happen until they grew to become young Talpi. I slinked back to the opening and fixed Creziel in my sight. I paused, then huffed a laugh. "I have *so* many questions right now. Why don't you tell me everything you know about this type of evolution, and I'll pick up from there."

Creziel scratched his neck, looking at the ground. "I... don't know much. They are exactly like us... but better. Our tales tell of these kinds of births, in our kind as well as other races. If we thrive, if we prosper, sometimes they are born stronger, hardier, *better*. And if we continue to thrive, more may be born." He grimaced.

"Then why is this not a moment of joy?"

He studiously avoided my eyes and did not answer. From behind him, another mental voice interfered.

"Because they bring discord to the tribe. Because we *remember*." Arthor's crass look confirmed his distaste. "Our ancestors have not experienced many examples of these evolved pups, but the stories are the same. Whenever they are allowed to be raised among normal Talpi, discord, unrest and blood are sure to follow... because they are not like us."

I couldn't believe my own ears. "Arthor. We may disagree from time to time, but I want to be crystal clear on this. Nobody is going to harm this pup. If they do, they will be exiled for good. This... this innocent creature in there is *exactly what you want*. Whatever the exact trigger is that led to the pup being born as an evolved Talpus, it means that your tribe is growing stronger, and the potential for the tribe as a whole to grow and obtain bigger and better things..." I shook my head in amazement. "I don't get it. Go. Fight. *Thrive.*" I stressed the final word. "You've told me yourself, those are Deyra's own words. What more do you want?"

It was a low blow, but the sense of shame and insult coming from the tall Talpus showed me that I had hit the mark. He raised a paw to point at me. "You may say this now. I will stay my paw. Mark my words, though. Not long from now, chaos will grow within our tribe, and it *will* stem from this so-called innocent pup." He turned his tail and strode away.

I blinked. Suddenly, I remembered something. I clicked Inspect on the Habitat they were resting in.

[Habitat
This construction converts an area of 10x10 meters into living space, optimal for any living creature to move into. Please note: While any race and species may take up the Habitat, not all are able to peacefully coexist. Increases health recovery for all creatures in the Habitat.
● Your Habitats now add a well-rested buff. Any minion sleeping in the Habitat for more than 4 hours will have an 8-hour increase to Toughness.
● Your Habitats now improve health and mana recovery.
● High-level creatures will now have the chance to spawn stronger offspring. The higher the level of the parents, the bigger the chance. Not all creatures have this option.]

Arthor was already out of sight. I sent a message to him anyway, knowing full well he'd be able to hear me just fine. "Well, you had better get used to the thought. Because this is in fact a boon from the Habitat. You are going to see more of them, and it's going to be *great*." I grimaced. As parting shots went, this one wasn't winning any prizes.

Later on, Timothy was nodding along to my explanation. "Uh huh. I get it."

"Of course. It's a crappy world, and they're afraid of anything that doesn't fit into their worldview."

"No. I mean, yes, but I doubt it's the full picture. So. Some of this is speculation, but it fits my headcanon."

"Head. Canon. Now you're just making up words. Say what you mean, Timmy."

His vague form became distinct enough for me to see his eyes rolling. "Old people. What I'm saying is, it makes sense with what else I've been able to fit together inside my mind. So, hear me out. These evolved pups supposedly tend to come in good times, right? That means when the tribe is well-fed and probably higher-leveled. So, whatever the exact requirements are for an evolution to happen, it usually means they're doing pretty good, likely also pretty well-established–for Talpi at least. However, an evolved pup like this is totally a threat to the status quo."

"A threat? It's-"

"I mean it. First off, it would be a clear threat to the leadership. Before we came along, at least, their leaders were typically the strongest, hardiest Talpus. I've asked. And any pup like this is going to eventually grow stronger than the chief, if he survives the first handful of levels. In a world like this, it would totally make sense to take him out."

He held up a translucent hand. "Don't make like I approve of it, because I don't. They have basically been keeping themselves down. Of course, there would be other factors, too. I mean, let's assume the tribe keeps thriving, and more evolved pups are born? Any survivors would be bound to band together with others of their kind, to the detriment of the other 'lesser' races."

I thought about his words. Considering what I knew of the place... it was harsh, dark, and bloody, but it sounded about right. However... I could feel a grin spreading on my face. "Of course, that's only if they don't have anybody telling them to play nice."

"Exactly. And once any evolved pups grow enough to earn their place in the tribe, we're bound to *have* a bloody society that's ready to receive and welcome them."

"Damn straight." I nodded at Tim. "Now we just have to survive this tiny issue with Selys."

"Yeah. No problem at all, right?"

"Maybe we'd better get back to work?"

"You're probably right."

Timothy promised me he'd make a round and talk with people, ensure that everybody bought into the "live and let live, or else..." policy. Meanwhile, I had runes waiting to be formed.

CHAPTER TEN

Busy. Everybody was so busy. We held a brief meeting, talking about time, and the conclusion was undeniable. We did not have enough, compared to all the things we wanted to complete. We were going to run short when it came to some of the largest projects. We wouldn't have the time to rebuild the Gallery completely the way I wanted to. Also, I had to admit that we couldn't upgrade the hoard in time either.

It frustrated me, but we would need at least five full days to be able to create the necessary constructions and Mana Crystals. With a mana regen of 2040/day and a Mana pool of 860, I'd be able to create a bit above two Mana Crystals a day. On top of that, I'd also have to build a handful of other constructions. Yeah. That wasn't going to happen unless I discarded the entire enchanting business. Tim had gone over the calculations twice, and it just wasn't going to happen.

All told, the usual buzz of conversation and regular work inside the domain held an undertone of frenzied business and stress that we usually didn't have. Every waking moment that wasn't required elsewhere to scout around the domain, work on the domain, or ensure the necessities for our survival, my people spent in the Training Chambers or Sorcery Chamber fighting to become stronger. Roth was reaching new heights of deviousness in his search for efficient training methods, but my minions bore it with few complaints. They knew what was at stake.

The litter with the Evolved Talpus pup wasn't the only birth. These days of relative peace granted us 12 new arrivals, most of them Talpi, a couple of Crawls, and three absolutely adorable Clencher pups. All the pups didn't add to my minion count yet, since they weren't old enough. Even so, once they were, we'd hit a minion count of 112 of my 150 max. There were more pregnancies, too, of all races. At this level of growth, we'd soon reach the limit, but I would be a fool to complain. I would have to investigate exactly what was going to happen when my minion count hit the cap. Would they be more likely to rebel and work against me? Would they not be able to take advantage of the beneficial boosts in my lair? I needed more information. This, at least, would be something Selys would be able to help with. With how many she had working under her, she had to know all the variables.

In my tiny breaks between enchanting, I experimented with the Ergul to find its limits, and the oozing monster did not disappoint. Old injuries, new injuries, complex breaks, it was able to handle almost anything. The only requirement was access to the wound in question because it had to have direct contact to heal it. Its limits were vast, and it appeared to drain the needed energy or mana or whatever it was from the healed person itself. Apart from that, any kind of meat kept the beast going, and it actually gained experience from the healing. I was still struggling to find some method that would allow me to enchant items for the Ergul. They just plonked right through its slimy mass.

Personal Info:
Race: Ergul. Level 3 – experience toward next level: 2100/3000
Size: Small

Stats and Attributes:
Health: 70/70
Mana: 40/40
Strength: 4
Toughness: 14
Agility: 2
Mental Power: 14
Mental Control: 8

Of course, Roth only took this as encouragement to up his training regimen a notch, and I wholly approved. The pain would be worth it if we could push our people a bit more. As some of the younger minions started growing up, the groups grew in size, and both Roth and his assistant trainers were kept busy trying to improve everybody.

The younger Crawls were the one exception to the constant training. While the older ones spent their time training with stoic single mindedness, the young ones divided their waking moments between training and staying with Timothy, learning. By now, it was becoming clear to everybody that Tim's teaching methods were working, and the gathered young ones were able to carry normal conversations. Not only that, but according to my translucent friend, they showed a hunger for knowledge that promised well for the future.

The young Crawls weren't the only ones who were improving in leaps and bounds. One of my infrequent breaks had me looking through the map as I ate a light luncheon of dried Dweeler meat. It was the last of the stores, and I relished the rich taste of the meal even while I tried not to think about the fact that it came from a semi-thinking beast.

It had become a habit of mine to check over the outskirts of my domain (just in case) and continue to look through the rest of the rooms, to keep myself up-to-date on any developments with minimal effort. My old boss would've loved it. Then again, he also wanted to install cameras in the bathroom. Bastard.

I found myself lingering when I came to the Sorcery

Chamber today. I'd apparently managed to land in the middle of the Sorcery training for the young Talpi, and it was a fascinating scene. What I'd seen of Arthor's training so far had stuck to his original theory. Manipulate earth with all your strength for additional Mental Power or create intricate work for Mental Control.

Today, however, they were subjected to another kind of training that made me look closer. They were divided throughout the bare room, Arthor and ten pups standing with equal distance between them engaged in something that resembled play more than the usual hard training. Wait. A Crawl? That was an actual young Crawl who had joined the training, and if I wasn't wrong, it was the one who'd accompanied Timothy earlier as he helped learn how the Mana Focus worked. Now I was *really* interested.

Between them, they were keeping a rock moving from person to person, like a ball game of sorts. The only difference from a kindergarten game was that they weren't using their hands, instead floating the rock from one person to the next. I observed, impressed with the level of control from the young ones. When I met him, Arthor had been stronger than this, but not by that much. There were definite differences between the students. Some dropped the rock from time to time. Others managed, but with a wobble, while two of the Talpi made it look smooth, effortless.

The Crawl? Not so much. In fact, he had to use his hands to help – but there was definitely something there. As I watched, the rock propelled out of control, bouncing across the ground. Arthor growled a low comment, while the young Talpi laughed.

I closed the map, thinking. So, some of the Crawls were actually training their way out of their natural racial deficits? There were some lovely long-term implications here for the future.

At a later point, the human fog cloud that was Timothy glided back and forth over the tile floor in front of me, his animated words making up for the lack of a solid form. "...honestly, I wouldn't even be surprised if whatever happens to slow down the development of the mental faculties of the Crawls did not appear with the young. They have already surpassed all their elders in terms of vocabulary and sheer cleverness."

"Though that's not saying much." I shot.

He snorted. "Too true. Still, at this point, you can hold a pretty normal conversation with all of them, and some can be taught pretty complex math. Like, 6th or 7th grade stuff, if I remember what I used to teach my niece."

I whistled, an accomplishment that was harder than one should expect with a too-long, prehensile tongue. "So, we've already surpassed the average Patriots fan. Well done."

"Har har, old man. What I'm really saying is… they're ready."

I raised an eyebrow. "Ready? Ready for what?"

"Ready for more. I believe that, from now on, we can count upon them to hold their own when we have important discussions. Gert especially; she has improved in leaps and bounds."

I blinked. That was *way* faster than what I'd expected. "Really?"

"Really really. I believe they always had the wits, and now we're finally breaking through the language barriers. I've got Gert doing the rounds right now with the other young ones, talking to the other races—showing off, really."

I gave it a moment's thought then nodded. "Well done, man. If you can show them that Gert's improvement isn't a fluke or a single lucky thing happening, then I believe they should be ready to give them a chance for more responsibility. Heh. I look forward to being able to chat with them without feeling the need to murder them!"

Timothy grinned. "Agreed. Also, this is only going to get better the more young Crawls we raise. We have two Crawl kids ready to join the ranks of the grown-ups and another five pregnant. Speaking of which, I have something to show you."

"Speaking of which? Pregnancy or murder?"

"Hah. No, Crawls." He floated outside of the chamber and

returned with one of the young Crawls in tow, the one from the Sorcery Chamber again. I took a good look at him. He was thin for his kind, and one of the first to be born in my lair. Still quite ugly, but the rolls of thickened skin had yet to grow on his thickset body. In his arms, he carried a lengthy roll of a leathery material.

"Oh. And who have we here?" I asked him.

"Lore." The answer was instant, and his mental voice was quite clear.

"Glad to speak with you, Lore. I saw you training in the Sorcery Chamber the other day. It's lovely to see a Crawl working on his mental attributes. How are you today?"

The rotund Crawl looked at me and then turned toward Tim. For a moment, I feared that he didn't understand me, but then his question rang out. "Does he always speak like that?"

Even with the blurry outline of his form, it was easy to see the smirk on Tim's face as he responded. "Onyx is a bit slow. Still, let's get on with it. He might catch up, eventually."

Frowning, Lore turned back to me. "Timothy wanted to show you what he has learned so far concerning feats and classes. I'm here to carry and find what he needs."

Still smirking, Tim beamed a smile at the tiny Crawl. "Don't underestimate yourself. You are also here because you are great at keeping order in our system." He turned toward me. "You remember Quipu, right? The system I invented to keep track of feats and everything?"

"Of course. I'm not senile, kid. I *am* curious to hear what you've learned, though. How far have you come?"

"I'm done cataloging everybody, at least every person I've been able to get the results out of. We should totally send somebody to Creive. He had Imps, too—we could learn from that. Of course, getting answers from him might be tough. Some of the older Crawls are... problematic, too, as you might imagine."

"Yeah. It sounds like you've done a lot of work."

"I guess. I haven't got anything but time, though. I can't train with the others, and I can't keep Lore and his friends occupied the entire day. That wouldn't be good for anybody's sanity. Talking with everybody and learning about the world and figuring out the system... it's pretty much the ultimate challenge!"

"...and?"

Tim always gave off a subtle glow. Now, the light shining from him intensified until I could use him for a lamp. "And you should bow before your new god of knowledge!" He burst out in laughter. "We are doing *great*! Roll 'em out, Lore."

The Crawl kid knelt down and meticulously unfolded the length of animal skin. Within, fastened to two horizontal strings, by means of tiny stone rings, were a large number of leather strips. Each strip was just that—a number of knots, interrupted by hollow rocks affixed along the way. Tim floated down near them and expanded a tendril that turned into a floating, disembodied hand that made its way alongside one of the strings. "Race. Name. Class. And then the fun stuff, Feats, arranged by level, so we can point out when they got which ones." He floated upward again and faced me. "We have another skin where we spell out the details of each feat as well as the known or speculated stat or feat requirements. That one is a bit more complex. But this... this is exactly what we needed to get to the fun part."

"You mean we can start using it?"

"Abusing, my scaly friend. We're about to abuse the crap out of the system!"

"That's what I'm talking about! So, what do we know?"

"Okay. There is some randomness to it, but the basic, wonderful point of the entire thing is this: It's fixed. The system is fixed. If you know what general direction you want to explore, you can aim to fulfill the requirements needed to pick up the best damn feats out there." He pointed at the Crawl. "Lore. Can you find Aelis?"

The Crawl let his fingers slide along the strings until he located a single string and separated it from the rest. My heart skipped a beat as I looked at the single reminder of my deceased friend.

Tim saw it and grimaced. "Sorry, Carl. It's just - she's a great example, and I talked to her in detail. See, she focused a lot on Agility first and Toughness second. No surprises here. However, she managed to pick two great feats. One was Enhanced Dodge, which only one other Talpus has, and Endless Stamina, which nobody else has."

"I remember. It allowed her to run like the wind for... an hour?"

"Exactly. Or, at least, it let her run without getting winded. However, knowing Aelis's attributes and feats at the time, we can now tell our scouts what they need to get that feat. And since it's an amazing feat for escaping pursuit, somebody *is* going to pursue it. And once they do? We can track their progress and eventually pinpoint the exact requirements. Like, maybe the minimum Agility isn't 24, like she had, but 15? Much more obtainable. And maybe there *are* no required feats. With heavy training, our scouts might suddenly be able to pick this one as their level 5 feat!" Timothy blurted the last sentences in a breathless rant and bobbed excitedly, looking expectantly at me.

A surprised snort escaped me. "Okay, maybe you need to sit down a bit. Except you can't. Heh. Chill, man. I knew you were excited about spreadsheets, but this isn't healthy!"

Timothy sent an affronted glare at me, then giggled. "Okay, maybe that got away from me a bit, near the end."

I tried not to grin and failed horribly. "A bit, yeah."

"The short-ish version is this: People gain feats at fixed levels. At level 2 and then at level 5, 10 and every fifth level from there on. Regardless of what happens, they *will* be offered feats. But the ones that they can choose if they meet the minimum requirements will typically be better! Not always, but usually. Also, we have some feats that are exclusive to certain classes. Like, only fighters can get Heavy Strike, but every class can choose Improved Strength if they hit 10 Strength, even shamans. This means that we can guide people who know which direction they would like to take and tell them which feats are available and which prerequisites they will need to gain it. Oh, and there's also quite a difference between what's offered for the different races, but I won't go into that."

"Thank you."

A hand with a single finger solidified in the white cloud, and he waggled it at me before continuing unperturbed. "The more we continue updating our system, the more accurate our knowledge will be. Meaning, at some point we will know exactly which requirements you will need to hit, and might also be able to calculate exactly which feats are offered and why. That one's still a bit iffy. But still..." Two pale arms reached victoriously for the sky. "We did it. We can start making sure our people get the most out of their points."

I shook my head in amazement. "I love it, man! Now, we have to make sure that people know about it... so, let's say this: We spread the word that every time somebody gains a level, they can see you or Lore here to learn exactly which possibilities they have." I thought out loud. "You may have to get an additional helper or two, so you're not inconvenienced all the time. Still, that would let everybody learn about the possible choices and decide for themselves. Hrm. One caveat. Do you believe this would, in the end, limit our people? I mean, if they only aim for the feats that they know, we're going to limit them to a select number of choices."

Timothy shook his head immediately. "No. Of course, there is going to be less experimentation, but in this case, that's for the better. Choosing a good feat can gain you a boost that would be the equivalent of *several* levels worth of gains. Besides, with all the training our people are doing at the moment, especially the young, they will be able to choose great feats at lower levels. Then they can choose to aim for other known feats with lower requirements or aim for the stars and try to find even better feats afterward by raising their attributes higher."

I nodded along. "True." I expelled my breath in frustration. "If only we were able to focus on this now. In the long run, it may be a game changer, but for now, we'll just have to start it up then focus on survival. As long as we keep updating and expanding the system, especially when we meet other tribes, we will be able to keep testing the limits. Hrm. And even if there are no obvious feats within reach, the boost from increasing attributes by itself will be enough to have some people raising their attributes higher than our known feats." I beamed a toothy grin at him. "Timothy, you've done an excellent job. Let it never be said that nerds are completely useless."

He glared. "I should have gone with the Poltergeist evolution, if only so I could beat your ancient ass!"

CHAPTER ELEVEN

"Can't let limits get ya." —— *John Froehner*

The days went by. We knew we had to move soon and toiled to handle as much as we possibly could. The piles of enchanted items inside my hoard grew and grew. Unfortunately, we were forced to conclude that the possible bonuses were limited to item quality, as none of the enchanted items in the hoard were getting any further increases.

The improvements in the lair were impressive. The Gallery of Illusions grew in size and expanded upward. It was a calculated decision. We might not finish it, but this way, we'd have it almost ready for if we ever made it back here. On top of that, they were rebuilding everything that had been ruined in the latest attack. It was a lot of work, but they went to it with a vengeance. What few complaints there came from the workers who were finally getting around to removing the rotting corpses from the pit trap.

One of my rare breaks brought me a pleasant surprise. "Are you kidding me?" I asked Timothy. He was doing his own thing inside the throne room today, performing some sort of undulating practices, having his features shift and waver, one body part solidifying and stretching after the other. It was disconcerting to look at.

He followed my gaze and chuckled. "Oh, them? Don't like the motif?"

I wasn't even sure what the motif *was*. An Imp hovered near the ceiling, maintaining a short blue flame as he traced an outline of what looked like...

"Is that one of those lightning-wielding critters we fought?"

"Yes. Apparently, Seira there got bored from the constant training, and she talked some of the others into helping her beside the training and work. They mean to turn the entire wall into a mosaic or something, showing off how you battled the two dragons. Kiss-asses, the lot of them."

Where the outlines were done, a few Talpi were chipping at the tiles on the wall, breaking them into tiny mosaic pieces that they removed and painted before reapplying them. The work had just begun with a tiny part of the wall finished, but it promised to be a huge undertaking.

"No. I love it! Hey, we can get somebody to create your likeness, too. Maybe if we get a frost dragon and have him fart on the wall."

"Up yours, scaly."

I couldn't drag my eyes away. One of the young Crawls was completely absorbed in applying paint to the mosaic pieces. The pup was covered with vivid colors everywhere, a vision to make any parent blanch at the cleaning ahead of them. "So, this was their own idea? Seira asked if she could be allowed to improve the room a bit, but I didn't envision... this."

"Yeah. They showed up earlier today, when they were done with their regular training, and got to it. Why?"

I looked at the three races, absorbed in their task, working together closely of their own volition. I knew I should probably be annoyed by the waste of time and resources, irritated by how they could be improving more elsewhere. Instead, I felt my heart soaring to see that they started striving for more than just physical improvement. "It feels good, Timothy. It feels really good."

We were attacked once. We'd pulled back most of our scouts close to the lair to be able to spend as much time as possible training, and a small group of Urten made their way undiscovered past the farms, almost all the way to the Gallery before we spotted them. It could have been ugly, but a handful of Crawls and some of the scouts sprinted in. Following a brief, but bloody clash, the monsters decided there was too much effort involved with the prospective meal here.

I found Wreil afterward. The tall, lanky Talpus wasn't alone. He sat with his back propped against the wall inside the tunnel where they had fought off the large carnivores. A throwing spear rested against his legs, but he had both paws closed around his necklace.

Another Talpus was standing above him, clearly berating him. Leith. The filthy one. Angry words flowed down from above. Wreil sat with his head bowed and took it. Once he was done with his stream of vindictiveness, Leith spat on the Talpus and flew away. As he passed me, his haughty look faded with a sense of shock. He looked down as he passed me by without saying anything.

I sat down in front of Wreil, waiting to see his reaction. He closed his eyes and folded his furry arms over his chest. The emotions coming from him were anything but hidden, though. Self-loathing. Fear. Shame.

Wryly, I asked. "So, I'm guessing Leith just told you his opinion on what happened?"

Wreil didn't answer, but gave a curt nod.

Softly, I asked, "What did happen?"

He bared his teeth, eyes still closed and growled. "I messed up. I should have had somebody here to watch the northern approach, but I... forgot. I was so busy trying to work out the issues between the Crawl scouts and Teyre. One of the wilder Imps. As a result, Laive was almost killed. She had to run for her life."

"It takes character to admit when you've made a mistake."

The sensations of fear deepened in him. "I must have a lot of character, then. Because... Onyx, you need to find somebody else. This was not a simple mistake. *I am not made for this.*"

I softened my mental voice. "Nobody's made for responsibility. I believe you can grow, though."

He shook his head vehemently, turned to look up at me. "You don't understand. We all have specialties. Something we're good at. Me? I work hard. Handle a spear well. Get along with others. That's it." He gave a soft, keening laughter that held no humor, and his paw clenched over the necklace. "I used to be proud of it, too. This tooth? It was an Urten. Slew it myself. Almost crapped my fur with fear, but I did it. Ate like a king for weeks and was lauded by everybody." He clenched his paws, expelled air hard. "This is different, though. Calculating risk? Thinking about who does what at which hour? I am not a leader."

I could feel his despair and inclined my head. "I understand."

"You do?"

"Yes. I have seen any number of leaders over the years. Not everybody is cut out for the work. Some have personalities that simply do not mix well with the responsibilities. Some dislike the work itself." I raised a claw in front of the set-upon Talpus. "Now, I have rarely seen Arthor be wrong about a significant decision before."

"Well, he is, this time around. Can't you do something? I'll end up messing up even worse next time, and somebody will suffer for it."

I grimaced. If he really couldn't, it might be for the best. If we were unable to rely on the scouts, we'd be in constant danger. Still... "Okay. Let's talk about this."

"Talk? What does that mean? Can you find somebody else?"

"I can. But I need your help. We do need somebody to oversee the scouts. So, you're not the right one for the task? I can respect you for saying it. Help me find out how we should handle it, and in the meantime, do the best you can."

Wreil still looked kind of lost, but he grabbed onto the proposal like a drowning man at a life buoy. "So if I come up with a good leader, you'll make sure it happens?"

"I will. But I won't have you make the decision now. You're too affected by what just happened." I made a quick decision. "A bit of air will do you good. I need you to visit Creive and tell him that we're going to need his help soon, tell him to get ready. He needs to know our plan. Who can take over your responsibilities in the meantime?"

Wreil stared at the hallway behind me. The flare of resentment from him was surprisingly strong. He kept his facial features composed, though. "Leith is the best at managing the tasks and schedules. He might cause trouble in the long run, but he can handle things for a while."

I nodded. "Good. While you're away, I want you to think about the best long-term solution. We'll make the best decision we can. I'm not expecting results right now, but think about it. Who's the best for it? And don't let yourself be limited by how things have always been handled. So, you have problems handling the schedules? Find whoever's good at that. Don't like talking down to the others? Sit down and agree to things among yourselves. There's no one set way to handle everything. You need to find what works for you and the scouts. Deal? I'm letting you quit, but only if you can tell me straight to the face that it's for the best."

The lanky scout still looked downcast, but he was frowning, and the mood from him was more pensive than lost. Within his paw, a tiny series of *clicks* sounded, as he thoughtfully prodded the teeth on his necklace. "Deal. I will talk to this Creive. Leith can handle the planning for now." He looked at me for the first time. "Thank you, Onyx. Please don't tell everybody what we talked about. It will make things easier for me."

I walked away, hopeful. I had a feeling Wreil would step up to the task.

My minions kept to their training and left me alone to work on my constantly replenishing pile of stone rings of various sizes. Then, at long last, the moment came when I reached out for the next item to enchant and found the table empty. I was done.

To celebrate, I went to oversee one of the training sessions of my minions. I had made a few inspection tours throughout the days to make sure that construction was proceeding as we wanted, but otherwise, I'd been single-mindedly and almost exclusively stuck inside the Mana Focus, enchanting. Even though it was the same air throughout my domain, the Training Chamber felt... less oppressive, somehow. I took a deep breath and wrinkled my snout. Smelled rank, though. Having three different species whipped through one inhuman exercise after the other would probably do that.

I looked at the scenery in front of me. We were in the Training Chamber that had been erected next to the Clencher Cavern. At first, it was supposed to be made only for the Clenchers, but the additional space actually made this place better for training than the other chamber. My only annoyance regarding the Training Chambers was that they worked only for my minions, not for myself. The Clenchers were still there, but it looked like they were being fed right now.

I shook my head in amazement. This was so far removed from the first days of the Training Chamber, where Roth had them lifting heavy weights and running in place, that I could hardly compare the two. Right this moment, Roth had piled the entire Training Chamber with rocks, creating a broken and difficult terrain to traverse. To either side, he had a couple of ranged fighters, ready to pelt the runners with, blessedly blunt spears, tossed from their atlatls.

The toughest fighters weren't the only ones who were forced through the terrain. Crawls moved carefully across, ducking behind hide-bound shields, right next to the agile forms of Imps who dodged and weaved through the air, using their speed to avoid the heavy missiles above the forms of Talpi who used both the terrain and the heavier Crawls as shields. They were also newly organized into squads, smaller segments of mixed races moving as one. They were adapting, incorporating the strengths and weaknesses of the different races to form a better whole. Right now, I saw three different groups, all different compositions of Talpi, Crawls, and Imps.

Roth stood on top of a large boulder and was yelling abuse at the people training in his high-pitched voice. As I watched, an Imp was hit simultaneously on his head and shoulder by throwing spears, and Roth let loose with a barrage of criticism. Bleeding and in pain, the Imp got up and dragged himself away from the obstacle course and toward my Ergul, who was waiting nearby. Next followed an intimate embrace by the disgusting blob before the Imp dragged his feet over toward the far wall and a pile of rocks and hefted one, lifting it above his head. Roth shook his head and spat, looking back to the obstacle course. Then he spotted me and jumped. "Oh. Onyx. What *is* your Agility score by now? A beast your size isn't supposed to be that quiet!"

I plonked down next to him, puffing up dust with my landing, and took in the sight of the trainees. "Heh. It's not half bad. Speaking of improvement—our people out there? They are getting good. Especially that group right there." I pointed to the course, where a Crawl took a sliding step forward, *slamming* his shield outward in a half-circle to deflect blunted spears flung from either side. An Imp used the defense to float upward and blast three fast fire bolts at targets.

Roth stood tall, beaming like he grew half a foot. "They are. I did what we talked about, trying out different groups. Two Crawls, two Talpi, and an Imp seems to work the best. Their levels also help, of course, but they are taking this seriously. At this point, everybody knows that the training works, and that slackers improve less than the hard workers."

"That is amazing and it gives me hope for the future. How about yourself, though? Can you find the time to train yourself, too?"

Roth rolled his shoulders, broad muscles rolling underneath the patchy fur. His eyes sparkled as he looked me up and down. "Why don't I take my sword and show you?"

The training halted within minutes as the news spread that Roth and I were going to face off. We agreed that we might as well make a spectacle of it and marked off a space in the throne room. It was large enough that I would be able to move without getting cramped, but the pillars, throne, and the hoard would give him some much-needed chances for outmaneuvering me.

My other minions kept pouring in, and soon both sides of the room were lined with spectators. I craned my neck to grin at the buff Talpus next to me, who was jumping up and down excitedly and stretching his muscles. His fingers were filled with stone rings, and while he carried no armor, I knew he was bristling with magic buffs. "They do know it's a friendly match, right? Heh. Of course they do. They're simply excited to see their tormentor get whupped around the room for a change."

Roth growled. He adjusted one of the rings adorning every claw on his paw. "Sure. You tell yourself that."

"Why no armor, though? You tell me if I'm going at it too hard. I've had a *lot* of increases lately. Oh, and I'll stay away from using my skills."

"Onyx." Roth's mental voice was, for once, entirely serious. "You're underestimating me. Don't do that. You may be big, but your fighting skills are still horrible. I don't *need* armor against you. It would just slow me down."

My eyes widened, and I nodded. "Fair point. We're staying away from using skills, though. We're supposed to showcase our abilities, not try to harm each other."

His teeth bared in something that could charitably be called a grin. "Alright. I'll go easy on you, dragon."

I shook my head in amazement. "You're a cocky little bastard, I'll give you that. I will try not to knock it out of you. Too much at least. So. No skills, just us. Fight to first blood?"

He snorted. "That's going to be two seconds. Until one of us gets hurt bad or you admit I'm a better fighter than you."

Again, I could only stare at the cocksure little runt. One side of my mouth edged up. "Alright, do your worst, fur ball!"

We moved to the center of the throne room and, with a simple nod of the head, exploded into action. Straight away, Roth's massive two-handed sword flew from its rest on his shoulder toward me as he ranged forward in an explosive lunge. I leaped backward, putting a safe distance between me and the Talpus... and immediately had to scramble further back, since his lunge led into a forward dash and another swipe. A growl escaped me as I went on the offensive. A sideward leap gave me a better range, and I slashed out in a horizontal attack. That would stop him.

Except, my massive leg tearing through the air didn't faze the tiny beast for a second. He ducked and *slid* under my attack, bringing the sword up and outward in a massive half-circle. I froze as the blade met with my stomach in a small twinge of pain. For a moment, I stared, wide-eyed, at the drops of blood dripping from the tip of the sword. Then Roth raised it one-handed in an ironic salute while he looked me in the eye with a massive smirk. There was a moment of silence, then the crowd went absolutely nuts, cheers, whistles, and roars exploding all around us. I bared my teeth at Roth. "Oh, it's *so* on!"

This time, I went on the offensive. All-out attack. And it was Roth's turn to scramble for defense. I kept in constant motion, always attacking with front legs, teeth, and claws. My massive Agility and our size difference spoke volumes now. While he might be fast for a Talpus, he wasn't as fast as me, and I chased him all around the throne room. Only problem was, he wouldn't stand still and allow himself to get *hit*.

I now sympathized with all the poor Sith who had to fight Yoda; this must be what they had felt like. The little ball of muscles was constantly moving, constantly attacking or dodging and constantly not fucking *there*! Oh, I got him a few times. A glancing blow with a claw. A dodge of his that almost, but not entirely, took him out of reach of my lower leg. And, finally, with one of the classics, as I turned around, letting my tail whip across the ground behind me.

Still, he always managed to partially dodge or turn the blow and prevent serious damage or a wipeout. And he got me, too. Soon, I had more than a handful of scratches from his sword. Nothing that would be more than an annoyance, but it was a testament to his capabilities that he was able to keep in constant movement and still attack with enough force to break my hardened scales.

We broke apart for a moment, putting some distance between us. A smile stretched across my face. It had been a long time since I had been in a match as challenging as this, and it felt *good*. I could feel my breath being a bit quicker than usual. He was giving me quite a workout. "You haven't been slacking either, Roth."

The strong Talpus bounced back and forth on his paws. "I know. It's good to see you improving, too, Onyx. You are becoming more careful with your movements. A few hundred additional cuts, and you might learn something."

I smirked. "Well, that would be boring for our audience. We wouldn't want to bore everybody, would we?"

He hefted his sword, bringing it in front of him. "I guess. So, are we going to finish this?"

I nodded, and we leapt into motion at the same time. This time, I didn't allow him the time to attack, though. I stayed in constant motion, claws and teeth constantly darting at him, and he fled. Leaping, sprinting, and weaving from one side to the other, he looked for openings. I gave him none. I knew, if I was going to beat the critter, I would have to keep him defending. He might not be faster than me, but dammit if it didn't feel like he could read my every move! I gave chase, continually searching for an opening.

He did not oblige, however. Rolling away from my strike to hide behind a pillar, he emerged swinging on the other side, and suddenly, I was on the defensive again. I pulled back first once and then three times in succession as the strong Talpus sprinted all-out against me in his offensive. Mid-dodge, I realized that I knew how to get him, though. It was embarrassing that I hadn't understood it earlier; I blamed the mental image of seeing a large, sharp sword swinging at me. Because, while the stabs and prods from his sword were annoying, even painful, as long as he didn't score a solid strike at me, there was no way he was going to inflict a real wound—and I would use that against him.

Abruptly, instead of falling back yet again, I stopped and used a claw to deflect his sword downward. It smarted a bit, but I put it in the back of my mind immediately. Straight away, I brought my teeth down toward him, forcing him to dodge backward and finally *struck* down on him while he was off-balance. Like a cat pouncing on a mouse, both my clawed paws smashed down in a circle of scaled flesh.

With my head near the floor, the surprise in his eyes brought a smile to my face. I retracted my claws slightly as my palms slammed down. I had no interest in perforating Roth, but I wouldn't mind teaching him a lesson... "Got youuuuu!" I thought, even as I saw his eyes narrowing, and he exploded into motion. His arms shot upward, protecting him from the impact, and I felt the shock as he took my descending claws straight-on. "Pinned you now, you oily little runt." I sent to him and pushed. A tiny bit of pressure, and I would...

He held my claws. A split second. An eternity. Then, with a grunt, the tiny Talpus *heaved*… and forced my claw to the side. I was still applying pressure to my claw, and it slammed into the ground with a low slapping sound. For the briefest of moments, we were stuck there, Talpus and dragon, staring at each other from feet away. Then I backed up several paces and *roared*. My triumphant yell reverberated throughout the room, disturbing the shocked silence, and I held one trembling claw up to point at Roth. "Friends! Family! *Look how far we have come!*"

CHAPTER TWELVE

"He held him back."

"Roth forced his arms to the side."

"He beat the dragon. He beat him."

The words rang through the chamber, amidst sensations of awe and shock as I gathered the leaders about me and we moved toward my old room. It took a while for Roth to be able to break free from all the people who wanted to congratulate him on his feat. Finally, he stumbled through the opening, beaming with pride and more than a little exertion. I welcomed him with a smile. "Join us, Roth."

He strode to join the others in the semi-circle facing me, but remained standing, twitching with nervous energy. "So. What is it you want that couldn't wait, Onyx?"

"We're leaving. I'll have to discuss the timing with you all, but we need to get going soon, so we won't have to face the three races unprepared. Your victory is the perfect proof of how far we have come."

Roth scoffed. "Victory? I didn't even beat you. They weren't the terms we agreed to."

I couldn't help myself. I coughed a deep, long laughter.

"Roth. You held off against my attack. You didn't dodge or divert it. You faced up against my strength and held your own. Do you have any idea how impressive that is, or how much it can mean to the other Talpi? In this moment, you're a hero to them. To me, too, you brawny little numbskull." For a split second, I had a fearful thought that his victory might actually convince them to move against me. I tamped it down, hard. That was not worthy of their loyalty.

The broad-shouldered Talpus gaped at me with his mouth wide open. As he turned toward the others and watched them nodding in assent, the sensation of victory from him grew even stronger. "So. Leaving? Why now, though. I think a week more with the Imps will finally give them enough Toughness to be able to keep up indefinitely, even if we march fast."

Grex rose into the air, hands waving. "Oh no. No more running. We need to go. Because. Because-"

"Because we're running out of time. But also because of who we are and how we fight." I took over. I smiled at those gathered around me. "We aren't like Selys, able to overwhelm with sheer presence and force of might. Neither are we like the majority of monsters inside this mountain, charging in without a thought to strategies or survival. We need to scout, to prepare the area we're going to hold, and prepare our traps. If we are going to take on all comers, we have to level the playing field. Erm. I mean, manipulate the terrain in our favor."

"That sounds like a proper Talpus strategy." The dry commentary from Arthor held enough scorn that I couldn't for a moment take it as a compliment. "It also sounds like you've already decided how everything is going to happen?"

I shook my head. "Everything is far from decided. Tim and I have a rough sketch, and we are going to decide it right here and now. Then we'll adjust when we see exactly what we have to work with. Tim, would you care to lay out what we know?"

My see-through friend solidified slightly as he floated into the center of the gathering. "I have spent a while asking around to gather what little information we have. It's not much. For obvious reasons, none of the races gathered here move through the upper layers much, and a lot of what we do know comes from the sparse information Selys herself gave Onyx or through past memories. But here we are. There are three races on the layer below Selys. Next to the Burning End herself, they are considered the strongest forces inside the mountain, and we need to force them all into submission."

"Why force, though? Couldn't we just... talk to them? Convince them that we are stronger than them?"

Creziel's thoughts were met with a heavy sneer from Arthor as he drawled his reply. "Because that's worked so well? To date, the lizard has tried that approach with how many foes? And we have been forced to fight them every single time. Even the two dragons who eventually gave in only did it when they realized that we were stronger than them. No, Timothy is in the right here. We will be forced to fight."

I interrupted. "That's not to say that we need to subdue them all, even fight them. Surviving under Selys means that they cannot be entirely stupid."

Tim shook his head. "They aren't. Dworgen, Aberrant, and Dragonlings. They are all known within the mountain, and none of them are mindless monsters. Regrettably."

Roth rolled his shoulders. "Dragonlings come close, though. We had a small group of 'em tear through our tribe a few years ago. They didn't stop to chat."

Timothy's form blurred. "Yes. They are, in general, regarded as the most ferocious of the lot and most interested in, well, fighting, eating, leveling. In form, they resemble, as the name implies, smaller, humanoid versions of dragons. There is little else known about them except that, like their, ahem, larger brethren, they have certain elemental affinities."

"Fire. Frost. Lightning. Shadow. Poison. Maybe other affinities, too. The most important thing is bearing in mind that they're supposed to be lethal at range as well as up close." I motioned with a claw for Tim to continue.

"Thank you. Dworgen are a bit of an unknown. They are

humanoids and craftsmen, first and foremost, and tend to keep to themselves. We may be fortunate that they can be reasoned with. However, if we do end in a fight with them, we know only that they smith and enchant their own items. They are bound to have excellent armor and weapons." He looked around, but nobody acted like they had anything to add. "The Aberrants are a known group. They are formed of the unwanted, the rejects, the cast-outs. Those who are, for some reason or other, cast out from their own kind can find a new home among the Aberrants."

Arthor spat. "A final home. Everybody knows that, if you join the Aberrants, nobody else will ever take you in. No intelligent Talpus would ever join them."

Creziel frowned. "You make it sound like they are weak. If they have been able to hold their own and join Selys, that cannot be the case."

Tim smiled at him. The smile was slightly off-center, but looked warm nonetheless. "Well put, Creziel. They are not. And that is exactly it. They *will* accept and feed anybody, regardless of race or past history." He smiled apologetically at Arthor. "Even Talpi who, I'm sorry to say, are generally looked down on. Inside the mountain, that is a warmer welcome than you can expect, well, anywhere. And they fight dirty. Exceptionally dirty. I don't know exactly what gives them the edge, whether it's superior knowledge or tactics. Still, they have a reputation for success in battle and nasty ambushes."

Roth rolled his shoulders. "Fliers, mixed races, and heavily armed and armored enemies. That's hard to prepare against."

The white form spread his arms. "It is. *And* we're under time pressure. Otherwise, we would be able to lay siege to each area and take them down slowly, one-by-one. As it stands, we have enough time to move up there and assault each of the groups separately, with little time to prepare. Or we can hole up, prepare an area well, and challenge all of them simultaneously."

That was too much for Arthor. "Are you insane? Is that the

best plan you can come up with? Why even insist that we move back here in the first place? We could have taken them one at a time otherwise in their homes!"

I shook my head. "It would have been a horrible idea. These are the three largest forces in the mountain except for Selys. Taking them on in their homes, where they have had years, even decades, to establish their defenses? Especially with the Dworgen known as competent craftsmen? It's a tragedy in the making. No. We need them out of their homes. And, regardless of what you may think, we needed the breather. We needed healing. And we have grown stronger for it. Wouldn't you agree?"

The tall Talpus bared his teeth. "You could not have known about the enchanting back then."

"No. I had a hunch. A hope really, that we could use what the Soul Carver left behind. I was not sure. Still, it does not matter. We have grown, and we will be well-prepared. Especially since the return here has taught us one thing that will grant us a huge advantage in the battles to come."

Grex waited for all of two seconds, then flew up in front of me. "Say it! We need to know. Why aren't you telling us?"

Tim guffawed. "Because the old man is a dramatic bastard, is why."

I shook my head at them. "It's the hoard. We now know that we can take the contents with us, establish a new hoard where we choose to create our defenses, then we will be able to have our defenses at our side to aid in the battle. They won't expect that!"

Arthor's eyes narrowed. "And, if we leave right away, we will still have a week or so to prepare the terrain to our advantage *and* build constructions."

"Exactly. So, this is my proposal. We split into two groups. One group moves straight to the upper layers, as quiet and undetected as possible. They search for a good, defensive area, fortify it, erect traps, and leave room for an escape tunnel in case everything goes wrong. Meanwhile, our non-combatants are going to go with me to visit Creive. They'll stay there, in relative safety, while the rest of us have Creive and the majority of his forces join us. Then, when we arrive, we'll erect the hoard, build all the constructions we can, then we challenge them all." I spread my claws wide. "So, what do you think?"

Their reactions were as varied as their personalities. Grex and Roth were ready for the thought of taking on the world, and Roth especially relished the idea of being able to plan proper ambushes. Gert simply said that her people would be ready, no questions asked. Leith stated that some of his scouts should have Professions in order to increase their attributes, because they would need good scouts and were already short-staffed with Aelis gone and Wreil away.

It was obvious to me, however, that they were not really considering any other options. The notion of me in charge was, at this point, simply a given. That left Arthor and Creziel to point out the potential issues with the plan.

"We will be outnumbered, Onyx. Badly. You said it yourself." Creziel's face was scrunched up, deep in thought. "These three groups have had a lot of time to grow, gain levels, and prosper. We have not. Your traps and constructions are without a doubt going to help, but they will not manage to outweigh the differences by themselves. We need more fighters. We will need some way to grind down their numbers."

I assented with an incline of my head. "Good point. I have a few ideas, but they depend on the terrain. We can talk it over before we leave."

"Creive." Arthor continued the thought. "We *must* have Creive and his flying minions. The Dworgen and Aberrants, we might be able to handle by ourselves. Regardless of their weapons and armor, we can use our usual strategies on them. However, the Dragonlings would tear us apart. Grex, do you believe that a single Imp would be able to stand against a Dragonling?"

"We don't know. We never tried. I want to try. Our fires have-"

"Pfah. The correct answer is *no*." He turned toward me. "Onyx, are you certain that Creive will join us?"

I grimaced. "Certain, no. Confident, yes. Wreil is there right now, preparing him."

The tall shaman blinked once. "What do you mean, lizard? He is your vassal. He must obey."

"Yeah, no. He swore to follow me, not work against me, even warn me if somebody was threatening me. Following me into battle was not exactly in the books when we talked. You know, with him just wanting to be left alone and all."

The eyes of the tall Talpus hardened. "You often say that we have much to learn from your world. You would do well to accept knowledge from us as well. Lizard, this is *not* how you should treat vassals. If he were one of us, sure. Not somebody you forced into servitude." He sneered. "Regardless, we need to find an approach, if we're going to do this. I, for one, would rather flee the mountain than face a large tribe of Dragonlings unaided, and I *will* confront you on that."

Across the group, others assented. Even Grex held up his claw, looking much subdued compared to his earlier boasting. I nodded. "No. You are right, Arthor. Right in that we need Creive's help. You're wrong in how to treat vassals. Sure, it would make our lives easier right now, but I have told you earlier. That is not the path I want to take. I want to build a better world."

Our discussions dragged on for a while as the original plan was improved and altered. Arthor pointed out that they couldn't afford to send away the apprentice shamans. Creziel and him weren't enough if they needed to manipulate a great deal of earth. I grudgingly concurred. We had to take a couple of breaks underway, first to have somebody check on our stores, and next to get something to eat while the talks continued. At times, I really missed Aelis. We had all become dependent on her being there, unobtrusively competent and keeping track of everybody and everything. Leith—well, he was here and paid attention, even if his scowl was almost as sour as his smell.

After several hours, we came to an agreement. The bare bones of the plan were unchanged, but we agreed that we would have to abandon it if we failed to convince Creive. But if that happened... no. I wouldn't start on that path. I was not going to live a life of constant flight, fearing for the day when we would be discovered by stronger enemies. *When* we had convinced Creive, we would hurry to meet the rest at an agreed upon meeting place and finish the preparations. Then, we would see about challenging Selys' vassals.

CHAPTER THIRTEEN

"B.M., it's almost like you have no understanding of adventuring at all. Without sidequests, you're not on an adventure. You're just a roaming band of thugs who bring terror and death to an otherwise innocent and peaceful world. The noble sidequest is what separates us from the monsters. Life is a sidequest!" – Red Mage, 8-Bit Theater

Creive was being difficult. Of course he was. Everything had proceeded as planned and something was bound to go wrong, it had to be the one moving piece I couldn't allow to miss out on.

I had left from my lair along with Timothy, the Ergul, a handful of Crawls, plus all the noncombatants, bar the apprentice shamans, a few days earlier. For once, I couldn't even complain about the tempo. Our march had been rapid *and* we had needed fewer breaks, both thanks to everybody being decked out with magic items and the gains from Roth's constant training. In short, we were looking to arrive at the meeting place before schedule - except Creive wasn't giving in.

"I made my position clear when we last talked, Onyx. I am not interested in the machinations of Selys or becoming part of the conflicts here. I have sworn to you. Hence, I will not go against you, and if anybody should attempt to force me to do so, I will take up the fight or flee. But I do not aim to join your battles, either." The blue dragon looked as majestic as ever. In the background, his massive stone domain hung suspended from the ceiling, intimidating and threatening. The damage from our earlier struggle was still clear to see, but the imposing dragon had learned from our battle. Last time, the sides of his upside-down fortress had been bristling with blue towers, ready to shoot lightning at any attacker. Now? He had expanded and moved some of the towers down on the ground, creating a circle of death further out.

Oh, and he was excavating the floor beneath the fortress, probably to get out of reach of any delvers like mine. I didn't see how that would help him if I asked my shamans to simply crash the entire structure from above, but... there was no need to speculate. Creive was not my enemy. He was just... being difficult. And Wreil had given me some good pointers as to how he thought we'd be able to convince Creive to accept our plan.

"I hear you, Creive. However, you are not seeing this. Think of the consequences of what happens if I fail."

"If you fail? I will still remain here. And I will not have wasted my strength and minions against Dragonlings who have grown fat and strong under Selys' rule. If you fall, any new invaders will have to face my powers. Forget it." The massive blue stood tall, chin raised, scoffing at my suggestion.

"No. You refuse to see the world as it is. If I fail, Selys will still continue with her plan. She will find somebody else to bring you under their claw. She may even force you into submission. Unless you believe you are stronger than Selys."

A trace of lightning played inside his mouth as he growled. "I would simply flee. I do not intend to-"

"So you keep saying. But don't you see? This is your chance to gain exactly what you want. If you risk this, you will come out of it a lot better. If I establish myself as the master of the mountain, you may remain my vassal, but you will escape from under the foot of Selys. I will let you rule your own corner, free of the threat of being discovered or forced to flee. Would you rather work with me or be chained by Selys?"

"Risk. That is the only word of that sentence that is a certainty. Spoken like a true shadow brother, you give nothing tangible, nothing real. I would rather risk surviving by myself. So, there is my answer. This isn't something I can agree to."

Except, that wasn't an answer, was it? That was... bargaining. Confirmation that Wreil had been right. I'd spent my time on work sites small and large. I'd haggled for better materials, for better pay, for time and conditions. I knew the difference between somebody saying "no" and saying "not at that price." A wide grin affixed itself to my face as I beckoned one of the Crawls with a claw. "Nothing tangible, you say? Let's see if we can't change your mind on that."

"So, let's sum it up. Once we're done, and I'm finally appointed, I'll make sure that you get the use of one of my shamans for two weeks, along with three builders to help with the manual work on your fortress. In addition, we will help with the initial work to get a farm set up. That way, you can ensure that you only have to worry about food for yourself and the minions that are meat-eaters."

"And these are mine to keep." The blue dragon glared at me, daring me to challenge his words. His earlier stoic facade had been revealed to be exactly that, and his eyes were currently fixed on the handful of rings and assorted weapons lying on the ground before him. I didn't even need to sense the strong feelings of greed coming from him. His claw curled possessively around one of the stronger of the bunch, a ring that granted +2 Mental Control.

"Yours to keep and use as you wish." It had been a matter of trial and error before I figured out what he really wanted. With his low Mental Power, I had no issues sensing when something interested him, and it also proved to be the place where his interests lay. While his overwhelming physical attributes would make him an absolute powerhouse in combat, it also stunted his growth, seeing as his mana regeneration and the growth of his hoard was many times slower than mine and his mana pool tiny.

Hence, growing his hoard with a large number of magical items, some of which boosted mental skills along with help in construction proved too much of a temptation for him. It also showed promise for any future cooperation between the two of us. He could see his weak spots for himself *and* stood ready to work to improve upon them.

"With those terms, my wings are yours to direct. I will not die for you, but I *will* kill for you." Grudgingly, he added, "If this all goes well, you can call upon me again. I would not serve under Selys, but an arrangement like this would work for me." I was about to respond, but sensed that he was not done. A long pause followed until his mental words appeared, haltingly.

"I must admit, I have been... surprised with your demands so far. You could have attempted much stricter terms. Of course, too strict, and I might have fled instead of swearing to you. But you have been more reasonable than I had hoped. Refraining from plotting against you and warning you in case I know something or somebody is moving against you? And you will look out for me? It was not what I expected."

One side of my mouth quirked up as I watched Creive stare at me. "Heh. My minions tell me that this isn't how these things are supposed to work. You, being a vassal of mine, should be attending to my every whim, jumping to uphold any demand I might come up with." A sense of unease shot from him, but I shook my head. "Honestly, I prefer this. A fair trade of services and goods, and we both end up richer for it. At some point, our working relationship might evolve into something even stronger, but I will not try to force it."

"Good. This works for me. Now, we simply need to survive."

I laughed. "Agreed. That's rule number one. Don't die."

On the whole, I found a lot to admire about Creive. He was business-like, honest to the point of rudeness, and efficient. Within a handful of hours of our agreement, we were off again, wandering toward our rendezvous point. Timothy was floating along next to me. He had been quiet for a while, and I was enjoying it. When we marched toward Creive's domain, he had spearheaded our group, flying first to warn us of any enemies, with the rest of us ready to react. Now, with Creive in tow, we had plenty of minions to keep an eye out for the few dangerous enemies that might pose a threat to us, and Tim and I spent the hours in easy companionship.

"-Anything you know can help, really. That's the curse of being the boss. You can't just go around asking people about their coworkers–that makes people nervous. That means you need to have some insiders who don't mind spilling the beans every once in a while."

Timothy pondered my question for a while. "Insider, eh? From what I've been able to gather, Wreil *is* a good scout and a hard worker. Gets along well with everybody. Most of the other scouts speak well of him, but he tends to get sidetracked easily."

I munched down on a side of meat. All unspoiled meat tasted good to my taste buds, but somehow, this was different from the usual. More savory. Weird. Maybe this Povel had been experimenting with the travel rations, too. "That sounds better than what I feared. Anyway, sorry for interrupting. You were about to ask me something earlier?"

"Yes. Horribly rude of you. So not in character of a big, scary dragon." He tittered. "So, I've been wondering. You're not going to let him in?"

"Let him in on what now?"

"Creive. You're not letting him in on our planning sessions?"

I shook my head. "Oh, that. Yes, I will. He's been pretty honest about what he wants here, and I doubt he's hiding anything. I should have been able to sense it otherwise. That's why I don't mind working with him at all. He's not the type to backstab us. I'll take everything he says with a whole damn handful of salt, though. Because, you know, he's quite alright with the world as it is.

"I mean, the whole 'alpha male calls the shots' thing? He's all-in on that. And he talks about his minions like resources, not people. He's more into success than survival. I think we can talk him over to our side, in time. We just need to show him that our approach is the best. Otherwise, he might feel pressured into doing something reckless."

"Huh. That's surprisingly insightful for a person who thought that a weighted average had something to do with how big somebody was."

"That was a *joke*, you bloody rain cloud. I'd sit on you and show you my weighted average, if only I could!"

His laughter rang out into the corridor. "That's a horrible thought. At least there are good odds that we'll be dead within the next couple of weeks. That should help me get that nasty image out of my head! Hey, I'll bob along and try to see if I can get some traction where Wreil failed, convince Creive to let me in on the attributes and feats of him and his minions. If he's as sharp as you say, a little quid pro quo might work with him, and I *need* to know more about fliers!"

"Good call. Hey, if you manage to convince him to share his own feats and attributes, I'll make sure you get the prime choice of steaks at the next meal."

"You're a right bastard, you know that?"

I blew him a kiss. "Only to you!"

CHAPTER FOURTEEN

Wings. They were a nuisance in cramped corridors, hard to use in a close fight, and more of a theoretical advantage inside the mountain than an actual advantage. Or so I'd thought. Our only match-ups against flying forces had gone in our favor. Even as I'd forced myself to practice, to improve my flying skills, I hadn't truly appreciated the difference it made in a tactical approach. A few days after leaving Creive's stone fortress in the hands of a few hardy defenders, I had to admit, my view had been skewed.

Creive was a serious person. Not one to waste his words on unnecessary blabber or idle talk. If one were to be unkind, they might even go so far as to call him simple. As I watched the way he reacted to the chitinous beasts his scouts had stumbled upon in the corridors, I was forced to reassess my thoughts both on him and winged forces in general.

It had taken him less than a minute to come up with the plan, and now, I observed as the attackers bore down on us. The enemy was a mindless one, a pack of Tearers. They were four-legged, horse-sized beasts with chitinous armor, sharp claws, and a blisteringly fast gait. The pack of close to thirty enemies was in heavy pursuit of the scouts who fled in our direction. It was a tall and wide dirt tunnel, straight as a razor. In fact, the very straightness of it made me suspect it was created by the Corren. I could see the winged, insectile Flitters–Creive's fastest-flying minions–at the far end in full flight, staying just out of reach of the ravening beasts.

Midway in the tunnel between my forces and the charging horde, the corridor met a side tunnel, a narrower, cruder passage which crossed the corridor diagonally before it disappeared to the bottom level. There, in both side tunnels, left and right, Creive's forces lurked.

I glanced at the blue dragon as the Tearers charged in. The closer they got, the clearer it was to see that these weren't low-tier critters. Their size alone meant that I didn't give good odds for any of my Talpi who were trampled. On top of that, their speed was impressive. Few of my people would be able to run away from them. Creive, however, had merely told us to hang back and prepare while he handled things. I could only watch while I kept up an illusion hiding my minions, Creive, and myself.

The silently pursuing beasts were nearly upon the Flitters when Creive's forces struck. One moment, the predators were charging along, jaws clicking in anticipation, as they savored the scent of the flying morsels before them. The next, they were met with a salvo of flying death from the Imps down the crossing corridor.

It was a nasty, impactful barrage. Reminiscent of riflemen shooting in unison, the salvo of fire impacted the charging Tearers, downing two right away. They crashed to the ground, tripping a few others. Still, the enemy was numerous and they were not unused to battle. Some took a hit and continued, others avoided the attacks.

Within a few seconds, the larger number of the galloping beasts swerved off and disappeared from view in an attempt to take down the new food that had suddenly appeared. A full third continued chasing the fleeing Flitters in our direction, oblivious to the new threat.

The Imps attacking from the side tunnel took one single additional shot, then they must have fled because the fire ceased. The remaining Tearers in our corridor rushed in our direction, silent and undeterred in their bloodlust. For a brief moment, I became anxious at the look at them bearing down on my forces. Then, the rest of Creive's forces struck.

They poured out from the other side tunnel, some pursuing the Tearers down the opposite side tunnel, some flying our way. Flitters kept themselves near the ceiling as they singled out beasts, getting into position, and Imps poured down fire on the charging Tearers. The Culdren were the ones who caught the attention, though. The ugly, brutish creatures frantically flapped their wings to catch up with the Tearers that were galloping our way. Higher and higher they rose as they gained upon the fast animals, until they looked about to hit the ceiling. Then they closed their wings and dove.

The beasts looked unimpressive and clumsy in the air, crude and heavy compared to the nimble aerial dance of the Imps and Flitters. But as the group of Culdren plummeted down claws-first upon the unaware animals, another word made itself known. Powerful. Their bulk and razor-sharp claws, along with the massive momentum they gained from the plunge, let the Culdren wreak havoc on the charging beasts.

Some opened their wings in the nick of time, slashing at necks and heads while beating their wings in search of height. Others trusted their heavy, armored hides and rode the Tearers as they crashed to the ground. I winced at the sight of one unlucky Culdren who was dragged below a crashing Tearer and rolled around in a bone-breaking collapse.

Within two seconds, the cohesive structure of the charging group had evaporated, and the single beast who had evaded attack was halting his charge to look for targets. Through it all, the Flitters struck, diving and piercing unarmored flanks with their poison-dripping stingers.

The Tearers didn't give in or flee. However, the chaos of the ambush was too much for them, and the few predators that survived the initial onslaught were like bodybuilders on a worksite. Large, noisy, and mostly ineffective. They milled about, unable to select good targets in the turmoil, as their flying opponents kept escaping out of range. One-by-one, they were taken down by fire, poison, or claws.

I blinked. They were dead. Every single enemy was down. From the triumphant yells of the Imps coming from down the side tunnel, the result was the same thing down there. This... was the exact opposite of my kind of fight. We planned our fights, chose our battles well. Then, even when we did fight, we fought to weaken our enemies, evade and stall, avoid them or wear them down until they were weak enough to take down easily. These flying creatures of Creive's had taken down a full group of strong enemies, and they'd done it on the fly and with overwhelming strength. This added a whole new angle to our strategies.

I glanced to my side, where Creive was exuding an air of self-satisfaction. I shook my head to myself as I prodded the Ergul to approach the first wounded. Yeah, this was not a dragon to be underestimated. Heh. As if those existed.

CHAPTER FIFTEEN

"Give me but a firm spot on which to stand, and I shall move the earth."
— *Archimedes*

In the end, my minions found us, not the other way around. In fact, we spent several hours navigating the confusing tunnels of the second-most layer before one of our scouts finally had the guts to approach us. Behind him, his scouting group hung back, eyeing Creive with distrust.

It was Leith again. The smelly scout sent dirty looks at the winged minions of Creive as he passed them by to approach me. He oozed nervousness and held a safe distance from the other dragon before bowing at me. "Onyx. About time you've come."

I frowned. "It's... good to see you, too? We were starting to become nervous that something had happened to you."

He grunted. "Not my fault. We've had to dodge a lot of monsters up here and, well, those winged insects look like they might belong with the Aberrants. When I spotted an Imp, I figured it was you."

"No issues. Please lead on. I look forward to seeing what you've built while we were on the way."

Leith filled me in on how they had done, all while scratching at a yellow-brown caked substance that seemed to have fused with the fur on one arm. They had been lucky, according to him. They'd lost one scout so far, and two Imps who'd decided to go exploring, but the main camp remained undiscovered.

They had been forced to flee quite often, however, and there was no doubt that both the Dragonlings and the Aberrants were aware that a new group had entered the area, because their activity had increased since our people first arrived at the layer. "It's getting to be a problem, especially when I need to handle Wreil's tasks, too. Good thing you finally showed up. Now, we don't have to go scouting all the time, but can close ourselves in and start the work for real."

I shook my head. "Yeah, no. You'll have to keep up the scouting. We're bound to see company soon. So, tell me. Have they all been able to keep the peace?"

He scowled in disgust. "They have. Not sure how, exactly. There's squalling pups everywhere. We had a new bunch of births, and I don't get how they can tolerate the noise. 'Nother one of those filthy evolved pups, too."

I glared at the dirt-covered Imp. At least he had the guts to be honest, but... "I won't have anybody doing anything against the pups. They'll grow up to bring us all to an even better place, help us build a better home for everybody. How can you dislike that?"

"Dislike 'em? I hate 'em. You tell me, once they're in charge, that they're not going to push down on us normal people. Evolved, my ass. They'll be working to cast us out before it's over, mark my words. That is, if we live that long. I think you should save your brilliant ideas for Roth and his ilk. They're bound to lap up your words... and we're finally there. Just aim for the noise."

He pointed straight ahead, and with his message delivered, he bounded forward. Soon, I heard his high-pitched voice engaging others on the other side of a narrow entrance that hid the sight of everything beyond. The narrow dirt tunnel was way too tight for my bulk, and I prepared to send somebody in to ask what was going on... but then Creziel came marching out with a huge smile on his face.

"Oh, we've kept the entrance mostly closed." Creziel spoke as his powers flowed, and the earthen mound slowly moved. "We've still had scout groups out, but we thought the best defense would be to simply not be found in the first place. It seems we were right. Phew." He straightened and pointed at a much wider tunnel. "Welcome to your new home, Onyx."

We walked side-by-side. Creziel was silent, but the joy coming from him was a good sign. At the end of the long, straight tunnel leading from the entrance, I started noticing signs of my shamans' earthcrafting. The walls looked smooth, too smooth to be natural. The ground, too, in places, as if it had been leveled or something heavy had been dragged over it.

Oh. I blinked, taking in the change in scenery. Before me, a tunnel narrowed down and split and split again. From where I was standing, I could see the first five tunnels ranging away. Had they made a *labyrinth*?

Creziel was more than eager to tell me about what they had been doing. "No. Not a labyrinth, Onyx. I mean, we are turning it into a labyrinth, but it wasn't before. In fact, you have seen this kind of construction before." Creziel gestured at the tunnel as if that was supposed to jog my memory.

My eyes narrowed to slits as I traversed the narrow tunnel next to him. I felt like I would have remembered cramped conditions like this, with the tunnel constantly winding and turning, disorienting and confusing. Hell, even the walls were curved, adding to the... wait a minute. "Is this like those insectile things... What were they called? Like those Hevrons who attacked us? The ones who had served under a white dragon before Creive killed her?"

Creziel smiled. "That is the case. It is long-cleared, obviously. There were remains further in, where they lived, though they are sparse. The moment we spotted the tunnels, however, we knew that this was exactly what we needed. We are almost done adding false walls and obfuscating the real passage through the place before we can get started on traps. Oh, here we are."

I almost asked him what he meant when we reached the cave, and I was distracted. Except... cave wasn't the right word. This was a ballroom. No, a damn cathedral. The walls widened to both sides and especially up. The walls were mostly smooth, packed dirt, but the ceiling above was hard rock. The entire cavernous area, easily the size of a football dome and twice as tall, was interrupted only by a handful of massive natural pillars that climbed all the way to the ceiling. It was also completely empty. Not a single one of my minions were present.

Creive had been languidly following me through the tunnel system. Now, he caught up to me as I stood and gaped and watched the area alongside me. I let my eyes slide from the open, tall room to rest on the massive beast of a blue dragon. He felt eager. I asked. "You approve?"

His eyes climbed to the far ceiling and nodded. "Yes. My minions and I will be able to tear our enemies limb from limb here. When do we fight?"

I smiled. "That isn't how we do things here. First we meet up with the others. Then we talk it over and improve the area as much as possible. Meanwhile, I establish my hoard and start constructing any defenses we all agree upon."

"What do you mean, agree? You will tell your underlings what to do, and they will do it. Why waste your breath?" The massive dragon honestly looked perplexed at this.

"I know a lot about construction. I *don't* claim to know as much about earth as a Talpus. So not listening to their advice would be moronic. And I'm going to be asking you a lot about aerial combat too, so you may as well get used to the idea."

He growled and craned his neck, taking in the area surrounding us. "If you insist. We will settle down in here, get accustomed to the terrain. Come find me when you are ready. Oh, and send one of your Crawls. I am hungry."

"Neither I nor my minions are your servants *or* your meals, Creive. Besides, the food is *right* there." I nodded at the Crawls coming up behind us. They were heavily laden with the carved flesh of the Tearers. We would have made it on the provisions we had brought, but the fresh meat did provide a pleasant variety.

I moved on, leaving the blue glutton behind. In truth, even after almost a week of marching with him, I wasn't sure what to think of him. He wasn't as bloodthirsty as I'd first envisioned, but he *was* single-minded and set in his ways. To hear him say it, the "lesser species" of the mountains only existed to serve him or become food. Working with him was doable; learning to coexist with him might be difficult. Still, that was a task for another day, when all this was over and I tried to bring him fully to our side. I could feel a smile making its way to my face as I heard the high-pitched voice coming from afar. Roth. And he was definitely not happy with whoever was on the receiving end of his tongue-lashing.

The huge cavern had a low opening at the far end, and I followed Creziel through it, emerging into a new cave. He looked and felt nervous, even for him, as he cleared his throat. "So, there is this one thing, Onyx. We prepared a little surprise for you."

Much smaller than the last one, this cave was circular and low-ceilinged. It was also rank with the smell of the many bodies that had lived here for the last days. There was a certain eau de wet dog that was hard to ignore. That was all I managed to take in before a yell rang through the room.

They were all there. Crawls, Talpi, Imps. And their chitters and whispers underlined the emotions stemming from them all. Happiness. Relief. Anticipation. Oh, and overjoyed glee from Ursam, who bounded across the room to slobber all over me. Once I finally convinced the big beast to relax, I turned back toward the rest... and then the crowd parted before me, revealing what they'd been hiding.

It was ugly. It was made of stone. It looked like it was about to collapse, and if I ever contemplated sitting on it, it definitely would. It was a throne.

"Personally I think it's a waste of resources, but Creziel insisted." Arthor walked forward to meet me. Regardless of his words, below the regular recalcitrance, a tiny sense of satisfaction bubbled.

Creziel looked at me, expectantly. "It *was* my idea. I mean, it felt like we were all alone and needed something... something to remind us of..." His voice trailed off, and the unspoken word hung between us. "Home." It would seem that the Talpi had, finally, found something worth fighting for.

I walked closer and, with a loving smile, patted the interimistic stone throne. "I love it. A reminder of what we've got waiting for us, as soon as we manage this tiny little obstacle in front of us." I stood tall, stretching my neck as I took in the small cave where my people had been toiling and felt a burst of pride in my chest. "So... who wants to tell me how far we've come?"

CHAPTER SIXTEEN

It was a blank slate, and I loved it. The place my minions had found was rough, filled with debris and signs of their former occupants—and rife with potential. This, Creziel had spotted right away and, in concert with the other council members, gone to work preparing the area. But they limited themselves to improving the overall setup, waiting to construct any traps, hidden tunnels, and the like until we were ready to discuss any battle plans.

And here it stood, two-thirds ready, prepared to be sculpted into a final, efficient meat grinder. The labyrinth itself would be excellent, both for ambushes, hit-and-run techniques, and smaller traps. The subsequent cavern would be perfect for our fliers to dominate. The, heh, throne room would be our fallback position if all went to shit and could probably become a good spot for a final surprise or two.

If I had hands, I would be rubbing them together in antici-pation. As it stood, I settled for a wide grin as I lowered my bulk to lie before my assembled minions. Creive was still in the large cavern, stuffing his face. "We are about to submerge ourselves in work, toil for our survival for the next handful of days. Before we do that, however, there is one discussion we need to take. One we've postponed too often. A discussion about the future of the Scoured Mountain."

The sensations coming from them varied wildly. Surprise. Enthusiasm. Even boredom.

Roth actually begged off. "I don't care. Let me fight and train, and I'm happy. You've done enough for us. I don't need all these talks."

I looked at him fondly. "This is the *exact* reason why we need to have this discussion." I let my gaze glide over them all. "You – everybody who's gathered here – are used to one mode, one reason to live. Fighting for survival. You may have had times of surplus and times where you were winning more than you lost, but you have never been *safe*.

"As such, it's no wonder that this hasn't really come up. But here it is: In the very near future, if all goes well, we will be looking at a mountain where we call the shots. Where we decide how society should be constructed. I want to start laying the first brick in that construction right here. Right now. With you."

Arthor frowned, suspicion and curiosity wafting off of him. Gert stared in rapt attention. Roth... scratched his head.

I laughed. "Okay. Relax. Timothy can tell you the exact point as to why you'll want to care." Tim and I had spent most of our march debating the exact idea we were going to set before them, and I loved it. Now, it was simply a matter of whether they'd accept the idea, too.

As the translucent figure faced the assembled group, his thoughts rang out as bright and clear as his countenance. "The world Onyx and I come from has had the debatable honor of being allowed to experiment with an untold number of governmental forms. From the simple tribalism of the earlier days, the widespread masses of our people have gone through every variation-"

I interrupted him. "Tim. You're obviously right, but... it's just us. A little less high-brow, perhaps?"

"Oh. Sure. Suffice to say, over time, we have tried a lot of different forms of rule and self-rule and figured out that most of them have... issues. We have spent a lot of time trying to come up with the best way to decide things for ourselves, creating a better system than letting the dragon decide everything."

I nodded. "Let me get it out there, by the way. I don't *mind* leading you. Not the least. I've helped you, but you have also saved me, several times over. The way I see it, we're in this together. When I say that I think of you as family, those aren't just words. That's why we need something more permanent than me calling the shots. Of course, a lot of the different types of government wouldn't be feasible here. Our future is unknown and filled with danger, we will have to fight for our lives constantly, and we have no clue what our group is going to look like in the near future. We are almost a hundred people now. In two years, we may be thousands. So, basically, anything we were to come up with currently probably would have to be changed as we develop."

I looked at those assembled. They were all hanging on my every word, even Grex, though he was jumping back and forth. "On top of that, the way we have been running things is already clashing with our old agreement. You decide the specifics for your own species, but I call the shots. That was the original agreement." With a sweep of a claw, I dismissed the notion. "If we actually practiced that, it would have me having to manage things that I do not know about nor care about. Until now, that hasn't been a real problem, but in time, it will be."

Roth yawned and plopped down on his behind. "I was supposed to get it? I have no clue why I am here. This is so *dull*."

Arthor hissed. "You're here to pay attention, fur-for-brains. Because if you don't, somebody else will make the decisions on training for the future."

Roth jumped up, growling. "What? Why? Is it Moiven? My assistant? I knew he would try something!"

Creziel took mercy on Roth and pulled him aside to whisper

into his ear. Meanwhile, Arthor frowned at me. "Are you saying that you are going to change all responsibilities?"

"Far from it. If anything, we are going to be better at pinpointing where the responsibilities lie."

Grex flew up to look me straight in the eyes, then crossed his spindly arms over his chest. "I can change. I am responsible."

I fought down a smile at the flabbergasted emotions that exploded from everybody at that blatant lie.

The Imp continued blathering. "Will you still make decisions, then? I am responsible, but you decide everything?"

Tim jumped in right away. "No. See, we are building toward the future. The positions we decide today will be the start of our government. We can always find a suitable word for the roles and positions that we will end up creating. As for the governmental form, we eventually desire something between a republic and a meritocracy. You see-"

I smiled fondly at him. "Seriously, Tim. I said *less* highbrow. You've already gone over my head with these discussions ten times over. No need to inflict it on everybody else."

Keeping my gaze fixed on Grex, I felt a smile building on my face. "So, the deal is this, Grex, if you all agree. Today, we assign responsibilities. We ensure that we've all agreed on exactly which areas we cover. As a rule, then, everybody gets to manage their own area of responsibility. The only exceptions would be when somebody disagrees or needs help or something. Then we can meet up, talk about things."

Grex beamed a huge smile, then, by degrees the smile grew smaller, until he squinted suspiciously at me. "But. That's what we do today?"

I laughed. "Pretty much. There would be one major difference. If we can't agree on something right away, those who earn the responsibilities here will have to vote on it. Then, whatever the vote is, that will be the final decision—regardless of what I believe."

The silence was overwhelming. Then, out of the blue, Grex released a high-pitched trill as he performed a spinning circle in the air. "You would let us make decisions over you? Us? Imps and Talpi deciding over a dragon because there are more of us? Of course! Let's start with the decisions now!"

Arthor ignored the antics of the Imp, staring at me. "Do you mean this, Onyx? Do not make light of this."

"I do. I have said this before. Dragons live long lives, unless they are killed. I do not plan to live my life as a tyrant. I want you to have more. Not just the struggle for survival, but something more significant. A life worth living. A world worth striving for."

Timothy added. "We have spent a lot of time on this. We believe it'll work, especially once we figure out what works and what doesn't."

A round of assents came from everybody, except for Roth, who glared at us all. "Still not giving up my training."

I smiled at the squat Talpus. "That sounds like a good point to move on to the more practical issues. We figured that we should start with a system that's pretty similar to what we have now then work from that. That way, Roth, you would only lose the responsibility if enough people agreed that you weren't doing your job."

Mollified, the bulky Talpus grunted. "Hrm. They can *try*. I'll have 'em running endurance training until they change their minds."

I was trying my best not to laugh at the affronted emotions coming from Roth. "So. These persons we choose today, these leaders, they might change with the times, but they will allow people a larger share of independence. And they might very well become a permanent part of our future realm, so think about this."

Arthor spoke up straight away. "So, you do not want to decide who you *allow* to earn a position?" The stress he put on the word was unmistakable.

"No. I did say 'we.' We have to be open to change, as our group expands or we learn what works and what doesn't. What Tim and I have come up with so far is this: to begin with, we would want to keep it more or less the way we already have it. One person represents the important tasks of our entire group. You know, sorcerers, scouts, fighters, training, builders, and so on. Apart from that, we'd want to have a representative for each race, which the races choose themselves."

"Can we choose as well?" The mental words were slow, but precise. The emotions coming from Gert, the young representative of the Crawls, were reserved but hopeful.

I glanced at Gert with a smile. She had joined the conversation a few times already. She had really grown a lot sharper than I had dared to hope. I focused on the small Crawl, trying to look past her ugly outer shell. "That actually leads us to our second point of discussion. So far, Timothy and I have argued that everybody who joins us and works for us should end up having a say in our society. We might end up with a number of different races or groups who join us in name only and work only to serve themselves."

Creziel was the first to react. "And we could end up as slaves or food again."

"That is a theoretical threat. It is, however, just that. Theoretical. I, for one, believe that we, as a group, are capable of vetting any future race or grouping that we allow to join our society. Gert, your kind has proven your strength in battle many times over already. I had my doubts about your minds, but those doubts are being put to shame every time you join our discussions."

Arthor stepped forward. "No."

I raised an eyebrow. "You'll have to elaborate on that, Arthor."

The rumbling sound from him wasn't quite a growl. "You are too hasty. Too quick to judge, to trust. So your see-through friend has managed to teach the Crawl to spit a few words?" He stalked over to place himself in front of the ugly creature. He looked down upon her, just barely, even if she probably outweighed him twice over. He sneered. "Still need to see if her mind's halfway *there*, or if it's all grunts and pointing like Erk was. The Imps lack common sense, but at least their minds work."

Gert bared her teeth at that. "I *can* think. We all can. The words are hard."

Tim and I had expected this to happen. I nodded and said, "Take your time."

Her gaze drifted toward Timothy, but the pale form simply smiled at her and motioned for her to continue. She frowned and shuffled her legs, looking at the ground as her thoughts reached the group assembled before her. "It's hard. Explaining, I mean. Doing is easy. We have always done. Caf hunts easy prey because she is quiet, for a Crawl. Ket guards us all, leads us in fights because he is tough and strong.

"Ort handles all the small jobs, but you have to prod him because he's lazy." She paused, frowning for almost a full minute, before continuing. "We need this. The talking. The learning." Her eyes looked back up, locking onto mine. "We will earn our place. We are strong, but will be stronger if we become a true part of this, this Council."

I smiled at Gert and said simply, "You have my vote." I looked at each of the others in turn. They nodded, one by one. Even Arthor had no objections, just a simple, grudging nod and a sensation of surprise. This was even better than I had dared hope for. Not only had her communication skills already far surpassed those of Erk, she also showed a level of thought I hadn't been sure their race possessed. "I appreciate your answer, Gert. That alone gives me great hope for the Crawls. For now, however, I merely have one final thing to add and then I'll let you decide."

I looked over each of them in turn. "You know where I come from. I used to work for a living, not fight. My experiences are definitely colored by this. Still, there are certain facts that you cannot avoid, like this: New beginnings are difficult and prone to issues. Nine out of ten new companies fail within the first ten years. I've been part of one myself. The same goes for us.

"There *will* be issues that we haven't foreseen and problems that we could not anticipate. We need to handle any challenges as they come and adapt. So, speak up, tell me what we need to improve, and we'll handle it. Together, there is nothing we can't do." I settled myself and looked expectantly at the group. "Let's make it official. Do you all agree that we should, from now on, make our decisions based on a vote, by simple majority?"

The room chorused with assent. Roth laughed. "Why wouldn't we? You're the one who's turning down the power, you crazy dragon."

I smiled as the others echoed his thoughts. And, like that, with a simple jab, the first Council of the Scoured Mountain was born. Grinning, I cricked my neck and purred at them all. "So. We have enough work waiting to keep half the mountain occupied for the foreseeable future. Any final comments before we get to the practical issues?"

I don't know what I expected. Definitely not Creziel walking forward to face the others. "I would like to say something." We grew silent, and they waited for the quiet Talpus to say his piece. "I never had any reason to grow. I was always the weaker fighter, the worst shaman. The time with Onyx has been the best of my life, and I feel like I am earning my place. So I will take up my responsibility, and I *will* bear it well. I really do believe that, if we work together on this, nobody will be able to hold us down... not even Selys."

Roth grunted. "Huh. I didn't expect that from you. What happened to the scared little runt I knew? I like the sound of it, though. *They can't hold us down.* Us against the mountain, we will take on any comers."

Creziel frowned. "That wasn't exactly what I-"

Grex interrupted, "We will fight them all."

Arthor sneered with a grin. "Pfah. We will outsmart them first."

Gert added, seriously, "We will learn and grow."

Wreil joined in, "We will stab them in the back."

Timothy entoned, "We will bring a new age to this world."

Roth repeated the words, and this time we all joined in: *"They can't hold us down."*

Ten minutes later, I was in shock. My time as a foreman had given me enough experience from dull, life-draining meetings to last me a lifetime. Here? Progress was smooth. Disturbingly so. I reckoned it was because everybody knew we couldn't afford to spend too much time blabbering about technicalities. Mostly, we had affirmed our already existing responsibilities.

Roth would continue as the resident trainer, and Creziel as the one responsible for building. Meanwhile, Arthor would handle all sorcery-related issues, Timothy would take care of teaching, Wreil the scouting, Grex would represent the Imps, and Gert the Crawls. Finally, I was in charge of the overall planning concerning combat.

I spoke up. "Alright, people. I think this is a good place to step back and take a moment to consider this. Look at what we're doing. With a brief discussion, we have started the creation of our own governing structure. If all goes well, we've taken the first step of altering the future of life inside the Scoured Mountain."

"If we survive the next month." The mental jab from Arthor came right on cue.

I took it in stride, bowing to all of them. "Yes. Now, with the thought of what we have managed in mind, maybe we should cut things short? Nobody says that we're supposed to handle all the large decisions today."

There was a general murmur of assent. Roth especially looked lost with the ongoing discussions.

"Good. Then let's turn our heads to survival. I want all of your ideas, both on which constructions I should make, traps and... anything. Just throw them out there. Then, we'll start sorting through it before we get to work. We have... maybe a week left to prepare. Now, remember, the moment we establish the hoard, they will become aware of our presence. That means that we will have to be mostly ready at that point. Right now, they may know that we're skulking about, but they are unaware that we're here in force. Once the hoard is up, it's game on."

Tim interjected, drily, "That means—"

"Oh we know what it means." This came from Arthor. "The lizard's speech is weird, but at least he is consistent. Now. If we can get started? The single most important thing is creating an escape tunnel. We do not want to get caught in here..."

Hours later, my stomach growled loud enough to interrupt Creziel, who was belaboring a point about the Stone Doors he wanted put in place. I grinned. "Let us take this as a sign. We have been working for quite a long time, and our basic plan is pretty clear at this point. We can always get back to this discussion. Let's get to work, then I can go get something to eat. Arthor, if you would join me? And Wreil, I'd like to talk with you afterward."

Most of them went straight to their own discussions and started splitting off in smaller groups or alone. From the mood, I could tell that they were eager to get on with the work. Creziel stood for a second, looking at the others walking away, and then shook his head before running after Roth. Timothy floated over the floor to join me and Arthor.

Arthor glanced up at me. The tall Talpus looked better than good. His fur was smooth and silky. I thought back to the dirt-covered, hunched-over Talpus I'd first met back in the domain and marveled. He had come a long way. Also, he must have upgraded his regular rocks for a new set. Right now, what was bobbing around him looked more like a quartet of hardened stone tiles. The tall animal let an eyebrow rise. "If we need to talk, we can do it as we walk. My stomach could do with something more than plants by now, and it sounds like you have meat to spare."

He turned and started walking. Two long steps caught me up to him, and I asked calmly, "The others have given me the general knowledge. Construction-wise, we're doing good, and we're even ahead of schedule. We have enough food to see this through. And the scouts have been able to keep us hidden, for now. What I wanted from you is simply this: how are we *doing?* What are your thoughts on the situation? What are the Talpi thinking?"

He looked straight ahead and sneered. "They are hopeful. Ridiculously so. They expect you to deliver a miracle, obviously. Pfah. They are blinded by the thoughts of what we *have* done as opposed to what we are facing right now. As if our successes in the past guarantee that we will pull off the same in the future." He shook his head. "They lose themselves in the work and do not think of the bigger picture."

"And you?"

He paused. The silence stretched, as we crossed half the gigantic cavern. The workers were already piling into the place, gathering to discuss their new plans. "Having Creive and his minions here will help. With them on board, we may have a chance, especially if we can take them on one-by-one. We still are not close to knowing their numbers, but we will be able to do our utmost to stack the advantages on our side. As long as we have an escape tunnel ready, our position looks as promising as it's going to get."

"Good. Arthor, I wanted to tell you that I appreciate your honesty. Others may try to hide what they think, but you give it to me straight. I like that. And you *know* I don't think I've been sent by Deyra like some sort of divine solution. I still do believe that this fight is worth engaging, with our end goal in consideration."

Arthor was quiet for a while. "I believe you may be right." He looked grim, staring at the floor as he walked. Then suddenly, he grinned. "Right until you do something stupid. Then, I look forward to telling you exactly how wrong you are, lizard."

I snorted a laugh. "I know you will."

Once we had finished eating, the shaman stalked off to continue the work on the escape tunnel. Wreil wasn't moving closer, for some reason. He looked to me and then down at his paws where he stood, fifty feet from me. Turmoil and satisfaction warred inside of me as I considered what had to happen. Now, I just needed to follow up on my plans, ensure that we beat our enemies, then get Selys to piss off elsewhere while we changed the world to a better place. I would have to...

"He's one opinionated little runt, huh?"

Timothy's voice came from right behind me, and I jumped. "For Chrissake, man. I'd totally forgotten that you were there. Can a dragon die from a heart attack? I think you almost killed me!"

He snorted. "Comes from not having a body. You get to be pretty sneaky." He bobbed up and down, clearly satisfied with himself. "So, sounds like you've talked him over to your side."

"Yeah, as long as we keep on not messing up, of course. That's a tall order. I mean, we could be attacked *right* now, and we'd be in trouble." I shook my head. "Still, we'll manage, and I have a bunch of ideas for how to make sure that doesn't happen. How about you? What's the plan?"

His visage grew less refined and a see-through appendage pointed back toward the large cavern. "That's why I'm hanging around, really. How much do you trust Creive?"

I frowned. "Now, there's a loaded question if ever I heard it. Hmm. Enough to not screw us over now that he's promised his help." I grimaced and rolled my neck. "Let me rephrase that, makes me sound less certain than I am. I don't feel *any* sense of deceit from him. Still, he's not part of the family. He's on the payroll, and I trust him to do that and not a bit more."

"That's a glowing endorsement right there. Hmm. That's the thing... he turned me down. Why would anybody say no to sharing knowledge, when it could mean that you would be able to improve your skill set and that of your minions? That's moronic."

"Oh. I did see you talking to him on and off, but I figured that meant that you had gotten to him."

"No. He kept on shooting me down. This last time, he threatened me to not pester him anymore unless I'd offer something *real*. Said he'd shoot lightning at me, too! I was simply explaining to him why he wasn't seeing the full picture."

I couldn't contain my mirth. A series of dry coughs escaped me as I laughed.

He glared at me. "This isn't funny! We are letting valuable knowledge escape through our fingers as we speak. How often can we get the chance to-"

"Relax, Timmy-boy. It's just... you're not seeing this. So, to you, the knowledge in itself is valuable, right?"

"Obviously. It can-"

"To him, it's a bargaining tool."

Tim looked at me with no obvious sign that he got it.

I smiled. "This isn't Earth, man. You're used to people putting value on brains or education by itself. Here, brains are a tasty snack. But Creive did let you come back several times over. That means he's not shooting down your idea out of hand. He's right there, waiting for you to give him a good offer for the knowledge."

Tim looked crestfallen. "Oh. But... that's so *ridiculous*. He could have so much more, help his minions grow."

"His minions, which he believes are expendable and his to order to the death, should he so please?" I smiled again, not mocking this time. "Listen, how about I take a chat with big blue there? I'm sure he can be convinced, with the right incentive."

"If you would? Seriously... that makes me distrust him even more. Who doesn't value knowledge? That's like... putting mustard on fries. Who would *be* like that?"

When Timothy left, Wreil moved closer. He was still staring down, looking like he'd found something extremely interesting on the floor. His paw had a death grip on the necklace. The overwhelming sense coming from him was shame. That didn't feel promising.

"I wanted to talk to you, Wreil, hear how you're doing?"

He didn't answer, merely frowned. With a sigh, he raised his head, stared up at me. "Can we skip this? I know I haven't done well. I've tried, but there's no one who can replace Aelis. At this point, it's better to let Leith run the show. I can go back to being part of the group, do what I do *well*."

"Whoa. What the hell? Where did that come from? That's not-"

He ignored me. "I'm sorry. I said I could handle it, but I can't. This is messing me up! I'm not like Aelis. I want to be, but I'm *not*."

"Wreil," I said, keeping my tone as level and reasonable as I possibly could. "I am not here to replace you, berate you, or try to turn you into a new Aelis. I told you before, I'll help you to make things work out right."

He looked shell-shocked. His hand froze on his necklace. "But then-"

"Did you delegate some of the scheduling to the others?"

"Ehm... Yes. Leith takes care of making sure that we have everything covered. He says that I'm supposed to handle it, though. That Aelis—"

I shook my head vehemently. "Leith isn't the one on charge. I am. Besides, you said it yourself. You're not Aelis. I don't want you to be. The only thing I want is for you scouts to be in the best hands possible. How are they doing otherwise?"

"They're... doing pretty good. It helps, having backup. We've been talking it over a lot, and we only go out in mixed groups now. The Crawls and Imps are noisy, but they stay back and, well, we can adjust pretty well as we go. Sometimes, sending out the Imps ahead in taller areas helps, too."

I nodded. Didn't push it. I was starting to get an idea and decided to send out a feeler. "That sounds good. And you did well in preparing Creive for our arrival. There was hardly any delay in our departure. Plus, the information you got from him helped me a lot in convincing him. How about you keep doing what you do well? Keeping everybody happy and making sure the group works well together?"

He looked at me and huffed. "That's not *work*."

"Believe it or not, it is. It is an essential part of being a leader, and from what I'm hearing, you're handling that part just fine. Keep that up. And if you need any assistance, tell me. For now, though, I'd like to ask you for help with a challenge. See, in order to catch our enemies by surprise…"

We talked. At first he merely listened, but then he started responding, coming with suggestions. Slowly, the clicks from his necklace became a steady background noise in our discussion. And his anxiety faded into the background.

CHAPTER SEVENTEEN

"I praise loudly. I blame softly." — *Catherine the Great*

The next few days disappeared like steak put in front of a Clencher. My time was mostly spent consulting, as most of the work at this point was grunt work, moving dirt, creating tunnels, and managing the layout. Since we weren't announcing our presence yet, I had loads of surplus mana, which I used to keep the scouts constantly camouflaged.

This way, even if the three races were aware that somebody new had made it to their layer, the odds of us being found were minimal. I could have closed the place off entirely, but I wanted to know what was going on out there. I also saved up enough mana to create two additional Mana Crystals. I expected that I might need them in the near future.

The escape tunnel was finished within the first day, and we got to work on the remnant corridors, turning them into labyrinths worthy of a minotaur. The first thing we did was agree upon the final layout. They had already done an amazing job. The already-confusing layout of the tunnel system had been twisted even further, filled with surprising turns, dead-ends, and paths taking winding roads back to the entrance. Now, we got downright nasty. We added openings for Stone Doors and Shadow Doors and started working on any and all traps we could come up with. On top of that, we added a winding layer of tunnels on top of the corridors of the area, where our ranged Talpi could attack through well-disguised holes.

Still, we weren't dealing with mindless attackers here. If all went well, we'd be able to keep them inside the winding paths and beat them there. The odds were good that the enemies might eventually break through, regardless of what we made. We needed to have a warm welcome for them, for whenever they made it through to the next cavern. So, obviously, the first thing we did was ready the area for a charge to meet anybody breaking through.

The next part was all Creive and the shamans. They worked on the large area, improving it with anything that could make aerial combat easier and tilted in favor of him and his minions. We added platforms for them to hide and bombard non-fliers, affixed thin strips of leather in places to tangle and disrupt enemy fliers, and created apertures for them to escape back toward the throne room if they were in trouble.

Heh – and regarding Creive – I'd been right. A promise of enchanting a full set of leather armor for him was all it took for him to agree to having his minions share their details with Tim. He didn't budge on sharing his own details, though, and I relented. For now. I didn't want him to think that I was trying to suss out his weaknesses. Still, it was definitely a win. At the very least, our Imps would learn exactly how to best select their attributes if they wanted the most powerful feats.

A handful of days after arriving, I had the Council and Creive gather in the throne room again. "Congratulations. You've done an amazing job. You should be proud of yourself."

They didn't look proud. In fact, most of them looked dirty, bedraggled, and tired –like they had spent every waking hour working in the dirt – which wasn't too far from the truth.

"Wreil. Our scouts have been amazing. Tell Leith he's done a great job, too. Though the enemies' patrols are constantly increasing, they have managed to keep us hidden and lead away anybody who looked like they were about to stumble this way. And everything else you've managed... I am very, very impressed with you." A click was the only response, but I did feel a burst of pride coming from him.

"Arthor. Creziel. You guys have performed miracles. Looking back to the first time I saw you working with earth, it's impossible to recognize what I'm seeing now. You have become absolute powerhouses. Whatever happens from here on, you have earned the power to sculpt the mountain as you see fit."

"Creive." The blue dragon's head rose, surprised. He did *not* expect to be singled out. "You have taught us a lot about aerial battles. Thank you. The same goes to you, Grex."

"I helped. So much. You should all be thankful." The Imp spun around himself and held his hands out. When no reaction came, he folded his arms over the chest and settled down again, insulted.

"Gert. Roth. Your fighters have assisted wherever you could. Your brawn is yet another reason we have been able to finish the first part so fast."

"The first part, Onyx? This means we are done waiting?" Roth jumped up and grabbed his sword.

"Exactly. This is where things are about to get exciting. Once we're done here, I'm establishing the hoard and starting to construct as fast as my mana regeneration will allow me. We're preparing for battle. I don't know how long it's going to take before they attack us, but I'd wager that we don't have more than two days at most."

Arthor frowned, eyes narrowed to slits. "We are ready, lizard. Still, you leave us with one topic that needs to be covered. You say that they're going to come at us, like that's a certainty. In fact, we need the three groups to attack us sense-lessly, with no thought to the consequences. How exactly do you think that's going to happen?"

"That one's easy. I'll just ask them."

Timothy's facial features solidified into clarity. He squinted at me and then shook his head. "You're doing that thing again."

I snorted. "Thing? What thing?"

"That thing where you have a plan, you believe it's excellent, and you're trying to force people to ask you about it."

I scratched my brow with a claw, keeping down the laughter inside me. "That does sound like me. So?"

"So... what?"

"So, are you going to ask me about it?"

Arthor scowled at me. I tried telling myself that I could feel the tiniest bit of mirth coming from him. It might be wishful thinking. "Pfah. You are insufferable, lizard. This is serious. If we can't enrage our enemies properly, we won't be able to meet Selys' timeline. Besides, everybody here knows that it has to do with the captives."

That really confused Tim. "Captives? What captives?"

I shook my head. "You need to get your head out of the clouds more. Alright, alright. Wreil. Tell them."

The scout stepped forward. "Well, for the past three days, on Onyx' orders, we have been ambushing any scouts from the three domains. We've got them stowed away in a safe place a short walk from here. We were despairing of capturing any Dworgen, but today, with the help of a couple of Culdren, we finally managed."

After the worst noise had died down, Gert was the one to ask. "Good. We can learn about them. Skills, strengths, flaws. Let us prepare. What else? They know their scouts are gone, time is running out. What *is* your plan Onyx? Create the hoard and hope they attack?"

I bowed my neck at the squat, muscular Crawl. A cool head and insightful mind. I could end up liking this one. "A portion of truth–and a bluff. I will simply tell them how it is. That Selys has approved of me taking over, and I will be showing them who calls the shots from here on out. That there is an easy solution, of simply accepting my dominance, and a hard one, of me slaying their people until they give in."

"And the bluff?"

"That I'm going to use all my abilities as a shadow dragon to besiege them until they cave. Haunt their patrols and warriors who leave their domains. Plant traps everywhere. Ambush their food gatherers... and so on and so forth." I grinned at them all. "Obviously, it's exactly what we *would* do if we had the time to take a leisurely approach. But they don't know we're working on a schedule." I looked at them all. "So. Any suggestions? Questions?"

The room exploded in chatter.

CHAPTER EIGHTEEN

[Do you wish to establish your hoard? Yes/no]

I clicked "yes" and watched as then tendrils of magic shot deep down into the ground and pulled - returning soon thereafter at a more leisurely pace as the hoard established its connection with Deyra. I was never going to grow tired of that sight. I watched the pop-ups appearing in a steady stream, patiently willing them away, one-by-one.

The last member of the Council had disappeared minutes ago. I had imagined that the debate would center on the overall strategy, but instead it had been mostly revolving around the order of constructions—-what would be the most important thing to build first. In the end, my initial approach had been downvoted.

I had spoken in favor of placing every available Shadow Tower inside the labyrinthine tunnels leading to the large caverns, but the others argued and voted that we would need a lot of Shadow Towers inside the main cavern due to the risk of one of the groups making it past the first area. With the Hoard planted, I was going to start the first of the constructions before I went out to intimidate the trapped scouts.

Blinking away the final notifications, I allowed myself a satisfied smirk. We *had* grown. The same went for our possibilities. It was hard to think that I had started with only a handful of possible constructions and barely enough mana to build a simple Stone Door. Now, with my insane mana regeneration and liberal use of mana crystals, I would be able to create between twenty and thirty constructions on the first two days alone.

It seemed implausible, and I had to check the math to be sure I was right, but there it was, clear as day. With a few exceptions, the constructions I'd be building cost between 100 and 200 mana, and I had a mana pool of 860, regenerating a massive 1920 mana a day. Add two mana crystals on top of that, and I had just below 6,500 mana to play with if they gave me two full days after establishing the hoard before attacking. That was pretty insane.

Except, of course, we didn't have two days. If we had, I'd be establishing a Gallery of Illusions right off the bat. I didn't see them giving us the time to establish it in peace, though. In fact, right this very moment, a Dworgen leader was very likely glaring at a map showing a new hoard that very much wasn't supposed to be there. Even if we didn't release the scouts, odds were good that we'd be seeing the first enemies encroaching on our area within a day's time.

I took the chance to glance at the map. It really was an excellent place they'd found. It was almost equidistant from the three domains, with the Aberrant domain being a bit further away from the others. On top of that, any pathways leading to the upper or lower layers were far away. As a result, this place should be far from most regular traffic. Heh. That was about to change.

"Alright. No time like the present."

I started walking through the domain, adding constructions and watching their magical glows spring into being as their countdowns began. A Stone Door here. A Shadow Tower there. Unfortunately, I couldn't create any of the Soul Carver's constructions myself. Pity. With an Essence Siphon, I might have been able to take on all comers myself, right out in the open. As I made it into the large cavern, I unfolded my wings and leapt into open air, carefully rising until I hovered near the ceiling, taking in the entire room.

I shuddered. I was glad that I wasn't the one who had to fight up here. While the room was large, the minute control needed to handle the stress of aerial combat while still being able to avoid the ceiling, walls, and pillars. *And* the traps… Yeah. I would leave that for Creive and his ilk. Still, there was no doubt that it would improve our side's chances. On top of the shielded platforms for our aerial forces to rain down damage on ground troops in relative safety, a good deal of the pillars had been altered, adding platforms for Shadow Towers. I circled the room slowly, starting their construction.

The tunnels were expensive in mana. I had to take a break to consume a Mana Crystal. The cost was annoying, but we'd agreed that it was necessary in order to have as overwhelming a battlefield as possible ready for when they'd come charging. And while I'd initially argued that Shadow Towers set along the ceiling to weaken all attackers was the right way to handle them, I had to cave to Creziel's suggestion. Because, as he'd argued, even if the towers managed to weaken a lot of the attackers, we'd already seen that they couldn't keep up with large numbers of attackers. If, instead, we changed the playing field entirely… I chuckled under my breath. Even if this should probably be a solemn moment, I couldn't wait to see our enemies' reaction when they finally understood what was going on.

In the end, I made it out of the tunnel with every single door created and a sliver of mana remaining, approached Wreil, who was waiting for me near the entrance tunnel.

"Are you ready, Onyx?"

"Yes. One final construction right… here." The final Stone

Door was birthed with a bright glimmer of magic. "That should do it. Take me to them."

The "safe place" where we kept our enemies hidden was a dead-end side tunnel to the entrance. We hadn't locked them up, since we needed to keep them tied up with a heavy watch over them at all times to ensure they didn't escape, harm themselves, or harm each other.

Several days of capture had left an impression on almost everybody we'd captured. I inspected them all. The first group was the Aberrants. Five of them. An Evolved Crawl – huh – nice to know that that was a possibility. A single, one-armed Dworgen, and a trio of Talpi. All of them above level 15–that was probably a requirement to even survive up here near the top of the mountain. Their attributes, though–the Dworgen was a powerhouse, but the rest were not at the level of my minions. Our incessant training was really paying off. Regardless of their attributes, they looked tired and bedraggled, and as I stepped into their sight, they shied away, looking scared.

The Dragonlings didn't flinch. They also looked less bedraggled, like they had been captured minutes ago, not like someone who'd suffered a beatdown followed by two days of too little food. Even covered with blood and with their muscular, clawed arms bound on the back under their folded-up wings, the trio of beasts looked battle-ready and ferocious.

Their coloration was different, as was their description. Red Dragonling. Blue Dragonling. Even a White Dragonling. We knew it already, this was bound to mean lots of different powers we had to handle. Apart from their colors, they had about the same build, though. That wasn't a good thing, because their average build was a cross between humanoid dragons and body builders, sporting the attitude of wrestlers on a steroid overdose. They looked *mean*. I went over the details of the latest Inspect again, pleased with the latest upgrade that allowed me to see their weaknesses.

[Personal Info:

Name: Czarny
Race: Red Dragonling, Level 17 – experience toward next level:
3230/17000
Size: Medium

Stats and Attributes:
Health: 420/420
Mana: 190/190
Strength: 38
Toughness: 42
Agility: 51
Mental Power: 19
Mental Control: 19

Weakness: Frost damage]

His attributes were really something. Clearly a scout, or focused on Agility, at least, he wasn't much slower than me. All told, he'd probably be able to overwhelm a newborn dragon by himself. The weaknesses were at the same time surprising and not. The red one being weak to frost damage, and the white to fire was to be expected. Traditional, even. But the blue was weak to poison damage? I guessed that meant shadow Dragonlings were likely weak before lightning, and green ones couldn't hack shadow attacks. I didn't really catch the logic behind it, but it didn't matter, either. An advantage to abuse, that was all that mattered. I was just happy that this only applied to Dragonlings, not real dragons. Further lightning weakness on top of the lightning weakness I already got from Creive? That would be dangerous.

The Dworgen looked like somebody tried to distill the essence of black knights into a humanoid. Their equipment was top-of-the-line, and they were crazy focused on Strength and Toughness. The four humanoids were half again taller than my Talpi. All wore full segmented metal armor that covered every inch of their low-set, squat bodies. One of the four had his helmet torn off, revealing a low-browed, neanderthal-looking face covered with scars. As my eyes fell on him, he *growled* at me, mouth parting to reveal sharpened teeth. Weakness… poison damage? Really? Well, a couple of Creive's minions did have poison, but applying it wouldn't be easy behind all that armor.

I tried engaging the captured scouts. The peace talks didn't last long. Two minutes later, I walked away, as my minions worked on releasing our captives from their bond before they were let go to make their way back home. What was that old quote? "Peace was never an option." It definitely fit the bill here. Both the Dragonlings and the Dworgen had felt like rage was boiling underneath their skin the entire time, and I almost believed that they were going to try to attack me, even while they were trapped. While the emotions from the Aberrants were more subdued, my offer of peace had also fallen on dead ears with them. Tim waited for me near the entrance, and I shook my head with a sad smile. "Yeah. It'll be war. Good thing we prepared for it."

CHAPTER NINETEEN

"To everyone battling a difficulty or under attack right now, smile, keep your head up, keep moving and stay positive, you'll get through it." — *Germany Kent*

"They are here."

Damnit. It was too early. The enemy scouts we'd released to light a fire under their asses had done their job *too* well. I'd done all I possibly could to construct everything. I used the two Mana Crystals I was able to for the day, spent every single mana point I regenerated, and the tunnels still weren't completely ready. All Stone Doors were ready, and the construction on the Shadow Doors had been started. We still needed the last handful of Shadow Towers to finish inside the tunnels for the plan to work optimally. Good thing we'd planned for this eventuality. "Are the shamans ready? And who is it?"

"They are waiting for you, Onyx. I ran as fast as I could. It's the armored ones."

"The Dworgen. Good." I made my way at top speed, zig-zagging my way past minions through the labyrinth toward the entrance tunnel. I found Arthor and Creziel mid-discussion in the center of a small crowd, fighters watching the far end of the tunnels anxiously as they fingered their weapons.

"Are you ready?" I asked without preamble.

Creziel nodded nervously. Arthor glared at the open Stone Door which was all that stood between us and the incoming enemies. "Yes. Have you seen their numbers?"

"No. Let me see if they are within range." Hurried, I opened the map and ranged outward. There they were. "We have ten minutes, maybe a bit more. They have just passed the offshoot with the dripping ceiling." The heavily armed and armored warriors moved as one flowing mass, uniform, darkened armors hard to tell apart from each other. None of them seemed in any way winded, even though they must have kept an impressive pace to reach us already. "I give it… between 80 and 100 of them. 110 at most. All with close combat weapons, some with shields and… a few ranged weapons, it looks like. Some are carrying large bags." I let my eyes drift back and forth, looking for people or items that stood out. "Found the leader. I think. There's one guy with a massive shield, right at the back. Looks like he is giving orders to the lot." I closed the map and turned toward the others.

"You know what you're supposed to do. Whatever happens from now on, it's been an honor getting to know you." I let my gaze slide over them all. "Alright, get to your positions. Wreil. Ready to close!"

Their presence arrived as noise first. A rhythmic, clanging thump slowly built in strength as the heavy footsteps moved closer. Soon, we could feel the vibrations through the ground. I glanced around.

Wreil knelt near the Stone Door in front, with another scout on the opposite side. I stood behind them, Arthor and Creziel waiting further back in the corridor, with every single Imp standing ready right behind me. All of us were illuminated by the weak light circle of Tim's being. Ahead, there was light, too, flickering torchlight in the tunnel ahead of us sending long shadows in both directions. The number of us assembled in the tunnel seemed horribly inadequate against the building thunder of the approaching army. From the built-up nervousness in the people around us, I wasn't the only one with a sudden case of nerves. I grinned to spite the feeling in my stomach and raised my head.

"This is all according to plan, people. One cheap shot, then we move back and wait." Nobody responded. The rumbling of the approaching enemies built to a clanging thunder. When the first Dworgen cleared the corner, closely followed by a wave of others, I could only feel relief. The wait was over.

As the Dworgen finally saw us, a barbaric roar arose from their ranks, and their pace increased from a jog to a run. No hesitation, even as they recognized a dragon waiting for them. They were only a few hundred feet away now. "Wait." My mental shout rang out through the corridor. I narrowed my eyes, focusing on the light flowing from the torches, washing over the incoming sea of armored forms. The metal of their armor was darkened and seemed like it swallowed the light.

The armor looked heavy, and was formed with few thoughts to aesthetics, except for the helmets that were shaped in bestial forms, tiny eye-slits adorning animal and demonic heads. I watched the incoming shapes break the light, leaving only darkness behind. Shadows. Shadows, which were mine to command. They reached the first marker.

With a mental effort, I grasped the shadows in the corridor, pulled them and *flung* them. Bestial shouts filled the tunnel, as the far ends of the tunnel were completely covered in magical darkness as thick as I could make it. The darkness ended a stone's throw before the Stone Door. "Now! Grex!"

Behind me, all our Imps fluttered into the air, hovering near the ceiling, and started shooting. Fire erupted from between their hands, and they flung it into the shadows. There was no aiming here, no deliberation, just speed and fire, boosted by Timothy's capacities.

From within the blanket of darkness, cries of pain and

surprise erupted. A few of my strongest ranged attackers joined the onslaught.

They kept coming, though. I couldn't see what was going on, but they did not flounder. Even as Dworgen fell under the continuous onslaught, and they were forced to move slowly, blinded as they were, they did not fall back, regroup, or falter. They emerged from the shadows, four warriors leading the way, wielding two-handed massive shields, protecting those behind them.

Damnit. Why couldn't they be mindless beasts? "Keep it up! We have to keep them defensive!" I landed a Shadow Whorl in their midst and pulled down another layer of shadows on them. Our Imps doubled down, and the blinding lights of their fiery onslaught had me seeing stars. Their effectiveness had been reduced, though, and the Dworgen increased their pace. They erupted from the darkness again and reached the second marker.

I raised my neck and *breathed*. The Weakening Fog spread out through the tunnel, enveloping the front of their formation in the debilitating droplets. Now, all my ranged attackers joined in, releasing an overwhelming assault of thrown missiles. Several fell, but they kept on. One of the shield-bearing warriors dropped to the ground, but another Dworgen grabbed the shield, leaving him behind. I took a few steps backward. "Ready!"

The shield-bearing quartet broke into a trot as a unified front. Through the uninterrupted barrage of fiery missiles and throwing weapons, they shouted and charged. I was impressed. I couldn't help it. The guts it took for them to attack like that… I wanted some of those as minions!

Still, guts weren't going to do anything for these guys. Seconds after they charged, they reached the first of the trip-wires and went down *hard*. The Imps and ranged fighters used the downed shield bearers as target practice. Spots appeared in front of my eyes, and when I could see again, the shield bearers lay finally, irredeemably still. The Imps redoubled their attacks on the Dworgen who appeared from the magical darkness. I breathed again, sapping their strength.

They were so close, though. The attackers were less unwieldy than their bulk suggested. Some of them went crashing down due to the tripwires, but others managed to keep their feet and press on through our attacks. In the back, two Dworgen appeared with heavy crossbows. I growled as a bolt glanced off my scales at an angle, leaving a bloody line. I sent off a final Weakening Fog, watching them slow down perceptibly, and then sent, "Now, Wreil! Stop the attacks!"

The scout touched the Stone Door and the door slid closed. Through the closing door, I gathered Shadows and dumped the entire corridor into darkness. On the other side of the door, I watched Wreil lock the door, and we moved back through the tunnel together. We didn't stop until we were well past our shamans, who approached the door, concentration written on their faces. From behind the door, a huge explosion and a smell of ozone disclosed that the Dworgen had discovered my surprise - my recently earned ability to trap the Stone Doors.

A few terse commands had the Imps and the scouts scrambling back to the winding tunnels and their positions. As I turned back to Arthor and Creziel to get them started, I gawked in amazement. They were already hard at work. Where they gestured, dirt flowed like lava from the walls, forming a wave from either side to slowly meet in the middle.

The Stone Door was under attack. Heavy booms rattled the construction from the other side, despite the shadows. The trap had bought us some essential moments, but now they had realized that it was a one-time affair and were hard at work trying to break down the massive construction. I really wanted to hurry the shamans up, but knew better than to distract them. They were both completely focused on their work, and the earth was slowly piling up inside the tunnel.

Their attacks continued unabated, but fortunately, they were unable to break the door right away, since they couldn't see what they were doing. Meanwhile, the earth moved and built up in the corridor on our side.

A heavy mace broke the first hole through the door at the same time as the final layer of dirt seeped in to fill the corridor entirely. The furious roars reverberated for a few seconds before more earth piled on, muffling the sounds. A few tense minutes later, Arthor stepped back with sweat-drenched fur. "We have this under control now, lizard. They might be able to dig away the earth, but we can fill the tunnel faster than they can dig."

I glanced behind me. There was almost a hundred feet to go before the entrance tunnel separated into the tunnel complex of our labyrinth. "Good. And I think you are right. Now they know we're here, and they probably know that you can't keep this up forever. We want to keep them here while our construction finishes."

Creziel grinned, panting at the effort. "It's fine. They have no idea what we are capable of! Now that the hardest part is over, we can take turns to catch our breath. We could even let them catch up to us once or twice, so they think we're struggling."

"Don't exaggerate, Creziel," the larger Shaman admonished. "We *will* run out of mana before we reach the end of the corridor. Still, we can bring in some of the pups to aid. They are slow, but growing fast. It will be good practice." He was still for a moment, glaring at the blocked tunnel. "I can sense them. They have started the excavation." He fixed his stare at me. " The Talpi will buy you the hours you need. Prepare the rest."

CHAPTER TWENTY

The hours seemed like days. With the shamans occupied, there was little for us to create in the way of expansions. The Talpi used the time to place as many simple traps as they could with the materials at hand and ensure that the numerous torches spread throughout the winding tunnels were ready to be lit. My other minions relaxed. Still, there was tension in the air. Everybody knew that the time was limited.

I spent my hours watching my mana tick in, creating new constructions whenever it was possible. At this point, I didn't want to save up for one of the larger constructions. It would simply take too long for it to be created. Instead, I focused on adding a new Shadow Tower whenever I reached 150 mana. They might not finish in time for the battle, but at the least, they were likely to be done for whoever arrived next. Apart from this, I drilled everybody on their responsibilities until I was certain that they knew them by heart.

I adjusted the Professions, ensured we had the best possible setup for the ambushes. I let my Shamans keep the Mage profession—we needed all the magical oomph that would give them. Apart from that, I granted Gert, Roth, and all the best ranged attackers the Fighter profession. I left a single one to grant the Ergul the Cleric profession. Nobody was going to die, if I could help it. I breathed a sigh of relief when we managed to hit the 24 hour cap since I first used a Mana Crystal. The next one would be available in minutes. That would mean I could use two of them again to ensure I didn't die.

Then it happened. The final Shadow Tower blinked into existence, nestled into a crevice, well-hidden in one of the approaching tunnels. I rushed toward the entrance, while, around me, the final details of our defensive plan fell into place. I checked in on the map. Our preparations were rough, but thorough. Everything inside the cavern was arranged to ladle punishment onto any invaders, with traps waiting for any aerial enemies who might escape the initial onslaught.

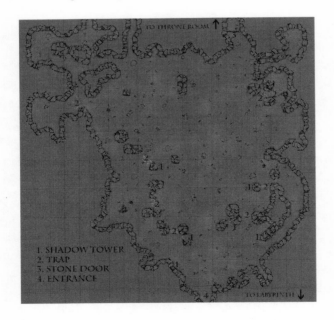

The labyrinth was little better for any attackers. Seen from the map, things looked rather straightforward. Having spent my share of hours working with shoddy light, I had little trouble imagining how different things would look from an invader's perspective. In my mind's eye, I could imagine stumbling through the tunnels under constant fire, searching desperately for that doorway you were dead certain you spotted when you were moving the other way. It'd be pandemonium.

Of course, I'd checked in on the Dworgen once in a while, through the map. The shamans were keeping ahead of the enemies, if only barely. However, as I found them now, thirty feet from where the tunnel system opened up, they looked less stressed than I'd feared. Creziel was slowly adding more earth to the barricade while Arthor was facing the young shamans, gesturing at the earth while he explained something.

As I walked up, Arthor faced me. "Is it time?"

"It's time."

A short barked order had the pups running back to safety on their short legs, while the shamans waited before me. They looked... better than I had expected, taking into account the volume of dirt they'd just handled. Both looked tired, but only Creziel dragged like he was struggling against exhaustion.

Arthor was more like one of those extreme runners after a marathon. Creziel spoke up. "We have maybe ten minutes, Onyx. They caught a glimpse of us twice. I would expect them to be pretty upset once they finally dig their way through." Creziel tittered, looking like he was about to lose his balance.

I snorted. "Angry is good. Makes them spend less time thinking. You've done an amazing job. Now, get yourself back to the throne room and take a break. You've earned it."

Creziel nodded, but Arthor interrupted. "I will be above the tunnels. This is my responsibility above all."

I shook my head. "I get you, Arthor, but no. Rocks will be of little effect against their armors. We need you well-rested. It's on us now."

He grumbled but relented and we moved back toward our positions. On the way in, I paused in the middle of the tunnel system and sent a mental shout to all. "Everybody to their positions. They're coming in a matter of minutes. Close the Shadow Doors." I kept the final Shadow Door open behind me as we entered the huge cavern, and I placed myself in the center of the cave and lost myself in the map.

I had spied on their forces from time to time, but now I really paid attention to the details. Our initial attack had killed more than a dozen of them and injured more. Still, more than 80 soldiers remained. They were digging in teams, taking turns to go back and rest. However, even having lost more than one in ten, there was nothing to spot on their attitudes. Standing or sitting, they looked battle-ready and attentive.

We almost hooked them. The first armored creatures who made it through the earthen piles roared in fury and charged forward, still liberally covered in dirt. Behind them, their comrades awkwardly shoved their way through the remaining earth and followed their lead. It was an unorganized approach, messy and bereft of formation–exactly what we wanted! Except a shouted command from behind stopped them, and they went into a defensive position, holding the line until they had cleared the tunnel entirely.

Five minutes later, the leader was staring down the corridor, where the tunnel divided into the labyrinth. Everything about him just *screamed* strength, from the way he stood to the agile movement despite the heavy armor and the natural deference all other Dworgen paid him. Oh, and the gleam of magic from his armor was a dead giveaway, too.

Alright, my favorite theoretical plan was shot. I'd been hoping to get them all fired up and distracted as they poured in small groups into the tunnels. That would've been perfect for keeping them confused and reacting instead of acting. As my old foreman used to say: "Keep waiting for dry weather, and you'll never get a roof over your head, son."

A minute later, they acted. Five groups of four Dworgen each moved cautiously into each tunnel. They behaved like professionals, sweeping fast and keeping an eye on every part of the tunnel. One shield-bearer first, then two with close combat weapons and a crossbow-wielder last. The first group was getting closer to the first set of torches.

I almost felt bad for them as I took a deep breath, gathered my focus, and plunged the tunnels into a sea of shadows. The moment that happened, my minions took action. From within the map, well zoomed-out, I could see the shadows shifting as my minions used the chance to go on the offensive.

Right this moment, ranged Talpi and Imps would be sending death and destruction down upon the shadow-covered intruders from the frequent murder holes in the ceilings. To keep their attention fixed on the environment and keep them from finding out about the attackers in the tunnel system above them, the floors of the tunnels were covered with traps, big and small. As a cherry on top, the first Shadow Towers started spitting bolts of energy-sapping dark matter at them.

I couldn't focus too much on the actual happenings. My control over the shadows had increased, but they were still not all-powerful. In fact, I was unable to dip the entire area in darkness, but maintaining coverage on five long stretches of tunnel was doable, if barely.

From inside the cavern, the sounds of battle and cries of pain were audible, but muted. I kept my attention fixed on the overview of the map, moving the shadows along with the troops to keep them constantly blinded. And it worked. Five minutes later, three wounded soldiers stumbled back from two different tunnels. The rest were left where they fell inside the tunnels.

Now, the survivors stood before the leader, presumably telling him about their discoveries. Right about now, they would inform him about the glimpse they had through the waning shadows, right into the large cave beyond, where the shadow dragon was waiting.

Everything was going according to plan. I allowed myself a smug smile. I'd lifted the shadows a bit on purpose, allowing them a glimpse into the large cavern. Now, when they next entered the tunnels in force, we would reactivate the Shadow Door and open the one right next to them, which would lead them straight into the next tunnel. Then we could guide them back into the remaining system, bleed them all the while, and have them spring all the traps. We had several more Shadow Doors ready to add to the confusion, and even if they eventually wised up to our strategy, we would likely have weakened them heavily enough that we could crush them inside the cavern.

I was debating sending a few runners into the tunnels to replace the two torches that had been accidentally knocked down, when they moved. They started out in force, exactly as I hoped. Clearly, there was a limit to their strategic wisdom. The moment they came within reach, I turned off the light. This time, it was easier to concentrate, as I only had to dispense shadows on a single tunnel. This meant I could lay on the darkness in a heavier layer, making it even harder for them to see anything. The occasional glint of light from the Imps' attacks only added to the chaos.

The Dworgen were acting predictably. They had shield carriers out front, and this time they moved a lot faster, making it far into the shadows where they, inexplicably, slowed down and rearranged. Then they continued onward at a slower pace.

On each side of the tunnel, a soldier with a two-handed weapon started moving along the tunnel, doing something with wide circular movements.

I had to look closer before I realized what they were doing. My mental shout rang out to the ambushers above the tunnels. "They're trying to take down the torches. Kill the ones along the walls!"

My minions tried their best. Within seconds, the first of the Dworgen near the side fell in a shower of fire and thrown spears. However, right away, the next soldier stepped up, grabbed his weapon, and continued. And like that, my strategy was ruined. Half a minute later, the first torch was knocked from its bearing inside the tunnel, and my grip on the shadows weakened.

My minions made them pay for it. Every step forward inside the tunnel, they were met with a deadly rain from my ranged warriors and Imps, and the tunnels were soon awash with the blood of the attackers. Still, they continued on. And where they had been, my control over the shadows was broken, and the unnatural cover that protected my minions inside the tunnels above was gone.

I made my ranged attackers and Imps return to keep them from being discovered. Even with the narrow holes, they would be sitting ducks against the heavy crossbows of the armored Dworgen. Soon, our enemies had cleared the entire tunnel, circling around to arrive back at the entrance.

When they moved back into the tunnel, I soon realized the second flaw in my plan. They didn't take any of the other tunnels where I could still maintain my shadows. No, they moved straight back into the same tunnel they'd taken the last time. Damnit. They were investigating all the walls meticulously now. The leader wasn't just a martial leader of some sort – he must be the actual leader of the Dworgen in the mountain. And as such, he would have access to a map. And if his people knew that the entrance to our cavern was in here somewhere... I cursed my lack of foresight.

Now, it was a matter of time until they located the Shadow door, unless their Mental Power was too low to see through the illusion. There was no way I'd take the chances on that, however. My command rang through the tunnels. "Everybody back. Into the cavern. Ranged attackers prepare. We'll meet them when they arrive. Creive. We will need you and your minions soon."

Unfortunately, I was right. While my minions and Creive's milled about around me, trying to get into position, I kept an eye on their progress. Within minutes, the pounding thunder from the other side of the Shadow Door announced their imminent arrival.

My people were ready, though. We had already taken down half of them, and we had never been stronger. Arranged in a half-circle surrounding the entrance, the Crawls lined up straight ahead, next to the Clencher cavalry. From the sides, the ranged attackers were ready, while the Imps and Creive's winged minions lined up on the shielded platforms throughout the room, like gargoyles adorning the facades. On the other side of the door, the Dworgen were busy emptying the large sacks they had been carrying, distributing huge shields and… what the hell was that?

The Shadow Door was already crumbling, collapsing under their frenzied attacks. I wasn't going to give them the satisfaction of ruining it completely. At a mental command, an Imp flitted through the air to touch the door and force it to open.

A boom announced the opening of the door, and dust spilled into the room, followed by a trio of armored attackers who stumbled in, surprised to see the door disappear in front of them. Behind them, their comrades followed, pushing them aside. Marching forward through the dust cloud with heavy steps, the Dworgen formation followed. They were arranged in a large semi-circle, huge shields protecting their front and sides, ranks right behind them armed and ready. Further back, soldiers held crossbows, aiming in all directions. In the absolute center, the leader stood, holding a dark banner. A moment stretched into eternity, until the tall form yelled a single word and *slammed* the banner into the ground.

At the same time, I sent a Weakening Fog into their midst and yelled for my forces to attack. Missiles rained down from the sides, and the air and my warriors were charging in. The Dworgen, unexpectedly, did not attack, but simply held their ground – and I immediately saw why. As I released another breath attack, dark light exploded out from the standard, covering the entire group in a circle - and my breath attack evaporated upon contact with the circle. My heart sank, as I watched throwing spears bouncing away from the circle, repelled by the same dark energy.

It was too late to warn everybody, but I tried anyway. My mental shout rang out, while Clenchers and Crawls charged. At first, our ranged fighters kept bombarding the center of the formation. With a resounding crash, the forces met, armored humanoids standing tall against the assembled might of my domain. Timothy was in the center of it all, boosting defenders, debuffing attackers, and attacking left and right.

Yet the Dworgen held. Their shield line buckled, but held as the soldiers behind them pushed back. And within those scant few seconds, the momentum turned. I watched a Clencher stumble back with blood spurting from a wide cut in its face. Next to it, a Dworgen *roared*, tossing two Crawls to the ground with a shield bash. Even Roth was stalled, the large swings of his two-handed sword made unhandy by the massive shields of the Dworgen and the close press of the combat.

Pain struck me two, three times in quick succession as crossbow wielders in the back of their formation started firing at the largest target present. Damn, I was a sitting duck.

I hesitated, then tried something. A Shadow Whorl came to life in the center of the formation of the ranged Dworgen. Good. At least I could start magic within the circle. I started moving forward. We would need to break them – somehow. If magic and ranged attacks were out of the question, I'd have to go in myself. If they managed to beat us back now...

"Pathetic." The single word rang inside my mind as well as that of the others. Above me, I spotted Creive, hovering near the ceiling. He looked like he had all the time in the world. His minions were flying too, surrounding him.

What was he doing? Would he stab me in the back? Use this chance to earn the throne for himself?

I watched him shake his head in disdain, and his poisonous words reached everybody, even as our line was buckling and started to break. "Shadow dragons. Plans behind plans and illusions. Yet this is the truth." The massive blue flapped his wings twice, almost colliding with the ceiling and then gathered his wings close. "You lack *force!*"

His massive form plummeted straight down, and mid-fall, he opened his mouth, blinding us all with a massive breath of lightning. Then, he fell like a rock, claw-first upon the shining black light of the dome.

The lightning had no obvious effect. It spread over the semi-visible dome and dissipated. However, for a few seconds, the spot where the attack had impacted glowed white. And that was exactly where Creive struck.

There was no finesse to it, no final spreading of his wings or attacking while he dropped. No, he simply hit as hard as possible, lifting up his legs to let his bulk do the damage. It must have hurt him like crazy. I couldn't imagine the kind of damage that would do to me, if I tried it. Still, it was nothing compared to what it did to the Dworgen. I expected some sort of impact with the dome, but it never happened. With a dull thud, Creive slammed down into the center of the formation. A handful of the attackers simply disappeared beneath his massive bulk.

There was a brief moment of shock, then my minions redoubled their attacks. The ranged fighters started sniping at the forms furthest from Creive, while my people renewed their push on the half-circle. I joined in, adding my bulk to the press.

Once the Dworgen moved past the worst of the initial shock, they took advantage of the fact that a big, fat target had impacted in their midst. Of course they did. Some fired their crossbows point-blank. Others let them drop, and hurriedly picked up weapons to strike at him. Except Creive wasn't done. Bleeding from dozens of places and with a glazed look to his eyes, he struggled to his feet, lifted his head into the air, and roared. With the sound, a glow built around him and burst. A blue and white circle of lightning coursed through everybody touching him. And wherever it touched, Dworgen dropped like they had been... Heh. Struck by lightning.

That was it. A few fought on, deep in the rush of battle, but the ones who realized that their center, and their leader, were lost, started throwing away their weapons and kneeling in surrender. Some fell, until finally, Roth rang the helmet of the last raging warrior with the flat of his blade, and silence grew throughout the cavern.

Our forces separated, ranged fighters and Imps keeping ready to move in, should the Dworgen try something desperate. Yet, they seemed to have lost all will to fight. Quite understandably, given that Creive was still in the center of things, surrounded by downed and dead Dworgen. He disentangled himself from the mess and stalked my way haughtily. The soldiers nervously cleared a path for him.

"I hope you have learned something today." The blue giant said, looking down his snout at me. The lower part of his body was a filthy mess. The impact hadn't been without cost to him. Two crossbow bolts were lodged deep within his abdomen and— was that a sword? Only the hilt stuck out of the center of his chest.

Shaking my head at his nonchalance, I ordered the Ergul to approach him and start healing his wounds. "I have to thank you for your interference, Creive. You were impressive. And in fact, I have learned something from this battle. I doubt it's the same lesson that you would have me learn, though."

He grunted as the Ergul started working and the first bolt clunked to the ground. "How can there be any doubt? Might beats intrigue. Without actual power, you are nothing."

The side of my mouth quirked up. "That's not my take on

it. Rather, that might *and* intrigue combined are better than either by themselves. Or have you forgotten how you lost to us in the first place? I would say that intrigue won that one."

He growled. "You took me by surprise. You would not be able to do that again."

Happily, I retorted. "I won't have to, my dear vassal." Even as he growled, I could sense his contemplation. Regardless of me half-joking, he was listening. Thoughtfully, I added, "There is something to be said for overwhelming force, though. At times, elaborate plans simply fall through. I will have to think on this lesson." He kept looking at me as I walked to my people. At some point, I might talk him into becoming a proper part of our alliance. Not for now, though. He was still way too feral.

"So, what do we do about them?" The question came from the side where Roth was marching up, frowning at a dent in his sword.

"I should think they're open to-"

Our discussion was interrupted by Wreil sprinting toward us. "Onyx! The Dragonlings! They're here!"

I looked at the Dworgen before me, broken but still alive. At the bloody faces of our fighters, still flushed from the combat. At the half-smashed Shadow Door sporting several gaping holes. "Well, fuck."

CHAPTER TWENTY-ONE

"Feel da power swallow you whole. Let go an' lose yo'self in it."
— Jason Medina, A Ghost In New Orleans

"Arthor! Creziel! Fetch the apprentices, start repairing the Shadow Door here. I don't care if it's pretty. Those holes need to be filled. All ranged fighters, I want you back in the upper tunnels right now. They may find us, but you need to make them pay for every foot. Imps stay here. Somebody get the torches back up. Everybody who's badly injured and can still move, pull back to the throne room. Assist those who can't. The Ergul is going to take care of you when we have time."

People were sprinting everywhere, and I took a deep breath and closed my eyes. Ten seconds I held them closed and held my breath as I shut out all sensations, counting down slowly. Then, I slowly exhaled and opened my eyes. Turning toward Creive, I continued. "This is going too fast. It's probably going to be an aerial battle, and it's going to be on you. Get your people ready – and include my Imps, too. If we have the time, we will talk more.'

The huge beast didn't comment. He nodded and jumped

into the air, gliding to the other side of the cavern as he called out for the fliers to join him. I let him handle his part and walked over to look down on the Dworgen. They were still being watched over by the Crawls and Clenchers, paws gripping their weapons tightly. The sound of cries grew from the tunnels. We were running out of time.

The Dworgen leader had survived. I had not expected that and mentally recalculated exactly how tough he'd have to be to handle a huge dragon dropping on his face. He stood up as I moved closer to their group. The emotions stemming from their people were surprising, to say the least. I sensed no fear. Anxiety, sure, disappointment in spades, and a good portion of resentment. He bowed his head. "I acknowledge your strength and that of your master." He pointed at Creive.

I ground my teeth. "He is my vassal. And you… are a problem for me right now." I decided to play it straight. "In a couple of minutes, we'll be attacked by Dragonlings. Did you plan for this?"

The dislike emanating from him was strong. "We tolerate the winged ones only because Selys orders us to."

I nodded. There was no untruth coming from him. Well, that was one issue I wouldn't have to fear. "Good. Now, I want you to swear allegiance to me right now, then I will let you leave."

A pang of distaste came from him. "I would. We cannot, however. Our oath to Selys is… strong. If you replace her as ruler, we should be able to swear to you."

I growled under my breath. Was it too much to ask for an easy out, for once? "If I let you go right this moment, will you come back to try to attack us?"

"No. You have proved yourself stronger than us. Also, you have mastered the large blue one. We have lost too many already to test your mettle again."

"For now." The unspoken words hung in the air between us. Still, I could sense no lies from him. He did believe that it was in his best interest to not try us again today – and I'd take that.

"Alright." I inclined my head. "Roth. Take a couple of scouts and lead them out the rear exit. Have them stay there to keep an eye on them. I will trust them in full only when they have sworn to me." My words were for the Dworgen leader as much as it was for Roth. I didn't want him to get any funny ideas about circling back and catching us unaware. I looked him right in the eyes as I added my final pointer. "Also, we're keeping their weapons."

Their leader looked like he was about to challenge my decisions, but reigned it in. Good. He was intelligent enough to understand his situation and control his temper. We might actually get along at some point. Theoretically. At the very least, it would allow us to defend ourselves without having to worry about our flanks.

The Dworgen got up and started moving, armor clanking as they struggled with their injured. I dismissed them from my mind and attended to my remaining minions. Behind us, the cries and sounds of battle were growing louder.

Our shamans were trying to fix the gaping holes in the Shadow Door, flanked by the young ones. They were slamming mud on the door, working to harden it. It was slow going – way too slow for my liking. It was likely because of their marathon performance earlier, but where the earth had moved like mud earlier, now the movement in the stone was barely perceptible. I glanced through the map and cursed. There were barely any torches up. The Dragonlings were out in force, and they were sprinting through all the tunnels *right* now. At least the door could still be closed. That might buy us some time.

Some of our ranged fighters had made it to the upper tunnels and started attacking, even though the tunnels weren't covered in darkness. My people wouldn't be able to get the torches back up in time to allow me to drop the tunnels into darkness again. A few foolhardy Imps had taken a risk and were baiting the encroaching attackers. Cries arose from where the divided forces stumbled into the remaining traps and were taking some damage.

"Arthor. Creziel. Stop. We won't be able to have the door properly repaired in time. Leave it open and be ready to close it immediately when we return. We will have to range out. Push them back while we erect torches, then retreat. Somebody, get torches ready. Creive, with me. Change of plans."

I gritted my teeth and glared at the crossbow bolt still stuck inside my leg, then growled, as Gert did as I asked, grabbing the missile with both hands and pulling it out without fanfare. No time for the Ergul to look at my wounds. I looked at my health. 395 of 570 remaining. No. I wasn't going to waste a Mana Crystal on that. I was certain there was more pain for me in the near future.

From within the dark, winding tunnels, scaled attackers charged down on us. I welcomed them with a Weakening Fog. A split second was all I had to take in the looks on their scaled faces–fury, surprise, raging bloodlust–before I dragged my head back, earning a nasty burn on the upper neck in the process. Damn. 360 health now. My mental shout rang out into the cavern. "Creive. Now!"

Even with my head averted, my vision turned white as Creive's lightning spilled out into the tunnel to welcome the charging enemies. With spots appearing everywhere in my eye sight, I turned back to the cavern to order my minions in, only to find Creive already charging, with the first Clencher riders charging in at his heels. I couldn't wait to move, to be able to do something. I wasn't going to let them finish us like this.

The noise as they clashed with the attacking Dragonlings was almost physical, but I had no time to focus. Behind the Clencher cavalry, I followed, with my Crawls at my side, eyes ablaze with battle lust.

At a furious pace, my Clenchers shot forward right after Creive, the spearhead that pierced through the incoming forces as they arrived in ones or twos. They rarely tried to kill, merely pushed the flying beasts aside, trampling, shoving past them, and hurting them in whichever way they could without slowing down.

As for Creive… I could barely fathom how facing him must feel. His lightning was often the first thing the attackers faced. It did not take everybody out of commission, but still left them reeling, half-stunned.

The Crawls and I handled the dirty work. Where Creive and the Clencher riders left the attackers shocked and shunted aside, the Crawls charged straight at them, howling and furious. There was no finesse here. They jumped on the reeling enemies, using raw strength and numbers to finish them off, accepting punishment from the Dragonlings as the due for being able to cause massive damage. Spears struck out, spitting confused enemies, leaving them bleeding and broken.

The Dragonlings didn't back down. Shocked and over-whelmed by the overwhelming carnage of our charge, they still fought back with claws, teeth, and breath, and they were no pushovers. My people suffered for it, bled to push back the enemy. I saw a Clencher rider slung from his perch on the massive beast by a well-aimed lightning spit. A young Crawl had his upper arm laid open by a savage slash. While my people fought hard and savagely, there was a power difference here. If the Crawls had been the only ones left to finish them, they would have been in trouble.

The Dragonlings were *not* ready for me. It had been a while since I had truly sensed the presence of the primal animal within me. I had been getting used to a position in the back of the conflict, weakening and disorienting the enemies, ordering my minions about while being far enough away to ignore the heady siren song of the bloodlust. I had made up my mind early on that giving in to that primal song would only lead to my demise.

Right now, however, I let it egg me on, just to give me an edge. Carl the foreman was getting used to savage violence, but he didn't like it. The animal inside me? He did. And opening up the door a little felt like opening a flood gate, as bestial rage threatened to overcome me. All around, savagery and blood flowed. I had been wounded several times already, and I burned a Mana Crystal. I couldn't stop now. *They were killing my people!* I tore through the tunnel behind Creive and my minions, slashing left and right to finish off anybody who had survived the initial charge. All around me, my people cleared the tunnel and paid the price in blood.

My claw *smashed* down on the ribcage of a downed Dragonling. I heard and felt the bones in its chest implode with the impact. I shook the claw, dislodging the corpse and seized the leg of a fallen, struggling enemy and *tore*. With a savage twist, the leg came off, and the screams from the owner increased only to bubble away moments later. A burning pain erupted from beneath me. He'd clawed long, bleeding furrows in my lower stomach before expiring. A savage joy thrilled inside me, watching him undone. Noise rang out from behind me, but I ignored it. The joy of battle rang through me. A single Dragonling remained within reach, right there. It was trying to hobble away on a broken leg. Hah. Pathetic! I pounced, growling in pleasure as he was flung back, limbs flopping about. Another enemy passed by me in the opposite direction. No. Not an enemy. This was Creive. Ignore him.

More! Hah. There they were. Amassed further back the tunnel in a large group. They must be too afraid to take me on. Well, I would teach them. First a Weakening Fog, then a Shadow Whorl to distract them – there – and then I would-

"Onyx! Come back!"

Who was that? I growled, fighting back the haze in my head. The shouting instinct inside my head told me to move on, continue my onslaught. The enemies were still *right* there, pathetic creatures. I needed to show them. A wad of poison impacted my lower leg, sizzling where it struck. Shaking my head, I fought it down again, focusing. There was nobody in front of me. When had I passed by the rest?

I narrowly avoided a lightning shot, dodging like the wind. Cursing, I shook my head, trying to dislodge the fog from my mind. I took a few steps back, trying to move away from the chaos of the battle. I suddenly noticed the wounds along my body as my mind slowly returned to me. 180/570 health? What the hell? I blinked, sending a final Weakening Fog into the darkness. Then, with a growl, I turned and fled.

I could now see how far I'd made it. I was farther outside the tunnel complex than planned. In fact, even as I ran, Dragonlings were glancing from out of the side tunnels, blinking at the sight before them. The carnage was disturbing. Bodies were everywhere. Most of them were scaled, but I saw the familiar forms of Crawls in places, too. A single Clencher was dragging its way back toward the cave, breathing heavily, missing the lower part of a leg. I cursed at myself. I had lost myself. I was never letting that happen again!

At least the outing had not been for naught. Inside the tunnel in front of me, hastily erected torches were back on the walls. I let shadow spill around me as I ran, covering the tunnel in darkness behind me. From further down the corridor, I spotted Roth. He was waving frantically, then turned around and sprinted away.

My leg wasn't taking my weight properly. I wondered what had happened. Hadn't I just taken a Mana Crystal? I limped on as fast as I could, using my wings to take the weight off of my hind leg. Meanwhile, I expanded my consciousness, dipping the entire area into shadow, ensuring our safety. Behind me, aggressive roars echoed from those following us as we disappeared from their sight. I reached the almost-restored Shadow Door. The moment I was through, a shout came up, and it closed, obscuring the entrance. Arthor and Creziel collapsed next to the door.

Roth was right there. He pointed frantically. "It's Grex. He needs healing, badly."

Mentally, I instructed the Ergul to attend me, and we were led to where he was slumped on the floor. They had done what they could. The ugly Imp looked like a particularly hideous baby as he lay, unconscious. A heavy leather cord was tightly wound around his lower leg, which was simply missing from the knee down. The trigger-happy Imp looked surprisingly innocent as the blood dripped from the wound. "Hang in there, Grex."

At a mental command, the Ergul swept over the ground and attached itself to his leg. As it started rocking, the light emanating from it rose in intensity until it illuminated a full third of the huge cavern. And then it slumped away, deflated, leaving the child-sized Imp sleeping on the dirt floor, the amputated wound red and swollen, but covered by skin.

I grimaced. Being an amputee inside the mountain was an unkind fate – but better than dying. At least he had his wings. Turning back, I noticed a crowd was staring at me. All Talpi and Crawls were hanging back, looking at me.

Roth was the one to break the uncomfortable silence. "Are you back with us, dragon?" He pointed with his sword toward the entrance, where hissing sounds announced the arrival of the first Dragonlings.

I nodded, shamefaced. "Yes. I lost myself for a while there. It won't happen again." I looked down at myself, at all the gore and blood splattering my lower body. At once, I felt like I could sleep forever. Quite a lot of the blood, apparently, was mine. 180/570 health and... a [Hobbled] debuff. Damn. Half running speed. I shook my head. There would be time to relax later.

"Alright. We earned ourselves a reprieve. Now, the entrance looks like it's repaired again, and I can feel we have some of the ruined torches back up. We can stall them for some time, get back to the plan, while we heal up and prepare a few surprises near the entrance. Creziel..." I took a look at the tiny shaman. He was still reclined next to the entrance door. It looked like the last push had knocked him out. "Nevermind. Wreil, you tell everybody to get back into the upper tunnels. Meanwhile, I'll see exactly what we're facing."

I sent my attention into the map once again. There were many. So many more than I had expected. Our attack had taken out a good deal of them. The shadows kept them from advancing in any organized manner. Good. They were milling about, shouting and raging. The main tunnel outside the labyrinth was filling up with Dragonlings. The confusion and constant movement made it hard to get an exact count, but I stopped when I reached fifty. Once they entered the tunnels properly, we would be able to grind them down, weaken… oh no.

"Stop everything, *right* now!" My mental shout made everybody pause. "They've made it into the upper tunnels." I should have seen it coming. When they first attacked, some of my ranged fighters and Imps made it out into the upper tunnels, raining attacks down on them. With the supernatural darkness gone, the murder holes and the defenders were *right* there for the Dragonlings to see. Some enterprising Dragonling had apparently leapt to the logical conclusion and now their claws were widening the openings in the ceiling with disturbing ease. We had expanded the tunnels enough that the Crawls could fit in. The Dragonlings were much taller than the Crawls, but not much wider. With their wings folded on the back, they were able to crawl through the tunnels toward us, even if the fit was tight.

My mind raced. I glanced up. The four separate tunnel exits that led to the hidden tunnels overlooking the labyrinth exited with a handful of feet of separation high up the wall above and next to the entrance. It had been convenient when we constructed it. Now, having to consider the defensive possibilities… I came up with, and discarded the first couple of plans to seal or lock the openings. There was simply not enough time. They would be here *now!*

"We need all ranged fighters ready to take them on as they enter. We will make them pay to make it out here! Crawls, Clencher fighters, I need you again. You will defend our ranged fighters, once we will have to pull back. Then take defensive positions further back toward the throne room where we can still punish them. Timothy-"

"Yes?" He floated forward, didn't hesitate for a second.

"Buff the ranged fighters and attack from the distance, but stay back. These enemies are a horrible match for you."

The sounds from the tunnels began to increase in strength. "We're out of *time!* They're incoming in ten seconds, the center tunnel." My gaze traveled upward, met by dozens of staring eyes. Every single winged minion was up there, staring down on us. Even the Imps were silent, for once. In the center of everything, hovering with slow, heavy beats of his wings, was Creive. I addressed him, anxious. "Creive. You-"

He interrupted abruptly. "No orders. Now is the time for battle. If they make it into the air, they are mine."

I hesitated, then nodded as I used my last Mana Crystal. The debuff blessedly faded away as my wounds closed. I hissed in pleasure, then sent my blessing at him. "Good luck."

He snorted. "I do not need luck." A shiver raced through his hovering body as lightning coursed across his scales. A skill? He bared his lips in a bloodthirsty grin. "I need a meal."

CHAPTER TWENTY-TWO

With a snarl, the first intruder spat fire and flung himself out of the tunnel. The red Dragonling dove into open air, beating his wings furiously to gain altitude, then a dozen missiles converged on him at the same time. The body that slammed onto the floor was a bloody mess. But even as the first one died, his brethren followed.

Within moments, we were reeling. The Dragonlings threw themselves from the tunnels, emerging at speeds and angles that made it hard to predict where to attack them. Some paused for long enough to spit elemental attacks at us from the tunnel openings. Whenever it was off cooldown, I shot a Weakening Fog at the tunnel exits, but since they came one at a time, I rarely hit more than one or two.

We might have been able to hold them inside the tunnels, if it were only a question of exchanging ranged firepower. Might. With my improved Mental Power, my Weakening Fog left them reeling and took most Dragonlings out of the fight with two hits. On top of that, our ranged fighters had gained in strength and skills. Their precision had become fearsome, especially with Timothy's improved buffs.

Add to that the sheer numbers we had arranged around the exits, and we had an overwhelming welcoming force. If only it hadn't been for one thing: the natural armor of the Dragonlings was something else. I grimaced as I watched a throwing spear hit a blue Dragonling on the leg. The force of the throw was enough to have the attacker's dive turn into a tumble, but the spear still glanced off and ricocheted into a wall at full speed. They were simply too hardy. And fast. They knew how to tuck a shoulder and turn a killing strike into a glancing wound or swerve in the air to present their well-protected back to a barrage of spears.

Even their wings were armored, though it was not as thick as the rest of their bodies and didn't cover everything. Some of them even carried small round shields. Bucklers, I believed. Tiny things, but disturbingly efficient at turning blows and deflecting spear tips. Still, we cost them, as they escaped the tunnels and launched into open air. A gleaming throwing axe tore through the throat of a Dragonling and immediately zipped back to Leith. That gift was paying off nicely.

As the emerging enemies made it through the initial killing grounds, they spread out and flew in all directions. But then Creive's forces made themselves known. First the Culdren. In twos and threes, they swooped in from above and descended upon the unsuspecting Dragonlings. Their attacks weren't pretty. They simply dove in, grabbed hold wherever they could, and got to work. Their bulky forms were even stronger than the Dragonlings, allowing them to seize and hold their limbs and their hardened skin protected them from the worst of the claw attacks.

Where the attackers managed to nail a Culdren with a breath attack, it suffered, but it appeared they weren't as sense-less as they looked. I winced to see two Culdren seize a keening Dragonling from above, fixing its wings with their massive arms and howling with laughter as they rode the plummeting form to a bloody impact with the ground. On top of that, Creive's Imps kept up a continuous rain of fire on the emerging Dragonlings.

Still, they kept coming. Soon, the entire situation grew out of control. Flying forms were everywhere, and I had trouble distinguishing between attackers and defenders. I wasn't the only one, either. Our ranged fighters had to retreat further back into the cavern as the Dragonlings survived the first attacks and were able to start taking potshots at our ground forces from all sides. Within minutes, we were forced all the way to the back of the cavern, forming a defensive half-circle in front of the exit to the throne room.

As for myself, I was feeling totally out of my depth. I was unable to keep up with the swirling, whirling forces; we had moved too far back for my breath attack to hit the exit, and my powers were pretty much useless against the fast attackers. If the third group hit us now, we'd be lost. Magical darkness would do nothing but add to the confusion. Whenever it was available, I tried to fix a Shadow Whorl to one of the intruders, but even that was hard to nail. At least my presence behind the ranged fighters was deterrent enough that the Dragonlings stuck with ranged attacks instead of charging in.

The aerial fight was... I had never seen anything like it. Everywhere, there was movement. A blue Dragonling spit lightning at a Culdren before diving at an unsuspecting Imp, but was forced to turn and present his armored back to protect himself from the poisoned jabs of a Flitter. Even following a single attacker, I had trouble keeping up.

On top of that, our arrayed Shadow Towers were in constant action, spitting weakening missiles at the enemy fliers. A few of our ranged attackers were able to challenge the confusing, whirling forces. Roth. Wreil. The Crawl holding the staff sling. Leith with the magical throwing axe. A few others managed to strike with steady precision, despite the confusion, helping whittle down their numbers.

Now, our plans kicked into motion, and the time we'd spent preparing the terrain turned the aerial battle in our favor. Hunted Imps and Flitters zoomed through tunnels too small for the Dragonlings, emerging elsewhere to surprise the assailants.

Our fliers led hunters through the far corners of the cavern, where they were introduced to the array of aerial traps we'd prepared. People tried to take advantage of the weaknesses of the enemies, Imps raining fire upon white Dragonlings and Flitters trying to poison the blue, lightning-spewing bastards. Scaled bodies impacted with the floor around the cavern as our fliers spent every advantage we had to take down the furious attackers.

But still, the Dragonlings kept coming. And, to our detriment, they weren't stupid. They had champions.

A large blue with a constantly crackling lightning force had taken charge of most of the blues who were harassing our ground forces. Wherever their missiles struck, our people were stunned, some falling to the ground senseless. Even our few shield-bearing Crawls could only take a single strike before the arm was entirely useless. Still, my people didn't cave. They managed a constant hail of ranged attacks on the Dragonlings. For now, we were stuck at a stalemate, barely keeping them back, even while reinforcements kept coming.

Above, an exceptionally fast green Dragonling had gathered a handful of his fellow greens, and they were playing tag with the heavy Culdren. Further up, a huge red Dragonling was, somehow, managing to keep Creive stalled with a constant barrage of fire from him and his fellow reds. A few dastardly ones were roaming the room, hunting down and destroying our Shadow Towers. White and shadow Dragonlings were airborne, too, performing an elaborate aerial dance, fighting for supremacy with our weaker flying units. Not only were they overwhelming our Imps and Flitters, they also aided their fellow attackers with debilitating and freezing attacks, especially on Creive.

I watched in dismay as one of the whites tagged two Imps with a freezing breath. They plummeted to the ground and impacted, badly. Behind us, a Culdren fled toward the safety of the Throne Room, poison dripping from his injured flanks. Narrowing my eyes, I came to a decision. "This will not hold.

We're going to change things up! Crawls, Talpi. Move forward–strike at my signal." I eyed the swarm of blue Dragonlings in front of me. They were keeping constantly in motion, but it *was* a formation of sorts, centered around the large blue who ordered the others in their attack. In short, it was a weak point, and one I needed to address.

Narrowing my eyes at him, I focused and, with a grunt of concentration, submerged the entire area in front of the Dragonlings in darkness. With a large leap, I bounded over my minions and sprang forward as fast as I possibly could. And with 79 in Agility, that meant *fast*. The enemies kept up their attacks, firing into the darkness as they kept circling.

I could not avoid being hit. Once, five times, more, the sizzling impact of blue lightning struck my skin, trying to force my muscles to seize up. My health was dropping at alarming levels, while notifications erupted all around me.

[Beware. You have taken lightning damage. 20% additional damage taken.] Thanks for nothing! Like I couldn't *tell!* I almost face-planted, but caught myself and pushed forward. Without my Magical Resistance feat, I would have died then and there. As it was, I still hurt. Right before the edge of the darkness, I leaped and beat my wings to lengthen the jump, pouncing out of the other side of the circle of darkness at full speed.

The look in the eyes of the Dragonlings when they realized that their enemy was within spitting distance of them was pure panic. I was not going to let them flee, however. I took all my pent-up fury and put it into a Deafening Roar, directing all my frustration at the attackers in a massive sonic attack. The blues who were further away wavered in the air, but were able to catch themselves. The ones closer to me, however, dropped like flies, gracelessly collapsing to the ground.

The leader of the blues took the brunt of my attack... and bore it. He dropped two feet and stabilized before turning toward me, murder in his eyes and growing lightning in his jaws. I flew straight at him and, as the charge built inside his jaws, dodged left with all I had. Somehow, I avoided his shot and, as I righted myself, I placed a Shadow Whorl upon him, beating my wings for all I was worth to close with him.

The half-blinded blue tried to dodge and weave to get out of the disruptive effect of my spell. Yet, to my luck, he had no time to realize that the skill was affixed on him. Right before the impact, he spotted me, eyes widening in fury and fear. The lightning around him blazed up in a white flash as my front claws closed around his form. I snapped my jaws, ignoring the sizzling pain as the lightning *leaped* around inside my mouth.

And, as sudden as that, the lightning went out, leaving me blinking away spots from my vision as I lowered myself to the ground. I tossed the corpse to the side, trying to ignore the clarion call of the lingering taste of blood inside my mouth. Beside me, Crawls and Talpi were moving swiftly, efficiently, killing the downed Dragonlings while, above us, the few surviving blues fled from our force to rejoin the aerial battle.

I was done. My health was at 160/570. Low enough that I did not dare take any further chances, and I had no more Mana Crystals to use until almost a day from now. I limped behind the ranged fighters, allowing them a full view of the room. I watched as my group advanced again, taking potshots at any Dragonling daring to move close to us. For a few moments, it worked, too. Even when our attacks weren't perfect, they hurt and distracted – a costly effect for the engaged enemies. And when Timothy managed to tag fliers with his Mental Attack, their forms locked up entirely, resulting in some spectacular crashes.

They were wising up to us, however. The retreating blues spread the news of their retreat to their brethren, and soon their circles closed tighter, avoiding our part of the cavern. At least, their numbers had stopped streaming from the tunnels. At this moment, we were dealing with the last of our attackers. We needed to finish them. To our detriment, the situation in the air wasn't looking good. As I watched, the final Shadow Tower fell apart from a concentrated fire bombardment of three reds.

Creive was a powerhouse. An absolute menace in the air.

Wherever he pounced on the Dragonlings, they fell from the skies, bleeding and ruined. But they weren't stupid. Creive was also huge and turned a lot slower than they did. So they kept their distance, attacked at a distance, and worked at battering the defenses of the massive dragon.

It worked. Creive was moving slower, and his attacks were less precise. He was roaring with outrage, spitting lightning at the enemies. I could see that he had already used his huge attack–the defensive shield of lightning was fading even now. We needed to do something. I just wasn't sure what.

Grex was in trouble, too. Apparently, he'd woken up from surviving his debilitating wound and decided that the only intelligent decision would be to rejoin the fight. He'd done a surprisingly good job of it, too, harassing one of the surviving blue Dragonlings. His wand helped him move explosively fast with bursts of speed, outmaneuvering the larger, slower beast. He managed to land a nasty hit to the beast's wings, impairing its already slow movement even further.

However, suddenly the tables turned as a lithe, shadowy Dragonling started tailing him. I watched the merry Imp falter and almost drop as a dark mass covered him, sapping him of his strength. Desperate, he folded up his wings almost entirely and dropped like a rock, aiming toward us, boosting his speed with a gust of air from the wand. Grex was way too far away, though, and the form behind him wasn't about to let his tasty flying morsel escape like that. Not when he had already been tenderized. The shadow Dragonling beat his wings hard, gaining on the fleeing Imp, stretching out his claws in anticipation.

One second, the Dragonling was gaining on Grex. The next, he veered off course and *slammed* into one of the pillars with enough force that small rocks were dislodged, tumbling to the ground all around the Dragonling, who had clearly broken a wing.

At first, I couldn't tell what had happened. Then I saw them. Missiles, small enough that they were not easy to spot. Three of them, to be exact. They were rocks. But they were not *just* rocks. Regular rocks didn't zip to and fro in the air. They definitely didn't hide in ambush behind a pillar, only to strike out and blindside a large red as he was zipping past.

I looked back to see Arthor walking up, and behind him… four, no, five young Talpi. And before the young shamans, rocks hovered. Up into the air the missiles zipped, like miniature airplanes flying to war.

I didn't like it. Having the young ones join the battle? Risk their lives? It went against any instinct in my bones. I kept my silence, though. We *needed* them. And they delivered. From their hands, missiles whizzed up to strike, to hurt, and distract.

The missiles of the pups were in no way as powerful as those of Arthor – but they didn't need to be. When you were flying, fighting for your life, finding an unexpected rock striking your face, even if it didn't move fast, it *hurt*. Even if it only produced a small distraction, my minions and Creive's were quick to punish the Dragonlings.

I looked straight at Arthor. His lips were clenched tight, paws locked in concentration, and I could tell he was hurting. He did not relent, however, and where his eyes moved, his rocks followed, lightning fast. And soon, the Dragonlings were reeling. Distracted, knocked out of the expected flight paths, stunned, they struggled to keep up with their attack.

Creive was quick to capitalize on the chance. First, one red flier dropped from the heights, then another, downed by his massive lightning breath. And quick, quicker than should be possible with his massive bulk, he closed in on the large red champion and *bit*. The huge Dragonling tumbled to the ground, spurting blood from an arm that ended at the elbow.

Just like that, the tides turned. The reds and blues were reeling. The shadow Dragonlings were still causing havoc among our Imps, but with the pressure of the shamans' missiles, they were struggling, too. The green ones, however… reacted. A shout from the lithe leader with the striped tail, and the entire group of green Dragonlings abandoned their assault and dove toward us.

I growled. "Defend the Shamans. Prepare to attack when I say so. Focus on their leader."

My minions closed up, Crawls moving in close to surround the shamans, while the ranged fighters moved back some. Suddenly, I realized the shamans had managed to do exactly what I needed—their realizing the threat of the shamans had made them bunch up to attack in formation. I growled in satisfaction and let a Weakening Fog fly straight at their leader.

Finally, they were playing my kind of game. My fog spread out and hit the majority of the approaching group. Instantly, three of them dropped to the floor. One wavered and veered off, while the rest continued, less precise in their flight. "Attack on my signal!" Eyeing the group, I waited. The greens were gathering their wings closer to the body now, gaining in speed to drop on us. "Now!" my mental shout rang out. At my word, every single minion carrying a ranged weapon released a shot, the moment after I dropped a wall of shadows in front of the swooping enemies.

It was a small wall. Maybe a handful of feet across. Not enough to really impede their approach or have them break off their attack. Barely enough to blind them. Still, the effect was undeniable. A couple Dragonlings swerved when the darkness hit them, adjusted their approach, or broke off entirely. However, the champion and a dozen others held their course. And the moment they broke out of the wall of darkness, they dove straight into the approaching hail of missiles.

The leader dropped like a rock, hit by a dozen different missiles. A couple of the other Dragonlings fell, too, badly wounded or killed, unable to adjust to the attacks in time. The rest panicked, veering off and gaining height. And as our missiles followed them, they didn't come around for a second attack.

All around the cavern, those Dragonlings not completely immersed in battle were starting to waver. They looked around to locate their leaders and found nothing. And, as Creive's roar filled the cavern, and he dove down on some of the undecided attackers, they broke entirely.

It started with a few winged assailants breaking off and fleeing. Within half a minute, it turned into a full rout. The Dragonlings realized that their leaders were down, while they were still facing off against two dragons. Creive made to pursue them, but I stopped him. We did not need any further bloodshed. We'd done it.

CHAPTER TWENTY-THREE

"Taking a break can lead to breakthroughs." —— *Russell Eric Dobda*

The Dragonlings were in full rout, and our people were dropping everywhere, falling to the ground exhausted and wounded. I wanted to sleep for a week. That wasn't going to happen, though. I stumbled drunkenly toward my minions. " Arthor and Creziel. Dammit, Creziel's still out. Arthor, I need you to take the shamans, the small ones and the builders out and repair the tunnels. We're not getting taken by surprise again." I let my gaze swing over the cavern, choosing not to focus on the corpses that littered the floors. "Roth. Wreil. Get Leith, figure out how we're doing. How many are ready to fight, how many wounded... " I bit back a curse. "How many dead. I will take care of the wounded first with the Ergul. Leith, get scouts ready. We want a secure perimeter as soon as we can. Also, find me some wounded Dragonlings among the fallen, if you can. We are sending them back to their own with terms."

I looked over to the other end of the cavern. Creive was busy crunching down on the body of a dead Dragonling. Meanwhile, his minions were gathered in a loose semi-circle around him. Some relaxed, tired from the ordeal. Others – "Creive. You will need your wounded seen to, also. If any need urgent attention, tell me, and we will take care of it."

The blue giant looked up from his meal, blood dripping from his fangs. He blinked at me, then inclined his head. "That was not part of our agreement. Even so, I will accept." He started addressing his minions, and I moved on, instructing Wreil to get his scouts out in force again.

The wounded were many. Most of them came limping or were carried to us, but some were too badly hurt to even move. We sorted them out according to the severity of their wounds and had the Ergul get to work. First, anybody with bleeding, life-threatening damage, bad breaks, or nasty poison wounds. Then, those with heavy wounds that would need to be seen to, but weren't in any urgent threat of dying, and finally the rest. And I *did* want everybody seen to. The lightning flashes from the blue Dragonlings were typically not life-threatening, but the areas surrounding the impacts looked nasty and charred – that had to cause some permanent damage to the nerves. The same for the fire attacks, but worse. Nobody was going to suffer any permanent pain or damage from this, if I could avoid it.

The Ergul wasn't doing too good. The ugly slime was flattened out, deflated, looking for all the world like a puddle of dirty dish water in an indent in the cavern floor. I had to hand it to the beast, though. It had toiled for half an hour, wobbling from one badly wounded to the next, canceling out the painful effects of poisons, joining broken bones, and causing open, bleeding wounds to flow together and close. The ugly soldier had done its job, though, and hit level 5 in the process.

Roth stood next to the puddle, prodding it slightly with a foot. It shivered, but didn't move otherwise. "Ugly thing. Practical to have, though. Would have liked to have one for the tribe, way back." He grimaced. "That was a nasty battle, Onyx. I'm hoping we won't have to fight right away. We need to rest. And heal. And rest more." He waved toward the tunnels. "And that's without mentioning all the work all our dirtheads have to do on the tunnel to bring the defenses back to where they were."

I smiled at him. "After today, I think you'll be surprised at how fast our fledgling shamans can work. I was impressed. I can't believe how much they've grown."

The buff Talpus grew half an inch. "You're welcome." Then, as I didn't react, he raised a furry eyebrow. "What? You think they'd be hardy enough to handle the constant casting, if I hadn't been all over them to increase their Toughness? And they really needed attention. Especially that Boider—lazy runt."

"Poor little furballs." I chuckled. "Good job, nonetheless. I hadn't expected for them to be able to contribute for a while still. Now, I'll have to see if we can convince Arthor to keep them out of battle, unless it's one of our ambushes."

Roth grinned. "Yeah, good luck with that." He sneered, mimicking Arthor's sardonic drawl. "Pfah. Life in the mountain does not wait. Either you find conflict, or conflict finds you. Always has been like this. Always will be, lizard." He glanced at the ground and then back at me. I could feel the earnesty coming from him. "In truth, I wouldn't mind if we could keep them from any conflicts. Not forever. Maybe… a month or two. I could have their Toughness and Agility high enough that their chances would be a whole lot better."

I smiled at him. So, there was a soft side beneath the bulging muscles. Maybe one of the pups was his? "I will try."

"Make sure you do." Suddenly, like a piece of wet garment dropping from a clothesline, he let himself fall to the ground, resting on the dirt with his eyes closed. "I want to sleep for *days*. You make sure those Aberrants or whatever they called themselves don't attack, alright?"

I shook my head. "Of course. I'll go right ahead and arrange that. It'll be—" A shout broke our banter. I immediately expanded my attention into my map, and found Leith racing through the main tunnel at full speed, shouting. Oh, hell no. Did we jinx it?

Yes. Yes, we'd jinxed it. They had spotted one of the Aberrants within the tunnels, and we could expect company soon. I cursed, set people to work, and sent my mental attention outward to see them approaching.

I ranged out through the map. I passed the tunnels, watching exhausted Talpi shamans, shaman pups, and builders running to reach the damaged area in order to restore the numerous gaps in the ceilings. From the looks of it, it was going to be a hopeless task. The Dragonlings had not held back. I moved further, moving past running scouts, past the Dragonling corpses left from our sortie, toward the ruined Stone Door at the very entrance. Further still.

I was soon approaching the edges of my map. There I lingered, unable to tear my attention away. It was foolishness, I knew. I should be calling for a retreat right now. We had managed two incursions, if barely. There was no way we'd be able to weather a third one. If we regrouped and rested, we might be able to pull off an assault on the Aberrants' domain in time. Still, I hesitated, eyes fixed on the empty tunnel.

And finally they arrived. I missed them at first glance. They moved languidly, slowly enough not to draw the eye. And they were smeared in dirt, blending in with their surroundings. It was a miracle our scouts had spotted them in the first place. A single female Ethium and one of the fur-covered beasts we'd fought when we defeated the white dragon, Aelnir. I grit my teeth, waiting for the rest to arrive, ready to call a full retreat. But there were still only the two of them.

I pondered the possibilities, my claws clicking on a rock on the floor as I rapped the ground. They were halfway toward the Stone Door by now. I let a message range out. "Enemy scouts incoming. Everybody move back into the tunnels, continue working." If they weren't going to send in attack forces immediately, we might have time to fix the ceiling. Hell, we might even use this to our advantage, gain some valuable intelligence.

I started moving myself. Soon, I met everybody who was going in the opposite direction of myself and checked the edges of the maps again. Still no other attackers. I grinned in relief.

Heh. At the very least, we'd end up with a couple of captive scouts. If only there weren't any reinforcements incoming.

Picking up the pace, I had the ruins of the Stone Door in sight within a minute and concentrated. I could feel the illusion blurring into existence. For anybody moving this way, they'd be looking down into a decidedly dragon-free corridor. Heh. They were going to crap their furs when I dropped the illusion.

I didn't have to wait long. A couple of minutes later, they were there, edging closer to the Stone Door. There was no hurried pace. The two Aberrants clearly didn't leave anything to chance, keeping up the slow pace, checking all areas for traps or surprises. Survivors, these.

To my surprise, they didn't move past the Stone Door. The Ethium knelt near the broken edges of the door while the fur-covered beast sat down on his haunches. He looked for all the world like an albino panda, clumsy and kind of silly. And then the world shivered. I'd have missed it if I wasn't staring straight at him, but a wave ranged outward from the beast, almost imperceptible, moving through me and continuing. I tensed, ready to attack, but felt no effect. The animal, on the other hand, stood up again and barked a long string of sounds at the Ethium.

She nodded and rose, jumping past the rubble covering the Stone Door and then... stopped. She took a deep breath, then her mental voice ranged out into the open. "Onyx. We bow before you. Please come forth. We wish to discuss our surrender."

Once I picked up my jaw from the floor and revealed myself to the unlikely pair, I learned a lot. Turned out they weren't *only* scouts. They were sent by the Aberrants with the explicit job to scout out the lay of the land and figure out whether attacking or joining forces with us would be the wisest choice.

"You did promise that you would accept us, right?" The Ethium by the name of Lieva asked, nervousness dripping from her. It was the first time I'd seen an Ethium up close. They were... disconcerting to look at. Like you'd taken a dark elf for a template and then dipped into a batch of hallucinogens. On a whim, you added multi-jointed limbs in both arms and legs, gave them a superhero-worthy upper body musculature and then *stretched* them. The proportions looked way off.

I huffed in laughter. "I know shadow dragons aren't exactly known for honesty, but yes. I mean to keep my promise. If you swear to me, I will leave you be. How did you know I was there, though?"

She indicated with her head at the yeti, named Red Fang. "It's a skill of his. Three times a day, he can sense who and what are nearby. No exact locations, but enough to learn if we're about to move into an ambush or which species holds a place. It makes him useful, when his attributes otherwise make him... limited as a scout. And when he learned that there were no Dragonlings or Dworgen nearby, but *two* dragons, even though we knew they had been here a brief while ago..." She shrugged.

Useful? You could say that again. I *needed* to have this Red Fang visit Timothy so we could learn what combinations were needed to have some of our scouts learn that. For now... "So, you say that you have the authority to decide for the Aberrants?"

The Ethium assented. "Yes. I'm not the leader, but they listen to me, and they know I am able to judge. And looking at it from my perspective, it's not a tough call to make. We're not like the Dragonlings or the Dworgen. We don't seek out conflict unless we need to, or unless there is a weakness to exploit. Judging from the remains in the tunnel, that's a lesson the others could've learned from. So, yes. We won't give you any trouble. If Selys has allowed us to do so without battle, we submit."

Her nervousness was subdued, but definitely there. It made sense. Regardless of my promise, it would be all too easy for them to picture me using it as a way to ambush them. "I have no intentions of attacking you. I meant what I said. For now, I will introduce you to some of my leaders, then I will let you go home to your people."

I called for the Council to come meet them. I wasn't going to let them enter and see exactly how close we'd come to being beaten by the others. However, I did want them to see what we had, see how we had several races working in harmony. While the other two attacking races were likely not going to be easy to convince into becoming actual allies, the Aberrants might be different. They already accepted several different races, even the weaker ones. While my people were inbound, I asked them about that.

Red Fang answered with a growl. "We take anybody who isn't helpless. Don't care what they did, who they were. Only what they do within the tribe. Aberrants are family. Take care of each other. Everything else is dirt."

I nodded. It sounded a bit single-minded, but I liked their willingness to ignore species and everything. "That's praiseworthy. We take care of our own, too. It's too easy to focus on race or strength and ignore how else we're able to help each other."

He scoffed at that. "Strength is important. If you're not strong, do not prove yourself, you will become food, feed the family in a different way. Or be chosen for the Culling. There are many kinds of strength, though. Some are still useful, even if weak." The furred beast reached out and punched Lieva, none-too-gently.

She laughed. It sounded a bit forced. "Yeah. We take care of our own. It's... call it a last chance inside the mountain. We have even had a couple of your Talpi become ours. They tried to attack you. They regret it now. Still, they have told us of you. We... believe you would be a preferable alternative to Selys."

Oh. It seemed like years ago now. The Talpi who thought that killing me was the right choice for the tribe. Somehow, hearing that they were still alive and kicking made me happy. And if they talked about me and the Aberrants still wanted to join me, they couldn't have been badmouthing me too badly.

Soon, my people were gathered around the Aberrant scouts, and I let them take over while I went back to help inside the cavern. My instructions were simple. "Feed them, help them relax a bit before they have to go home again. Have them see how we get along. And pump them for information." It was a gamble, but I felt pretty assured that they were more likely to relax and speak their mind if there was no dragon perched above them.

At the other end of the cavern, a pair of heavily wounded Dragonlings were suffering a much worse service, as they were reportedly agreeing to every term we threw at them. Soon, we could send them back to their own with the message that they were now my underlings, pending confirmation from Selys.

We'd done it. But there was still work to do. I got to work figuring out the toll of the battle. Our losses were ugly. Three Talpi, four Crawls, two Imps, and one of the Clenchers had died during the protracted conflict. We'd weathered the Dworgen pretty well, but the elemental attacks from the Drag-onlings had been lethal. As for the wounded... we had even more of those. We had been fortunate in that only a few suffered permanent damages. We'd have to see about getting them work as crafters; that would be a task for Arthor. Creive's forces had taken worse casualties, bearing the brunt of the damage from the aerial battle, but he didn't seem to mind. In fact, he was already asleep with a full belly after gorging himself on the Dragonlings. And why not? We had made it! That fact overrode any other consideration, burned through my mind, and I had to sit down.

We made it. The mountain was mine. Heh. Apart from that tiny detail with Selys.

CHAPTER TWENTY-FOUR

As soon as Timothy and the rest returned and learned that we were safe, having sent the Aberrants back with the message to their leaders, they flung themselves to the ground, spent. We handled the absolute necessities, healing the worst, leveling up, and ended with a huge feast to celebrate. In the general food coma afterward, we hung around in the large cavern, marveling at our survival.

The experience from the battle was incredible. I'd been a part of the first heavy decimation of the Dworgen, but my participation against the Dragonlings had been more limited. Even so, I had still earned a full 27,100 xp. That got me right past the barrier to level 27. On top of that, I was gifted another 2,800 from Creive, who'd been in the center of both battles. I reckoned I was getting a straight ten percent from him. I definitely needed to get myself some more vassals. I spent every single point on Mental Power, like last time.

I was not the only one to level up. If I was impressed by the experience I'd gained, my minions were euphoric. The gains were crazy. My choice to invest in my minions was already paying off as they gained an additional 50 % experience on top of what they otherwise would.. Every single person who'd formed part of the battle leveled up, and most gained at least two levels. A few got even more. Gert, who had still been fairly low-leveled, jumped from level 9 to level 12. Once they got over the worst of the food coma, they started crowding around Timothy to hear what their recent levels might be able to bring them. Looked like business was booming for the opaque Quipu-enthusiast.

We were back inside the Throne Room. Nobody, except for Creive and his minions, wanted to spend the time in the gore-covered cavern. Every spot in sight was filled with people, relieved from our victory and sated from feasting and celebrating.

Roth sighed, burped, then sighed again. "Soooo, we have a decision to make, right?"

Grex leaned back against a pillar next to Creziel, eyes closed. "What decision? Talpi kids joining us on the Council? They saved everybody!" He roared with laughter, like it was an incredible joke. He hadn't mentioned his wound with a single word so far. Any hope of Grex growing more cautious from the near-death experience seemed ludicrous.

Roth laughed, then groaned and tenderly touched a wound on his chest. "Nah. Timothy. That fog cloud over there has helped everybody find good ways to level up instead of simple guesswork. You all saw everybody gather around him. No need to hide it. We might as well make it official; that's part of his responsibility on the Council."

I wanted to jump in, but decided not to and see how this played out.

Creziel got up on his elbows, then clearly thought better of it and flopped back down. "I agree. He is performing the work for it, and it helps. We had *two* builders gain Increased Strength. You all know how rare that is. I say we do it."

They chimed in until only Arthor and I remained. He just grunted. "I can see I'm outnumbered. Let it be official, then. Doesn't mean I have to like it."

Then I spoke up. "I'm agreed and glad to hear it. You deserve the position, Tim. And the work. I'm not taking over, that's for damn sure. Now, unless any of you has something important to say, I've earned a nap."

Arthor spat. "Pfah. A paddling is what you've earned. Your plan fell through in the most horrible way. Still, I guess you cannot be entirely blamed for the way things developed. Go sleep. Do better next time."

I slept and the world, for once, did not see fit to throw any curveballs at me. We rested, ate, healed, and talked. Everybody knew it was a temporary breather, and it was all the more precious for it.

"Why are we still here?" The angry words were the only warning I got.

"A warm welcome to you too, Arthor." I lifted my neck to nod at the Talpus, who strode straight through the cluttered throne room at me. His rocks were whizzing about him as usual.

"Pfah. Dispense with the needless chatter, dragon. I want an answer."

I waved a claw at the rest of the throne room. "Plenty of reasons. I have been working to create Mana Crystals, to make up for the four I had to spend. Besides, our people have earned a break. They have been through some heavy battles and need the rest and distractions from risking their lives. And while the weapons we got from the Dworgen were of excellent quality, you *know* they will need training to be able to use them well."

That wasn't an exaggeration in the slightest. My Talpi favored spears in general–easy to craft, good range and it was easy to learn the basics. The Crawls had used whatever was at hand: spears, crude clubs, scavenged weapons. Now, however, the inclusion of sturdy, high-quality close-combat weapons, some strengthened with rune magic, meant that the Crawls finally had the gear necessary for preparing for true ranked fighting. It was going to be a learning experience for both trainer and trainee.

"Beside all that training, a lot of them are busy talking to

Timothy and Lore, trying to pick a clever way to increase their attributes from the levels they have gained. Especially the Imps, since I talked Creive into having his Imps share their details with Tim. Only cost me the promise of three Mana Crystals, too. Hey, you heard about that scouting skill that white Aberrant had? If that one isn't exclusive to their species, one of our scouts should be able to pick it in a single level, according to Timothy. Picture that. No more going into hostile places with our eyes closed... we'll be able to figure out what's waiting for us."

Arthor bared his teeth. "I will not deny that the ghost's skills can be useful... pfah. You are trying to distract me. We healed the last of the badly wounded two days ago. Also, you have admitted yourself that we will not be able to construct everything needed to upgrade the hoard in time. Why are we lingering?"

"Like I said, we need a break. Besides, we don't *have* to leave until tomorrow. We have quite enough time to still make the deadline Selys gave us."

The shaman shook his head and walked over to stand right in front of me. He pointed a claw straight at me. "You're lying. Besides, I know why you're stalling. You don't want to face the decision we have to make."

I prepared a retort... and stopped. "You're right. Almost." I held up a claw, forestalling his reply. "We've handled everything the mountain has thrown at us. We have beat down or subdued the only challengers to the throne and the prize is right there, waiting for us to accept it. I am not one to shirk from action. But, if you start building without knowing all the measurements, you're going to spend twice as long repairing it afterward, and the result will *still* be crap. The moment we enter Fire Peak, we make our decision, and I will have to swear Selys' oath. And that will have consequences for all of us."

My low growl caused some of the others in the throne room to look at me askance before turning back to what they were doing. "We don't know *enough* to make a good decision. So, I'll have to swear an oath the Soul Carver fled from?" My tail whipped back and forth behind me in agitation, raising up dust. "And the alternatives *stink*. Try to hide inside the mountain and avoid Selys' reach? Not going to happen. If I can sense her hoard; she can damn well sense mine, too—and that's beside whatever surprises the Blessing of Deyra grants her. Flee outside the mountain? Try to survive as best we can while Selys tries to take over the world?" I shook my head. "Take Selys on?" I let the idea trail off.

Arthor's mental voice was uncharacteristically mild. "I know. It is a hard choice. And for once, the Talpus way isn't optimal. Run and start over? That works quite well, but not if we have to flee the mountain entirely. We have never gone into details, but there is a reason we entered in the first place. The Scoured Mountain is a harsh place, but the benefits outweigh the dangers. The surroundings are dangerous, and the predators around here are lethal. Even with all we have grown, the challenges outside will be hard to handle. The few who prosper outside are... dangerous."

I grimaced. "You are right, though. I'm glad you came to give me a nudge. A poor foreman is one who does not face reality, grim as it may be. Let us gather the others. It is time for the Council to debate the most important decision they are likely to ever make. Should we move against Selys or not?"

"Have you lost it?" Roth was fuming. "Did you hit your head in the battle? You want to attack *Selys?* After we finally succeeded in doing what we needed to take over? "

The assembled group was staring at me with differing degrees of disbelief. Even Grex was more astonished than anything.

I kept my tone relaxed, level. "I don't. I really don't. What I do want is to have a *plan.* And right now, going into Fire Peak, trusting the goodwill of Selys doesn't feel as much like a plan as boundless optimism. So, I intend to plot and prepare contingency plans in case negotiations go bad."

Arthor nodded, approving. "For once, you're talking sense,

lizard. If you go into a Dweeler nest, you do it with a bolthole ready. Let's make sure we know what we're going to do if Selys does plan to enslave us all."

Gert looked bewildered. "I agree. Only… how do you plan to do it? We will be inside Fire Peak, cut off from help, at the mercy of the Burning End. There's nothing we *can* do."

My eyes met with Arthor's. He nodded at me, and I grinned. "Oh, that's where we'll have to disagree. Our people have managed to outsmart and outmaneuver half the damn mountain by now. What's one more time?"

CHAPTER TWENTY-FIVE

"When you travel, remember that a foreign country is not designed to make you comfortable. It is designed to make its own people comfortable." —
Clifton Fadiman

The travel back to Fire Peak was the most uneventful one we'd had. By now, it felt like the mountain was used to our passage, and challengers shied away from our route. We did delay three times, in nod to our precarious situation, leaving some of the provisions Selys had given us in hidden stashes along the way to the top. If we had to leave quickly, we couldn't afford having to waste time on foraging. The hoard we dismantled and kept on us, distributed among all of us. While we'd be able to hunt down food with a little time, replacing the item stash we'd amassed by now would be harder.

The only major incident during the trip was when Wreil dragged Leith before the Council and asked them to make it official that they were splitting responsibilities for the near future. Leith took the expanded workload surprisingly well. It likely helped when Wreil started commending him for his skills in front of everybody. For now, Leith would handle the scheduling and dividing work and Wreil would handle... everything else.

Taking in the vista of the city, it was no less impressive the third time around, especially with a new gate and an approach that was free from broken corpses. We reached it in the late afternoon and paused for a while, watching the walled city bathed in the warm sunlight coming through the crater above.

Roth shuddered. "I don't like this. No place is supposed to be as bright as this. It feels like entering a lair of Clenchers willingly."

I couldn't entirely disagree. Now that I knew of them, I couldn't ignore the large towers interspersed around the city. Entering below the canopy of that fire shield... It felt like walking willingly into prison. Even though we had handled everything as best we could, it still felt wrong. Still, sometimes, that was the best deal you were going to get. Your materials were sub-par, but there was no money for anything better. You'd better shut up and get to work.

The sorcerer was waiting for me again as we arrived. He bowed as I entered the huge gates, his face hidden behind the mask. "Welcome back, Onyx. Walk with me. Your minions will be taken care of."

A large group of armed guards escorted my people away. We started walking–not toward the fortress, but along with the wall. I made no comment, content to wait until he revealed the purpose of the walk. The sensations from the human were muddled. He was likely powerful enough to hide them from me. After a while, we turned away from the wall, aiming for a part of the city I didn't know.

"So. You have succeeded, I assume."

I grinned. "Yes. We beat back the Dragonlings and Dworgen. The Aberrants didn't need any lessons–they surrendered willingly. I am ready to take up the position as the master of the mountain."

He nodded. "All in good time. Selys is busy right now. She

will admit you in a few hours. I aim to show you more of Fire Peak while your people wait."

"I'd appreciate it. Selys showed me some last time, but the majority of the layout and inhabitants are still unknown to me. I would like to see who the builders are, for instance. I mean, not the original ones, but those who do the maintenance and created the wall."

"That will be of no issue. We have time. I will also introduce you to the leaders of the Guard. Those who are chosen to defend the city are the highest-leveled fighters from the entire mountain. The best of those rise again to work for Selys herself."

I couldn't hide a grimace at the memory of the Soul Carver obliterating guards left and right inside the throne room. "That would be nice. What and who will she take with her when she leaves?"

"That is not for me to say. Now, if you pay attention, you will see some of the few remaining constructions left from the Corren, the original builders of the mountain."

The city was theirs. The layout, the towers. The Corren, original dominators of the mountain, had definitely left their mark on Fire Peak. There were precious few actual buildings left. Still, what little remained stood out from all other constructions, and they did not deteriorate fast. A silo of sorts, tall and cylindrical. A honeycomb-looking structure, 40 feet tall. A huge, wide, warehouse-like structure with a confusing interior. As we walked, the sorcerer pointed out any constructions of interest.

It appeared that the dwellings in the city were quite heavily segregated, racially speaking. The different species interacted within their functions, but slept and stayed with their own. The one exception was the slaves who were everywhere. And *their* emotions were easy to read.

Hopelessness. Fear. Suffering. Pain. I tried to tune them out. I couldn't do anything about them yet… but then the smell hit me. Blood. A lot of it. We were slowly crossing a large plaza and at the far end of it, an overwhelming stench of blood and *prey* made the animalistic part of me cry out in hunger. "What is going on over there?"

The sorcerer barely reacted. "Oh, that? It's the Culling."

"Which is?" Was he being deliberately obtuse?

"Well, Selys has a number of ways she controls the stronger groupings in the mountain. The Culling is one of those. Once in a while, their leaders are called to visit Fire Peak and tell of the state of their groupings. Then Selys informs them how many of their kind or other kinds of tribute they will have to deliver for the growth of Selys and Fire Peak. Apart from this, and from when Selys needs them for something, they are left alone to grow and prosper."

I stopped, squinting closer at the gathering at the other side of the plaza. What did he mean? "I would like to see this." He shrugged and we walked closer, letting us look closer at a grisly sight. Four large cages were placed at the back end of the open area, filled to the brim with... all kinds of races. Smaller races were present, but there were others, too. A dozen Dragonlings filled one entire cage, while another was filled with large beasts, chained to the sides of the cage so they couldn't reach each other.

In front of these, a large, wooden raised area held a rowdy crowd. At our arrival, the busyness of the plaza subsided, but a single, sharp word from the sorcerer soon had them continuing the auction. Because that was what it was. An auction. The single, bestial Urten in the center of the plaza growled the benefits of the next sale, while the onlookers talked, cursed, and jeered among themselves. The Urten indicated a huge Clencher that occupied a full fourth of one cage by itself.

In the center of the crowd, a smaller group stood out. Stronger. Better armed and armored. Quite a few of them wore the golden armors of the elite guard. And in their hands... "Are those coins?" Some of the people present were waving something at the Urten, gold flashing from within their fists and claws.

"Coins? No. There is no money inside the mountain. In

fact, I am surprised that you even know of it. Except... you would know of money, wouldn't you?" The sorcerer shook his head. "Those are chits. Every worker in the city gets one a year. Some get more, if they please Selys."

The bidding had intensified. Within a single minute, bidders dropped out, leaving a scarred Dragonling glaring at a dark-furred beast as they faced off, trying to outbid each other over the Clencher. I took a look at the animal in the cage. It was a huge specimen, almost as large as Ursam. I would've liked to have it and add it to my forces as well. The sounds of the crowd grew as the bid war ended, leaving the Dragonling to stroll back and forth in front of the onlookers, sneering at the loser with his arms raised in victory.

A handful of workers, white in their eyes, took hold of the chains that were attached to the Clencher and dragged it closer to the edge of the cage. I could sense hints of fear mixing with bloodlust among the crowd. The Urten faced the Dragonling and received the chits. Then, they held a subdued conversation, until we could see the Dragonling shake his head and grin before he strolled closer to the ferocious beast. The Clencher sensed his presence and struggled to move away, but the workers managed to keep him in place. Indifferent to their struggles, the Dragonling moved in closer, reached in...and with a single, powerful stroke, tore out the Clencher's throat.

The crowd let out a sigh, and the emotions from the crowd hit me like a wave, almost physical in their intensity.

I wavered. "What the *hell* was that?"

The sorcerer seemed unperturbed. "That would be one of the guard leaders. Crefring. He must have saved up for quite a while. That Clencher was at least level 10. The experience from it should be enough for at least half a level for him. Oh, and he will receive the flesh from the animal as well, obviously. Selys does not believe in undue waste."

Undue waste. "So, what, the groups are culled to keep their numbers and threats down and delivered here to be slaughtered as a reward?"

He tilted his head. "That was a decent summary, if lacking in detail. A rare few are spared, if they can aid the owner better alive than dead. Dragonling slaves, for instance, are not easy to come by." He turned and started walking without waiting for me to follow.

I stood there for a moment, struck by the sheer animalistic cruelty of the idea. The Culling. Such a crude name, yet so accurate. Like a medieval tithe, but a tithe of blood. A crude chain, wrapped around the throats of those under Selys' yoke. And soon it would be mine.

We spent the next ten minutes in silence as we slowly traversed the city. The sorcerer turned and turned again, his relaxed pace at odds with my dark thoughts. I knew there would be a lot of work to do to turn this place into a decent place to live. But I couldn't push the sensations from the crowd to the background. They were so strong. Bloodlust, thrill, envy, and *hunger*. So much hunger.

This was so different from my people. Even the most prag-matic of them had grown far beyond this. But there were *thou-sands* to convince, and... I shook my head at the sheer task before me. The sorcerer turned again, and I followed. We were approaching the northeastern side of the wall, walking closer to a large, crude building that saw constant traffic from armor-clad beasts. The guards' building, likely.

On an impulse, I stopped and brought up my map. The path from today crossed where I had walked on my earlier visit to the city. But... this was off. We had taken a large detour on the way to our destination. It wasn't like he'd introduced me to anything especially interesting... unless. "Did you take a detour to show me the Culling?"

It was tiny, but I caught it. The hesitation before he answered. Then the outright lie. "No. I merely wanted to intro-duce you to a larger part of the city."

I squinted at him, then lowered my head to look him straight in the eyes. "You're lying. I don't see why, though. Unless..." I thought back to our former conversation. The warning. The hints that I'd be better off elsewhere. "You don't want me to join up with Selys." He froze up. His posture was standoffish, hostile even, with his arms crossed over his chest. But he didn't deny it. "Listen. I don't even know your name. I'm not about to call you Pet."

"Mordiel." The response was grudging.

"Alright, Mordiel. You already know that I'm not some bloodthirsty dragon by nature. I'm a simple guy. You know my secret, and if you're telling the truth, I'd do well not to tell Selys I was a human. So, give it to me straight. Why did you show me what they were doing then try to hide it?"

Mordiel took off his mask and faced me. The somber face inside was that of a middle-aged man, mouth creased with wrinkles and downturned lips. He looked almost... sullen. "I believed you would be able to get the hint!"

I smiled. "Sorry, Mordiel. I'm slow. And I prefer straight talk."

He took a deep breath, closed his eyes and then nodded, as if to himself. "I feared we would have to do this. Come. We will visit the city guards, then I will tell you."

The guards were... everything I'd expected. High levels. Skilled in combat. Much brawn. Less brain. They were also well-organized into combat teams and trained for any emergency. Or so the guard captain, a dirt-smeared Culdren, postulated. Heh. I was sure that "sneak attack inside the fortress" had also been added to their list of contingencies after their failure when the Soul Carver attacked. As a force of power, they were indubitably strong, and their numbers were impressive: a hundred and forty guards, with trainees on top of that, divided into divisions and subdivisions. The guards themselves were clearly marked with their golden armor, while their numerous trainees were decked out in less impressive garments.

As people, I found myself less impressed. They were hugely confident in their superiority over everybody else inside the city and not afraid to show their disdain in action as well as in speech. I had seen guards throughout the city, strolling along like kings, pushing lesser creatures about like they owned the place. And, in truth, they did, as long as they did not overreach and invite the wrath of Selys or meddle with one of the other few important people in the city.

The guard captain talked and talked, spinning one story after the other to add to the same conclusion. "Look at us," they said. "Look how strong we are, how necessary." But all I could think of was how difficult it would be to turn these sociopaths into actual people. My thoughts turned dark as I thought about what could be done when I came into power. I kept drawing a blank. Reform for these would not be easy.

When we left the place, I was the first to talk. "Are they all like this?"

"What do you mean?"

I scowled at the building we were leaving, searching for the right words. "Tiny lords, trying to abuse the power they've been given at the expense of others."

He laughed then. It was not a happy laughter, but a pained bark. "I don't know how I ever mistook you for a dragon. You are so soft, it would make a Calvuz mother cry for harsher education. *Of course* they are bestial. This is what they are inside the mountain. Animals. Animals given speech and quick minds, perhaps, but animals still. They will carve and claw at each other for a better piece of meat."

I shook my head. "I disagree. My minions are anything but. They are people, with all their flaws and egoism, but they're still people. They strive to improve, to grow, and are even selfless at times. One sacrificed herself for her own kind. For me. That is *not* an animal."

Mordiel sneered. "You go ahead and believe whatever lets your scaled head rest at night. So, you want to know why I wanted to show you the *real* heart of the city as well as its guardians? That was it. Because you were a human. To give you a chance." He sniffed. "Call it weakness on my part, or simply longing for my past, for when I was not a dragon's plaything."

He fixed my eyes with his, unblinking, unwavering. "I have

your undivided attention? *Run away!* Go to the meeting with Selys, then flee. Flee before the ceremony tomorrow. Do not take over after Selys. Do not stay here. For the love of Deyra, do *not* swear the oath. Die first." The final message arrived with *weight* as Mordiel's eyes bored into mine.

I hesitated. Damn. Regardless what I'd told him so far, if I went any further, this would have repercussions. But warning me like he'd done... he was risking everything as well. On a whim. For a second, two, I held back. Then I growled and addressed him with the same fervor he'd held. "You don't *get* it. I'm here to help! You think I'm blind? I have eyes. But, I intend to fix this place. Once I hold the place, I'll put my people into position, make sure that we can repair what's broken."

Mordiel looked at me with an incredulous look in his eyes, but I continued. "You think I don't know it's going to be tough? Looking at the people in this place, I despair. But I've already succeeded. I have four races working together and thriving. And I will build a *new* goddamn society. One where people aren't enslaved or killed for their meat or simply for being a different shape than the others. I can do it. Just help me."

"But Selys..."

"*Screw Selys!*" I regained my composure and continued. "Eventually, this will bring us into conflict with Selys. I am well aware of that. But Selys will be gone soon, and while she is away, we can prepare for her. Institute change. Grow in strength. Prepare our defenses." I lowered my head to his, repeated my plea. "Just help me."

He stared at me. Shrouded eyes wide open, he didn't say anything, only stared, as if he were trying to figure me out. Then, he said, as his face fell. "I cannot." I started to repeat myself, but he interrupted, grinding his teeth. "You do not understand. I am not able to betray Selys. And by this time tomorrow, the same will apply to you, unless you flee." He shook his head, then continued, less intense.

"Why do you believe the Soul Carver refused to swear the oath? Because he knew. He knew what it would cost him and refused to pay the cost." He grimaced and spat. "Even if I wanted to, even if I thought it were feasible, I could no more move personally against Selys than I could kill myself. She has ensured so. Back then, I believed swearing an oath was better than death. Because I had hope. Hope."

The look on his face was a horror to behold. Finally, a single tear ran from his eye, and he looked up, with a smile so filled with self-loathing I had to look away. "Hope is a waste of emotion, something for humans. Good for me I don't have that problem anymore. Because I *took the oath.*"

We finished the tour with few words. In truth, neither of us had any interest in conversation, and I couldn't spark much interest in my surroundings. My mind was in turmoil. Mordiel would not, *could* not tell me the exact words of the oath. Was he right, though? Would I be signing away my future, my humanity if I swore the oath? Would it be worth it for the chance to rule the mountain? Even if I would have to obey her direct commands, might I be able to eke out some liberty to act as I wanted? I went back and forth over the subject, without becoming any wiser, until, finally, Mordiel stopped in the middle of the street.

"Onyx. We're done. We will be going to see Selys now."

I simply nodded. Whatever else happened, I would have to make my way through a chat with Selys without stumbling or giving away anything. It was a simple chat, nothing more. No way that could go wrong. Right?

CHAPTER TWENTY-SIX

She was magnificent. There was no denying it. Even though she had been on my mind quite often the last few months, the sheer majesty of Selys was hard to handle. Her golden armor gleamed in the fire of the oil lamps in the throne room. Together with the glittering opulence of her hoard, it turned the closed confines into bright daylight. The Burning End. It was fitting. I took her in, towering above me at twice my height and several times my bulk. There would be no doubt that she would become the end of me, should she decide to make it so. Facing her directly in combat... no. That wasn't even a question.

Her smile was large as she welcomed me. "Onyx. My son. You have returned, and in triumph, I hear."

I almost stumbled at that. Had somebody been listening to my conversation with Mordiel? I hadn't talked to anybody else.

She merely laughed. "Oh, do not act so surprised. I know what happens inside the mountain. And when the Dragonlings and the Dworgen are broken within the same day... I know. So come, let me celebrate your success."

I approached her and bowed my head deeply before her in deference. "You're right, Selys. I've returned, and we made it."

"With a single day to go. You were pushing the limits, Onyx."

I nodded. "We did take a good deal of casualties during the battle. I dedicated the time I believed I could spare with the Ergul, ensuring that my minions were healed and ready to travel."

Selys frowned. "What a waste of time and effort. They could have made their way by themselves, if they survived."

I bowed my head again. "Respectfully, I disagree. I've spent a lot of time raising the levels of my minions. They are part of the reason that I've made it this far. I don't believe in throwing away good tools when it can be avoided."

She bared her teeth. "There it is again. You do think too much of those weaklings. Imps. And Talpi, even." She shook her head, reflecting blinding pinpricks of light all over the room. "Still, I will not debate your results. You have done well. Today is a day of planning. Tomorrow, we celebrate!" A wide grin from her took me by surprise. "There is no reason why we cannot celebrate a bit today." She looked at one of the guards. "Felux. Bring us a meal. And something to drink. I have good news to impart to my son."

Two guards near the doors left the room and we spent the next minutes observing as a large crowd orchestrated an incredible meal in studied business. Several small wheeled trolleys were rolled in, holding large raised bowls. The bowls carried different forms of liquid. I tentatively lapped at one of them. The strong taste of the drink burned in my mouth, but the lingering aftertaste was very pleasant, carrying notes of plum and cherry. Was that... alcohol?

"What is this, Selys? It's excellent."

Smirking with satisfaction, she responded. "I have my own craftsmen, Onyx. Enough of them that I can spare a handful to make sure that I eat and drink well. That, I believe, is a brew made from mushrooms and some choice flowers. It leaves you relaxed and merry, as long as you do not imbibe too much."

I tasted it again and took a larger mouthful this time. "It's really good."

She nodded. "Soon, you can have it anytime you would like. While I plan to take a lot of my winged followers with me, many will have to stay. Speed will be necessary for my success."

I held up a claw. "Ah. I've been meaning to ask you. The minion count. How does it work? I am already nearing my limit. What happens when I reach my limit?"

She inclined her head. "That is a good question. Shows you think ahead." She drained a bowl, and a minion sprinted to remove it right away. "You will be able to choose who are designated as your minions. Who gets to earn the right to the gifts and increases your reign can bestow upon them. It allows for good competition. Keeps them focused on the possible rewards." She lapped at another bowl, then grimaced and lifted a claw at one of her minions. "This one goes down even better with a solid meal."

A short procession entered and halted before us. Two guards with clanking chains holding two Talpi.

My stomach sank. Selys sent a wide smile at one of the guards and waved them off. The Talpi kneeled on the tiled floor before us, groveling and shaking, abject terror overwhelming any other emotions coming from them. Selys smiled. "It has been a while for me. I rarely enjoy Talpus–the fur, you understand–but your minions gave me the inspiration. Go ahead."

She indicated the meal–no, the persons, shaking on the ground before me. My mind roiled with the cold, no the evil of it. What could I do? Deny outright? Claim I wasn't hungry? She would be able to tell that I was lying. I decided to go for a half-truth. "Ah. I appreciate the offer, Selys. I must admit, though, my time with the Talpi has left me with a certain fondness for the species. I wouldn't kill any without need."

Her lidded eyes looked at me, and her tail whipped back and forth. It felt like a pressure pushed down on me. "You are a curious one. Capable, inventive–but so weak. You are hungry.

What else would you need?" Her eyes flashed, and her claw shot out, carving through the neck of one of the Talpi. "You are welcome. Now, eat."

I considered flat out refusing, but I could feel I was treading on danger-filled ground. Several emotions warred for primacy within me as I lowered my head and ripped a mouthful of flesh off the still-warm corpse. Shame, hatred, defeat, hunger… it didn't help that it tasted so damn good. The Talpi had clearly been treated with some sort of seasoning before they were forced before us.

Selys waited until I had started eating before she impaled the still-living Talpus with a claw and effortlessly dragged it closer to her. Then, she lowered her head and slowly, almost gently, ripped off its arm and chewed, blood spilling from her maw as the tiny creature cried out in suffering. "I do not understand why you would turn this down. The sensation of fear and vital energy improves the flavor. Ah, well. You are entitled to your own habits, how strange they may be. As long as you can follow orders when I am gone."

I nodded, taking another mouthful, keeping my head down so she didn't see my emotions. I couldn't wait to see the last of her. "So, when is this going to happen?"

"Are you that eager to see me go?" Suddenly her eyes sparked with danger.

"No. I mean. Of course, I am eager. I want to take over here, but…" I halted, unsure how to continue without putting my foot in my mouth.

Selys showed all her teeth and got up from her rest, stalking closer. "Impatient, are we? I might become suspicious of you. Fear that you were planning to plot against me when I was gone." She lowered her head toward mine. For a moment, I feared that she would jump me then and there. But she veered, taking a drink from my bowl. Languidly, she moved back to her rest, all sinewy grace. "This is entirely normal. Of course, a youngling wants to grow up and decide for himself. Still, you will need my help, a guiding claw to ensure that you do not fall from something a more experienced dragon could have told you. And you will have it."

There was nothing I could say to that but thank her. So I did. Trying with all my might to appear as if I meant it.

She might have felt my lack of sincerity, but ignored it. "Now. As to the practical aspects of it. Tomorrow, we will hold a ceremony to celebrate your accomplishments and introduce you to Fire Peak properly. The guard is out in force, instructing everybody that they will be present. The same goes for your minions, obviously. It shall be, when the sun sinks near the edge of the crater. Fitting for the transition from fire into shadow."

She continued. "There will not be much to it. Most of them will already be aware of what is going on. Whatever else happens, lesser beings will gossip. Regardless, we shall inform them about your succession, then you will swear your vows. Once that is done, we will have a city-wide feast for a week before we start the preparations for my departure."

I took great care not to appear too eager, and lowered my head. "What can I do?"

"Nothing much. I will not take much in the way of goods. Armaments for my winged minions and most of the magical items we have stored. Meanwhile, I shall allow you access to the hoard and give you the chance to familiarize yourself with the new possibilities. Obviously, you will need to spend some time to handle the transition smoothly."

I nodded. "Of course. A change in leadership is never easy. Some are bound to test the limits of the new leader. And there will be much to learn."

"Yes. I am glad you see it clearly. Some blood will be spilled when underlings test your mettle. That is unavoidable. More, when we integrate your minions into our system. I shall be entertained to learn how they fare against those who are already established and secure in their positions."

I blinked. This would ruin everything. If my groups were

divided all around the city and mixed into the existing group-ings… I thought rapidly, trying to find an argument that might work. "May I ask why? I mean, I have spent a lot of time working on their cooperation. At this point, they work together pretty much flawlessly, as you can see from my results. I would hate to break them up, maybe even lose some useful minions needlessly."

She didn't give an inch. "We will not change the systems in place. Once I have left, you will grow accustomed to handling Fire Peak and be ready to get the rest of the mountain properly under claw. If your minions are that useful, they must surely be able to prove themselves against the minions inside the city."

Fuck me. I tried changing my tack. "If only I could show you what I mean, Selys. I would pit one of my groups against those in place in the city, show you that splitting them up would harm more than help?"

She smiled. Not a single part of her smile reached her eyes, though. "Let us focus on tomorrow. Later, once the ceremony is handled properly, we can discuss specifics."

My heart fell. We can discuss it when you've sworn the oath to obey, in other words. I felt the walls closing in on all sides. Maybe she was feeling my inner turmoil and fencing me in. What to do?

Somehow, I made it through the rest of the discussion. The talk turned to specifics, to practical issues that needed to be fixed before she left. I could concentrate on that and ignore the issue towering before me. Before I knew it, I was stumbling out the front gate of the fortress, with the sky above turning orange as the sun fled beyond the crater. My mind was racing with possibilities and plans, far-reaching consequences, and I barely noticed Mordiel until he addressed me. "So. Onyx. You are still here."

"Yes. And you were right. Damnit, but you were right." I turned my head toward him, focusing. "What happens if I run?"

He grimaced. "You mean, even if you can somehow make it

through the gates? You were with the Soul Carver. Did he talk about what she did when he turned her down?"

I shook my head. "Not in any detail, no."

"It was bad. For a while, she turned the whole mountain upside down to find and hunt him. She sent me out, as well as others, ranging against him and his minions when he tried to attack on several fronts. For a while, nobody dared act against her, such was her fury. Still, when she learned that he had fled the place, she relaxed. Set safeguards in place and moved on. If he had remained inside the mountain, he would keep lingering as a threat against her. Outside, the chance for growth is a lot less."

"So, if we do flee the mountain, she's bound to forget about us for a while." I looked at the human from the corner of my eye. "What will this mean to you? Talking about this with me? She would not handle it well if she learned about it."

The mask was in place, hiding his features. The shudder that went through him, however, gave him away. "I... know Selys. She ignores those beneath her most of the time. She would not expect it. I should be able to avoid attention."

We walked in silence for a while. Now, there were no detours. We marched straight for the same plaza as last time. The gleaming in the distance told me that my people were guarded, yet again. I broke the silence. "Why don't you flee with us? With us, you'll be treated like a real person, not like a leashed animal. I will show you what we've done to bring back humanity to the mountain."

He turned to me and watched me without words as we walked. "I believe you. I do believe you. And I would, in an instant. Except, I cannot. The oath forbids me from doing it. Forswearing myself—it would see me dead. And there are other safeguards. Please, take this as my warning and flee. Take your flying minions with you, if you can. Otherwise, just leave. Take to the skies tonight. And let this be my single attempt at being human, for once."

I wanted to answer him, but couldn't find the words. The

guard surrounding my minions was heavier than last time. "Mordiel. If I ever have the chance, I promise—"

"Stop," he interrupted. "I have found my peace, such as it is. I do not wish for hope at this point. It would be too much. If we meet again, it will be as enemies, and I do not want that. Please. Flee."

CHAPTER TWENTY-SEVEN

*"If you are made for flight, intended for it, you had better find a pursuer,
fast.
Otherwise, all that fleeing is going nowhere."*—— Dan Chiasson

It took me little time to have my people gather around. The
Council surrounded us, while the rest of our minions presented
a wall between us and the numerous city guards that lazed
about, keeping their eyes on us with weapons in hand. I took in
the postures of my people. Careful. Guarded. Ready. Even Grex
was looking at his surroundings like he was itching for a fight.

I didn't beat around the bush. "We're in trouble." A brief
explanation had them informed of Selys' machinations and our
own issues.

Like so often before, Grex was the one to react first.
"Alright. We flee! Cut a path to the gates. Surprise them. Big
bastards with nice armor—we can take them. A simple ambush,
then we run."

"Oh yeah?" Arthor's comment was piercing. "And once
Selys takes to the sky, what's your plan then?"

"Uh. Hide?"

Nobody had expected the laughter, but it washed over us all at Grex's suggestion. A bit hysterical at the edges, sure, but once the noise died down, and I was drying a tear of mirth from my eye, a bit of the initial panic gone from the emotions surrounding me. I spoke to them. "Okay, apart from Grex's excellent idea of hiding in three miles of surroundings that have been *entirely leveled* - how about we stick with our actual plan? We'll go over it once again, make sure everybody knows their place. Before that, though: Can anybody come up with a situation where we'd be able to stay or even *want* to?"

There was no reply. Finally, Gert spoke. "We have endured much. If you could think of any way to reverse or remove the oath, get out of it, yes. We Crawls would be able to handle any challenges of being spread out. We would survive. And whoever survived could rejoin you stronger afterward."

I gave her a kind smile. "In enduring, grow strong?" I shook my head. "The fact that you are offering makes me damn proud of you... and of the rest of you for seeing the light and accepting the Crawls on the Council. Unfortunately, I'm not seeing it. If Selys is able to make the oath hold, I will have to bow to any command she comes up with afterward. I'll have no way of knowing exactly what she will demand. She may even have a different oath, tailored specifically for me. I don't see her leaving many loopholes, however. As for removing Selys... even if we were to chance it, and the oath would permit it, she's going to leave the mountain! We wouldn't have a chance for who knows how long."

Roth asked, with a big grin, "So, we do what Grex said?"

"Oh, hell no. We're not going to be dumb about it."

"Hey!" Grex fluttered up to face me and looked affronted for all of two seconds. Then he grinned. "Remind me. What was the plan?"

I got comfortable. "Yes. Let's do this right. Whatever else happens, we're not going to run away while there's still daylight. So, let's reiterate this plan and make sure we get out of here safely."

Night had fallen. We had been granted a stroke of luck. Heavy clouds moved overhead, and there was little light to brighten the plaza. At night, Fire Peak did not live up to its name. Some far plazas and central areas looked like they held torches or fire pits to illuminate the area, but ours was limited to a handful of torches carried by our guards. As for the guards, they had changed twice, but had not seen fit to reduce their numbers at night. Rude.

Still, we had spread the word and arranged for everybody to go to sleep if they could. It would be the last chance for rest in a while. The guards were much less attentive now that their prisoners—or wards—were sleeping. Even so, twenty-two guards surrounded us in various states of attention. Wreil had also spotted watchers inside two buildings, farther away.

My attention had been somewhat scattered earlier on when I talked to the leader of the city guards. Knowing that my primary plan wasn't going to work had that effect, apparently. Even so, a handful of things stood out from the conversation. Especially the one detail: City guards were no pushovers. You wouldn't even be allowed to try for city guard trainee unless you'd hit level 10, *regardless of race*.

On top of that, they preferred the stronger, more martial races. They wanted people with the attributes to survive, who already had experience fighting. This meant that a fight wasn't going to be easy. We'd have to hit 'em hard and take 'em by surprise. One solace lay in the fact that the guards looking over us were trainees or at least lower-ranked guards. Few golden armors. There were no higher-ups, or we would have an even tougher fight on our hands.

It took a long time for my illusion to take hold. Even if the discipline was lacking in the guards, they still couldn't be entirely comfortable at having to take care of a dragon. This meant constant eyes on me. I was in no rush, though. Our only real deadline was dawn, and it was hours off. I was more concerned with doing it right.

Then, with no fanfare, the illusion took.

I almost lost it then and there, due to the surprise, but grabbed the threads of magic with a mental clutch and held tight. Then, I allowed myself to breathe regularly again. Slowly, ever so slowly, a huge grin grew on my face. We were ready. I could feel it. Right now, the few guards who were looking at us did not see us, but my carefully maintained disguise that overlapped the resting forms. Inside the illusion... Well, right now, there wasn't any real difference between the two images. We needed everything to calm down completely before we tried anything.

I settled into a more comfortable position. I was *not* going to rush things. As I lay, silent, I activated my Mana Manipulation. I wouldn't put it past Selys to leave some magical trap, some unseen trigger to catch us if we were to try anything untoward. Compared to the last time I'd really used it, my Mental Power and Mental Control were almost doubled, and I could feel the difference immediately. Without any form of effort on my part, I could stretch a thin, intangible finger of mana out and sense my surroundings, searching for any magical residues. I let it range out through the top of the ground for as far as it reached and covered almost half the courtyard.

To my relief, there was nothing to be found. No runic diagrams, arcane traps, or unexpected surprises. Now for the real test. One-by-one, I let the near-invisible pseudopod snake out through the dirt, then let it roam through the nearest guard. No reaction – Roth had been able to confirm that you couldn't feel the presence of the feeler. Nothing magical, either.

The next guard sported a dagger with a bit of magic inside. The fifth, a ring with a taste of... power. No, Strength. It probably boosted his Strength. The twelfth guard, a brawny Urten, however, was different. On a piece of string hanging on his armor rested a whistle that sang with magic. Standard procedure or Selys' paranoia – I didn't care. He would be the first to die.

It was a long wait. Still, I'd had plenty of practice maintaining an illusion over a long time on my past trek with the

Soul Carver. The only real issue here was the size and intricacy of the illusion. If I didn't keep up my focus, details would start to blur, and some of the guards might start wondering why they couldn't see the sleeping beasts clearly. Good thing that the size of the illusion didn't impact the cost, only the difficulty of maintaining it. Heh. The cost of 2 mana/minute, I could handle for a full day, if need be.

I checked over my stats before we got started.

[Personal Info:
Name: Onyx
Race: Young Shadow Dragon. Level 27 – experience toward next level: 8600/26000
Size: Very large

Stats and Attributes:
Health: 570/570
Mana: 910/910
Strength: 32
Toughness: 57
Agility: 80
Mental Power: 91
Mental Control: 122
Mana regeneration rate: 2074/day
Health regeneration rate: 57/hour]

I loved it. With my Mental Power increasing, I pretty much had the build I wanted. Mental Power enough to pack a magical punch, Mental Control high enough to keep it up pretty much forever, and Agility high enough to avoid most attacks. Of course, if Selys caught us tonight, that would do me a fat lot of good.

Peace remained over the plaza, and the guards mostly ignored us, chatting between themselves. They might be proficient in combat, but that didn't stop eight of them from starting an impromptu game involving tossing daggers near each other's feet. There were no other guards in range that I could see. After what felt like hours, I decided that we were ready. Most of the guards seemed to be completely convinced that we were sound asleep, and only the occasional glance at us showed that they were still on the job. Inside the illusion, I moved my tail sideways and silently prodded one of the resting Imps. He reached out and tapped the Talpus next to him, while slowly getting up.

The illusion held. I spared a moment to thank Deyra that my ability to see through my own illusions was extended to my minions as well, or this could've been a mess. Right now, for all the world to see, we were all merrily snoring away. Yet around me, the huge circle of minions who had been faking their sleep silently got up, except for the Clenchers, who were actually asleep with Eamus, the trainer, to keep them under control. Slowly, they reached for their belongings, arming themselves and moving outward in preparation. A few low noises arose, but nothing to give away the game. A silent minute later, there were no new sounds. Every ranged attacker was standing at the edge of the illusion right now, waiting. I grimaced. The timing on this was going to be a *bitch*.

The shadows around us were hard to work with. The torches in the plaza were far away, and I had to struggle to draw the darkness closer, pool it on the ground, fold it and make a huge circle... but I had time. A few grueling minutes later, it was ready. With a grunt from the mental effort, I *heaved* and all the way on the outside of the guards, a circle of magical shadows came alive.

It did nothing to any of the guards surrounding us, since the circle was cast behind them. In fact, some of them noticed right away that the lights from the city beyond faded and disappeared. Within seconds, however, the outbursts of confusion began, then were silenced.

Every single one of my ranged attackers and Imps rained death on the guards! Throwing spears, bolstered by Timothy's boost, flew true and hit the unsuspecting soldiers hard and fast, aiming for heads, elbow joints, backs–any spot that wasn't armored. Besides the spears, firebolts flew, lighting the targets on fire and outlining their silhouettes even as they burned. All around, rocks circled, striking from the sky to knock out any survivors. I stretched my neck and sprayed a Weakening Fog right at the Urten with the whistle, keeping my focus solely on him.

It wasn't silent. Our attacks were deadly, unfair, and surprising, but we didn't get them all. An Urten bellowed in pain from a spear to the shoulder, and a smaller beast cried out in mortal fear as his fur lit on fire. Still, the whistle-holder dropped like a log, removing the worst threat. The cries of pain from the remaining survivors bubbled into silence within seconds as my minions charged right at the unlucky guards and bore them down. Good. Now!

I ignored the headache coming on from the concentration and focused on the next part. We were so damn close. Now, all we needed was... I remade my illusion. Larger this time. I gritted my teeth as it pushed my control to the edge and... it was done. I dropped the shadow circle and sighed in relief as pressure receded a bit. It was still one of the largest illusions I'd ever made, but I could skimp on the details now. Time seemed to flood back in as the plaza went back to where it came from: guards standing around in a circle, keeping an eye on sleeping forms. Well inside the illusion, I squinted, on edge as I tried to get a sense of the rest of the plaza.

Wreil was the one who came with the verdict first. I recognized him by the click as he flicked his tooth necklace. It sounded loud in the silence. "We made it, Onyx. Nobody's reacting."

A wave of relief hit me. "Good. We can't relax yet, though. Let's clean up and get moving fast."

"Arthor's way ahead of you." He pointed, and I turned. True enough. Right there before us, an Urten seemed to sink into the ground, along with the cobblestones of the plaza. Within seconds, all that remained was the dirt itself, smooth and without a trace of the corpse. Wreil *sniffed*. "There's no getting rid of the smell. Anybody with half a nose will be able to smell the blood that's been spilled here. And we can't simply rearrange the cobblestones. Even so, it should confuse them quite well, keep them from spotting us right away."

I smiled. "We're not even started, though. Let Arthor and the shamans finish, then we can start *really* ruining Selys' day. Meanwhile, I'll rest a bit. This is going to be draining."

A few minutes later, we started moving. Not like we usually did, though, in combat formation, with everybody in the optimal position for a fight. No, this time we were all clumped up tight, walking as close as possible to present the smallest profile we could. Surrounding us all was a circle of shadows to keep any hostile eyes from glancing closer at us. The only people we allowed outside were Wreil and the scouts, half-hidden behind my Camouflage spells as they raced back and forth to plot a safe course.

We moved like that for what seemed like hours but may have been twenty minutes. Less. The burden of the illusion spell grew only stronger the further away we got from the plaza. A month ago, I wouldn't even have been able to leave the plaza while still maintaining the illusion. Now, with my Improved Spell Control and improved attributes, I managed. The weight still grew heavier with each step. The silence around us was heavy, only interrupted as scouts broke through the thin layer of shadows every other moment to inform us of the path to take.

"Hold to the left here. Somebody's still awake in the house on the right, and they have light."

"Wait. Somebody is crossing the street further along. It will be a minute, at most."

"There's three guards coming. We need to turn right down here."

At first, I was tense, keeping up with the terse instructions, but the further we moved, the more I retreated inside myself. The pressure *grew* as the illusion became harder and harder to maintain. At some point, I jumped at a touch and looked down to see Creziel touching my flank with a sympathetic look. "You're doing great, Onyx. We're there soon."

I grunted and doubled down. The mana cost from the illusion was quite alright. The distance, however, and the control needed... I half-closed my eyes, keeping my full attention on the illusion. *The shadows were simple to picture. Mine to command. I just had to grasp for them. And the torches like this. The contours of the bodies were harder. It would have to do. Grasp and tie it off, like this. The guards like so. Large, but immobile. No need for added complexity. Our people... relax here. I let them be blurs. Nobody could see from a distance. Now, flex and... hold.*

I had no clue how long the remaining walk took. It might have been minutes. Maybe half an hour. The next thing I noticed was when something nudged my leg. The web of the illusion unraveled as my eyes widened in a panic. "Godsdamnit, I-" I flailed and managed to maintain the shadow circle by a hair. As I opened my eyes, I glared at the offender.

The smiling face of Creziel stared right back at me. He pointed ahead of us. "We made it, Onyx."

He was right. Straight ahead of us was the wall surrounding Fire Peak. We actually did it.

CHAPTER TWENTY-EIGHT

Her roars were overwhelming. Bestial. Loud enough that you could hear them from outside the city. They were also way too late. Near the wall, I created another illusion, keeping ourselves unseen as we slowly eked closer. The shamans needed little time to expand a rough hole in the wall large enough for all of us to pass through. On the other side, we waited, anxiously, while they closed the hole behind us again.

We were almost to the edge of the cavern when we were found out. It might have been a guard change or somebody wondering how come the plaza was suddenly empty. Regardless of what the reason was, they figured out we were gone, and the news made its way into the center of the hill and up... up to the throne room and Selys.

We left by means of the tunnel the Talpi had created last time to spy on the Soul Carver. In theory, Selys shouldn't know of this tunnel, and we would be safe, for the moment—especially once we closed it after ourselves. By sealing up the city wall after us, we also hoped to confound any trackers as much as possible. As we crossed the plain, I had some of my minions break out torches. Then, I was finally able to drop the large illusion and call upon the shadows to guard our presence in the dark night. Not only did the shadows not cost me any mana, with my improved Shadow Control, they came easier to me than the illusions.

Now, as we made our way further into the tunnel systems beyond the crater, deep enough that the light wouldn't emerge into the cavern outside, I finally allowed myself to relax. I slumped on the tunnel floor as the shadows faded around us. All around me, my minions dropped, too, spent with the stress of the escape. Above, Creziel and Arthor worked in concert to seal off the entrance behind us.

Timothy stood right behind, staring as the walls slowly moved closer and huffed. "Well, that's a relief. I was never a fan of the whole 'take over the leadership of a few thousand psychotic murderers' scheme in the first place."

I refused to move from where I lay, head surprisingly comfortable reclined on two boulders. "Yeah, when you say it like that, *everything* is going to sound bad. Truth be told, I didn't exactly love it myself. Heh. You know, beggars and choosers."

He laughed. The laughter sounded the tiniest bit hysterical. "Yeah. And speaking of choosing, are you sure what we're about to do is the wise choice? Splitting up and all that?"

I raised my head wearily and gave him a lopsided smile. "No. I'm not sure. But the die is cast, and they all agreed. It feels right, too. We're going to piss off Selys then we're going to rig half the lower layer with traps to take her down when she comes. As soon as the wall's closed here, we're continuing... except for Arthor and a lot of the scouts."

He winced. "Yeah. I get it. And I get your reasoning, too. Still. I mean, killing a bunch of guards and running is one thing. The Soul Carver killed a lot of her minions when he fled, and Selys went after him with a vengeance, but... when she finds out what you're planning, Selys is going to *end* us."

I snorted a laugh. "I know. Well, she's going to try, at least. But we agreed to this. It's either flee from the mountain or try to take her down—and I'm not quitting."

"Spoken like a good old macho man. And you did manage to talk everybody into this. I still say you have a death wish. So, when she comes after us, brimming with fire, how do we take her down? You have a plan for that, of course."

"Not exactly a plan, as much as a to-do list. Lots of moving pieces. It's like... Okay, when the higher-ups give you the go-ahead to start on a new site, foundation, it's not like they have all the key workers and materials ready from the get go. You need to get started working on what you *can* do and plan for everybody to arrive when they're supposed to. Then you cross your fingers and try to fit everything together while you work. It's a puzzle, and something *always* goes wrong. You need to roll with the punches and adjust. If you want to wait to have every-thing in place, you'll never get anything done."

"Sure. Sure. I get the point. Except, if the project's delayed, you get fined or fired. Here, you get fired in the literal sense."

I smiled at him. "Heh. I've been threatened with being fired before."

"Carl." His vague form solidified, letting me see his eyes rolling.

"Don't you 'Carl' me. It's enough that my ex did it constantly!"

He barked a laugh. "Alright. Have it your way. Anything I can help with?"

"Not too much, at the moment. We're already trying to run damage control. In fact, I think some of the scouts already left. They'll tell the Dworgen and... well, everybody on the second layer, to run off. Otherwise, Selys is sure to use them against us."

"You think that'll even work?"

"I can't be sure. Depends on whether they're more afraid of Selys than of dying in battle, I guess. But we did beat them, and I doubt there's any love lost between Selys and them. Might work."

Companionable silence grew between us. Then I continued. "Wreil's off, too. I sent him to visit Creive again, tell him what's happening. We could use his help again for sure, and we're keeping the non-combatants there for the time being."

Tim nodded, then grimaced. He was getting *good* at grimacing. Too much practice, probably. "Good plan." He hesitated. "How about the final group? Sending off Arthor. Are you really going through with it?"

I grinned. "Are you serious? That's the best idea of the lot. She told me herself. The Blessing of Deyra flows through the exact center of the entire mountain, encapsulated in some vertical tunnel or other. If Arthor breaks that flow? No more fiery defenses working in Fire Peak. No more boosts to her attributes. No more fancy constructions. And she's going to be furious. Hopefully, so much she doesn't stop to think but simply flies off to kill us."

"That's... a pretty weird thing to hope for. But sure, in theory, it might work. And meanwhile, we're running off to fortify the domain and ambush Selys when she gets there." He sighed. "I can't believe you actually talked everybody into it."

"To be fair, they were under a lot of pressure at the time."

"Too true." He sighed again, a much-suffering sound. "And apparently, it's spreading. Now, since you evidently have a death wish, I'll have to stay close and make sure you survive."

"Awww. I love you, too, my tiny fog horn. Get it? Because you're see-through and noisy? Besides, it's not like I had any plans of letting you run off on your own. I need somebody around who can appreciate my wit."

He huffed. "Appreciate is such a strong word. But yeah, I'm hanging around. Let's call it temporary insanity. Or the fact that I don't know where else I'd go. Besides, at this point, I'm probably the only person in this world who knows how much the Dolphins suck. Somebody needs to tell you once in a while."

"Hey. Don't make me go Ghostbusters on your ass." I grew pensive. "I'm not suicidal, though. The odds aren't looking too good. I know that. And if worse turns to worst, we're definitely running. But fleeing and hoping for the best when we have a chance to make a difference? I won't do it."

His image grew crisp, and the serious expression on his face intensified. "I'm with you. This is a once-in-a-second-lifetime opportunity to do something important: create our own home with some real rules, not this dog-eat-dog crap. Besides, you won't be able to do it by yourself. You might need to use words with more than two syllables to convince some of the other races to join you, and we all know how well you do at that."

I snorted. "Insults aside... Thank you. It means a lot." His expression softened, and I continued. "Want... want a hug?"

"Screw you."

"Aw, don't be like that. High five?"

"I hate you."

CHAPTER TWENTY-NINE

"People talk about fight or flight? That's nonsense. It's fight and flight."
— *Amanda Bouchet, A Promise of Fire*

Our escape was the fastest we'd ever gone. The scouts knew the route almost by heart by now, where we could find water, even a few areas where farming on the run was an option. This time around, we didn't need to send people foraging. We still had a few stores to keep us going and the emergency stashes we left on the way up came as a godsend.

Morale was...mixed. We had just gone from several major victories to running for our lives. Roth, Creziel, Gert, Timothy, they all spent time trying to explain to everybody why the world had turned upside down. There were murmurs everywhere. My minion count was reduced by one, then three, as two Talpi and a Crawl slinked away during the run, deciding that it would be safer to seek safety with somebody who was not wanted by the Burning End.

I couldn't entirely blame them.

On the second day after we fled, it happened. It started as an almost imperceptible shiver in the ground under us. Then, a tremble followed, and a wave of light rose ahead of us and rushed over us all. In a split second, it passed, leaving me with a cold and warm feeling. The sensation waned as quickly as it had appeared. Still, I roared in triumph. "He made it! Arthor's disrupted the Blessing. Don't gawk. We need to hurry! Selys is sure to come after us now." Miles and miles and half a mountain separated us. But even so, in the distance, I swore I could hear the lingering echo of a roar filled with frustration and hatred. The rest of the tribe did not seem to think that earning Selys' enmity was such a positive thing, and we lost another Crawl that night.

We made it back safely. I hadn't dared to believe it. All the time, as we fled through the tunnels, cautious, on the alert for ambushes, I expected the call to go up that we had been spotted, that the first of Selys' forces had reached us. Instead, I could follow on the map in equal parts disbelief and relief as the tunnel systems around us got more and more familiar - and suddenly, we were there.

As I re-entered my domain, I viewed it with nostalgia. I had been here for such a short period, but I had missed the place. There was no time to reminisce over the good old days, though. We needed to get to work.

As my minions entered the throne room behind me, groaning from the heavy pace we'd maintained, I addressed them. In the background, they started spilling the items for the hoard back into its regular place and the notifications poured in.

"Alright, everybody. No time to relax. You can bring your stuff to your rooms, then we'll get to work immediately. Creziel, you know what to do. We need to get the place up and running and *fast*. Fortunately, we got most of the physical work done before we left. Still, there's a lot to be done, especially on the Gallery. Arthor will work on the main trap when he comes back.

"I know you'll have to move a lot of earth to get it done, so you had better get to it. You can decide where the builders need to go. Now, I know we had to leave this place before we were done, so we have a lot of unfinished business - especially for me. I have a lot of constructions to create. For you, we're going with quantity over quality this time. We need a *lot* of traps and surprises."

He assented and moved on, and I searched their faces for the other people I was looking for. "Roth. Good. I need you to get to training. Push them hard. You should focus on drills on... hey, what did you call it again, Timothy? Fighting while running away?"

The blue form settled in next to me, watching everybody arrive. "Tactical withdrawal? Or maybe strategic retreat?"

"Yeah. That's the one. Roth, we'll be facing overwhelming numbers here, meaning we'll need to run away a lot, but hurt them while we do so. Make sure that they bring in their main force."

Roth grunted, twirled his sword a couple of times, while he thought. "Hit and run? Ambushes? Nothing new to that. I'll push them hard, Onyx, don't worry about that."

"Good. We'll talk again soon. We will need to start sending out troops and scouts. We can't just wait for them here. You can get Arthor and talk that over too... No, wait. Arthor's not back yet. Ask Leith. Sorry. Too many moving pieces." I saw another Talpus aiming straight for her room and dismissed Roth. "Laive. Good to see you. I have bad news. You should prepare your room for an escape. Get anything that you want to keep ready. Regardless of what happens, we're not likely to come back here, so any soil or seeds you don't want destroyed, you'll have to bring with you."

She nodded. "I'm not stupid. I knew that all along. That's how things are. Talpi flee. I can have them ready in an hour. What else?"

"Your poisons. We will need them. All of them. Whatever you've got, we're going to use it. Maybe talk to Roth about who gets what and how to handle the poisons right."

"I will. Some will probably poison themself regardless, when they try to apply it. Like the Imps. Stupid beasts." Behind her disdain, there was a feeling of... was that concern? Surely not.

"Do your best, Laive. That's all we ask."

Laive returned to the flow of returning minions and I settled into place, watching them as they moved by. When I thought back to the group of dirty, bedraggled Talpi I'd found in a tunnel months ago, the difference was uncanny. Not only the physical differences, no. My minions moved with self-assurance, some even with grace. There was an air to them that spoke of people who knew what they were capable of and no longer feared any moving thing within the mountain. Good. We'd put that to the test soon.

Timothy interrupted my thoughts. "So, old man, riddle me this. You've probably gotten Selys truly mad now. She's going to come running with everything she's got. But you're talking about tactical withdrawal and strategic retreats and whatever soldiers like to call it, but not about fighting. Why *not* fight and hold? We've got a pretty impressive army here by now. I mean, we took down those guards pretty fast."

I smiled at him. "Good point. And sure, we've grown, man. We've got a lot of advantages and magic items and whatnot. But there's two simple reasons why it won't work. First is numbers. I know houses. I've worked on a number of large construction projects. And Fire Peak, even if the outskirts are mostly used for construction and storage, can hold thousands. My guess is somewhere between five and ten thousand."

"Ten... no way?"

"Yes. No more than ten, I believe. They're not likely to give proper housing to their slaves, but there was a lot of space that wasn't occupied. Now, if you spent a while thinking about it, you could probably crunch the numbers better than me. But it's not as completely overwhelming as that implies. Heh. We'd be screwed otherwise.

"I mean, of all those inhabitants, most are bound to not be fighters. Construction workers, hunters, butchers, you name it. Selys might bring them out as cannon fodder if they were attacked by an overwhelming force. Trying to bring them all on a week-long trek through the layers of the mountain, keeping them fed and watered and controlled and preparing them for assault? Nah. Not happening."

Timothy frowned. "But still. That leaves... maybe a thousand? A thousand soldiers about to attack us?"

"That's not likely. My estimate is that it's going to be on the low end. In the city, I learned that the number of actual soldiers, guards, and trainees is relatively small. In the hundreds. She's bound to bring a good percentage of them, as well as many of the other combat-ready inhabitants of Fire Peak. Then, like we talked about, she might pay a visit to some of the other large groups on the way and force them to join her attack.

"Still, think of it like this. Our scouts have already warned the three groupings on the second layer that Selys is going on the war path and leaving Fire Peak free for the taking. Who knows how they're going to act? Will the Dragonlings try to take the city? The Aberrants? Will they go elsewhere and try to not become a part of the battles? Will *we* try to make a run for Fire Peak?

"For every group of reinforcements that Selys *must leave* to guard her city, she'll have to weigh her odds. And she's going to have to leave a lot of forces to defend Fire Peak. Moving further down past the second layer doesn't really help her. We hit a good deal of the camps that were right on the route when we marched toward Fire Peak with the Soul Carver in the first place. We won't have to worry about those. So, my guess is that her actual number of forces is going to be a lot lower than her full numbers. Maybe five hundred."

"Five hundred." He repeated the words as if they tasted bad. "That's still enough to wipe us off the map."

"Exactly. We still might hold 'em, though. Dig in deep somewhere, stack the odds. It might work, if it weren't for the second reason."

"Selys?"

I grunted, agreeing. "Selys. And her sorcerer. Both of them

are horrible matchups for us. The Soul Carver told me how they'd managed to beat him. They simply torched him and his minions from afar. Everywhere they met. They refused to commit, instead burning his monsters and avoiding any close combat. We... can't answer that. So we're going guerilla tactics here. Hit and run, hurt 'em and fade away. And, most importantly, piss them off enough that they fall for our trap and decide to pour in to take us out."

Timothy didn't seem entirely convinced, but he nodded. "In that case, I'd better go talk to Lore. A couple of our ranged fighters leveled up from fighting those guards and haven't decided on their choices yet. They might be able to get [Sprint] if they choose right. That should be helpful for this kind of fight. I'll see you around, old-timer."

I smiled at the floating bag of air. Heh. Windbag. I'd have to remember that one for later.

The next couple of days, we drowned in work. We sent scouts out in force, along with groups of fighters to prepare the best ambush spots and plant some simple traps. The initial constructions in the lair were done quickly, but then we got to the *real* challenges. After two days, the trap layers started expanding beyond the domain, placing traps everywhere. Simple rope traps to trip and hurt. Poisoned spike traps, falling rocks. Anything to delay, hurt, and annoy. We started marking the safe approach to the lair after a clumsy Crawl triggered a trap, almost losing a hand in the process. Arthor returned from his side trip to the Blessing, but I barely had a chance to talk with him before he got to work.

Everybody who wasn't kept busy building or preparing? They trained. No exceptions. I smiled to see the Evolved Talpus pup join the older Talpi pups in the Training Chamber. According to Roth, he was uncannily coordinated for a pup of his age. I asked him to treat the pup the same as anybody else and moved on. That would be an opportunity for the future, if we survived. When. Damnit. I was going to be optimistic about this.

Creziel finished the rough work on the Gallery of Illusions. We talked about options, then he went on to focusing exclusively on expanding the traps. Usually, Arthor was the one I would go to when I wanted to discuss the larger plans outside of actual combat. But now, he was busy. He spent the entire time in the tunnel system beyond the Gallery of Illusions, toiling, working the soil and moving the dirt.

I watched him once, in passing. He stood, eyes closed, with his hands on a wall, completely absorbed in whatever he was doing. I couldn't *see* anything, but even so, my senses gave me the impression that *something* was happening. Almost imperceptible tremors from within our surroundings, like the feeling of movement you get when you're on the higher floors of a skyscraper in windy weather. I shook my head and moved on. This was a far cry from the simple pit traps we'd had when we first began working together.

Soon, the scouts started returning from meeting with the races on the second layer, one-by-one. They had all managed to deliver their messages without being killed, an accomplishment in itself. Their reports were a mixed blessing.

"The Dragonlings tried to jump me. Scaly goddamn bastards! I managed to tell them, and then they tried to eat me. Maybe they understood that killing some of us would earn them standing with Selys. Or they were just hungry."

"The Dworgen told me that they could not afford to get involved in this kind of conflict. Still, I have [Enhanced hearing], and they talked out in the open where I could overhear some. They were discussing the wisdom of spending some time mining for ore elsewhere. We may not have to deal with them."

"The Aberrants did not respond. But they thanked me for the information. I am unsure what that means, Onyx."

That was... good news? Probably. If two out of three groups decided that joining the attack on us wasn't in their best interest? That would mean that Selys would have to account for them, maybe keep back a sizable part of her guards.

At a certain point, Arthor returned from his work and

started helping with the traps with little fanfare. He'd done his job. The main trap was ready.

As for me, I was on construction duty. And supervision. There were not many constructions that would help us here, but I constructed anything I could get away with. I maxed out the number of Shadow Towers, built an Outpost, then another Outpost, then... stalled. The Outpost was nice and useful, but that was really the last combat-oriented construction I could come up with. I could theoretically make one more Outpost, but with the battle plans we had, only two would be really efficient, since we'd attempt to focus our fights inside the Domain on two spots.

[Outpost.
With the growth of lairs, the need for guards and defensive positions increases as well. This construction allows you to define a spot where your minions will be more effective in combat.
Regardless of the name, this construction can be positioned anywhere within the domain. It adds a field, giving a slight boost to the physical attributes of all minions within range and mildly decreasing those of any hostiles.
2/3 Outposts created
Size of field: 25 x 25 yards
Mana cost: 350
Construction time: 36 hours]

The only construction I had yet to attempt was an Illusion Defense

[Illusion Defense.
This construction comes in the form of an illusion generator, covering the entire Domain. It can hide any entrances to your Domain, envelop your lands in shadow, and severely impact the detection ranges of any hostile domains.
Mana cost: 500

Construction time: 96 hours]

While it was lovely, it would also be a waste of mana right now. Too little, too late. They knew exactly where we were hiding. The only reason to build it would be to try to upgrade the hoard in time for their arrival, hoping to get some amazing upgrades. It was either that or enchant more weapons, create mana crystals, and stock up on throwing spears for my ranged fighters. In the end, I opted for the safe gains and started enchanting. I simply didn't think Selys would give us the time.

Wreil returned triumphant, alone, from visiting Creive. He was covered in dirt and sweat and reeked to high heaven as he stumbled into the domain. All the same, he laughed and smiled. "I did it, Onyx."

Enchanting was second nature to me by now. Nevertheless, I wanted to be entirely sure that I understood this right and laid the weapon aside. "Creive agreed to help?"

He flicked his necklace, beaming. "Yes. He agreed to keep an eye on all descents from the upper layer except the main one. That's not all, though. I couldn't talk him into going up against Selys *and* her main army. That was simply too much for him."

One side of my mouth quirked up. "Can't entirely blame him for that."

The lanky scout grinned. "So, I talked him into roaming the place instead and taking on any stragglers and small groups he might meet... and send somebody with a message if they sent any larger forces."

I slammed a claw into the tiled floor. "Hah. That's excellent work, Wreil. This way, we can keep our focus entirely on her main group! What was the final cost of it? What do we have to do for old Bluey?" The emotions stemming from Wreil were exuberant, bubbling with anticipation. "Wait. Why have I got a sense that you're still holding something back?"

The message spilled from him in a burst of self-satisfaction. "Because I am! It was so easy! Creive may be strong, but he has no concept of worth. We agreed to five Mana Crystals, to be delivered after the battle. Also… I convinced him to tell us about his feats and attributes."

I blinked. Then chortled. My mouth lolled open in disbelief. "Oh, I am looking forward to hearing that story. For now, though, let's fetch Timothy. This is going to be amazing!"

The hours flew by with constant, feverish activity. Moods were starting to get tense. People were snapping at each other, working in any waking moment. Time was ticking, and every-body was aware of it. I chanced upon Creziel and Arthor, who were standing near a Training Chamber, arguing. As I walked closer, a furious Talpus passed me by. He turned around, blazing with anger, and delivered some scathing reply to the two shamans before striding off.

Arthor sneered at the Talpus then dismissed him. He talked to me. "The nerve of some wastrels. All Raivel knows is carrying dirt, and now he wants to lecture me on strategy? Me? Pfah!" He growled at his retreating back. I took a good look at Arthor. He looked… ill, feverish even. The skin of his face was pale, and his fur was sodden and matted with dirt. For once, his rocks lay unmoving at his feet instead of buzzing around him. And he *reeked*. He nearly stumbled as he fixed me with his eyes. "I'm done, lizard. The large traps are done. In the Gallery and outside."

"Excellent. You're incredible! Now, when we're done here, you need a break, Arthor. You look like death."

He waved away my suggestion. "I am fine. We need to prepare more. I have been helping Creziel with his traps. He is precise, but he's so *slow*."

I looked at the traps. It was a leather bag, filled with… spikes. Simple as that. Tiny stone spikes, about four inches long. They weren't even edged, but did look like they had a nasty point to them. "What is the plan with those? I would think that you'd need a good handful of those to bring down anything, unless you hit an eye."

Creziel knelt, smiling, and picked up one of them. "It was my idea. First, we take a spike, like this." He slammed the end into the ground and frowned, squinting at the precariously placed pointed end. The floor flowed, burying the lower part of the spike with maybe two inches protruding from the earth. Then he sprinkled some dirt over the spike. "There. It's difficult to spot, and the point is tiny enough that it should be able to penetrate most feet. Then he pointed at a stone container and a simple fur brush. Handling the closed container like it was death itself, keeping his paws steady, he held it up. "This is one of Laive's poisons. We brush a layer on the tips - carefully - and then we take great care to not impale ourselves. Whoever is wounded by one of these will not be able to join any fight any time soon. The Blood Purge will take care of that."

"Blood Purge." I repeated. "You know, I don't even want to know. But is it effective?"

He nodded. "Slow-working, but horribly effective. You will live, but for a few days, you will wish that you had not." He indicated the opening where the retreating Talpus had left. "To be honest, that is probably the reason Raivel was incensed. Going up against Selys' forces scares him, as it does most of us, but he does *not* enjoy handling the poison."

He shrugged. "Regardless, it has to be done. We will leave shortly. We are taking a longer route out this time around. There is only one descent from the higher layers nearby, and I want to have them hitting traps steadily from then on. Then, once I'm done with that, we have found a place that we are going to pay extra attention to."

"That sounds like a great idea. Please talk to Roth. We need everybody to know where the traps are. Also, I want you to be sure that you're coordinating, so the ambushes are timed well with the traps to the best effect."

Arthor's mental voice was oozing with sarcasm. "Oh, traps should work *together* with ambushes? Who knew? How good that we have you to tell us how to best handle *what we have done for our entire lives*."

"Sarcasm ill becomes you, Arthor. In fact, no, that's not right. You're pretty damn good at it. But you need sleep. And that's an order. We don't want you to keel over in the middle of the attack."

"I thought we were going to decide everything as a group?"

Wow. He *was* tired. That was as close to whining as I'd ever heard from him. Ah, well. If it worked with my daughter, it would work here, too, when she tried to pull the old "I'll go ask Mom" on me. "You want me to talk to the Council? Explain to them *in detail* how you're being too stubborn and prideful to take care of your body's needs? Because I will."

He glared at me. "You're a pest, you know that?"

I smiled. "Maybe. But it's for your own good. Now, are you done with the spikes? I want your opinion on something before you go to bed."

CHAPTER THIRTY

Unfortunately, time proved me right. We did *not* have the days we wanted. I was enchanting a few throwing spears when it happened. The rumor made its way to me by way of a group of agitated workers yelling, panicking. Their stories didn't match up. They were incoming. The scouts had clashed with the first attackers. We were lost. No, we had beaten them back, but took heavy losses. No, it was a flawless win.

Wreil and Arthor were arguing in the throne room when I entered. "They're coming?"

Wreil glared at Arthor, who in turn ignored him and addressed me. "Yes. They were morons, believing that we wouldn't be ready for them. Mostly fliers, and our ranged attackers had the place well-prepared. They wiped them out."

I smiled, relieved. "Well then, why—"

Arthor continued, "Then *this* moron decided that they could handle everything by themselves, and left them alone to run home to safety. I'm just telling him what I think of him."

Wreil exploded. "That is not what happened! I am the fastest of us, and you needed a full explanation right away so we could react properly. Besides, Leith is back there to take care of things." I inclined my head to Wreil, waiting for him to continue. Mollified, he glared at Arthor, then faced me again. "The Dragonlings joined forces with Selys. We managed to overwhelm the first group, and we removed most signs of our attack. Still, we might be outmatched in the air, and we need numbers, now."

"You'll have it. Arthor, knowing the Dragonlings have joined in is valuable—and being informed fast even more so. Wreil chose well." I grimaced, then continued. "Do we have injured?"

The scout nodded tersely. "Only a few. They can still fight."

"Once you've run back to them, I want you to send the wounded back from their positions. The rest of us will be following. Every single person who is ready to fight. We'll create a backup camp, along with the Ergul and our reserves. That way, instead of risking wounded and tired fighters, we can heal them, rest them up, and rotate them out again. They'll be nearby in case the help is needed. Let's turn this into a proper grindstone." The ugly blob had finally become a minion the day before. The Ergul took up a full 8 minion count, leaving us at 112, but I'd have sacrificed triple that for the life-saving chances it gave us. I asked Wreil, "Can they surround us? Attack from elsewhere? They're likely to have the numbers to overwhelm us if that happens."

He gave a curt shake of his head. "I don't think so. Not with Creive on the prowl. Also, the nearest path to the higher layers would add several additional days to their travel."

I bowed my head, then raised my mental voice, letting everybody inside the domain hear what was coming to pass. "Selys' forces are descending to the lower layer now. Be prepared. All fighters will be moving out soon. You know what you're supposed to do. Roth, please come to the Throne Room. We will plan our excursions now, then leave."

Having said that, I moved to the side of the room, projecting my map of the lower layer, large enough to fill up half of the wall. We would be able to use that for the details.

"Arthor, one question? We have lost another two since yesterday?"

He grimaced. "Yes. Raivel and another. Even with all our plans and preparations, they apparently feared Selys enough that they would rather risk the mountain by themselves. Cowards."

I grimaced. Raivel was one of the builders, and lately, trap layer. Steady, always in motion. Dependable. I never thought he'd defect. I forced a sardonic smile on my face. "Listen to you, Arthor. Calling somebody a coward for not wanting to tangle with the mightiest dragon in the mountain?" My grin died, and I continued, somber. "I can't even say they don't have the right idea. But, I think we are doing what we need to. And even if we fail in the end, I'll make sure their forces are hurt enough that Selys won't have the spare soldiers to go out looking for us if we flee."

The next minutes were loud, controlled chaos as a lot of people converged on the throne room, anxious to hear what was going on. They were summarily arranged into groups or told to get back to work. A few were then sent off immediately, while others stayed, waiting for orders.

Roth stood, discussing with Arthor and Wreil. "So, there weren't too many in the first group. A group of eight, Dragonlings and Culdren."

Arthor spat. "Accursed Dragonlings. Of course, the bloodthirsty beasts had to join Selys."

I winced, then growled. A moment's focus opened the map, then expanded it to the nearby wall, visible for all to see. "They'll pay for that decision. Question is what Selys sends now. Wreil, any help from a scout's perspective?"

Wreil tapped the tunnels near the ascent to the higher levels. "With the races we've seen, I believe she'll send more fliers at first. Depends on their numbers, though. They might simply triple their number of fliers and try to overwhelm us, or they may send some stronger forces forward to accompany the scouts."

"Arthor, anything to add?"

"Yes. I believe she will go for numbers. The Burning End cares little for her minions."

I nodded. "Agreed. So, we need to be prepared for mixed units. We'll also need to have people standing by so we can adapt to different scenarios, though. So, we send Grex and some of the faster Imps, ranged attackers... what else?"

"I'll be at the front." Roth flexed, beaming.

"Good. I'll adjust the professions again, make sure those at the front are as strong as we can make them."

He nodded. "I'll take the two Crawls with [Sprint] too, a couple of Clencher riders. Make the Clenchers into Fighters. Also, I'll take that blue blur of yours, if he agrees. With them, we should have the speed we would need to escape if it's needed and the strength to hold back the worst of them. Can you handle the rest? Make sure you send in reinforcements as they're needed?"

I smiled. "You think I'll stay here in safety? I'll be right at the backup camp, ready for if we need to hurt them or to ensure we won't be overwhelmed. I'll try to stay out of sight as well as I can, though. If they spot me, Selys is bound to join the battle." I growled. "Make sure to not overextend, and don't take risks, if you can help it."

Arthor scoffed. "Pfah. For somebody who wasn't born a year ago, you sure try to act like a parent."

I grinned. "You're a weird family, but... it still counts."

He rolled his eyes, but didn't say anything. "This leaves us with about half our fighters on the reserve. Are we keeping them back entirely?"

"No. The rest of the Crawls and the Clencher riders will be with me in the backup camp. The ones who need more time to recuperate will go back to the cavern we prepared." I pointed on the map to an innocuous-looking cave, lit up from the presence of some of my people. "Here. Then we keep retreating, and if they make it this far, we'll join forces and put the hurt to them. You make sure to make them mad."

Roth's eyes burned with an inner fire as he hefted his sword. "Oh, I can do better. I've already tangled with you, Onyx. It's time to test myself against somebody *really* strong."

I huffed. "Knock yourself out. Only... please don't go up against Selys by yourself."

Soon, we took off. The frontrunners left us behind, hurrying to reinforce our ambushers. This time, the feeling in the air was different. As we walked, the discussions and squabbling had stopped and there was a sensation of... expectation. Oh, and fear too. Plenty of fear. That sensation lingered, even as we marched rapidly for almost six hours before settling down, creating an interimistic backup camp minutes away from our fighters. Here, we would be ready to react to what happened. If only it had been close enough for a final Outpost, but no... this was far outside my Domain.

We waited while I cursed at being downvoted once more. Initially, I'd argued that I would take part in the battles, but the idea was shot down repeatedly. They didn't want to risk everything collapsing because I happened to overextend, or lose myself to battle frenzy again. I could only grumble and bear it. Around me, the uncertainty was ever-present. Uncertainty and a question. You could almost taste it hanging in the air. *Can we do this? Can we really do it?* The minutes passed without any call for reinforcements, and the wait grew into hours. Then, the answer came... in the form of wounded.

I watched them coming through the corridor. Wounded Talpi running despite their wounds. Imps chittering, unable to keep quiet as they flew. I saw Grex doing a weird, stumbling kind of one-legged run, howling with a furrow of deep cuts down his back. Why the hell hadn't they called for backup? I prepared for the worst as they moved closer, glacially slow. When they came closer, however, I heard it. Grex wasn't howling with pain. It was *laughter*. And somehow, regardless of everything, that was the sensation they brought with them. Elation. Satisfaction. *Pride.*

Grex aimed straight for me and sank to one knee next to

me. The wound of his missing leg looked good - better than the rest of him, at least. He didn't mind any of his wounds, though, new or old. "Onyx, you should have *seen* it. There were so few of them to begin with. We ruined them. Then, they kept coming, on and on. Larger waves each time. So stupid! They wanted to fight us close. Did they not see our wings?"

Wreil was there, too. He was cradling his arm. The shoulder looked... ugly. Like something had bit down on it. Still, his weak grin didn't waver. "How could they see your wings from way down there on the ground?" He snorted, then addressed me. "They were mostly ground troops, Onyx. Scouts, lightly armored, same as us. Not ready for a battle. They should have run." Then he turned back to Grex. "The Dragonlings did see your wings... right before they ran into our throwing spears, right? Funny that the armor on the wings is so light, right? Spears punch *right* through." He made a piercing motion, then winced.

Grex bobbed his head eagerly. "Yes! That was fun! And then they saw our fire. They did not miss that." He chortled.

Wreil grew somber for a moment. "Still, it is a good thing you were ready to help, Onyx. There were many. Not too many for us, but close. We hit them hard, three times. But it cost us, some. I doubt there are many fliers yet, but we will be moving back. You need to move the camp."

I nodded. "We'll move camp, then rest. The Ergul is with us. He'll take care of you once we're safe. Rest then. You've earned it. How about the rest of our people? Roth?"

"He is still there, along with the unhurt ones. He will be pulling back soon, ready for the next ambush."

"Good to hear. Do you need my help? Any sign of Selys?"

"No, we can handle it. Nothing from Selys so far. Now, unless you have anything else, we need to get going."

I acquiesced. Within seconds, the camp was ready to move. The Ergul handled Grex and Wreil's injuries. Wreil would be fit to rejoin the battle soon, Grex would not. Grudgingly, he started the long way back to the domain. Wreil promised they would be quicker to send for help next time.

Soon, we had the next temporary camp installed while, ahead of us, our people fought for their lives.

The next day was a blur of constant movement and snap decisions. The Ergul earned its weight in gold and leveled up twice as wounded fighters were healed and rotated back into the retreating defenses. Our backup camp did its work many times over, allowing us to swap in attackers to overwhelm and change the setup on the enemies.

We pulled back all the time, sometimes at a run, in order to stay away from the front. Twice, Roth called for me to intervene, and I moved up to help with their ambushes when the incoming groups were too large. Twice, we hurt them badly, illusions cutting them off from their reinforcements, their forces crushed as our combined might ambushed the enemy forces. Still, every time, I moved back to the back-up camp. We did not want to push them into a concentrated attack too early.

We started losing people. The Ergul's energy was low, and even with an unlimited supply of meat, it couldn't keep up the deeper heals. Our ambushers started slipping. My minion count dipped lower by one, then three. Yet more than that had to stop fighting entirely, retreating to the domain. Over a long stretch, our forces spread thin. But if the protracted battles were costing us, it was even worse for Selys' soldiers.

Wreil dipped back to tell us to retreat again. "They are becoming smarter. They move in larger numbers now, mixed forces. We need to pull back and then commit."

I swallowed at the thought of it. "Are you sure? It's earlier than we planned."

"Roth seems to think so. He's ready for the big push, as we planned. You need to retreat past the central chamber. Everything has been prepared. Then, if you can, create a huge illusion that shows an innocent cavern, and keep it up until they're inside. We'll want the enemies unprepared for what we've readied for them. If this fails, we can only fall back to our domain."

I nodded and looked around me at the two Crawls who were resting from the deep wounds they'd suffered. Within minutes, we were fleeing again while Wreil moved back to the fight, preparing for the pushback.

I finally had a chance to see the true numbers that Selys had sent against us, and it was chaos. These might not be the crack troops that defended Selys' fortress, but they were still strong enemies.

The terrain looked innocuous and familiar. In fact, it was the exact same tunnel we'd used to take out the Dweeler tribe, what seemed like ages ago. Wide, tall and relatively clear, it was perfect for our purposes.

The few remaining Dragonlings were attacking from a distance, unleashing elemental damage on my forces from the far side of the large cavern. Urten advanced slower, shields and armor keeping the worst of the damage at bay. Other races were everywhere, adding to the confusion. Crawls, Stick Kin, even Hevrons and some type of snake people.

It wouldn't be too bad if they were like in some games, nameless, predictable enemies, each race having only one or two abilities. But these were leveled-up fighters. Each of them held feats, skills or magical abilities to aid them. The ability to self-heal. A supernatural capability to dodge, if only for half a minute. Like our own people, the enemies were far from power-less, and they were charging in their scores, throwing in everything in the attempt to overwhelm us.

Our position looked dire. We were entrenched behind rough defenses at the far end, defenders firing from behind rocks and boulders, desperately unleashing what they had.

The moment the Dragonlings moved in closer to capitalize on our poor positions, I let the illusion drop. The boulders turned into earthen barricades, hardened and almost vertical. Wide and solid, with the glow of an Outpost buffing our forces surrounding the construction. On top, my forces unleashed hell on the fliers, dropping them from the skies.

The ground forces, enraged that they'd been cheated, charged in. That's when they discovered the real threat of the long, wide cave. Because if Creziel had spent a lot of time trapping the tunnels, he and his builders had practically lived right here. A floor that had already been uneven and broken had been turned into something even worse. Pit traps. Poisoned spikes. Falling rocks. The ground, the ceilings, the very *walls* couldn't be trusted. And, if you managed to make it to the far side of the cave, you'd still have to climb the barricade with an enemy that was ready to cause you pain for every inch of ground you'd win.

This time, we stood together. I'd managed to convince them of this much. If we were to make them pay, I had to be a part. Timothy and the Outpost boosted our attributes as all ranged fighters unleashed their payloads on the invaders. I shrouded areas in darkness, causing enemies to fall into traps, dropping them with my breath attack when they moved closer.

We held them. We actually did it! Three times, they swarmed against us, and we threw them back. There were not many flying enemies left, and they brought few ranged attackers, allowing us to cause them to suffer all the way toward us. Our Imps were death incarnate, keeping up a constant barrage of fire that soon had the floor covered with bodies. Still, the attackers kept on, regardless of traps and a staggering death toll. And it happened. In the background, we heard *her*. A dragon's roars egged on her forces, driving them into fits of frenzy.

When they reached the barricades, Roth kept them off. Crawls on his flank, the squat Talpus was indomitable, throwing back anybody who braved our defenses. They still came on, dying by the dozens just to reach us. We started losing people, though. Defenders dropped back and out of the battle, too injured to continue.

And still we held them, killing them from afar, weakening them and grinding them down. In the end, they started falling back, their forces unable to break through. We laughed at their backs, giddy with elation. Then *he* came.

This time, there was no end to the wounded. I counted them. Five. Ten. Twenty. More. They kept streaming by in ones and twos. This was not the controlled flight of the first group. These fighters fled, running without looking back, sprinting, with not a thought for anything but what was chasing them. Bleeding and broken, they fell back. I did not stop them. I merely paid attention to see if anybody needed the aid of the Ergul before we could start falling back to the lair.

There was a group of Imps, flying faster than I thought possible, looking mostly unhurt. There were two Clencher riders, mounts and riders liberally covered with wounds. Two of them shared a few words, turned, and charged back down the corridor. The others fell back, too spent to fight on. The rest continued. Good.

I had ordered them to pull back the moment I spotted the sorcerer, but he had still torched us. If we had been the least bit slower, he could have torched half our forces. As it stood, many ran with painful, oozing burn wounds, but we'd made it away.

The wall of flame that filled the place was still there if I closed my eyes, though. And we hadn't even seen Selys yet. I shuddered. There was one consolation. We now knew she had come. The plan was viable! Not only that, but even with the numerous wounded, we had gained a lot in the process.

Since I hadn't spent that much time on the front lines right until in the end, most of the others had gained more experience than I did, but I'd still gained a full 18,300 experience there. On top of that, 1650 additional experience bleeding over from Creive told me he was keeping busy as well. Every single one of my surviving fighters was gaining in levels, growing stronger for every fight, and I was no exception. I hit level 28 and, with a wince at the memory of the wall of flame, threw all five points into Toughness. I had a hunch I'd need it. For now, I could smile at the thought that we'd grown, while Mordiel's forces had experienced nothing but losses.

Mordiel! I knew his oath compelled him to do it, but couldn't quite contain the sensation of betrayal. Regardless of our talks, of how he'd warned me, he had stepped up and torched the entire cave, waves of flames burning and hurting my people. Suddenly, we were the ones fleeing, badly wounded with the enemies right at the back. I had to remind myself that it wasn't his own desire to attack, and he had no choice with Selys right there.

A young Crawl dropped to the ground next to me. He grunted as he peeled at an oozing burn wound. He looked at me, pain in his eyes. "They come soon. Cannot fight anymore. You fight them off!"

I called the Ergul, mentally pointing him at the Crawl. "We can't fight them off here. Don't worry. This was part of the plan, though. We'll make sure they regret coming at us! You stay here, rest a bit, help others who are worse off, if you can. I will aid in the retreat. The next time we fight, it'll be in the center of our home, and we will finish them!"

While I said the words filled with bravado, I didn't feel self-assured. We'd been doing so well, and we'd *hurt* them. Really. But we hadn't even made Selys come forth. If we couldn't even beat Mordiel, how would we ever succeed with our plan? I gritted my teeth. Poor Mordiel. I should have done something about him before I left. I didn't like it, but I would have to hurt him, enough to have Selys risk her neck. I left to rejoin my retreating forces to help protect them as they fled.

CHAPTER THIRTY-ONE

"It's not that I'm so smart, it's just that I stay with problems longer." -
Albert Einstein

They had reached our home. In the distance, roars and cries heralded the first wave of attackers, and the map confirmed it. The leading enemy soldiers were running through my halls, and they looked *pissed!* My mental message rang out into the domain. "If you're not able to get into position within the next two minutes, you need to move to the exit right now."

I blinked the map away and glanced around me. The Gallery of Illusions was crowded. All surviving Crawls and Talpus close-range fighters were slumped on the ground, taking the last chance to rest before the attackers hit. Two Clenchers and their riders were still able to fight, and Ursam rubbed my flank affectionately.

Next to me were Timothy and a severely singed Roth. He had retreated as one of the last fighters, ranging out again and again to make the attackers think twice about following right behind. I shook my head in amazement. "I can't believe you ambushed a group of Urten by yourself. Is it even called an ambush if there's just one attacker?"

Roth held a water skin up and tipped his head back. He gulped down the liquid eagerly, letting half of it run over his fur, drenching him and washing away soot, blood, and other, nastier residues. At least it looked like not too much of the blood was his own. He sighed, exhaustion wafting from him, and shook his head. Droplets flew all over me. "No. If a Talpus attacks more than one Urten, it's usually called suicide." He grinned. "Those bastards'll have to find new words after today, I'm sure. I mean, they're strong and all, but so *slow!*"

I smiled and addressed them all. "Today's not about suicide. It's not about defending at all costs, either. We need them to expose themselves. First the sorcerer, Mordiel, then Selys. So, we stand here and make them pay for every inch of ground. You've already done it once, and with the Gallery, it will be easier. And once they make the wrong move... we make them pay!"

Shouts of assent and war cries rang out throughout the Gallery. From inside the walls, movement was visible through every single murder hole next to the Shadow Towers. Above us, Imps dominated the air, turning an upward glance into a confusing whirlwind of motion. On either side of me, two magical circles glowed on the floor. I'd moved both the Essence siphon and the Outpost in here to aid in our defense.

I could see the effects of the Outpost - a solid boost of ten percent to all attributes. The Essence Siphon was still inactive, though it stood ready. The fresh blood grooves the young shamans had carved trailed out from the center of the magical creation like a particularly thirsty sun. Once it kicked in, it was going to do a hell of a difference. In short, we'd tipped the scales as much as we possibly could. If we couldn't hold them back here...

Timothy pronounced my unspoken feelings as he floated closer to me. "What the hell are we going to do about that sorcerer bastard?"

I growled "Leave it to me."

"What? But he'll torch you."

I checked the map once again and snarled. We were running out of time. I expanded my mental message to include everybody nearby. "The sorcerer is *mine*. We work together and we beat them back, but the moment the human sorcerer comes forward, I want you all to move back to the throne room and await my orders. I'll handle things.

"Now, get ready. They will arrive in less than a minute. Everybody move back. We want to give the Gallery a chance for its effects to come into play, then we hit them." A few of them yelled or squeaked, ready for battle. I growled and glared around at my minions, my people, my *responsibility*.

"So, they underestimate us because we are small and weak? Today, we'll teach them a lesson. We will show the Scoured Mountain what we can do when we work together!" A roar built up from within my throat, building until it nearly shattered the ears of those nearby. And I roared, my mental shout reaching for the heavens, miles above. "Let them come! Let them bleed! Let it be known: *They can't hold us down!*"

They roared their approval at this. Talpi, Crawls, and Imps united in their fury, bellowing their defiance at the incoming armies. And into this cacophony of noises, they came.

Selys' forces charged. Before, according to my defenders, they had attacked with abandon, eschewing tactics, knocked out of any sense of order from traps and constant ambushes. Now, knowing that they had arrived at their destination, they attacked in an orderly fashion. Ranks of armored forces approached the Gallery.

These weren't the random beasts they'd sent at us until now. These were the Guards. They didn't quite walk in step–their military decorum only went so far–but they did keep their formation and had large defensive fighters on the front, with others I assumed were ranged fighters or mages lurking behind the front ranks. Not everybody looked good. In fact, quite a lot of them were wounded or carried themselves like they were sick or in pain. Courtesy of Laive's poisons. They poured into the room, tens at the time, ready to take us on and... kept moving straight on, ignoring our forces moving in on all sides. They would, of course, given that every single one of my people was hidden behind a veil of illusion.

From the center of their formation, a panicked shout rose up. So, somebody in there did have the Mental Power to at least partially see through my illusions. Heh. I wasn't going to let them use it. With a glance and a mental nudge, I flicked the tiny, intangible switch on the Gallery of Illusions and activated its effects. And, in a second, the world went nuts.

The attackers suddenly exploded into action. Nothing coordinated about this, though. No, this was pure chaos, a hundred different people bursting into as many varied actions as the effects of the Gallery of Illusions hit them differently. Some simply ground to a stop, confused or doubting whatever their mind was attempting to tell them. Others attacked some intangible foe, lashing out with physical attacks or spells. A few blinked with half-closed eyes as if trying to see through the illusions.

I didn't give them the time. My Weakening Fog was the first attack to impact. With my increased Mental Power, it tore through their ranks, leaving attackers dropping to the floor or heavily weakened with its effect. At the heels of my breath attack, the entire room burst into motion. Throwing spears filled the air alongside fiery missiles from the Imps zipping around under the tall ceiling. As rapidly as possible, I mentally selected each Shadow Tower, and they started unleashing their weakening barrages from above.

Toxic clouds erupted where clay containers hit, releasing harmful contents, courtesy of Laive. The area where they entered was instantly turned into a killing ground as the attackers were struck from all sides. They didn't take it lying down. Regardless of the effect of the illusions or their Mental Power, they continued on, attacking with abandon. Within moments, almost every single attacker was doing *something* to try to answer our onslaught.

It just didn't work. At this point, my close combat fighters were well-trained and powerful. The pincer maneuver they pulled off as they ranged around on either side to enclose all the charging enemies looked effortless. A Crawl lashed out with his spear to trip a charging Urten, instantly moving forward to face another attacker, while a Talpus right behind him jumped in to slit the downed fighter's throat. Within a couple of heartbeats, the Talpus was back on her feet behind the Crawl again.

It wasn't perfect. Initially, very few of the attackers could see through my own illusions, but their effects burst the moment we went on the attack. Mid-combat, the Gallery's illusions were less powerful, too. At least one in three of the attackers had the mental attributes to resist at least part of the effects. And while the first group was slaughtered in a matter of minutes, reinforcements kept pouring through the entrance.

I roared out, "Move back. Follow the plan!" I'd been very clear on the approach. "Don't get trapped. Let ranged attackers and towers weaken them first, *then* strike." Following up my words with action, I let my Weakening Fog envelop a dozen newcomers, grinning as almost a full squad of Urten dropped senseless to the ground. That would never grow old.

We suffered losses. I grimaced as a trio of Crawls overextended. Suddenly, they were surrounded by enemies, fighting for their life to move back to the relative safety of our ranks. They were too numerous to contain. A small group of lightning-wielding attackers moved at incredible speed, starting to threaten our flanks. A stray attack from them caused an Imp to drop from the heights in the middle of a group of enemies. The blast of lightning stunned the Imp, and I was unable to retaliate before the Imp was torn apart by the battle-frenzied beasts. I instantly retaliated, landing a Shadow Whorl into the center of the gathering of fragile fighters. Within moments, two Clenchers smashed into the group, barreling them over.

The battle raged back and forth for a while. The constant

reinforcements threatened to overwhelm us, but we fought cautiously, trying not to overextend, letting our enemies move themselves into trouble. I weakened as many as I could, and I noticed my ranged fighters and Imps starting to single out the invaders who managed to see through the illusions.

The rest of them were... not easy pickings, but fighting an enemy who was essentially blinded or fighting an illusion was easier than somebody out to kill you. And the Outpost combined with Timothy's boost... I watched as Roth, touched by one of a dozen of Timothy's boosting pseudopods, whirled and sawed through the arm of an enemy Urten, before he moved past and grabbed the other arm, *throwing* the enemy fighter back into the center of their forces. The little bastard was half his size, and he tossed the large beast like he'd been a baseball.

The illusions, our boosts, traps, and hidden fighters–they all combined to grant us a huge advantage. Our attacks came in harder, we dodged a little faster in every single struggle.

Meanwhile, the Outpost did the opposite for the enemies, weakening and slowing them ever so slightly. Without it, I believed that we might have faltered. As it stood, the invaders painted the cavern floor red as they entered, fought, and died in quick succession. Now, on top of that, the Essence Siphon grew in size and tapered over, starting to send its life-giving essences my way and healing any cuts I suffered. As soon as that happened, I moved further forward in the lines, accepting wounds that closed almost immediately. The battle didn't last long. Three minutes. Five at the most. It felt like an eternity, however, one where my every focus was on the enemy and could mean the difference between life and death.

As suddenly as they had arrived, the remaining attackers turned and fled. With screams and roars, they caved and *broke*, running for the exit. There weren't many left in the cave at this point–three dozen perhaps–and only half made it out alive. Once they were down, I didn't waste any time. "Remove any wounded. Pull further back, apply any level ups, and prepare for anything. I'm recreating the illusion, but we need to get ready. Move *now!* They may send in the sorcerer!"

They did, and he was not alone. Roars rang through the Gallery, and my pulse quickened. She was coming! I scrambled to make sure I was ready. My minions were scrambling back, helping the wounded away to the escape tunnel. My health was completely full. The Essence Siphon was now running at a continuous pace, and I was feeling the difference as the life essences of the attackers ran across the floor, causing my wounds to close rapidly. I took the opportunity to open my mini-map and observe her approach.

There they were! Further down the tunnels leading to my domain, about two dozen wounded and exhausted invaders were strewn along the sides, looking pitiful and beaten. Next to them, another group stood, ignoring the plight of those who had been defeated. There were not many of them compared to the numbers we'd seen before. Maybe thirty were there, ready for battle. Right now, the battle-clad attackers were standing to the side, bowing and scraping as they made room for Mordiel and... a *white* dragon?

My mind was reeling. It wasn't Selys! Who the hell was it, then? Did Selys know what we were planning? No. I had to focus. They were arriving right now! We had to follow our plan.

My people were back in position while those who were too wounded to continue had been helped to the exit. I looked at them. There was hardly anybody there who hadn't suffered some kind of wound or other. Even so, they formed up the ranks, collected their throwing weapons, and held on tight. The fire in their eyes was undiminished, and I was damn impressed. They weren't going to back down. We would hold the goddamn line!

This time around, however, no forces arrived to test our mettle. None of the thirty attackers came roaring against us. Instead, we were struck by a sudden increase in light and heat - and moments later, a fire storm roared through the opening of the Gallery.

The blaze of the fire grew and grew as the flames roared closer. They did not look or act like any natural fires I'd ever seen though, or even those from movies. In fact, they seemed almost fake in their constancy. Filling the frontmost third of the chamber, their fast expansion stopped, and the wall of fire halted. Then, as if at an afterthought, the fire started expanding at a leisurely pace, constantly burning and roaring like a flamethrower left to burn until it expended all its fuel. The heat grew as it started moving closer. "Flee! Move out of here! Wait near the exit! I'll handle this!"

I took a last look at the wall of flames that slowly grew closer, expanding unnaturally over the earth and the numerous blood-filled grooves and thought to myself, "This is a horrible idea." Then I covered my snout with my front leg, draped my body in shadows, closed my eyes, and braced for the worst.

CHAPTER THIRTY-TWO

I was burning. I heard cries behind me from those who had been too slow to run from the cavern. All reason gone, the pain of the fires that beset me was beyond anything I'd ever experienced before. I screamed as the fire enveloped me on all sides, assaulting every available surface and removing all sense of control or coherent thought. At first, I could only think of how I simply had to endure it for a while, with my Magical resistance halving the damage, before the Essence Siphon would kick in and heal me. And it did start. But even as I felt my flesh reforming, charred scales rebuilding under the assault of the magical flames, the pain did not diminish in the least. In fact, if anything, the suffering increased. I could feel myself whining, gibbering under the relentless onslaught. My health dropped rapidly, and I had to use a Mana Crystal as the Essence Siphon couldn't keep up with the damage. My struggle reduced itself to my personal circle of torment, and my entire being focused on staying here, on forcing myself to weather the pain and not run. I needed to stay, or it would all have been for nothing.

It was a few seconds. Minutes. An eternity. The suffering

increased unceasingly until, suddenly, it died and disappeared entirely. The first couple of seconds, I just lay there, whimpering, while I felt burned flesh regenerating, cracked scales righting themselves and popping into the right places with audible clicks. My health was down to a quarter. And before me, at the entrance, stood Mordiel, flanked by the unknown white.

His eyes were wide open as he approached. He stared at me and removed the golden mask, panting from the effort. He had to halt to gain his breath and spoke haltingly. "Incredible. I cannot believe you survived that." A frown adorned his face. Though he was not burned by the fires, he was still flushed from the heat. The white dragon stepped around him to face me, one small form and one large one, mere dragon lengths apart in the center of the Gallery.

I glared at Mordiel. "I knew you would come after me. I didn't want to have to face you, but..." I shook my head, acknowledging the futility of my hopes. "Who the hell is this? Where is Selys?"

"I am your demise, silly shadow creature. Did you really believe Selys would move for somebody like you?" The haughty message came instantly from the dragon, but he didn't attack. No, he actually looked sideways, as if waiting for Mordiel's approval. Frost started spreading around his feet.

Mordiel shook his head, sneering. "This... is Selys' backup plan. She is quite furious with you, you know." Sweat dripped from his face and steamed on the cracked dirt of the cavern. His fires had burned away all blood running toward the Essence Siphon. I wouldn't be able to rely on it again. "Selys was meaning to use our white friend here elsewhere. If he manages to end you, he may be allowed to take over your place. I am here to see to it that it happens."

"So Selys is still in Fire Peak?" I growled, watching my plans fall apart.

"She didn't want to leave the Peak defenseless." His arms

twitched upward, and he *jerked* them down. Hard. His grin was a rictus. "She miscalculated, though. Ugh. Not attacking you right now is harder than I thought."

At this, the white turned on him. "Why are we still talking? Let us *end* this!"

"You have cost us dearly. More than half our forces lie dead or wounded, but the rest... He is right. Let us make an end of this, Onyx!" He spat the words, trembling with effort.

I gaped at him. "Are you-"

He spat the words. "Don't *wait*. Do you think this is easy? Come at us already. Finish this!"

The sorcerer was panting, and a burst of fire erupted from him, only to be suppressed with a grimace. The white started growling, as frost built inside his mouth. I could do it. Mordiel even wanted me to. Wanted to end it on his terms. Kill them off, grind down the rest of the invaders. It was doable. Except... With a quick mental movement, I opened my map and checked on the positioning of my enemies.

There they were, less in numbers, but still powerful. The remainder of the unhurt attackers stood arranged in orderly fashion, sending long glances down toward us, eagerly waiting for the conclusion. A handful of them were arguing, waving in our direction, as if debating whether they should check and see what was going on. That wasn't important. The fact that they were in range of our trap was.

"No." I fixed him with an apologetic look and shook my head. "You're not my enemy, Mordiel. Selys is. Come find me after."

His response was a growl, almost a shout. His hands burst into fire as he gritted his teeth. "A-after?"

I grinned and sat up. "Oh yeah. After." I let my mental voice range out to the edges of my domain, gleefully, triumphantly. "Let it fall. Bring it all down! Now! We run!" Then I turned on my heels and fled. As soon as I moved, Mordiel and the white reacted. Flames and frost licked at my back. It *hurt,* and my health plummeted even faster than last time. I used a second Mana Crystal. It was my last resort, and I wouldn't be able to use any more today. Regardless, it granted me the seconds I needed to widen the distance between us, sprint down into the entrance tunnel to escape the direct streams of their attacks.

Regardless of his powers, compared to me, Mordiel was *slow.* The white had clearly been taken by surprise as I fled. As soon as I got up to speed, I outdistanced both them and their powers swiftly, even as the white started running to catch me. Meanwhile, behind me, the mountain collapsed.

Tremors ran through the ground under me. I only focused on speed as I looked ahead of me and ran for safety. A slow rumbling sound slowly grew and turned into a roar... and then stopped. I raced past the Gallery, through the entrance tunnels and into the throne room. There, at the end of the room, stood Creziel, anxiously bouncing from one leg to the other. I called out as I ran. "Move already. Move! We need to do it *now!* They're right behind me."

True enough, as I raced from the throne room and into my own room, I glanced back, and saw vivid colors appearing behind me. Creziel, running in front, was approaching the exit tunnel. He slowed down for a brief moment, groaning with exertion. The tremors started again, closer this time. "Quick! Grab on!" I lowered my left wing as I ran, letting it drag along the ground. A tug and a sudden weight almost tripped me. Then he was there, hanging on for dear life. I carefully lifted the wing as I sprinted on, bringing him in relative safety onto my back. The air filled with the rich smell of earth, and suddenly dirt clouds exploded all around me. I ran on, half-blinded, holding my breath as best I could while the mountain fell behind me.

It felt like minutes, like we were running for our lives, staying right ahead of an avalanche. In reality, it was probably a lot less drastic, but half-blind, half-choked by the dirt in the air, I struggled on. And as suddenly as it started, we emerged, sprinting from the steep tunnel and into a small cave. Past a half-wall that hid the tunnel exit, we continued, out of the cave, past a bend in the continuing corridor. There they were. My entire force was there. Some were down and out with horrible wounds, some resting against the tunnel walls panting with exhaustion. But most were... ready. Braced for anything, hefting their weapons and preparing for yet another fight, defiance in their eyes.

I slowed down, panting, then craned my neck to look at Creziel, who was still hanging onto my back with a death grip. He caught my eyes, blinked, and seemed to come around. He gave me the slightest of smiles. Then he nodded. My roar filled the air. "We did it! They are trapped! Rest and get well. You've earned it."

We spent hours resting and allowing the Ergul to gain enough power to heal the worst of our injuries. Then we met to discuss our fates. We had failed. Selys had not taken the bait. But we had still succeeded in defeating her forces. What were we going to do now?

Arthor was the last one to arrive. He was, like the rest of us, covered in a thin layer of dirt. He was clearly exhausted, too, wavering slightly as he stumbled closer. Still, the tall Talpus held his head high and oozed confidence. He took in the group gathered in a large semicircle on the floor of the tunnel and grunted. "What are you all looking at? Tell me what happened! Did you manage it on your end? Is Selys trapped?"

Arthor didn't know. There was no way he could have. He had been hidden from the main tunnel behind a thin wall, waiting for their forces to pass him by before he could bring down the ceiling. It was a desperate plan, deadly for Arthor if they had somehow managed to notice his presence. To make it to us at this point, he must have run all the way around from the other tunnels.

I held up a claw. "We're safe right now, Arthor. I'll tell you everything. How did you handle it on your end? Did you manage?"

He gave a grudging nod. "We cut it close. Pfah. Too close. A number of the attackers were caught *inside* the first earth slide, but thanks to Deyra, nobody escaped. The rest went off as planned. I brought down three separate blockades. They will be tunneling for a *week* to get out, and we can keep building on it and hardening the earth. We have them!"

A sigh of relief escaped me. "That's great. Well done, Arthor. Creziel managed on this end, too, even if we were almost caught in the collapse." I smiled at the rest of them. "Well done, *everybody*. You held your ground against Selys' forces, and you actually beat them! If anybody would try to contest how strong we've grown, this should be proof enough."

I let my head sink. "Unfortunately, Selys didn't take the bait. Or she was too cautious, didn't want to risk leaving Fire Peak to the predations of the other groups. Whatever her reasons, she only sent her soldiers along with the sorcerer and another dragon... which leaves us... at an unfortunate impasse."

"I... Yeah." Grex hovered about. "The earth looks impassable, that's true. What's the trouble? We starve them out, as planned, eat the dragon meat, and grow. Selys... who cares about Selys? We own the lower layers. She can come!"

The others looked at the bragging Imp, staring. Roth was the one to answer. "Don't be daft. If we give her time, next time, she'll bring twice the numbers. Three times. She might not have many left among her personal troops, but the mountain still bows to her. The third layer, the fourth. If she forces all others to join her, we're done for. We didn't make it unscathed through the battle. There's no way we can outgrow the entire mountain."

I bowed my head in assent. "Roth is right. We need to figure out what we do now. Selys will not hold back. She will keep sending minions after us until we are dead. So, that leaves us with a choice. Where do we go now?"

They spoke up all at once. After a moment, Arthor glared at

the others until they kept silent. "You said earlier that the choices would boil down to attacking or fleeing. I agree. Still. Attack Fire Peak? I know we have leveled, but I don't see it, lizard. There's a short list of creatures who've tried to fight against Selys. They're all dead. So, if those are the choices you place before us, the conclusion's as simple as Grex. We flee the mountain."

Creziel nodded, as did the others. Even Grex agreed with a look of resignation. I looked at each of them in turn, and in the end, gave a single nod. "I agree. But I don't think we should flee."

Arthor glared at me. "You agree? But you don't? Then why bring it up? Is this something from your world that is supposed to make sense?"

Timothy jumped in, grinning. "No. Carl, you need to start making sense. That was weirder than the final season of that show with all the white walkers." Bastard. We'd talked about this.

I glared at Tim, then shook my head. "That's because I haven't even started to make my argument yet. You expect me to recommend charging Fire Peak with all their defenses? Attack her and her minions in her seat of power? Don't be daft. Even if I weren't a shadow dragon and patently unsuited for direct confrontation, that would be the height of idiocy.

"Now, I've had a couple of hours to think about it. This didn't pan out the way I hoped it to, but it also wasn't a horrible result. Right now, we deprived Selys of a lot of her forces, and she can't expect reinforcements right away. On top of that, the Blessing of Deyra is still disconnected, removing some of her most efficient defenses. So, here's what I've been thinking..."

I was used to the attention of my minions. Nothing new there. Yet, facing their unblinking scrutiny, I felt something emerge that had only been there in fits and start before. Devotion. Whatever came from here on, we would handle it as one.

"We have been blessed with many gifts lately. Struggling through adversity, we have emerged on the other side bigger and better. I'm not only talking about levels, physical, or magical strength. We *have* gained those. Yet, they pale compared to the cooperation and teamwork we have learned.

"We've just proven it. Selys' forces were stronger than ours, but still we managed, through organization, tactics, and a proper application of force. I've been on many sites, but I've never had as damn good a team as I have today." I looked at them fondly. "Still, that's not all. We've also gained some allies that may help, and most importantly, Selys has given us an opening… and she doesn't even know it yet. If we do this, it could give us one shot at removing Selys from her throne without risking it all."

I spoke for a good while. They were quiet, taking in the ideas, offering occasional questions and suggestions. Finally, I rounded off with a solemn tone. "It won't be easy. It won't be safe. And to make matters worse, I will have to ask for your acceptance that I call the shots for the entire affair. It will be a mess, with a lot of risks and moving pieces, and we won't be able to gather everybody to adjust things once the ball starts rolling." When I stopped, they looked around, as if waiting for somebody to start talking. Then, all at once, their mental chatter exploded.

Grex yelled the loudest. "That sounds *incredible*."

"Incredibly insane, perhaps. Count me in!" This from Roth, who laughed and rolled his eyes.

"We will be able to do our part for that, even if it will not amount to much." Gert frowned.

"*Enough!*" Arthor spoke over the others. "Onyx's new form of deciding is suitable for this. Even if he is the one up front, we will all be risking our lives for this. This is a decision that will affect all of us, and might mean our destruction—or salvation. It should not be something that we decide without having talked over the implications. Pfah. Even if it is suicide." He motioned at the collapsed tunnel. "For once, we are not in a hurry. Let us discuss the decision and come to the best possible solution."

"Onyx. We have voted."

The finality of the words caused me to sit up right away. We'd discussed the matter for hours, going back and forth over the possibilities, until they'd asked me to move while they voted among themselves. Arthor stood there, a somber look on his face. A sense of decision came from him, and resignation. He was clearly not entirely happy with what they had decided.

"You wish to go against Selys–face her down, outsmart her, and do battle until one of you is no more."

"That's the essence of it, I guess. I really don't want to face her, though. That's pretty much the point of the whole thing."

He ignored me. His words were somber, formal, not as pointed as they usually were. "You are aware that I put the tribe first. Pfah. Even if you argue that our new tribe isn't just Talpi, but also Crawls and Imps."

I nodded. "Not everybody's going to agree. But, to me, you have all become family. Some of you closer than others, but still people I'm ready to fight for."

He bared his small teeth. "You don't have to like family. Family just is. And I agree."

I felt my heart soaring. "Agree that it's worth the risk?"

"Yes. Had you suggested that we fight her straight on, I would have voted against you. But traps, hidden weapons, ambushes?" His eyes gleamed. "Those? Those are what the Talpi revel in. We will take the risks we need to give you your chance. And should you fall… we will mourn you, but will be able to flee, carry on."

A chance. The words were tantalizing, intoxicating even. I asked Arthor in earnest. "Are you serious?"

"Yes. We all agreed. The risk is worth it. Besides, you are the one taking the burden of the risk. Should you fail, we have a chance to escape, hide, and hopefully escape Selys' wrath." He continued, suddenly somber. "Besides, dragon. Whatever else I might say about you, we owe you. If we have to start over from nothing outside the mountain, that would still leave us in a better position for survival than anybody could have hoped for half a year ago. So, we will give you this. One chance. One attempt to bring her down. We will give it our all. And afterward, we create a new world, together."

I could feel the glory rising inside of me. Bringing down my head until it was level with Arthor's, my eyes stared intently into his. I said, "Arthor, I love you. Now, let's go kill a tyrant!"

CHAPTER THIRTY-THREE

"If thy heart fails thee, climb not at all." – Elizabeth I

We took a full day before we started moving. Part of that was due to the sheer number of wounded. *Everybody* had some minor injury or hurt, and we had rushed the healings earlier, favoring the heavily injured. Now, we did a thorough check-up with everybody, ensuring that the Ergul handled them all. The beast leveled up twice in the process, reaching level 7. I wanted to be entirely sure that nobody started the march with wounds that would worsen with time.

The other part was on the shamans' authority. They decided that a tour around the domain to ensure that they hadn't missed any possible exit points was necessary, and I agreed. The conclusion was that Selys' minions inside our domain were well and properly trapped. Unless they revealed some unexpected control over earth, they were unlikely to be able to tunnel out in time to cause us trouble.

Everybody took the chance to level up. We gained massive experience from the fight. No surprise there. It had been like shooting fish in a barrel. I already knew that using area effects on groups of enemies meant I'd receive experience for every single enemy to die. What overwhelmed me was just how much experience we actually gained. A full 51,700 experience points flung me from level 28 and straight to level 30! Time to grow!

As for the surviving adversaries, they were locked up tight, but unlikely to die. They could still reach the stream inside our Clencher cavern, and their own fallen would provide them with food for at least a couple of weeks. It was barbaric, but pragmatic. Arthor argued that he wanted to cave in the area with the stream, but I talked him down. If Selys died, Mordiel would be on my side, and his underlings would be mine. The white dragon… that was an unknown, but one we would be able to handle.

When we did move, it was as two groups. This part, we had all agreed on right away. If we were to do this, we would not take everybody for the assault. Only those who'd be able to flee quickly. And this was important: whoever decided that, for whatever reason, had no intention of marching on Fire Peak would be allowed to join the other group, no questions asked. I had enough on my conscience without forcing people to go against the most powerful monster in the mountain against their will. To my surprise, the number of the other group was less than a fifth of our numbers.

Even if they did not want to fight, they would still do their part. Led by Wreil, they'd move back toward Creive, inform him what was going on, then… wait, work on Creive's domain, and keep our non-combatants safe. Meanwhile, Wreil would continue his march, hopefully with Creive in tow. Within his domain, they would be as safe as anywhere else in the mountain, and there was an exit to the outside nearby. If they learned of our demise later, well, it would be easy for them to flee the place. The rest of us marched. Up. Toward Fire Peak, and a final confrontation.

We didn't *just* march, though. We had a week ahead of us and a safe head start. We needed to use every spare moment we had to gain whatever possible advantages we could. As such, our forces split up once, twice, three times. We talked about tactics, about skill choices, ways to boost our attacks and get any advantages, unfair or otherwise. We knew what we were facing, and we were going into it with our eyes open and of our own volition.

On the second day after we left, Timothy floated alongside me, expanding merrily. "You won't believe what happened. There's one of the Imps who got a new feat. Dix. She's a bit of a freak, apparently, by Imp standards, in that she prefers *silence*. Yeah, sounds weird, I know, but we're not only talking about when they're hunting. She just doesn't talk much. Anyway, she's a complete Agility build. A lot of the others focus on Mental Power, too, since that aids the damage of their fire attacks, but she's all in on Agility. And her new feat is called Unseen Attack."

I frowned. "So... she's able to stay invisible while she attacks? That's-"

"No. Even better! Her fire *attacks* are invisible. She is still there, for all to see."

I thought about it "That's... quite the advantage. She can probably get a few shots off before any enemy spots her. Oh. And in combination with my illusions or my Camouflage..." I let my thoughts trail off as I considered the possibilities. "So, how many others could possibly get that feat soon?"

"Finally! You're starting to think the right way. Took you long enough." Timothy's features solidified so I could see him winking at me. The silence stretched for a bit between us. Then he started again. "You know, I really thought you were a blockhead when I first came to my senses. Me build. Eat enemies. No like books." He laughed at my glare and continued. "You're alright, though. A bit single-minded, but alright. And you actually do have a head for strategy... if only because you're good at listening to others and picking out the right suggestions."

"You're seriously starting to lose me here, Timmy, my boy. Are you practicing your backhanded compliments, or is there a point to it?"

His indistinct smile faltered for a moment, before quirking back up. "Yes. There is. And it's this. Your plan won't work."

I missed a step. "Seriously? What am I missing?"

His blue hands waved vaguely at the air. "Most of it makes sense. The distractions and everything, the *trap*. But you're downplaying one thing. Regardless how many of their guards we've taken out, Selys is still bound to have her personal guards... and they'll be big and strong."

I frowned. "I know. I do have my shadow and illusion skills, but... yeah. It's an issue. My plan is to move fast enough that they haven't got a clue what hit them. It's not perfect, but... heh. It's what I've got."

"It won't do, old man." He shook his head. "I was hoping it wouldn't have to come to this. I'm... coming with you."

My tempers started fraying at the edges. "Like hell you are. I know what I'm going into. It might not be the smartest, but I'll give it a chance. I'm not about to risk your life, too."

"Well, guess what, old man? It's not your goddamn choice. You ever think about the result if you fail? If I'm left by myself in this shitty world? I know you dig this whole leadership stuff... that's not me. I want to make the best of it, maybe create a life that doesn't suck. Nothing more." The smile that formed on his face, while see-through, showed, without fail, the fear he was holding back.

"How do you think I'm going to fare if I'm left alone, and we're left without a domain? I can tell you. First, we're going to be outside the mountain. We won't be able to hold any domains or areas, and whatever farming they've learned will be crazy difficult, because, apparently roaming, powerful monsters is the *norm* out there. So, that pretty much removes the only easy way we have of getting food. Oh, and that tendency of the Imps to fly around and get into trouble? In here, that's pretty much contained, because the tunnels keep them close. Out there? They'll have monsters coming in every other moment. And we won't have the growth rates of the mountain to help us."

"Whoa whoa whoa. I get it. It's—"

Timothy continued, unabashed. "No, I don't think you do. I give it a week until they let the Imps fend for themselves. The rest might be able to hold together a bit longer, but they'll have to attack monsters for food. And that is going to cost them. They..."

"OKAY! Okay, I get it. But... I can't leave it. Being thrown from the mountain would be a worse experience than a New York cab ride. But the alternative is worse and..." I paused, trying to find the words. When I failed, I opted instead for honesty. "I wanted to give you a chance to survive."

Timothy's infuriated crisp features suddenly relaxed, and everything but his face blurred. He was quiet for a while. Then he snorted. "Is that it? That's the only reason why you're trying to keep me back?"

"Yeah. I mean, odds are already looking kinda crappy facing up against her. Still, you have a chance to flee if it fails. If you go in with me, you're all in. Do or die. I figured it would be better for you guys to be able to get away, start over elsewhere, than risk *both* our lives. Even if life outside would suck."

He tittered. Then laughed aloud and dissolved into a fit of laughter.

I struggled for words, then gave up and went for it. "That was *not* the reaction I expected."

After a while, he subsided. "Dude. That was hilarious. Have you got any idea how stereotypically heroic that was? We're talking manly man, flannel-shirt-wearing, axe-wielding, macho hero stereotypes here. I'll make it easy for you, man. I'll be helping. I get your point, and I *agree*. Selys needs to go. And you need me. Besides, you're the one who told us we were like a family. Family can be a pest, but they're still *there* for each other."

He was serious. I considered how I could convince him that it was an awful idea, then reconsidered. "Okay."

"Okay? Just like that?"

"Yeah. It's not like I *like* the idea of going up against Selys by myself. And I don't want to be a saint or something. I kinda want to survive, you know? So, we'll have to adapt the plan a bit. How do we do it? I mean, I'm going to be moving *fast*, and you're intangible. You're also vulnerable, though. They do have sorcerers, and if Selys catches you, you're a goner."

His eagerness was contagious. "Meh. Already forgotten the feat I took last time? Improved Speed. It's literally in the title. I think you don't quite understand exactly how fast I've become." He burst ahead and sprinted through the procession of our people, ignoring shouts and roars from the people he ran around and sometimes *through*. And he was *fast*. On top of that, when he really let go, the blue color of his form was a lot more unrefined, harder to pinpoint as an actual person.

When he came back, an uncanny grin taking up half his face, I shook my head in amazement. "That'll do, nerd. That'll do. Do me a favor, though. You may have that Path of the Resistant feat that protects you somewhat from magical damage, but it's still your kryptonite. Keep the hell away from Selys and any mages if you can."

We discussed practicals for a while, then the talk turned to me. I grunted in response. "Yeah. I actually need your help. After the fight with Mordiel, I made it to level 30. I don't know which options are coming, but since I get feats every fifth level, there's bound to be something good - if I qualify. I've got 10 spare points to use. Soooo, if you've got those leather rolls handy, I want to find out if our cheat codes work for dragons, too. I mean, if we learned something useful from Creive."

"Oooh. I've been looking forward to this. Be right back!"

Minutes later, we were walking alongside Lore, who was struggling to simultaneously walk and hold up the large leather pelt to show us the leather string that displayed Creive's feats. Tim was hovering right next to it, mumbling to himself. "No. That won't do. No, that's crap. Hah. Maybe..." He paused and turned toward me. "Hey, what's your Toughness?"

"62."

"Damn. Too low for this one. Agility? Above sixty, right? And that Toughness... Yeah, this could work."

"Stop talking to yourself, man. Talk about stereotypes, nerd!"

"Patience, Old Yeller. Daddy's trying to think here." He acted like he was thinking, tapping his chin with a finger. Of course, the illusion was somewhat ruined by the digit going halfway *into* the chin. Also, I could feel that he was messing with me. "So, Creive's a powerhouse, right? Built for combat, aerial fights, and head-butting brick walls. You... aren't."

I snorted. "Don't sugar coat it on my account, kiddo. I go for fast, evasive, and magical."

"Yeah. Well, Creive has speed, too. And he has three Agility-based feats that you might be able to get. Lore, show me Onyx's string, please. Hmmm. Okay, you were already offered Improved Flight at Level 10, but turned it down for Hardened Scales. Decent choice, by the way."

"Thanks. They've saved my butt at least once with how many beatings I've taken."

"Alright. You've got the attribute requirements for Winged Shield and Aerial Burst of Speed. However, since you turned down Improved Flight, and Creive didn't, you might not be able to choose the Burst of Speed one. Read the descriptions for us, please, Lore."

The Crawl took another skin out and started deciphering the information contained on the strings.

[Aerial Burst of Speed.
This feat allows you to fly twice as fast without any detriments.
It does not affect your turning speed.
Duration: 30 seconds
Cooldown: 5 minutes.]

[Winged Shield
This feat adds a shimmering, thick, layer of magical armor on both wings, forming a weightless shield, defending the bearer against physical, magical, and elemental damage. The layer is

easily broken but allows for a single-use avoidance of damage and regenerates after a while.]

Timothy *harrumphed*. "So, what do you think? Aerial Burst of Speed is pretty much a perfect getaway skill. All it takes is for you to bump an additional eight points to Strength, unless you needed Improved Flight, too." He shrugged and smiled. "Sorry. This isn't an exact science.... yet. Improved Flight is simply a lifesaver. You might get that one presented for free, since you already have the requirements. Creive got it at Level 20. He's got [Magical Resistance], same as yourself, and I'm thinking that may be a prerequisite, too. He said his Agility was around 60 back then."

I rolled my shoulders, thinking. "It's an entire science, isn't it? One thing's the prerequisites, but another's which ones you get to choose from, right? But yeah, both would help. Hmm. I'm thinking I'll have to take the chance and invest in Strength. I like Winged Shield, but let's be realistic here. Saving me from a single hit won't do anything against Selys. The one thing I'll need above all now is speed."

"Good point. Well, go for it."

"Now? Well... okay." I jumped into my character info, selected Level Up, and dumped an additional eight points into Strength. The other two points went into Toughness - regardless of what happened, I'd need survivability.

I closed my eyes, took a deep breath, then looked... and there it was. Alongside the option for a short-range damage spell and a feat that could double my mental attributes for 30 seconds, Aerial Burst of Speed stared right out at me. I grinned and chose it, growling in satisfaction at Tim. "Nerd?"

"Yes?"

"You're a genius."

CHAPTER THIRTY-FOUR

The remainder of the march back to Fire Peak was largely uneventful. Or, as uneventful as we could hope for. We jumped a trio of roaming Tainted Shamblers, scared a tribe of Dweelers away with our numbers, and avoided any large settlements. There was only one occasion where we were left reeling—when our scouts chanced upon another scout team, this one sent from Fire Peak.

When I learned that Leith had somehow managed to discover the band running in the opposite direction *and* made it back to us fast enough that we were able to duck down a side route to avoid notice, I praised him and promised him a gift from the hoard. Later, once we had decided what we were going to do with the scouts.

We were about two days out from Fire Peak, and I tried to put myself in Selys' place. At this point, unless she had any godly scouting skills I was unaware of, she would probably be wondering what was going on. Her minion count had steadily dropped during the battle, but they had survived. In her spot, I'd probably assume that they'd won the battle and would be returning triumphantly to Fire Peak. *Trust but verify*, though.

Or, in her case, there was probably no trust except for trust in her damn oaths and how scared her people were of her. Of course, she would send somebody to check on the deal, see what the result was. After a moment of deliberation, I told my people to pull back even further as I built an illusion of an empty tunnel that we could hide behind, just in case. Yeah, the scouts might very well be able to help Mordiel and their troops escape earlier than expected, but I didn't care, especially if it meant that Selys remained unaware. We were going to blindside that wicked beast.

We made it back to the upper layer, undetected as far as we knew. Our position was good. We created an opening into the crater of the mountain again, a few tunnels over from where we'd escaped . This allowed us an amazing vantage point we could use to decide the finals of our approach... and wait.

Unsurprisingly, Grex was the one who hated the wait the most. He sat on a small outcropping, halfway up the wall, leg and stump kicking a rhythm at the rock. "Let's attack! Now! Blasted dragon will be taken with her wings wet."

Roth didn't move a muscle as he stared out the small opening in the tunnel side. The flat, pockmarked landscape filled the view, with not a single thing of notice within sight except for the city. "Stow it, Flitters. This is horrible terrain for an attack. Some of us will be able to sneak onto the plain without problems, find some smaller holes to hide in. Maybe dig them for ourself. That can give us a single surprise attack.

"Still, the moment we're spotted, we'll be in it deep. Once the big red knows we're there, she can find us in her map, and we'll be aflame. You, Grex? You're screwed. In this place, you'll be a flying snack for whenever Selys gets peckish." He sneered. "Remind me again why we agreed to get out there in the open?"

Creziel was right near the opening, too. The tiny shaman wasn't looking at the view, however, but on his knees, both hands roving over the dirt floor. "You're worse than Grex some-times. You really should learn to pay attention, Roth. We are *not* going out there." He turned toward me. "We can handle this, Onyx. They may have tried to create a defensible environment, but it's still *soil*. Not many rocks either. This will be easy to work with."

One less thing to worry about. "Great. We have... a little less than two days until Arthor is going to put the plan into motion. Then we'll have to act. You get to work. I'll handle the camouflage, maintain illusions, and make sure we're not spotted."

It was a waiting game again. So many moving parts, and I needed to handle it right. The wait was tedious. We couldn't range about for fear of being spotted by roving scouts and spent most of the time engaging in discussions about strategy. Who should move first? How should we distribute our forces? How about the close-combat fighters? We went back and forth over the options so often that soon, even Timothy was tired of discussing theoreticals.

Leith was the first one to return along with his Crawl bodyguards. He grimaced the moment he reached me. "Onyx. Bad news. We found the Aberrants. They let me talk with their leader. They're cowards. Too afraid to go against Selys."

"Damn. I was hoping for their support. I had them figured for the most reasonable of the lot. You gave them my offer, right?"

He spat and leered at me. "What, you think I'd forget? They weren't interested. It makes sense. If we lose and Selys spots even a single one of them, she will wipe them out." Leith grimaced and gave a bright smile. "It's not all bad. Their leader said that they were due a scouting tour about these times, and if he were to find any wandering monsters, Dragonlings or the like, they might have an accident."

"You mean they'll make sure our backs are free?"

"That's exactly what I mean. And apparently, the Dragonlings aren't the best of neighbors. Huge surprise, right? Sounds like the Aberrants will use this chance to get theirs back."

"That's... pretty good, actually. With how many Dragonlings

have been killed, the Aberrants should be able to come out on top. Plus, we won't be risking any ambushes. Thank you for risking it, Leith."

Gert was next to return. The two Crawls with her moved slowly, burdened with heavy sacks, which they dropped, clanging before me. Gert knelt. Funny how she hadn't started growing the nasty rolls of hardened fat or skin that the older Crawls all sported yet. "Onyx, the Dworgen simply said no. No explanations. They respect your strength, though."

I cursed. "And this?" I pointed a claw at the bags.

She started undoing the string keeping the rough sacks closed. With the help of the Crawls, he extricated the contents. Heavy, rectangular, metallic shields, lined all around the edges with gleaming runes. "These lay in our path when we turned around, piled up in the center of the tunnel."

My grin grew wide. "Heh. So, they're not about to risk an attack, but they don't mind playing favorites? Well, I'm not turning down a gift. Grex, you mind flying down to Creziel and tell him we have something for the ambushers?"

"Right away."

I thanked Gert and returned to muttering for myself, considering the odds. It could have been worse. At least Selys wouldn't be reinforced, and there was little chance we'd be ambushed from behind. We were only waiting for one group now.

I was looking through the opening at the sky above when the final group of scouts returned. Twilight arrived in a weird way down here, observing from within what was shaped like a massive volcano crater. First, the sun disappeared from the sky, but everything remained bright for hours afterward. Within the crater, however, light fled the ground and shadows deepened as the remaining rays of the sun fled higher and higher up the side of the crater.

Then, real twilight arrived, painting the skies with outlandish colors that you couldn't find on earth. There was beauty in this place, too. It was easy to forget that, down inside the mountain. With a last look, I turned toward the sound of footsteps. The five Crawls veered off and dropped to the floor to rest. The trip had exhausted them to the point where they didn't even react, just closed their eyes and rested. The final person continued toward me, his steps still springy.

Click. The sound of his tooth necklace clicking sounded louder than it ought to. Why the hell would a scout, who was supposed to move silently, even *wear* that? I'd have to ask. Later. I nodded at him, trying to keep my anxiety in check. "Wreil."

"Onyx." He bowed, searched my eyes for something, then beamed a splitting grin at me. "He said yes!"

I could hardly credit his words. Without this, it had felt like suicide. With him on our side... "Alright! This is happening! No turning back now. Wreil, I cannot thank you enough. When is Creive coming? We're running on a schedule."

"He will be here in time. He insisted."

"Alright. We will have to trust in his timing. Anything else, Wreil? We're committed now, every single moment counts."

I was almost turned away, but he stopped me. "One thing, Onyx. When you make it—and you had better make damn sure you succeed—this is what I need to be doing. It took me some time to be sure, but I know it now. Being a leader? The planning, keeping everything fixed in your head, all those details? That's not for me. But the other half of it. Making sure everybody is doing good? Talking to others on behalf of the tribe? Finding their weak points and pushing until they give away more than they wanted in a trade, making friends? That I've always been good at."

I beamed at him. "I love the idea. One of the reasons we asked you in the first place was that everybody talked well of you. That seems to be a great quality for the first ambassador of... whatever we are."

"Ambassador." He tasted the word with pleasure. "You'll have to talk me over exactly what that means... but it *feels* right." He grasped his necklace tightly. "Does that even make sense? I... I even gained a feat I can use to move around undisturbed. [Cone of Peace] means that most animals and monsters are less likely to see me as a target."

I laughed. "That's amazing, Wreil. And yeah, I know what you mean. Once we've survived this, I'll make sure to talk with the Council and make it official. Don't think for a second that means I won't need your help keeping the scouts happy."

He grinned. *Click.* "Too true. For as long as Leith's there to make them cry, you'll need me to cheer 'em back up. And you've got it. One thing, Onyx. This becoming reality means you need to survive. Promise me. We need you!"

I looked at the tall Talpus, intensity burning in his dark eyes. Then nodded. "Promise. Selys will burn." Abruptly, I stood up, turned around. "Everybody! We move in... a little less than half a day. Creziel will be preparing the tunnels all this time. The rest of you, get ready. Rest while you can. Roth, get the best close combat fighters. We'll want them protecting our ambushers with the shields. Grex, you make sure that your people stay here. If we attack before time, everything will be ruined." I walked among them, calling out orders, watching them spring into action, a feverish murmur running through the gathered people. This was happening. We were actually doing it.

Everybody was resting. It was the middle of the night and the clock was ticking down. A mere two hours to go. I didn't need much sleep, and had taken to continuing the plotting, perusing the map to make sure I had my route memorized. There were still a lot of unknowns, but we were decided now, and there was no turning back. All around me, forms were unmoving, sleeping soundly. This was life inside the mountain. Even with the perils at hand and the very real threat of possible death, my minions slept like the dead.

There was one exception. A small form extricated itself from the rest of the people resting on the rocky soil and slowly wound its way toward me. I smiled in welcome at the tiny furball. "Creziel. Good to see you. Couldn't sleep?"

He shook his head. "No. I was too excited, thinking

about..." He waved at the sight of Fire Peak in the far distance. "Everything."

I smiled at him, patting at the ground next to me. "I completely understand. Keep me company? I could do with some distraction as well."

He sat down and looked up at me. "Did you also spend a lot of time planning everything where you were a leader back in your world?"

"Yes... and no." I smiled. "We were a large company. That means most of the details were already set in stone when they brought me in. Sure, I could point out if there were some glaring errors with the plans or schedules, but my bosses weren't incompetents. Heh. Not all the time, at least. No, I usually ran with a smaller crew, five to ten people at most. I was pretty good at that, though. A set number of tasks ahead of me, and a well-known bunch of workers to help me—that's easy. This, scaling up, planning things from scratch? It's been a learning experience, let's just say that."

Creziel looked at the ground, then up at me. The fondness stemming from him warmed my heart. "At first, I didn't know what to make of you, Onyx. A dragon who cared? Who took the time to help the weakest of the weak? I didn't dare believe it. But then I saw you with Jazinth and again with Aelis..."

My heart ached at the thought. The two Talpi appeared in my mind, shining and vivid, as if they were still alive. Jazinth, haughty and unrepentant, laughing and confident. And Aelis. Proper, straight as an arrow, delivering one of her reports with her paws behind her back. "Damn, what I wouldn't give to have them with us."

Creziel nodded, head downcast. "Me too. Jazinth was... not an easy person to get along with, but she cared. Aelis—we are less for seeing her dead. Still, such are the ways of the mountain." He sighed and took a deep breath. "Onyx. That is why I came to speak with you."

"Because of the ones we've lost?"

"No. Because you *care*." He expanded with his arm toward

the resting forms. "Roth is ecstatic with the possibility of fight and growth. Grex loves the thrill of it all. The other day he told me that the unexpectedness of our travels was the most wonderful thing he'd ever experienced. Arthor... Arthor cares, too, but only about odds and survival and strength. You care about *us*. And that is why we cannot let you go. The others might only think of the advantages we lose. They are learning otherwise, but if you die, we might go back to what we were. And that will not do."

The earnesty oozing from him was almost overwhelming. I summoned the fondest smile I could. "I'll do my best, Creziel. I promise that. I have no intention of dying today."

He huffed. "That is not what I mean. I mean that your life is more important than mine. When we move, today, I will be going with you, and I'll use my powers to protect you."

I would have laughed at the absurdity of his comment. Except, his sincerity was steel-set, as was his decision. I softened my tone and asked. "You're not making this offer lightly, are you? No. You aren't. How would you do it? I will be flying. You can hold on to my harness, but I doubt that it is viable when I have to move quickly."

"They can fix me to the harness with ropes and belts. I do not care about comforts. Our powers combined may help all of us survive and thrive."

By our powers combined... I shot down the thought. It was unworthy of the moment. And I knelt and bowed my head to the tiny creature. A creature, no, a friend who was ready to risk his life against Selys to spare mine. After a while, I spoke up. "In truth, your offer is a huge relief. I'll make sure that some of the others take over with the digging, keeping you fresh for tomorrow. And I know exactly where your powers can come in handy. See, I'd been planning to cut back here, run this way..." My words sprang from my mind to his as I raised a map on the dirt floor of the cavern. Small, so as not to disturb my resting minions with the glow. We plotted to save our lives, end a monster, and free a mountain.

CHAPTER THIRTY-FIVE

"Lesson taught by History: do not fight Russians in their own territory."
— *Victor Bello Accioly*

Controlling my telepathic powers wasn't hard. There was a mental component to it, deciding where to apply them, who to stretch out to, who to include. Even which general area I wanted to shout out to. Heh. And since my mental force grew right along with my mental attributes, my telepathic shout could be damn loud, indeed!

"Face me, Selys! Come out here! You feeble old lizard. You would send your sorcerer and pet dragon against me, while you quake in fear inside your walls?" I hovered in the air, wings beating slowly to keep me level. The morning was early enough that there was little light. Torches still lit Fire Peak in the distance. "This is what the mighty Selys has come to? Hiding behind her walls as she sends her minions out to fight her fights? Well, guess what, coward! I *beat* your precious guards, the white, and your little sorcerer. The Burning End? Don't make me laugh! Looks like you burned out years ago!"

Before me, Fire Peak turned from a sleepy nest of inactivity into a veritable ant hive. Guards moved everywhere on the walls and horns sounded from within in a chaotic mess of sound. There was no doubt my mental voice reached them all. The panic of the inhabitants was soon drowned out, however.

Beyond it all, it grew. Her roar. It grew louder and louder, deafening enough that it seemed to set the very air to vibrating. And her response landed with all the grace of an enraged Shambler. "You dare? You really think you can take me on?" The seconds grew, turned to minutes—then she rose.

Selys. The Burning End. The mightiest creature of the Scoured Mountain. She climbed from her fortress as huge and unstoppable as the sun. The fires of the city reflected off of her glorious golden armor, and every single set of eyes drank in her glory.

Below and behind me, half-hidden within a narrow tunnel in the wall of the mountain, Timothy gaped. "We're supposed to fight... that?"

She looked larger than I remembered her as she hung mid-air, the center of everybody's attention. Still, I showed off my teeth. "Heh. No. We're supposed to *trick* that. Be ready." With those parting words, I started slowly flying forward, staying low to the ground. My mental shout rang out again. "The all-powerful Selys! Hiding behind her walls and guards and defenses, afraid to come out. Afraid to face a young dragon. Her own offspring, even."

She did not move. Indeed, she hovered in place, above her fortress, letting out a plume of flame toward the sky. That... was not good. I needed her out of there. Having to attack her and her forces within the city *would not do*. Well, according to my dear old ex-wife, I could be one infuriating son of a bitch. Time to test that in practice.

"You actually *do* intend to wait us out? What a joke! Relying on your defenses to hold against us? Have you already forgotten? I destroyed the Blessing! Your old fire towers are worth nothing. Oh, and your walls? You would trust them? My shamans will tunnel their way there, turn them to dust. Even if

I should fall, the Dworgen or the Aberrants will be free to invade Fire Peak and take the mountain for their own. Hah!"

"Youth." Even from across a distance of miles, the contempt in her message was clear to hear. "You think you know so much. I did not survive almost a century by launching into combat unheeded. This is something you have yet to learn. It takes only one unfortunate battle for your good luck to turn sour. A dragon–a real dragon, not an upstart hatchling–plans for the long game. However, even in your arrogance, you are right. It would not do to face the Dworgen without my defenses. So, it would seem you force my claw." Selys rose, higher and higher, climbing in the air. The first rays of sun of the day glinted off her brilliant armor, and she dove. And the battle for the mountain was on.

She did not come alone. The gates clashed open, and forces poured out, armored forms moving in formation toward us. A quick glance confirmed that there were few golden armors among them. So, she was still keeping back the elite troops. These were city guards at best. They didn't take any chances,though, closing the gates again after them. Not giving us a decent chance to enter. Well, at least we'd have a while until their forces reached us. The same could not be said for Selys, who came at a speed that seemed impossible with her massive bulk.

Within seconds, I knew that I was outclassed. Of course, I'd known that all the time. A dragon who'd dominated the mountain for *decades*, even forcing other tribes to deliver their kin for her to slaughter like so many chunks of xp? Oh, and with the Blessing of Deyra on top, to double her experience gain. Yeah, she was out of my league.

The degree to which Selys had me beat still surprised me. Damn near cost me my life, too. As she dropped from above, I threw a Shadow Whorl to ruin her vision and confuse her. I also summoned the heaviest shadows I could find nearby to blind her approach. And even with that, her flames still reached out to seek my life blood from a hundred feet of distance... and they nearly managed. Even a desperate evasive swoop didn't let me escape entirely. I fought to ignore the pain in my hind legs and keep my focus on Selys.

She climbed the heights again, darting outside of the reach of my breath attack. "This is ridiculous. Surely, a shadowkin isn't Crawl-brained enough to think he can match me in open combat. What is your *play?*" She initiated another dive.

I sped up, flying lower, away from her along the wall. Despite the threat, I couldn't keep myself from grinning. "Oh, if you insist. Let me show what I have." I shouted for everyone to hear. "Now!"

They appeared - from everywhere. Dirt and rocks tumbled down, revealing openings in the nearby cavern wall, as my people emerged into the open. It was an ambush, and a well-concealed one. All the way along the cavern wall and in a number of spots in the ground themselves, cramped tunnels appeared. Within those tunnels were everybody we had who'd be able to do damage at a distance. They didn't waste time, but immediately opened fire. Spears, rocks, and fiery missiles erupted from everywhere, seeking Selys, an overwhelming barrage reaching out to hurt the behemoth. I acted as well, turning and climbing as fast I could to send a Weakening Fog at Selys. Perhaps we could get to her, hurt her enough that the risks of my plan weren't even necessary.

The spears and rocks bounced off of her armor and dark red skin. Where the Imps' missiles impacted, they hissed and faded away, leaving little evidence they'd even been there. A single spear hit near her eye, carving a thin line of red in the soft flesh. Selys roared in fury, and I turned tail, creating distance between us again. I sent to everybody "Aim for the weak spots! You won't hurt her otherwise." Inside my head, I cursed and beat my wings faster.

"Gnats! You would challenge me? Me? *I will end you!*" Fire exploded from Selys to roar against the cavern wall, hitting three of the holes. For several seconds, the flames roared, obscuring the tunnels from sight. Then they dwindled, exposing a blackened swath of wall and... a handful of faces that reappeared inside the tunnel opening and immediately started throwing spears again.

In her astonishment, Selys held still in the air, and a single spear actually stuck in the thinner part of her left wing. Her furious roar reverberated in the cavern. Step one of our plan was definitely a success. "Piss Selys off." Heh. Done and done!

Now, from one of the tunnels rose a tiny, ugly being, flapping his small wings to face off against the giant form of the red dragon. Grex? That was *not* part of the plan. He climbed steadily, releasing firebolts every other moment while he moved straight at Selys on a death-defying course. At first, she ignored him and his attacks. But the next time she released her fiery breath, she let the tail end of it wash toward him. The tiny Imp would have no way of avoiding the wall of flame thundering at him.

Grex careened through the air, moving unnaturally swift, tumbling end over end before regaining his balance, now on the far side of Selys. I gaped in astonishment, then continued. The wand. Of course. He was using the wand to propel himself faster than otherwise possible. He maintained his attacks, tiny firebolts spitting at the more vulnerable parts of her head. She growled, beat her wings, and her massive jaws snapped at him. But a fresh blast of air carried him out of range.

While she was distracted, my people rained fire and missiles up at her. Another spear stuck, this one in the soft flesh under a foot. She hissed in pain and spat fire again, this time at a number of the tunnels on the ground. Her fury was almost palpable when my people popped back up to attack after the wave of flame had passed. Adding insult to injury, I sent a new Weakening Fog at her, not that I could see any difference as the debuff landed.

I grinned to see my minions emerge unscathed. Wonderful! We'd created the tunnels with this exact scenario in the mind. Long, inward-reaching corridors to allow the flames to enter and burn away safely, all created with a chamber to the side, where our fighters could drop in when they were attacked to shelter from the flames. A small enclosure with an entrance to the far side where physics would insist that flames would burn down the open corridor instead of trying to work around corners to reach our people.

Of course, theory was one thing, and practice was quite another. Any number of things might go wrong. The heat of the fire might crack some of the walls. The fighters might be too slow in reacting. Selys might dig at the walls themselves. But then again, she had no clue what we'd been preparing.

Selys had started dodging and juking, her massive body moving with surprising speed, avoiding the majority of the attacks. Still, a lucky firebolt from Grex managed to explode right near her eye, and she cried out in pain. Then she realized something and turned her long neck toward me. "Maggots. They cannot harm me. You are trying to wear me down, Onyx."

Ruh-roah. She was onto us. My mental shout rang out into the caverns. "Plan B! Keep it up!" I fled, activated the Aerial Burst of Speed, and followed the wall of the cavern. I moved in the southward direction, at full speed, barely keeping ahead of her with the boost active. Every other second, I changed directions, filling the air behind me with magical darkness to impair her movement and avoid any flames coming my way.

On my back, Creziel held on for dear life, hovering a skull-sized rock in the air straight in front of Selys' eyes. I narrowly evaded a plume of fire, confounded her once... and then I was there. I moved closer to the western of the three tunnel openings leading to the second layer. A short glide would lead me into the tunnel system.

Selys' voice played in my ears, tense with anger. "Think you can flee into the tunnels? This is *my mountain!* I know every curve of the corridors, every single chamber. Here I thought you had a plan."

A terse smile played on my lips as I dove toward the exit, covered the air between me with darkness, and swerved at the last second, beating my wings to avoid colliding with the cavern walls.

Selys tore the darkness apart with fire, emerged, diving with her claws outstretched... and stopped. Growling, she veered and started flying in my direction again.

Creive struck. As Selys turned, the lightning exploded from out the tunnel opening, turning the half-darkness into day. Selys was caught in the center... and caught off-guard. For a second, her muscles seized, and she dropped toward the ground. Creive moved in. He had been slightly singed by Selys' unaimed shower of flame, but charged fearlessly, tearing and biting, savaging Selys. Blood dripped from her flanks where his razor-sharp claws dug into her body and tore. All too soon, however, Selys regained control, buffeting him away with the beat of a wing.

It had been costly. Convincing Creive to come here, risk his life against Selys? He was arrogant, but he knew his limits. He knew he'd be outclassed. Still, Wreil had managed to get to him. The price had been freeing Creive as a vassal and promising him free reign over his corner of the Mountain without any intervention. That, and protection if anybody should choose to move against him. I might rue the cost if I survived. For now, however, I used the distraction and flew for my life. For Fire Peak.

The burst of speed was spent now, unable to be activated for the next five minutes. Damn. I'd hoped I could save it for this part, where I needed to move fast. Below me, as a glowing, magical shadow, Timothy ran. His blue form was vague, indistinct, but lit up the darkness. On my back, I could feel Creziel's fear mixing with the thrill of the headlong flight.

Ahead of us, Selys' forces halted, slowing down to confront us, preparing for battle. They reorganized into formations, dug down, spells shot up, and shouts erupted. They grew closer, and I started to see the separate squads readying themselves, magical weapons and armor glowing in the near darkness. A nice mix of warriors and spellcasters, it looked like. Even archers. Maybe... a hundred of them, all told? I'd give bad odds on my taking them on myself, even with Creziel and Tim to help. Heh. Good thing I wasn't about to do something as stupid as that.

"*We go dark!*" This message only ranged out to one person—Timothy. With my full focus, I spun shadows around me, surrounding myself fully. And this time, I wove them thick, as heavy as I could, then I pushed out. Cries rose as the darkness covered the entire area around me, almost reaching the enemy squads. And fear tinged the cries as they realized one thing. *It moved with me.* Seconds later, the outer limits of the area I was able to handle enveloped the first of the soldiers.

They didn't take it lying down, of course. Shouts and orders rang out, and arrows and spells filled the skies, reaching out for me. Except, they fired blind, and I - I belonged inside the darkness.

Still, I would not have wanted to take them on. These were not simple enemies, but the cream of the crop. The highest-leveled of Selys' forces, including some of her personal guards, unless she'd brought them here. There were a handful of enemies who actually were as tall as me and a single ogre-looking huge bastard who might outweigh me too. They might end me in actual combat. *If* I had any intentions of stopping.

I let the shadows fade to orient myself, veered slightly to stay on course, then beat my wings, avoiding a large swath of frost that rose out to envelop me. Then I dove, avoiding fiery tendrils erupting from the paws of a robe-wearing Urten. I grunted at the sting of two arrows impacting my midriff, but they were repelled by my scales. And like that, I was past, flying for the city.

Underneath me, a series of cries followed Timothy's progress. There was no finesse to his charge. He simply ran and attacked, stunning anything in his path. He'd chosen his direction well, going between any sorcerers. Within seconds, he passed their rows, too, running slightly behind me.

"Incredible." I thought. "It's actually going according to

plan, so far. Now, I can only hope that Arthor did his part." I spared a moment to look back at where we'd left Creive, and instantly regretted it. The large blue dragon was reeling, flying as fast as he could from a brilliant, fiery vision. Selys had overcome her initial shock, and was fighting back. She had used her defensive skill, creating a fixed ring of fire around her, and even the arrogant blue didn't dare approach those flames. He fled, shooting lightning to defend himself.

On the offensive, Selys outmatched her challenger. Drastically so. It had been a minute at most, and Creive was fleeing for his life. My minions still kept up their attacks, and missiles ranged out to attack Selys constantly. However, the fire shield consumed anything that even came close. Creive took a fire breath to the torso and dropped almost to the ground. With heavy beats of his wings, he narrowly escaped another breath and fled for the tunnel.

Damn. Time to go. Creive had done his job. He had bought me a moment, a minute's distraction, as had my minions. Now, they could flee in relative safety and... everything was up to me.

Us.

I took a moment of comfort from the tiny weight tied to my back and the blur below me. Speeding up, I flew over the thick walls of Fire Peak, taking care to keep out of range of the defenders. A swoop allowed me to reconnect with the glowing form of Timothy as he *slammed* through the wall, erupting out of nowhere. We moved together, an unlikely pair, darkness above, light below, aiming straight for the fortress above.

I could feel my nerves building. We were doing great! Sure, there were bound to be a ton of enemies between us and the goal, but Selys still hadn't noticed us. If only we managed to make it inside, we could–

"*Onyx! I see you!*"

Damnit. So much for that thought. Okay, now the race was on.

CHAPTER THIRTY-SIX

I flew across Fire Peak, and the world tried to stop me. Or, at least the part of the world that wasn't fleeing. I'd been right in my musings. Not everybody in Fire Peak would be ready for a fight. In fact, for every defender who raced to defend the city and kill me, ten ran the opposite way. I helped it right along, shouting as I went. "We're taking down Selys. This is your chance for freedom. Fight!" I doubted many dared take me up on the offer, but it added to the chaos and confusion. We needed to move, though. It looked like half the entire city was on the move, either away from us or toward us, brandishing weapons. Still, they were so *slow!* As I flew, Timothy raced below, blasting energy at anybody who came close, punching his way through.

Through the air, Selys' furious message thundered. "Why do it? You pathetic hatchling. I was ready to give you this entire mountain. Why throw it away?"

Even as a handful of guards converged on Timothy, I couldn't keep a grin from reaching my face. Because they were too slow. As for the few lucky defenders who were able to momentarily catch up with Timmy-boy... I laughed out loud as a lizard-like critter halted, shocked at the sight of his throwing axe flying straight through Timothy's form to no effect whatsoever. No, they were not prepared for us. In any normal situation, we would never have gotten this far.

I spat back, my mouth twisted in a wide grin. "Maybe you should focus more on how easy it was to find people who wanted to join the attack? Have you ever considered that, maybe, you're the absolute worst?"

I passed by one of the Fire Towers, currently unoccupied. From what Selys had told, under normal circumstances, the magical web would already be in place over the city, burning any attacker from the skies. Or the towers themselves would be busy, their winged tenders manipulating the towers to fling fireballs at any intruders. But, with the Blessing of Deyra out of commission, they simply stood there, inactive, unguarded. There'd be no need for the tenders to stay up there, if they couldn't even use the towers. The fiery glint in the depth of the crystal ball on the platform laughed up at me... and then I was past. I looked at the dark fortress hanging ahead of us, and my mirth disappeared. Because somebody up there *was* ready for us.

The gates were closed. Not only that, but in front of the gates, a heavy-set handful of guards with glowing, clearly magical weapons were waiting, backed up by two robed creatures wielding fire and lightning. We would be able to take them down, though, probably. Only... I glanced at the air behind me. Selys was flying my way. She was gaining fast and already looked closer than she had been moments earlier.

We were short on time. Taking the direct route would allow her to catch us. "Timothy. Course change." I dove below the levels of the rooftops, hopefully obscuring the direction I took from Selys, and veered to the left. One street later, I turned right again. Again, we were looking at the fortress, but this time around, we were heading straight for the wall. The gray, defensive, very unguarded wall. It grew in size as we neared, and the huge construction slowly grew more imposing. I prodded the shape on my back, who was still making tiny mewling sounds, sending out waves of feeling really small. "You're up, Creziel. We need to get in!"

I took to the ground, landing at the same time as the translucent form of Timothy arrived. Somehow, he'd kept up with me. I had to give it to him. His speed was really something else. However, where I halted, he continued running, slamming into the wall and disappearing. He returned seconds later. "No guards on the other side. The wall isn't too thick. Fifteen inches at most."

"Great. We'll need to move. Fast." A few hundred feet away, the guards near the front entrance had noticed our presence, and a handful of them peeled off to run at us.

Creziel didn't need more pressing. The wall shook, bricks moving slightly as the mortar softened and ran from between the bricks in the wall like sand. I added to the damage, turning my side to the wall and starting to *slam* my tail against it as hard as I could, dislodging bricks with every strike. In a mere ten seconds, we had a hole gaping at us, except... it was still too *slow!* A glance at the air confirmed my fears. "Selys is coming! Move faster!"

As if in response to my thought, her voice slammed into me, almost taking solid form. "What plan is this? Tunnel into my fortress while your forces kill me? Do you mean to ambush me, like a Pinhead waiting for prey? This is my city. *You cannot hide!*"

She was right there! The gleaming gold of her armor rose over the walls of the city in the first, weak rays of the morning sun. Like a portent of... something I did not want to look at too deeply. I turned around and looked at the widening hole. We were not fast enough! I slammed my tail against the wall again, feeling bricks give with every strike as dust rose in a cloud around us. "Creziel. We're not going to make it. I need you to do something. Widen your approach if you can. Weaken more. You don't need to remove all the mortar."

"Okay, but—"

"Don't ask! Just do it! Tim, move through the wall." My

strikes fell in a quick rhythm now, like a drum beat. Three strikes to loosen the bricks and a fourth, harder one to clear them away. Still, it was too slow. She would be here any moment. I leapt back. Creziel cried out on my back. I ran. The guards were close now, and one of the mages had joined them. He was preparing something. A bright haze glowed about him. No time for that. I turned, skidding and almost losing my balance. Then I sprinted at the hole, with everything I had. The wall closed in so fast, behind me a roar built. The opening seemed so tiny. It would never-

I smashed into the wall with every ounce of speed I possessed, lowering my head at the last second. Bricks flew everywhere. My body was pressed down, but I pushed against the pressure, trying to spare Creziel as well as possible while fighting to break through, and then... pain. My legs were on fire! I scrambled onward, dragging myself through. They couldn't carry me. I swallowed, then I used a Mana Crystal and breathed, as the flesh of my feet knit itself back together. I ran, unseeing, away from the opening. I was in a small room, cold, filled with fire, steam, and... cauldrons? A kitchen. At the far side, a few workers or slaves were cowering in fear.

Behind me were footfalls and louder sounds. Roaring. The crackling of flames. The mental shout of Selys. "You coward! Trying to slink away like a snake? Face me!"

I yelled back at her while I ran. "Face you? Not until I have the Blessing of Deyra to bolster me!" Then I sprinted, while behind me, the sound of her roar slowly, ever-so-slowly faded into the background. "Creziel? Are you okay? Tim?" Both replied in the affirmative as we emerged from the kitchen past a series of smaller doors into a rough hall. "Alright. Selys might be able to force her way through, or we may get lucky, and she'll have to go around to the main entrance. Regardless, we need to keep moving and find our way, quickly."

A single guard with a polearm ran into the hall but blanched at the sight of us. Tim moved for him, bombarding

the unlucky bastard with stuns, effectively keeping him unable to move, even as he was brought down.

I furiously looked through my map, trying to figure out where I was. I'd studied the turning, winding halls of the fortress so many times over the past couple of days, I almost knew it by heart. *Here.* "Got it. Let's move. And remember. Whatever happens, *we keep moving.*" And we ran for our lives.

We moved like lightning within the hostile fortress. And this was a fortress, created for war and defense, not a palace dedicated to pleasure and luxury. Defenders came running in pairs, sometimes in groups, trying to halt the intruders. They would've been able to make it, too, if we'd allowed ourselves to be dragged into battle. They could have brought their numbers to bear, held us back until they were too many or Selys arrived.

But we didn't pause - merely sprinted through the halls, ahead and always up, with one single goal in mind. Not the Blessing. That was a misdirection. Something to maybe make Selys waste a minute in catching up to us. We'd debated diverting the Blessing to another place, maybe even using its powers for ourselves, then dropped the idea again. It would remove the single greatest weapon we had to use. We continued running straight for our actual goal. *The throne room.*

Timothy let out a cry as an enemy sorcerer managed to tag him. But his Mental Attack did not waver, and he downed the enemy Dragonling. I allowed myself a second to rake a claw at the sorcerer's che*st* as we sprinted past, puncturing his scaly chest. My breath was coming ragged. My Toughness was impressive, but I'd run at a dead sprint for the past three minutes, and it was starting to take its toll. Except... "We're almost there. One additional turn. You know what to do."

I almost lost my balance as I made the curve at way too high of a speed, knocking over a pedestal with a golden amphora in my hurry... and there they were. The huge, golden double doors lay ahead, guarding the entrance to the most protected of the entire fortress, the throne room holding the entirety of Selys' treasures. In front of them stood a group of guards. The strongest of Selys' defenders, the best trained… but there were just three of them. Again, I thanked the heavens for Selys' actions. Sending Mordiel against us, unleashing some of her forces against my minions in the belief that it was a full-blown attack. It had all left the fortress understaffed, under-defended. I unleashed all I had on them. A Weakening Fog, followed by my Deafening Roar left them reeling, weakened, and Timothy's Mental Attacks stunned them, bringing them completely out of balance.

I struck fast, mercilessly. I tore the throat out of one defender with my claws and seized another with my teeth, tearing his arm off. The thrill of the blood rushed to my head, and I rode it. Pain blossomed in my shoulder, where the final guard struck me. He backed off, moving into a defensive position, braced against me. In response, I enveloped him in darkness and swept his feet from under him. He died quickly, messily.

The doors slammed open, and the view almost stunned me. The splendors of the Scoured Mountain were arranged before me: gold, magic, and gems arrayed artfully before me. And surrounding it all, the blue, magical glow of a Hoard Defense. "Creziel, prepare the exit." This was a critical moment. We knew Selys was after us, catching up with every second, and we had so little time. I leapt forward and flung a claw at the defense. Pain raced through my claw, removing a sliver of health. I gritted my teeth and continued. This was going to *suck*.

Blow after blow fell down upon the Hoard Defense as my health plummeted. The pain was incredible, but I'd suffered worse. The torment of teeth ripping into me, of fire burning me to the bone. This was negligible in comparison. But the time it took me to beat down the defenses while dust arose all around me was *not* negligible.

From time to time, cries arose behind me as Timothy darted around behind me, firing painful and distracting barrages at the attackers who tried to approach the throne room. I attempted not to focus on him—no time for distractions. And I *was* winning. A third of my health had been shaved off, bit by painful bit, but the Defense was diminishing. Already, the gleam of the opaque shield was a lot weaker. If it was anything like the Hoard Defense I'd smashed back after killing the first dragon I'd ever faced, the big red, it was just about to burst.

It held. Even as my health dropped below 200, and my claws started feeling numb from the pain, the damn forcefield held, repelling me.

Finally, it exploded, enveloping the room in a shimmer of blue sparks. A treasure without match, large enough for me to gain huge powers if I took it for myself. The gathered treasures of the Scoured Mountain lay free for the taking. I ignored it completely until I found it. There it was! The option I'd risked my life for. I purred like a happy kitten and selected it. [Take ownership of hoard?] Oh hell yes!

CHAPTER THIRTY-SEVEN

"I am not afraid of death. I just don't want to be there when it happens." -
Woody Allen

I could hear her roars. She knew where I was, knew that the
Blessing had just been a distraction. And if she'd been angry
before, now she was furious. I... had what I needed, though. In
fact, once the defense died down, I'd been able to secure what I
aimed for within seconds. "Creziel? How are we doing?" Saying
that I was glad for his presence right now would be the worst
understatement. I might have been repelled at the entrance to
the fortress. At the very least, I'd have had to take the long,
winding route toward the skies and freedom. *And I was out of*
time.

Razor-sharp focus was the single emotion coming from the
Talpus on my back. "I... think I have it. I just need a moment."

"You do not have a moment." A wash of flame followed the
words, coursing into the throne room - followed by the furious
form of Selys herself. She rammed her shoulder into one of the
half-open majestic double doors, slamming it fully open with a
resounding boom. I stared at the ceiling above with a sinking

heart. *So close.* Selys towered in the entrance to the throne room.

She was not unhurt. The golden armor was scuffed and singed, marked by hundreds of attacks. She was bloodied too, hit by countless strikes and puncture wounds. One flank was badly impacted, deep, bloody furrows down to the bone indicating where Creive's claws had carved at her. Her left eye was half-closed from the blood constantly dripping from a deep wound.

But she still stood tall, looking every bit as intimidating as she had before. And she was *furious,* though her fury was cold, controlled, as she glared at me and her treasure which lay displaced, scattered all around me, buried in dust and bricks. She touched the center of her armor, and something within disappeared. Her injuries flowed, healed. A mana crystal. Damnit.

From my back, I could only feel complete concentration. Creziel was entirely focused on his work. Sand dripped from the ceiling.

"So it ends. An attempt to empty my hoard. How petty. Still, you are ambitious, I will give you that. Tell me, before I end you, why? What did you so desire from my treasury that you would go against me? Was it merely a wish to build a hoard large enough to defy me? Or are you still just a pawn of the Soul Carver?" At her side, I spotted movement, almost imperceptible. Behind, no, *inside* the door she had slammed open. A white-gray haze. She hadn't managed to hit Timothy dead-on with her flames, then. Bobbing forward slowly, he almost got right up next to her, when she finally spotted him, turned with incredible grace... and the world exploded.

My vision was completely ruined for several seconds. I blinked furiously, and slowly, through blotches and spots, the form of Selys reappeared. Explosive Redistribution. That had to be it. Tim had literally blown himself up to reappear somewhere else. Outside the throne room. Wise choice. Selys was even more infuriated now. Blood flowed freely from the right side of her neck. "Now, I will skin you first. *Then*, I will get my answers."

I laughed. I couldn't help it. The stress, the incoming death, everything, the laughter just bubbled to the surface. Contemptuously, I kicked at some of the treasures on the floor and pinned her down with a grin. "Catch me, and I'll tell you."

With that piece of suicidal smartassery, I launched into a jump. This time, straight upward, at the ceiling. My health took another hit as bricks exploded to all sides, and I flew for my life. On my back, Creziel cried out in pain. I had no time to check if he was okay, however. Behind me, flames blasted out of the aperture as Selys suddenly realized I might escape her. I banked, escaped the worst of the pillar of fire. My health dropped close to ten percent. With a grunt, I activated the last Mana Crystal I could use. No more lifelines. There was just my final gamble left.

Activating the Aerial Burst of Speed again, I fled. As fast as possible, I flew for the walls to escape the city. Every second I gained on Selys would improve my chances. I just needed to-

Behind me, the ceiling of the fortress erupted with fire again, as Selys breathed on the hole. Then, with a massive collapsing sound, the fire-heated bricks flew to all sides, as Selys burst through the ceiling and instantly followed after me.

Damn! Damn! No fair! I'm so goddamn close! The wall was right there ahead of me, maybe half a minute away. But now, she was on my tail, and I did not have any additional time to spare. I needed more speed, or the trap would fail!

Timing it had been the largest gamble on our part. To begin with, we didn't even know if it was possible to repair the ruined funnel leading the Blessing of Deyra through the mountain up to Fire Peak. Still, Arthor believed he would be able to do it. With the help of Timothy, we'd been able to find two Crawls with suitable abilities—feats with two-day timers. The effect of the feat was underpowered—a minor Endurance boost—but ultimately irrelevant. The important part was that it allowed us the chance to arrange the timing, the oh, so delicate timing. If

Arthor repaired it too early, Selys would have her defenses live when we arrived. Too late, and I'd be left without a weapon.

If we managed to time it just right, though, make sure that Selys was already outside Fire Peak when the connection reestablished... Selys had said it herself, though we were talking about Creive, back then. "You didn't even secure access to his hoard." Now, with full access to the hoard of Fire Peak, I fled, looking around for the single thing that could save me.

As I flew, I concentrated, enveloping the skies behind me in shadow, as deep as I could build them. I craned my neck, spotting one of the fire towers surrounding the entire city. Selecting Inspect, I located it... and there it was. Just like with my Gallery of Illusion. In the corner, as a small, almost imperceptible button, it was just waiting to be selected...

And it wasn't greyed out.

[Activate Fire Web]

I spared a second to look at the wall that was still several hundred feet ahead of me. Behind me, Selys appeared from the darkness, in attack range now, covered in the magical effect of some skill or feat. Damnit. Even with my feat active, she was somehow catching up to me. It would have to be now! With a curse, I mentally selected the button.

Nothing happened. The fire web did *not* come alive to burn the two of us out of the skies. Except... a Fire Tower blinked and ignited below me. I pushed the [Activate Fire Web] button again. Was it even working? Maybe... maybe I could make it. I put in everything I had, beat my wings as hard as I possibly could to give me the final bit of speed I needed while I spammed the stubborn button. On either side of me, towers in the distance grew brighter.

The world exploded.

Behind me, around me. Everything was pain. My sight reduced to whiteness as I closed my eyes and flew. For a second, I thought Selys hit me, but no. The flames were everywhere.

Through the burning roar all around me, I flew, fighting to stay aloft as I could feel my body burning, being carved *away*. And I was dropping, falling.

The muscles keeping my left wing functioning stopped responding, and I was thrown into an uncontrolled spin, blinded and almost crazy with the pain. All I could see was a fiery inferno, all around me. And then, as suddenly as it had appeared, the fire faded away, and I hit the ground. *Outside* the walls of Fire Peak.

I survived. Somehow, I survived. I marveled at the sensation, mired in disbelief as I lay on the ground, broken and beaten. My health was down to 115/640. My left wing was charred, and burned and my hind legs refused to work properly. From my back, a sensation of horrible agony told me that Creziel was still there. I tried to focus. My leg muscles worked. I could feel that as I lay, painfully testing my battered body. My feet, though. Hesitant, I lifted my head and looked at them. They were lumps, fused into something that did not resemble my clawed feet. My front legs worked alright, though, even if they were tender, as did my neck and head. Until I healed, I would simply have to drag myself around. And at least, Selys-

Out of the fiery, glimmering haze surrounding Fire Peak, she dropped. She fell like a comet, straight at the crater floor, and impacted. It wasn't like on TV, with a massive explosion or the earth becoming a crater three stories down. The dusty earth covering the crater around Fire Peak did erupt in a dust cloud, but her massive body smacked into the ground and turned over twice before sliding to a halt a few hundred feet away.

I dared not breathe. She made it out. Somehow, she survived the insane fires for... how long had it been? Ten seconds? Twenty? More? Somehow, she hadn't succumbed to the pain, but fought her way through, even as her body was burned away. But was she still alive? The dirt slowly settled around the queen of the mountain.

A claw moved, weakly, and I almost cried. Too much. It was too much! My plan had worked, but it still wasn't enough? As if from a distant place, I heard cries. That would be the city's defenders, rushing to the defense of their overlord. I grunted and summoned my strength. The pain threatened to bring me to my knees, but I refused to quit! I could rest when this was done. Growling under my breath, I started dragging myself toward Selys. Searching for an end.

A few hundred feet. It could have been several miles, for all I knew. The distance felt like forever. My attention was fixed on Selys, where she lay, twitching, heat and smoke rising from her body. Now, I could see a magical sheen surrounding her slowly fading. I'd seen that once before. In the battle with the Soul Carver, she had summoned that skill to consume nearby fires to momentarily boost her own strength. So, that's how she had survived the inferno. And, as a red dragon, she probably had some innate fire resistance to top it up.

Well, resist this! I thought and pushed myself up on my shaking front feet and exhaled. She lay at the very edge of my limit, but my Weakening Fog hit her, and this time I could *see* the difference. The magical sheen dimmed down and died, and I could finally see Selys clearly.

She was ruined.

Whoever came up with the Burning End would be able to appreciate the irony of it. The Mistress of the Mountain had burned. Lumps of scales had simply burned away or fused together, leaving horrible, red, oozing patches. Her armor had joined with her body, melting into a grotesque, glimmering patchwork quilt. As for her wings... they were closer to stumps. Only part of the wings remained, flapping as the tattered sails of a shipwreck. Still, even with the disfiguring wounds, she was majestic. Majestic and alive, unmistakably alive.

I dragged myself closer. I could not let her aim her fire breath on me. I wouldn't be able to survive even a single direct hit at this point, if only I could keep her from turning. I breathed again, the Weakening Fog enveloping her entire body and sapping her remaining strength. She had to be running low on energy. No way she could endure much more. Maybe I could capitalize on her state. I focused, worked as fast as I'd ever done. Magic, shadow, illusion, built as hard and fast as I could.

Her eye, the other melted away, flicked open. Slowly, ever so slowly, it rotated and then fixed on me, fully enveloped in a sea of darkest darkness. Like a snake, her massive neck arose sinuously, while her body turned over, with kinks and pauses, to face me. This time around, she didn't waste her time on threats or questions. She gulped huge mouthfuls of air, breath rattling in her throat and unleashed a wave of fire at me.

The fire burned harder than a furnace, afterimage lingering even after it winked out and disappeared - taking my illusionary alter ego with it. Selys' astounded grimace almost made me grin, even as my single advantage was consumed. Even rattled as she was, she wasn't falling for that again. *This was it. Either she died or I did.* As the cooldown ran out, I breathed again. One last Weakening Fog. Her eye blinked, the neck slumped and dipped, and she caught herself. Her head lolled, but stayed up.

Cries rose louder nearby. That was it. Her army would arrive any moment now. I lifted myself to face my death head on, front legs trembling under me. I'd given it my all. At least I could rest now, and somebody was sure to take her down, crippled as she was. I glared at the red monster, daring her to do her worst.

Flames built in her mouth. It was coming. Finally.

Selys' head took a massive blow, and the flames spilled onto the dirt. She had missed. Somehow. And then I saw it. Next to Selys' head, a pointy rock the size of my claw arose and struck down on her unprotected eye. Blood and worse spurted and she bellowed in pain.

I finally noticed the growing sensation from my back. Pain. So much pain. But also concentration. Satisfaction. *Creziel.* I had just had time to entertain the thought when a blue burst arrived from out of the corner of my eye and hit Selys, causing a shudder to run through her. *Timothy.* His translucent body was tattered, almost gone, but still he sprinted closer, firing Mental Attack after Mental Attack at

Selys. I caught myself, then summoned another Weakening Fog.

Together, we took her down. We bludgeoned Selys to death as we sapped her energy and stunned her in turn, in front of her own city, bereft of support, friends, and defenders. It must have been only seconds, but felt like an eon. Finally, the massive, bloody head slammed down on the ground and stopped moving. The Burning End... ended.

For a moment, there was only silence as we blinked at her corpse in disbelief. Then, we stared at each other. Timothy looked like he was about to fade away, like a projector running out of energy. I told him to take some mana from me to heal, but he shook his head. I craned my neck to take in Creziel. He looked back woozily, equal parts road rash, blood, and astonishment. Oh, and that paw was definitely broken.

"We did it." The words came from me, but they were reflected in their eyes. I could taste the victory. We'd managed... and now we would pay.

The guards were few in number. Less than fifty, all told. Even so, they would be more than enough to end us. Selys' guards ran at the easy targets before them. Cheap experience and dragonflesh. Who wouldn't want to partake? I felt the hurts of a thousand cuts and burns all over my body and winced. "Timothy. Creziel. You can still run, hide. Help them protect the tribe. Maybe even take over this damn place—"

Creziel scoffed. "I'm not running anywhere with this foot. Let's make something of this, a tale for the tribe to remember." The decisiveness coming from him made me smile. A smile filled with pain, but heartfelt.

Timothy scoffed. His words were hard to hear, and tinged with exhaustion. "I'm with the furball on this, old man. I told you, I'm not doing this alone. Besides, you said it yourself. We're family, dysfunctional though we may be. Family sticks together. Let's end this."

Then, the exhaustion was suddenly replaced with a wave of surprise and awe. The mental message sprang from him.

"There's one good thing about dysfunctional family." He suddenly sounded like he was holding back tears or laughter, or both. "They tend to have a shitload of cousins."

I craned my neck to look at him, but he stared out over the wastes. Openmouthed, he glared dumbstruck at the forces spilling over the plains, running for the city. For us. Except, those weren't Selys' forces. They were Crawls, Clenchers, Talpi, and Imps, swarming over the dead plains. Roth raced at their forefront next to the Clencher Cavalry, high-pitched yells audible at a distance as they challenged the defenders of the city. The defenders, in turn, finally realized that their easy targets were about to be reinforced by a force who dwarfed theirs and turned tail.

I looked on in disbelief as Roth raced past us with the Clenchers, halting to establish a defensive perimeter. Then... then, I finally let my head slump to the ground and closed my eyes. I'd earned my rest.

CHAPTER THIRTY-EIGHT

We had a feast. It seemed like the thing to do. Obviously, quite a few things had to be handled before we got to that point. Fire Peak's unconditional surrender, for instance. That part was surprisingly easy. They might have closed the gates and prepared the walls for defense. They had not realized one thing, however. *I already owned the damn place.* It took them a while before they really understood that, with all its implications.

The details weren't what mattered. Wreil volunteered to go talk to the defenders. In fact, he insisted. It did sound like fun, to be honest. I'd have liked to deliver that message myself. "Oh yeah, guys, so, Onyx already has full control of your hoard and your defenses. He can destroy Selys' constructions at will, and he totally controls that Fire Web defense, too. Notice how he turned it off? What's that? You can keep us away from the defenses? Remember how he's a damned shadow dragon? Illusion skills are his bread and butter. And we've got flying forces too, unless you missed that part. We can have Imps on all the fire towers in minutes. Unless we already have. Want to test us?"

The gates opened not long after that. Meanwhile, I spent

the time with everybody on the plains outside the city while the Ergul worked over my wounds and heard what had happened.

"What happened to the plan? Arthor's going to chew you *up* when he comes back!"

Roth grinned at me. He was covered in cuts and looked a mess, but he vibrated with joy. "He isn't. The old, mangy bastard is cautious, but he takes the chance to level up whenever it's there. I mean, there was no reason to run away entirely. The moment Selys left, we weren't in any imminent danger. Those attackers of Selys... Well, they were big and all, but they weren't really a match for us. We marched out against them, but any time we got in trouble, we'd be able to move back into our tunnels and slink away. Those big bastards wouldn't be able to get to us. Besides, we knew if we didn't finish them, and Selys won, they'd be hunting us in the days to come, anyway. It was the only smart thing to do."

I smiled fondly at him. "That's a horrible excuse, Roth. Arthor's not going to buy it for a minute. Heh. I'm not complaining, though. You saved my life. I would've been so annoyed if we killed Selys only to be offed by a bunch of her underlings."

The squat, furry creature patted my flank, carefully avoiding the wounds. "Yeah. We'd have been a bit annoyed, too."

In the end, our victory procession was not a noisy one. Selys' former city guard, decimated, beaten and humiliated, opened the doors then got the hell away from us. We walked the length of the city. That is, I had to stumble, painfully, as my wounds didn't allow me full use of my legs or wings yet. We took over the fortress and installed our forces everywhere. For now, I'd ordered everybody except for my minions away from the fortress. Later, we would address the city, start handling the situation, and bring their forces to heel. However, right now, we were only interested in one thing.

Celebration.

It was weird to think, but with the hoard under my control, I could suddenly see... everything. If anybody were to try sneaking in to attack us, they'd be in for a rude surprise. They knew it. Hence, we were left to lounge and lick our wounds surrounded by the utmost splendor and luxury to be had inside the Scoured Mountain. It was an incredible experience, watching Crawl and Talpi play around Imps in the midst of stacks of gold and gems.

I looked at my people fondly and found, to my astonishment, that they had all made it. Wreil looked like a freak, with half his fur burned off after a particularly close dodge, and others sported ugly wounds. The Ergul had spent all of its juice on me, for now. But still, somehow, we'd made it. Throughout the room, that was the sensation that was the most prevalent. Disbelief.

Creziel was the one to put words to it. When they untied him from my back, they found him in surprisingly good condition. Half his fur was evaporated, his back was covered in oozing burn wounds, his foot was broken, and he might be concussed. Yeah, surprisingly good. "So... what happens now?"

"Now?" I thought about it. "First, we are going to level up. I know I'm not the only one who might have some interesting choices ahead of me." Understatement of the frigging millenium. I'd gained 89,400 experience points from the battle. That was about a fourth of my former experience points combined! Every single one of my minions who'd managed to tag Selys would be looking at a similar increase, with an additional frigging 50% on top of that. Some of them would effectively double their experience. For me, it meant three full levels, leaving me just past the level 33 threshold.

I continued. "Remember to ask Lore and Tim for recommendations. After that, though? Well, we're forcing the city to accept our rule. Then, we're going to make sure that none of the nearby threats dare go against us, make sure nobody's planning to try to take over the place. Next, we'll send Wreil out to make the Dworgen and Aberrants join our forces. Then deal with any remaining Dragonlings. Following that... I don't know."

Gert blinked at me, mouth hanging open in shock. "You don't know? We just took down the ruler of the mountain, and you don't know what's going to happen?"

I laughed. "Come on. It's not like anybody thought we were actually going to succeed?" My eyes glinted with laughter as I looked at them all. "Fair enough. I guess, if there's a time for resounding statements, it's now. I aim to make the mountain—the entire damn mountain, yeah, you heard me—a safe haven for intelligent species to coexist in peace. I intend to build a fair home and force everybody who intends to rule through violence to submit or flee.

"But I have no plans of doing this alone. This is going to be a place of equal rights and opportunities, and we'll manage, together, to ensure that nobody is downtrodden. And, once the mountain is safe..." I let the words trail off, looking at them hanging on my every word. "Well, who knows what the limit is?" I stared at them all, at the magnificent, strong creatures who would be ushering in a new era to this dark world. With a sensation of joy bursting from deep within, I roared, and they cried with me. Their roars and shouts spread throughout the throne room, past the half-empty corridors of the fortress, onto the torch-lit streets outside.

"They can't hold us down!"

ABOUT LARS MACHMÜLLER

Lars Machmüller lives in Denmark with his wife and three kids. Family comes first, and as such, he spends a lot of time perfecting the art of packed lunches, cleaning food off the floor and delivering kids to and from school, kindergarten, playdates and whatnot.

Whenever somebody is *not* crawling on his shoulders, he dedicates every waking moment attempting to exorcise all those LitRPG plot bunnies that keep finding a place to live within his skull.

Whatever little time remains, he distributes evenly between his towering to-be-read pile, his trusty PC, and music.

Connect with Lars:
LarsM-Writes.com
Instagram.com/LarsMachmuller
Facebook.com/groups/357145749698735
Patreon.com/Moulder666
Mailchi.mp/94863280f513/Cranky-Chronicler

ABOUT MOUNTAINDALE PRESS

Dakota and Danielle Krout, a husband and wife team, strive to create as well as publish excellent fantasy and science fiction novels. Self-publishing *The Divine Dungeon: Dungeon Born* in 2016 transformed their careers from Dakota's military and programming background and Danielle's Ph.D. in pharmacology to President and CEO, respectively, of a small press. Their goal is to share their success with other authors and provide captivating fiction to readers with the purpose of solidifying Mountaindale Press as the place 'Where Fantasy Transforms Reality.'

Connect with Mountaindale Press:
MountaindalePress.com
Facebook.com/MountaindalePress
Twitter.com/_Mountaindale
Instagram.com/MountaindalePress

MOUNTAINDALE PRESS TITLES
GameLit and LitRPG

The Completionist Chronicles,
The Divine Dungeon,
Full Murderhobo, and
Year of the Sword by Dakota Krout

Arcana Unlocked by Gregory Blackburn

A Touch of Power by Jay Boyce

Red Mage and
Farming Livia by Xander Boyce

Space Seasons by Dawn Chapman

Ether Collapse and
Ether Flows by Ryan DeBruyn

Dr. Druid by Maxwell Farmer

Bloodgames by Christian J. Gilliland

Unbound by Nicoli Gonnella

Threads of Fate by Michael Head

Lion's Lineage by Rohan Hublikar and Dakota Krout

Wolfman Warlock by James Hunter and Dakota Krout

Axe Druid,
Mephisto's Magic Online, and
High Table Hijinks by Christopher Johns

Skeleton in Space by Andries Louws

Dragon Core Chronicles by Lars Machmüller

Chronicles of Ethan by John L. Monk

Pixel Dust and
Necrotic Apocalypse by David Petrie

Viceroy's Pride by Cale Plamann

Henchman by Carl Stubblefield

Artorian's Archives by Dennis Vanderkerken and Dakota Krout

Vaudevillain by Alex Wolf

Made in United States
Troutdale, OR
08/30/2023

12506496R00205